I0665785

# Malic Slater

*To all my friends and family members that supported me. I would have never thought that I'd be able to write a novel. Your endless support in my work is what helped me push through tough times.*

*Thank you to my close friend and his mother for being there on my side and helping me get here. I couldn't have done this without your help. Thank you.*

# CONTENTS

# Prologue: The Cloaked Metallic Crusader

*April 17, 2134*

Beneath the inky, star-studded expanse of the night sky, a vast and foreboding forest lay shrouded in impenetrable darkness. The colossal trees, their bark resembling Earth's woods, concealed hidden hatches and traps. They were guardians of secrets, poised to ensnare any unfortunate soul who dared to enter their enigmatic realm. A bunker lay hidden within this alien wilderness, its purpose shrouded in mystery. Two guards stood, wearing tactical suits and masks that covered their mouths as their eyes darted nervously through the obsidian curtain of the forest, a feeling of being watched by unseen forces haunting their every move.

"Why did we get this assignment? Standing here, guarding something we know nothing about."

One guard grumbled.

"You heard what the boss said."

Replied to his partner.

"It's classified."

"Classified, my—"

"Keep it down, man!"

His partner hissed, glancing around nervously.

"I just want this to be over with. This place gives me anxiety."

The first guard sighed, shifting his weight.

"I don't like this. Keeping a base away from the mainland might be a switch, but they could have added some security cameras. This organization can surely afford better protection. We're wasting manpower here."

"You know why we can't have special accommodation."

The second guard responded with a bitter tone.

"Ever since URDT started scrutinizing every move by The Excesses, they've been tracking our every purchase and acquisition. They're watching us like hawks."

"We can't catch a break."

Muttered the first guard, clenching his fists.

"We're practically fighting with sticks and rocks now."

"It's not just sticks and rocks anymore."

The other guard whispered, a voice dropping to a conspiratorial tone.

"Whatever the boss has planned, it's bound to provoke a response from URDT, but what worries me is their resurrected 'toy.'"

The first guard looked at him, puzzled.

"What are you talking about? URDT has a new weapon?"

"Not just any weapon."

His partner said, his voice barely audible.

"The Melancholic Knight."

The first guard's eyes widened.

"You can't be serious!"

"I can only assume that's why the boss moved operations away from the Republic of Melancholia."

The other guard replied.

"They wouldn't dare cross their borders or send their secret guardian after us."

"So, we're up against a metallic warrior now?"

The first guard scoffed, though unease crept into his tone.

"They really want us gone, and we're first in line to be its victims."

"We'll be fin—"

Before he could finish, a colossal force slammed down upon the first guard as if gravity had unleashed its wrath. The massive figure turned toward the other guard, who barely had time to react before it seized him by the collar and hurled him into the air. He crashed back to the ground, stunned. The first guard lay immobile, as the shadowy figure loomed closer, partially illuminated by the base's spotlight revealed the Melancholic Knight towering in gleaming silver armor, every inch polished and fortified with bolts, exuding a blend of elegance and menace. Sporting a streamlined and powerful silhouette. Small blue lights pulsed at his knees and waist, casting a faint glow over the metallic plates. The helmet concealed its face. The suit resonated in a subtle metallic clink as it got closer to the guard.

"This can't be true... the rumors..."

The downed guard managed a weak gasp.

The Melancholic Knight knocked the guard unconscious. He dragged the bodies into the dark and concealed them in the dense foliage around the base. Retrieving their keycards, the Knight unlocked the building and slipped into a seemingly endless, dark corridor. The Knight's headlamp illuminated his path. His visor HUD sending images back to URDT.

"Good job. Silent and swift."

A radio voice echoed inside the Melancholic Knight's helmet.

"Find what The Excesses were hiding."

The voice continued.

"And remember to remain concealed in the shadows. We cannot afford any attention. Be cautious."

The Melancholic Knight stared down the dark path, feeling the gravity of the unknown—a blend of trap and salvation.

***

Meanwhile, far from the infiltrated base, another location buzzed with activity as workers operated communication systems, analyzed data, and monitored life support. Images of the Melancholic Knight's movements flickered across several monitors, observers scrutinizing every step. The leaders surveyed the mission from above. On the wall, a sign declared: "URDT Tactical Operation of Military."

"He's hesitating, Akarui."

Kenryoku said, concern evident in their voice.

"He's not ready for this."

Akarui responded, her gaze fixed on the screens.

"He'll come through; we just need him to stay focused, and everything will fall into place."

"Remember."

Kenryoku replied sternly.

"I won't be responsible for your work or any mess you create. You will have to clean it up."

Akarui's eyes narrowed.

"I don't want to hear it from you, Kenryoku. You and Premier made the decision to entrust the suit to the boy."

Kenryoku's expression hardened.

"We shall see."

***

In the corridors, a shivering wind whispered secrets through the base's confines. The once-reflective floor now bore a grimy sheen; neglect cloaked every panel and wall. Fluid leaked from pipes that hadn't felt the touch of inspection in eons. A thick haze veiled the already limited visibility, plunging the labyrinthine passages into abyssal darkness.

The Knight maneuvered through the gloomy tunnels, each step a cautious dance. Occasionally, wiring crackled and sparked, illuminating the area with a vibrant display reminiscent of fireworks. His eyes darted incessantly, scanning for signs of movement—real or imagined—instilling an unsettling sense of being watched or pursued.

Akarui's voice pierced the eerie silence, laden with disbelief.

"This place... it's like a forsaken tomb. Are we certain this is the right location?"

"Our intel led us precisely here—these are the coordinates of the stolen ARC equipment."

Kenryoku's response was resolute but tinged with a hint of unease.

The absence of any sign of life or presence was perplexing. Had The Excesses fled at the sight of the Knight, or were they gathering forces for a counterstrike?

An electric burst of light exposed an obstructed path of broken furniture strewn like jagged defenses hanging in tatters, its destruction fresh.

"The entrance... it was blocked, seemed recently."

Akarui noted with a tremor in her voice.

Kenryoku scrutinized the camera feed, his gaze on the Knight's surroundings.

"There's a vent above you—find it. See where it leads. It seems this warehouse was a refuge during the planet's colonization."

Kenryoku observed.

"But why is it abandoned? Destroyed?"

Akarui questioned.

"The area was perilous, with harsh weather."

13

Kenryoku explained, his words tinged with grim recollection.

"It was a deadly time when humanity sought rebirth."

The Knight's gaze settled on a damaged elevator. Its flickering light revealed a series of posters adorned with slogans: "Renewal Rally: Rebuilding Together." "Uplift Humanity: Uniting for a Better Tomorrow." and "Harmony Revival: One World, One Family." all emblazoned with the URDT logo. Yet, amid the hopeful messages, graffiti marred their surfaces, spelling out a chilling word: "Lies."

As the Knight entered an empty room, recorded voices began to broadcast. "To anyone hearing this, please! We need supplies; the weather is preventing us from escaping this cold place. URDT, we need help!" The Knight stared intensely at the radio.

"They didn't come. They were busy on their own interests while the people suffered."

A harsh voice out of nowhere erupted.

Akarui's voice cut through the static.

"Who's talking?! I need an immediate scan around the perimeter—NOW!"

At the URDT, the crew sprang into action, fingers flying across keyboards, monitors lighting up as they scrambled to get results. Tension filled the room, everyone fully aware that whatever threat loomed was closing in fast.

Suddenly, a harsh voice crackled through the communication line.

"So, the URDT finally arrived. Not too busy anymore, huh? Are you ready to suffer?"

Akarui shouted into the comm, her voice almost desperate.

"Get out of there, now!"

Before the Knight could react, an enormous object smashed through the wall, debris raining down as it barreled forward. The Knight was slammed into the opposite wall. A mighty hand clamped around the Knight's legs, swinging them violently through the air and crashing him onto a series of tables, shattering everything as though it were nothing more than dry twigs.

Heavy footsteps echoed through the wreckage, accompanied by a hiss of steam released with every stride. The towering figure advanced, each mechanical step resonating like a hammer striking steel. Its massive form dwarfed the Knight, casting a long, ominous shadow as it stopped just a few steps away.

The mechanical figure slowly lifted its massive, helmeted head to the fallen Knight.

"There you are… The lost weapon of the URDT, finally making an appearance."

With a calculated motion, the figure raised its visor slightly, revealing the face underneath— one they'd been searching for.

"You came all this way just for me."

The figure sneered.

A voice crackled through the Knight's helmet, filled with dread and disbelief.

"Jax Maddox."

Akarui whispered.

Jax's eyes glow a sinister yellow, sharp and predatory like an owl's, piercing through the shadows with a malevolent intensity. A long, jagged scar ran from his forehead to the top of his head, revealing a damaged, hairless scalp. A short, uneven beard shadowed his jawline, further exposing his face's rough, scarred tissue.

"You didn't think I knew you were coming? Those guards did their job well baiting the mouse to find its cheese."

He paused, a wicked grin spreading across his damaged face.

"And me? I'm your trap."

Jax's voice was cold and taunting.

Grabbing the Knight's arms, Jax threw him across the room near the stairs and then charged the Knight. Grabbing him again, Jax lifted him up like a surfboard, throwing him through the wall to where the Knight started his investigation.

"I don't need The Excesses army to deal with you; two were enough to lure you in."

Jax's voice reverberated through the chaos, dripping with disdain.

With a swift leap, Jax bolted to the Knight's entry point. The Knight, barely mobile, dragged himself toward the exit, each movement sending waves of excruciating agony through his body.

Jax's accusations cut through the air, carrying the weight of betrayal and despair.

"Where was the URDT when we needed you? What were y'all doing while people covered themselves with damaged blankets? You only show up now because I leaked my coordinates."

The Knight's gaze fixed upon Jax, locked in a battle of wills. Despite his agony, determination gleamed fiercely in his eyes.

***

Akarui's voice trembled with urgency.

15

"Hang on! We're sending reinforcements!"

"It's too late. He'll be dead before they arrive."

Kenryoku's response, cold and callous, struck like a blow.

"We can't just let him die! The suit he wears is a prototype; it is not sturdy enough!"

Akarui's plea dripped with desperation; Kenryoku remained steadfast.

"This is what he signed up for. He knew the risks."

Kenryoku said in a firm voice, but the underlying conflict haunted his expression.

Akarui's frustration spilled over.

"You're heartless..."

Kenryoku's indifference pierced her, and his response was steeped in a chilling detachment.

"If that's what you feel, so be it."

Akarui's thoughts were a fervent prayer for the Melancholic Knight, a silent plea for strength and resilience. She closed her eyes, hoping that the Knight would rise, fight, and endure.

***

With a tremendous effort, the Knight rallied, standing resolute despite the searing pain coursing through his body. Every movement was a symphony of agony, but his resolve remained unyielding.

Jax slowly advanced, a sneer playing on his lips. His hand hovered over the label "ARC." an ominous sign of imminent danger.

"You know, our intel has been busy tracking your fancy gadgets. The return of The Melancholic Knight since the world's end is thrilling, but facing you now, it's rather anticlimactic. I hope you provide the fight I'm anticipating."

The Knight grappled with the grim reality of the situation. There was no escape, only the impending battle. He fought not just physical pain but the emotional torment of helplessness, a crushing weight of solitude amidst the chaos. Akarui's faith was a flicker of hope in the darkness, but even that seemed like false promises, amplifying his desolation.

Amidst the sizzling wires, the Knight's mind raced. What could he do?

"Well, time to end this. I don't want to waste this perfect machinery we, The Excesses, made."

Jax sneered, preparing to end the dance.

The tension surged as Jax took aim, the ARC charging up with deadly intent. Smoke curled from the barrel, signaling an imminent shot, but the Knight stood firm, anticipating the moment.

Suddenly- the Knight dodges incoming bullet with lightning reflexes, rolling along the corridor.

"This party isn't over yet. Care to dance some more?"

He taunted, adrenaline fueling his defiance.

At the URDT, Akarui, enthusiastic and supportive, encouraged the Knight as she observed through his camera feed. The URDT room flickered in the dazzling light of the ARC, revealing the intensity of the battle. Kenryoku remained stoic, his hand resting thoughtfully on his chin, analyzing the unfolding action.

"The suit he wears is just a prototype. He knows the risk of playing with fire."

He commented, assessing the precariousness of the situation.

Despite his valiant efforts, the Knight's movements began to slow, bullets closing in on him.

A bullet struck the Knight, the armor absorbed the blow, but it stung and momentarily impeded his motion. Defeat loomed as Jax charged forward, overpowering the Knight and pinning him against the wall.

"It was fun while it lasted."

Jax taunted, relishing the impending end. His mocking gaze locked on the Knight's helmet, a smirk of satisfaction tainting his expression.

"We modified the ARC but improved. I want to show how much damage it can do now; this bullet can break through your fragile armor."

Jax sneered, pressing the ARC barrel firmly against the Knight's helmet.

Seizing a split-second opportunity, the Knight broke from Jax's grasp, catching Jax off guard. With fast reflexes, the Knight punched Jax's ARC, sending it flying.

Then an explosion missed the Knight's helmet by a hair's breadth. Taking advantage of the chaos, the Knight headbutted Jax, causing him to stagger backward. The Knight grabbed a wire, tearing it fiercely from the walls. Sprinting towards Jax, the Knight leaped onto Jax's back, evading Jax's attempts to reach. With decisive strikes, the Knight pounded Jax's armor, prying open different plates until he exposed Jax's vulnerable spinal cord, the link to his machine.

17

In a daring move, the Knight stabbed the wires directly into Jax's spinal cord. Jax convulsed violently, his body lost control and fell into immobilization. The Knight, overwhelmed with relief, gazed down at him.

***

"YOU IDIOT!"

Kenryoku's outraged shout pierced the air, startling everyone, including Akarui.

"You killed him!"

The outcry echoed.

"Wait."

Akarui protested vehemently,

"Check for Jax's pulse, now!"

The operation crew swiftly examined Jax's condition through the Knight's HUD, monitoring the BPM label for any signs of electrical activity in his heart.

"Barely at 62, ma'am."

A crew member shouted back to Akarui.

Akarui's emotion was palpable.

"That was too close."

She sighed, a mixture of shock and relief clouding her expression.

"He nearly sabotaged the entire operation, Captain!"

Kenryoku fumed, his gaze fixed accusingly on Akarui.

"What else could he have done, Kenryoku? He was outmatched, and that suit wasn't in sync with him. He was defenseless!"

Akarui retorted, frustration evident in her voice.

"No means of neutralizing a threat! He's learning nothing from his training."

Kenryoku criticized, unrelenting in his scrutiny.

"You should be grateful he volunteered to become The Melancholic Knight. You and your superiors rushed him on a mission to capture a dangerous target with little intel!"

Akarui exclaimed, facing Kenryoku defiantly.

Kenryoku, collecting his thoughts, walks down the stairs.

"This was the only opportunity; capturing one of The Excesses leaders will bring us closer to stopping their schemes."

Kenryoku's gaze lingered on Akarui, registering the doubt and disdain she harbored, yet he pressed on despite the tension.

"Our troops and FIREBIRDS are occupied maintaining order in our city; we must determine his commitment to being the Melancholic Knight."

Kenryoku announced, turning toward the colossal monitor showing the Knight's HUD, fixated on Jax's motionless form.

"He's in conflict, doubting."

Kenryoku remarked, his eyes reflecting concern and resolve.

Akarui's gaze was also fixed on the screen.

"He's still young. What more can we expect?"

She sighed, a trace of sympathy in her voice.

Acknowledging her words with a nod, Kenryoku gruffly,

"Results."

Akarui's gaze lowered, her hands motioning absently over the communication panel. She pondered the weight of their decision, questioning the rationale behind sending someone so young into treacherous waters, allowing them to struggle while gathering data. She hesitated for a moment before pressing the button.

"He's still breathing, Aiko. Bring his body outdoors and await further orders."

Akarui commanded a mix of determination and concern lacing her words.

***

"Yes, ma'am."

As the knight's visor opened, Aiko's face was covered by his mask. The mask, a deep blue akin to a pure sapphire, concealed his visage in the darkness. The interior of the helmet, adorned with wires and connected parts, burdened him, causing a throbbing headache.

Drawing a deep breath, Aiko attempted to alleviate the pressure the helmet imposed on him. Summoning inner strength, he shut the visor, rising from a brief rest to haul Jax's massive suit. Each movement felt akin to dragging a pickup truck without wheels, etching deep marks on the floor. Straining against the weight, Aiko exerted all the might the Melancholic Knight suit afforded him, giving him a semblance of superhuman strength. Aiko gradually maneuvered Jax's unconscious body toward the entrance. When they settled outside, the Knight opened the torso of Jax's suit to reveal a mechanical implant integrated with his throat, leading down to his bare, heavily scarred chest.

At the URDT, a radar tech reported.

"Ma'am, an unidentified vehicle is heading towards The Knight location; it is entering at dangerous speed!"

Akarui quickly tried to warn Aiko.

Aiko heard a pitched whistling slice through the air, a shrill sound cutting through the silence, signaling an ominous turn of events.

The deafening whistling grew louder, a warning that Aiko struggled to discern.

Before Aiko could react, a rocket hurtled towards him, shattering the peace with a resounding BOOM! The explosive shockwave slammed Aiko across the ground, smashing him into a tree. His suit lay motionless and damaged, and he remained utterly still inside.

"Aiko!"

Akarui's anguished scream echoed through the chaos, a desperate plea slicing through the turmoil.

From the darkness, a truck emerged, barreling through the wreckage towards Jax's inert body at breakneck speed. The vehicle, cloaked in the midnight shroud, almost melded into the surroundings. Shadowy figures leaped out, swiftly hoisting Jax's unconscious form into the truck before vanishing into the night without a trace.

"I told you... I don't need any backup."

Jax weakly whispered from his prone state, an air of defiance tinged with resignation.

"Without you, our entire operation will crumble, and you've damaged our new 'toy.'"

A voice crackled from The Excesses walkie-talkie, its tone ominous, hinting at imminent repercussions.

With relief and apprehension, Jax closed his eyes, anticipating the reprimand he'd soon face, his value to their organization bittersweet knowledge.

Meanwhile, Aiko lay with his body weakened by the explosion's impact, bones still reverberating from the shock, and a throbbing headache worsened by the collision with the tree. He made a feeble attempt to raise his hands towards the sky, yearning to glimpse the stars amidst the encompassing darkness.

Amidst the haze of pain and confusion, faintly remembered voices echoed within him, murmurs of comfort and hope.

*"Hold on to Hope..."*

A familiar voice whispered, though Aiko, fatigued beyond measure, couldn't place its origin.

Lying there, gazing up at the night sky, he sought solace in the faint glimmers of light that punctuated the vast expanse, a fragile lifeline amidst the turmoil that enveloped him. He slipped unconscious.

***

In the aftermath, the heavy burden of responsibility weighed upon Akarui's shoulders. Her form slumped, her head buried within her arms, and her breaths came out in soft, desolate exhales.

"I'll report what action has been taken, Akarui..."

The unfinished sentence hung in the air, trailing away like a ghostly echo.

Kenryoku departed, ascending the stairs with measured steps, a calm facade masking his turmoil. Meanwhile, Akarui remained seated, enveloped in disbelief and resignation. The crew members, witnessing their captain's distress, were struck with astonishment. Some retreated, while others observed the scene, unsure of what to make of their leader's apparent breakdown.

"He wasn't ready."

Akarui murmured, her voice scarcely audible.

"I wasn't ready."

She said her words laden with unspoken burdens and the pain of unfulfilled promises.

The monitor displayed Aiko's condition, a stark reminder of the dire circumstances: "Unconscious." Simultaneously, the suit's synchronization registered a bleak "13%."

# ACT 1: I Thought About It All

# Chapter One: Embarkment

*January 5, 2134*

The water cascaded from the willow's branches, their shadows casting gentle yet intricate patterns on the earth below. Towering proudly in the meadow, the trees stood sentinel, their branches weaving tales of varied existence. Their purpose was singular: to thrive, relentless in their journey through any obstacle. They sheltered tents, absorbed the warmth of campfires, and slowly reclaimed abandoned vehicle parts, embodying nature's omnipotence.

"C'mon, Albie. I can't leave you stranded in this storm."

Aiko called out, glancing back at Albie, who was lagging. Albie trailed along, sketching the ground with a stick, a rhythmic dance of water, the earth-like minerals leaving a smooth, tangible trail.

"Albie, don't make me return there."

Aiko warned. Albie's movements abruptly grew sharp, disrupting the ground in an agitated flurry. His breath echoed heavily, punctuating the air with audible tension.

"This isn't the time."

Aiko declared, seizing Albie's arm and pulling him back onto their path. The stick dropped from Albie's grip, etching an imperfect yet distinctive drawing on the ground— a triangular shape topped by a box, two squares flanking a small circle, resembling a door. The interruption shattered Albie's concentration.

"Get your cap on. I won't share my jacket again."

Aiko ordered, retrieving the cap Albie had dropped and firmly placing it on his head, urging him forward into the watery forest.

"We're almost there. Keep moving."

Aiko insisted. Albie nodded, conceding to Aiko's persistence as the forceful tug softened into a gentle pull. His gaze lifted skyward, raindrops assaulting his senses, his lowered eyebrows forming a protective barrier against the relentless downpour. All he yearned for was a reprieve from the relentless wetness.

The path they traversed seemed unending—endless walking, steps upon steps toward the destination Aiko needed to reach.

The rain's barrage on Aiko's hood, pounding on it endlessly. The jacket's thickness offered a shield against the harsh elements, but the relentless raindrops were a constant torment, urging him to press onward.

"We're close; keep moving."

Aiko quickened his pace, tugging Albie's arm along, the latter yielding to Aiko's authority with a loose grip. The hill loomed ahead, gradually revealing a grayish light peeking through the clouded trees—a guiding beacon for Aiko. Climbing through the muddy terrain, softened by the perpetual downpour, they persisted, Aiko taking the lead. Reaching the hill's summit unveiled Aiko's sought-after sight. His mask gleamed blue, reflecting the faint light, as he gazed upon his destination. Across the expanse, billowing smoke filled the sky, swallowing the raindrops in its wake. The smoke funneled down to where the trains lay, dormant yet poised for their journeys. Brimming with cargo and life's essentials, many containers stood behind them, awaiting their rightful owners. Workers bustled about, maneuvering cranes and forklifts, ferrying various packages. Aiko seized Albie's arm again, forcefully pulling him down from the hill, his satisfaction palpable after surveying the scene.

At their destination, Aiko clutched Albie's hand, the tension thick in the air as they stealthily maneuvered through the outdoor facility, evading vigilant security. They trailed alongside a forklift, using it as cover to inch closer to the awaiting trains. But amidst the constant threat, a brief respite allowed Aiko to peer up at the rain-laden clouds, his masked face the only visible part amid the downpour. However, his grip found nothing but empty air in a split second—Albie was gone. Panic surged through Aiko as he frantically swiveled around, retracing their steps, scanning the area for any sign of Albie. But the rain played tricks, obstructing his vision. A glimmer of a cap caught his eye atop a cargo container. He had to be there.

Without hesitation, Aiko bolted towards Albie's suspected location, his heart racing faster than his feet through the muddied terrain that hindered his movement. He strained to overcome the rain's impediment, its constant pounding obscuring any sound.

The mud clung to Aiko's shoes, impeding his mobility and further complicating his search for Albie. As he reached the container's rear, he found Albie playing with a wrench, pressing it into the mud, creating an unnecessary diversion.

"ALBIE."

Aiko's whisper carried a tone of urgency.

"Stay close and stop that!"

The echo of boots in the distance jolted Aiko's heart, intensifying his anxiety. Peering cautiously around the container, he spotted a guard headed their way. Adrenaline surged, and Aiko whirled around to Albie.

"We have to move, NOW!"

27

Albie became an anchor, resisting Aiko's grip as if rooted in place. But Aiko, driven by urgency, pulled harder until Albie finally relented.

The wrench in Albie's hand collided with the container, the noise reverberating like a thunderclap. A surge of adrenaline rushed through Aiko, prompting him to peek around the container, only to find the guard charging toward them. With an iron grip, Aiko forcibly tugged Albie and sprinted away, desperation fueling every stride.

"STOP!"

The guard's commanding voice echoed, igniting a determination to capture them. Aiko raced through the maze of towering containers, using their massive shadows as cover, but they now seemed like colossal barriers, trapping them in the labyrinth.

"STOP!"

The guard's relentless pursuit closed in, his presence a looming threat that quickened Aiko's heart. His chest heaved with each breath, his veins pulsating with every beat. Pushing Albie to match his pace, Aiko dashed, their hands locked in a struggle. Albie followed, matching his steps but still resisting Aiko's grasp. As they narrowly escaped the container maze, something caught Aiko's attention.

The trains rumbled to life, inching away from Aiko and Albie. Time was dwindling; they had to make it on board.

"STOP!"

The guard's shouts grew louder, closing in. Aiko grabbed Albie's wrist, propelling him toward a container with an open door, the train serving as their fleeting chance. With a swift motion, Aiko hurled Albie aboard the cargo car, ensuring his safe landing before he prepared to follow suit.

Aiko stumbled over rocks, crashing to the ground on his knee, a jolt of searing pain shooting up to his brain. He gritted his teeth, suppressing the urge to cry out. No time to waste. The train was in motion. The guard drew nearer.

"GET BACK HERE!"

The train whistle as it started to depart. Ignoring the agony, Aiko pushed through, his limp turning into a determined sprint. With a final burst of effort, he leaped.

"OOF."

Aiko clutched the handles, straining to haul himself onto the train. He made it just in time as the speeding locomotive picked up pace. The guard, conceding defeat, halted his chase, watching helplessly as the train and the boys slipped from his reach. As the distance widened, Aiko glanced back at the shrinking figure of the guard, a surge of relief flooding through him before turning his focus to Albie, who was still toying with the wrench.

28

Aiko swiftly plucks the wrench from Albie's grasp. Despite the mask covering Aiko's face, his stern gaze conveys everything to Albie. Aiko shifts his attention to the left, observing the scenery morphing as the train barrels ahead. His hand delves into his olive-green jacket pocket, retrieving a folded piece of paper—a map. His eyes trace the terrain around them, following the train tracks as they stretch northwestward into a new region. It appears vast, enclosed, yet promising. Aiko scrutinizes the map further, focusing on the destination's name: "The Republic of Melancholia."

# Chapter Two: Harmony Fall Station

The wind persisted in its haunting whistle as the train hurtled forward, the trees outside performing an ethereal dance amidst the swirling mist created by the train's velocity. The constant rush of wind and the rhythmic sway of trees provided an ongoing symphony of motion, a never-ending melody that echoed through the speeding train.

Aiko found himself entranced by the mesmerizing motion of the passing landscape. Despite the train's rapid pace, time seemed to elongate, each passing moment stretching as the scenery flickered in and out of view. The jostling of the train along uneven tracks caused the containers to sporadically crackle and shift, prompting Aiko to lean back against the cargo for stability, yet unable to quell the unsettling sensation within.

Meanwhile, Albie's curiosity led him to explore the cargo's contents. He sought something intriguing, reminiscent of the excitement of finding a simple stick during their journey or discovering a wrench that elicited a chuckle. But among the boxes and packages, there was nothing.

"Stop poking around, Albie. Find something to do with your wrench; just don't break anything else."

Albie's gaze dropped further, a sly grin tugging at the corners of his mouth, unnoticed by Aiko. With a swift motion, Albie retreated to a distant corner of the compartment, securing his wrench and tinkering with it. Skillfully, he adjusted the tool, fashioning it into a makeshift mouth. He manipulated it up and down, crafting a crude puppet-like movement.

Peeking over at Aiko, who seemed lost in thought with his head reclined, Albie concocted a playful idea. Placing the wrench mouth at a spot where Aiko's head could fit, he moved it up and down, creating an illusion that made Aiko's head seem to disappear and reappear playfully.

The wind gradually transformed from a gentle breeze into an icy, biting gust, and the once cloudy sky dissolved into a serene, moonlit night. Yet amid these changes, the train's relentless motion, the trees swaying in the wind, and the persistent whistle remained unaltered. Aiko, still rooted in his spot, remained entranced by the trees' perpetual dance and the wind's ceaseless whistle. The night cast a reflective hue on his mask, revealing its serene blue amidst the shifting shadows and flickering light. Aiko tore his gaze from the evolving scenery, turning towards Albie, who clutched the wrench in a corner. Curled up as if in bed, Albie seemed relieved, finding solace amidst the ceaseless rattling that pervaded the surroundings.

Aiko approached Albie, observing his trembling body and closed eyes, his teeth clenching against the chill. Kneeling beside him, Aiko nodded, understanding the discomfort Albie was experiencing. Swiftly, Aiko removed his jacket and draped it over Albie's frame, meticulously tucking it around him to shield him from the relentless drafts. Retreating to his previous position, Aiko leaned back, his gaze fixed once more on the scenery outside. The looming shadow cast by the mask played across his face as he stared at the scene, a colossal mountain dominating the landscape. The mountain's silhouette cut through the sky, enveloped in a chilling aura. Aiko focused on the mountain's motion against the backdrop, then shifted his gaze upwards, fixating on the rattling ceiling of the train. The rattling persisted, unyielding.

The night persisted, the relentless rain drumming ceaselessly against the roof, its rhythmic pattern echoing throughout the cabin. The continuous rattling of the train's movement grew wearisome with every passing moment. Then, as swiftly as it had begun, the downpour subsided, leaving behind a tranquil stillness. The train had come to a halt.

"Get up; it's time to go."

Albie remained unresponsive to Aiko's words. With a nod of acknowledgment, Aiko lifted him by the waist, intending to carry him. Yet, Albie remained motionless, deliberately ignoring Aiko's request. Disregarding his companion's reluctance, Aiko hoisted Albie off the side of the open container, warily scanning his surroundings.

Navigating a steep path up the hills, Aiko bore the added weight of Albie's body, doubling his physical strain. Upon reaching the summit, he dropped Albie abruptly onto the ground, causing him to land awkwardly on the side of his face. Though a pained cry escaped Albie, he stifled it, meeting Aiko's unwavering gaze. Their silent acknowledgment spoke volumes.

Retrieving his map from the jacket, Aiko traced their current location. After traversing extensive trails from the previous day to their present position, they found themselves within five miles of the Harmony Fall Station, drawing at last tantalizingly close to their destination. Aiko advanced toward the dense, towering trees that loomed overhead. Meanwhile, with dirt smudging his cheek and around his eyes, Albie picked himself up from the ground and hastened to catch up with Aiko's determined stride.

Aiko raced through the air, his mask slicing through the rushing wind as he surged forward. The trees blurred by like tall grass, a promising sign that his objective was within reach. The pulsating energy of the open landscape fueled his determination—he knew he was on the brink of reaching his destination.

Beside him, Albie struggled to keep up, his breaths ragged, rasping against the biting chilly air. His lungs felt constricted, causing him to cough intermittently. Despite the discomfort, he knew he couldn't afford to lag behind Aiko's relentless pace. Regretfully, there was no other option but to push through the physical strain and continue the sprint.

As they approached the train station, dark figures on the horizon gradually transformed into people moving about purposefully. Upon closer inspection, Aiko discerned individuals converging toward the Harmony Fall Station. Finally catching up to Aiko, Albie was overcome with emotion, tears streaming down his face.

"We're here."

Aiko turned to Albie, finding him bent over, one hand clutching his knee, as he struggled to catch his breath. His throat noises attracted Aiko's attention.

Albie's tears shifted from anger to a poignant sorrow before tearfully facing Aiko.

"We're so close, Albie; you can rest again when we get on the train. Now, c'mon."

Aiko's steps carried him into a bustling crowd, the throng resembling a herd moving in sync. Each stride felt like another step in an endless journey for Albie and everyone around them. Albie hurried to Aiko's side, reaching for his hand, but Aiko instinctively pulled away. However, a glimpse of Albie's expression, the uncertainty etched on his face, made Aiko reconsider, allowing their hands to intertwine.

"Albie, stay close to me."

Aiko said towards Albie while looking at the sea of faces around them, a mix of the unfamiliar and the recognizable. Some were dressed in elegant garments with intricate textures that stood out to Aiko and Albie. Among them, figures in farming attire passed by, a stark contrast to the impeccably dressed crowd. Aiko noticed many carrying gas masks around their necks, a curious sight that puzzled him. Nonetheless, he forged ahead, making their way towards the gates for the train, the uncertainty of what lay ahead looming over their journey.

As Aiko and Albie approached the train gate, the personnel managing the trains stood guard. The swarm of people shuffled towards the train, each undergoing scrutiny upon entry. Scanning their surroundings, Aiko feared their streak of bad luck had caught up. They were next in line for inspection.

"Ticket, sir?"

The ticket agent peered down at Aiko; palms open. Aiko, unable to speak, merely met their gaze. His trembling hands in his pocket did not escape Albie's notice.

"If you lack a ticket, you can pay with credits."

The ticket agent offered.

Aiko remained motionless, causing a delay and drawing stares from the people behind him.

"Sir, do you understand?"

The ticket agent pressed.

"I'll cover it!"

A voice emerged from the crowded line. A boy appeared, reaching past Aiko towards the personnel. Aiko was caught off guard by the boy's intrusion and noticed an odd birthmark on his right cheek.

"I'll pay for them; it's okay."

The boy assured.

The personnel, eyebrows raised, inspected a card retrieved from the boy's poncho pocket, displaying his name and ID. Handing it over, the boy's offer was reluctantly accepted.

"Well, if you insist. Go ahead, boys."

The ticket agent relented.

Aiko glanced at the boy who had come to their aid and received a small smile in return. After processing the payment, the ticket agent returned the card to the boys.

"Apologies for cutting in line. You must return back since it's unfair to those waiting. But your generosity towards these two is appreciated."

The ticket agent explained.

"It's fine; I'll wait."

The boy replied, resigned to his place in line.

The boy, casting a final glance at Aiko and Albie, returned to the perpetually busy line. Meanwhile, Aiko and Albie entered the train, finding a maintained but well-worn interior. Footprints littered the floor, and windows were scratched, yet offering a decent view outside. Sideways seats facilitated quick movement, while overhead spaces became storage for passengers' belongings. An electronic screen displayed changing destinations, morphing from "Harmony Fall Station" to "The Republic of Melancholia."

Amid the rush, Aiko and Albie navigated through the crowd, finally securing available seats. Suddenly, someone took a seat beside Aiko, catching him off guard. Signaling Albie to sit, Aiko remained standing near the luggage area, observing those who missed seats. The estimated travel time of two hours sunk Aiko's spirits; the rush for seats now made sense—avoiding the discomfort of standing.

"Travel begins in T-minus 2 minutes."

The announcement echoed, the train brimming with eager passengers. Albie smiled, recalling Aiko's earlier insistence on resting. Aiko, gazing around, realized their fortune was thanks to the boy's help. He searched for the boy in the crowded train but couldn't spot him amidst the mass of people.

As the train smoothly started, Aiko felt a sense of relief compared to their prior experiences. Despite the overcrowding and the impending two-hour stand, Albie seemed more at ease. Aiko couldn't shake the guilt, pondering why the boy had extended such kindness. Questions swirled in his mind, unanswered. He simply wished for the journey's end, longing for resolution.

The crowd gradually thinned out as passengers disembarked at various stations on the way to The Republic of Melancholia. Aiko finally found a seat next to a slumbering Albie, giving his legs a much-needed reprieve from the cramped confines. As two hours dwindled to one, Aiko could finally relax, mirroring Albie's peaceful sleep.

"Hey."

A voice jolted Aiko from his reverie. He turned to find the boy who had offered assistance.

"Do you mind if I sit with you guys?"

The boy ask, to which Aiko nodded in agreement. The boy settled a few inches away, giving Aiko space. Aiko stole glances, observing the boy's appearance. He appeared older, clad in a tan poncho that cascaded over his shoulders and down to the top of his pants. The fabric of his pants bore signs of outdoor wear. Dark blonde hair framed brown eyes, and he stood slightly taller than Aiko with a slender frame. A prominent birthmark adorned the bottom of his right cheek; his eyes, a captivating hue of green, held a depth that seemed to have stories untold.

"I see you noticed the mark. It's unsettling, isn't it?"

The boy's question caught Aiko off guard. How did he know Aiko had been looking at his appearance, especially since he couldn't see Aiko's face?

"I've noticed the lingering gazes people give me; it can be unsettling for others, I understand."

The boy explained, acknowledging the unspoken query in Aiko's stare. Aiko listened but remained silent, simply recognizing the boy's words.

"The name's Quentin, Quentin Reily."

He introduced himself.

Aiko glanced at him again but avoided eye contact, unsure whether to respond. He remained puzzled, relieved that his lingering thoughts about the boy's whereabouts had been answered.

"I see you're the quiet type, then. It's okay if you don't want to speak."

Quentin remarked.

"Aiko."

Aiko finally stated.

"Aiko Ashin."

Quentin was slightly taken aback by Aiko's response.

"That's a nice name. And I assume that's your younger brother sleeping over there."

Aiko turned to reveal Albie dozing on a stranger's shoulder, the person seemingly undisturbed.

"Albie!"

Aiko called out in a hushed yet urgent tone. Albie stirred, slowly opening his eyes and adjusting his position.

"Albie Ashin, I presume."

Quentin interjected, amused by the exchange between Aiko and Albie. Almost about to scold Albie, Aiko checked himself and settled back to refocus on Quentin.

"So, where are y'all from?"

He continue addressing both Aiko and Albie. Aiko hesitated, wary of revealing too much about the recent troubles he and Albie had faced. He needed to craft an answer that satisfied Quentin's curiosity without divulging too many details.

"Somewhere from the outskirts of the nation."

Aiko responded cautiously.

"Near the Division zones or the Inhabitant zone?"

Quentin probed further and was keen on extracting more information.

"Yeah."

Aiko affirmed, relieved that Quentin didn't press for specifics.

"That explains it. You and your brother are away from civilization. Hence, no ID cards."

Quentin deduced, offering Aiko a sense of relief by not delving deeper into their journey.

"I know there are still people living outside these zones, but I've never seen someone like you, especially with a mask."

Quentin remarked, observing Aiko's appearance.

Aiko acknowledged Quentin's observation but remained silent.

"You guys don't have any ID cards or means of payment?"

Quentin continued.

"No, we traveled here on foot for like 3 days. I didn't anticipate the need for payment for the train ride."

Aiko admitted.

"I can imagine how difficult walking through those zones must have been. The temperature and terrain can be unforgiving."

Quentin sympathized.

"Thanks."

Aiko replied softly, feeling a sense of gratitude. Quentin's mention of ID cards triggered a question in Aiko's mind, prompting him to wonder what Quentin meant.

"Thank you for paying for us. I didn't know how to react to the ticket agent."

Aiko expressed his gratitude.

"Nah, you're good. I just noticed you were troubled, so I offered my assistance."

Quentin replied, his hand resting on the back of his head, grateful for Aiko's response. He chuckled lightly.

"What do you mean by the credits or ID?"

Aiko questioned, seeking clarification from Quentin.

Quentin looked at Aiko, reaching into his poncho pocket to retrieve his ID card.

"The URDT issued citizens a form of identification since the beginning of the colonization of this planet."

Showing Aiko a card with Quentin's photo, the tag number, and something that says PSC.

"It's called a PSC, for Personalized Score and Credits. It's quite intricate. The system evaluates how much you contribute to society, mostly gauging your value to the Republic of Melancholia and then designing this system, replacing the old paper currency with instantaneous credit transfers. It covers all activities, including the educational system, rewarding academic excellence, contributions, skills, and achievements. Your score also affects your social reputation."

Quentin explained.

Aiko studied the cards intently before turning to Quentin, a sense of confusion lingering. Quentin met his gaze, understanding evident on his face.

"What do you do to earn those credits?"

Aiko ask Quentin who tucked his card back into his poncho.

"I engage in community work across different regions here. Also, I finished high school about a year ago, which helped me accumulate many credits. Earning credits depends on the job type, but ultimately, it's about the quantity and quality of the work you do. The credits earned are essentially hours worked, and there's always endless work everywhere."

Quentin shared; his gaze fixed on the passing scenery outside. His words drifted out slowly.

"Is the work exhausting?"

Aiko probed.

"Everything is exhausting."

Quentin replied with a sigh, capturing the weariness of it all.

Quentin leaned back, his eyes closing as he uttered those words. Aiko observed Quentin's posture, grasping the sentiment behind his statement.

"But maybe not."

Quentin remarked, suddenly sitting up straight.

"I'm going to apply for the URDT military. They offer endless opportunities—new friends, new experiences, and plenty of credits for your service!"

Quentin declared with contagious enthusiasm, rising from his seat, his words resonating with an appealing fervor.

"Things might look up in the future. The URDT military needs recruits. Have you heard of the famous FIREBIRDS program? They're the elite squad—the best of the best!"

Quentin continued, energized by his own words.

"What's FIREBIRDS?"

Aiko asked, caught off guard by Quentin's sudden declaration.

"It might sound funny, but it's meaningful. Stands for Federal, Initiative, Regiment, Elite, Bold, Reconnaissance, Integrated, Dynamic, Soldiers. They were formed during Earth's final stand. I don't know much about Earth's final days, but I've heard that the FIREBIRDS offer a lot—transforming individuals beyond themselves."

Quentin explained, his admiration evident.

As Quentin finished his praise, he settled back into his seat, his gaze shifting from the floor to Aiko, who was now lost in the train's motion.

"I'm joining the military to be like my dad."

Quentin disclosed. Aiko, surprised by Quentin's revelation, felt Quentin's eyes on him and acknowledged his sudden reaction.

Quentin's voice choked with emotion as he shared.

"My dad used to... be part of the FIREBIRDS. He'd return home to me and my mother, brimming with amazing stories about his adventures. I admired him greatly; he always looked so content when he returned."

Apologizing for losing his composure, Quentin regained focus and continued.

"I'm sorry if I seemed scattered. It's been a while since I heard from him. Neither I nor my mom know where he's gone. I've never spoken of this before, but I want to join the military—to be like him and seek answers."

There was a momentary hush, the train's rhythm, and the rushing wind filling the space. Albie, now awake, glanced at Quentin and then gazed down at the floor, silently understanding Quentin's words.

"You know, you can come with me."

Quentin broke the silence, addressing Aiko, who was still lost in thought by the window, contemplating the passing scenery.

"Do you know where you're headed, Aiko?"

Quentin asked, trying to gauge Aiko's thoughts.

Without much outward expression, Aiko gazed into the distance for a while, prompting Quentin to infer that Aiko did not know where he was headed.

"No, I'm not sure."

"Want to travel with me?"

Aiko's was surprised by Quentin request but only gave him a response to quiet his mind.

"Okay."

Aiko's answer was a bit unsure; he felt he needed someone to help him get around the unfamiliar nation.

As Aiko's intentions became clear, Quentin relaxed, relieved by the decision. He leaned back, gazing at the train's roof. Quentin glances at Albie, who is resting peacefully.

"How come he doesn't talk like you do?"

Quentin catching Aiko's attention, Aiko, unamused, answered back.

"He can't speak. He has a condition that prevent him from speaking."

"I see. Unfortunate then..."

A hooded man swiftly entered through the rear door, his face obscured, dressed in all black. Following closely was a girl, younger in appearance and of similar height to Aiko. She is wearing a skirt with a jacket covering her whole body, and her hair is elegant and long. Her demeanor was focused, displaying little emotion.

Both moved swiftly through the train compartments, passing Quentin, Aiko, and Albie. Quentin watched them, intrigued by their presence and the connection between the two. However, Aiko and Albie remained oblivious, lost in their thoughts and rest.

Suddenly, a thunderous thud jolted the train, its suddenness tossing Albie off his seat, causing him to injure his knee. Aiko was shoved away from Quentin, who tumbled to the floor.

"Something's wrong with the train!"

Quentin exclaimed, scrambling to his feet. Aiko rushed to assist Albie, who winced in pain from the fall.

The train's interior lights turned an ominous red, casting a foreboding glow over everything.

Quentin declared in shock, his face reflecting the gravity of the situation.

"We're being hijacked."

# Chapter Three: Turbulent Ride Part 1

The sudden halt of the train jolted every corner, with warning signs flashing across the screens. Quentin, Aiko, and Albie stood up, taking in the caution signs surrounding them. Quentin, quick to react, drew a conclusion.

"We're being hijacked."

"How do you know?"

Aiko, checking on Albie and ensuring his well-being, Quentin glanced back at them both.

"Are you guys okay?"

He asked, his concern evident.

"Yeah, I'm fine, but Albie hurt his knee."

Aiko replied, relieved as Quentin handed over a gel labeled 'Skin Soothe.' Aiko carefully applied it to Albie's injured knee, soothing his pain.

"I've heard about an organization behind these activities."

Quentin continued.

"They've been hitting places crucial to people's lives. I don't know much about their goals, but they're troublemakers. And right now, we're in trouble. We've got to get out."

Turning back to Albie, Aiko found him exhausted, lying back on the seats.

"We have to leave, Albie. It's not safe."

Aiko urged, but Albie shook his head weakly, signaling his refusal. Frustration tightened Aiko's fists. When Aiko tried to pull Albie to his feet, Albie resisted, turning it into a struggle.

Albie's tearful mumbles rang out amidst the chaos.

"You're making me do this; we have to GO!"

Aiko insisted, tugging at Albie's arm more determinedly. Suddenly, Albie delivered a sharp kick to Aiko's chest, sending him reeling backward and Albie landing back on the seat. Aiko, stunned by the unexpected move, looked at Albie with wide, dazed eyes. From Albie's perspective, Aiko's blue mask concealed his expression, yet he sensed

Aiko's surprise and distress, understanding Aiko's emotions without seeing his face; the mask hid it all.

"Look."

Quentin stepped in between them, approaching Albie and kneeling beside him.

"How about a piggyback ride? Come on, it'll be fun."

Quentin tried to ease Albie's nervousness, mentioning the promise of delicious frozen treats at their destination.

"I heard there are delicious frozen cotta where we're going. You just need to cooperate, and I will get you one. What do you think?"

Quentin's compassion enveloped Albie, who glanced down briefly, his gaze darting around before closing his eyes for a few seconds.

Albie nodded reluctantly, and Quentin offered his back. Albie jumped on, holding on tightly. Now carrying Albie, Quentin glanced down at Aiko, who remained on the floor. Extending his hand to help Aiko up, Quentin awaited his response.

"Okay, let's head out."

They proceeded toward the front door, where the incessant red light continued flashing, accompanied by blaring alarms. Quentin attempted to open the door, but it was locked and refused to budge.

"The doors are locked. It's either a safety feature, or the hijacker has control."

Quentin deduced, scanning their surroundings while carrying Albie. Aiko, recovering from Albie's action, began searching for an escape route. He noticed a hatch and a switch above the roof.

"There's a door up there."

Aiko pointed out.

"Okay, I'll give you a boost up there."

Quentin offered. He knelt with his hands open, allowing Aiko to jump onto his hands and providing extra force to pry open the hatch. With a mighty push from Aiko, the hatch immediately gave way.

"Go to the other side of the door to see if you can open it from there."

Quentin instructed Aiko. Aiko navigated to the roof of the moving train, feeling relief as the train resumed its high-speed journey. Spotting a ladder, he descended to the other side of the door and exerted force on the handle until it creaked open.

The door swung ajar, granting Aiko, Quentin, and Albie exit from the compartment. Now outside, caught between where they had come from and where other passengers sat helplessly.

"So, what's your plan?"

Aiko asked Quentin, who scanned their surroundings, seeking potential routes.

"Well, the compartments inside the train are locked, so we can't pass through them. And we're in the middle of nowhere, high above the ground and streets. We might just have to walk on top of the train roof."

Quentin's confidence seemed to waver as he spoke.

"Let's just do it. We need to sprint towards the front of the train. We have to try."

Aiko urged Quentin, who hesitated before agreeing.

"Alright, let's give it a shot."

Quentin consented, with Albie concerned.

Nodding determinedly, Aiko started climbing the ladder, followed closely by Quentin. On reaching the top, Aiko had initially focused on opening the door for Quentin and Albie, paying little attention to the vastness of the Republic of Melancholia's. The cold breeze made one of them shiver, and the scattered clouds hinted at the recent rain.

Looking around at the cityscape sprawled beneath them, its mini towers gleaming like beacons amidst the mechanical vehicle noises and blaring horns.

"Alright, let's make our way."

Quentin declared confidently, cautiously testing the slippery roof's stability before picking up speed while carrying Albie. Aiko followed suit.

They moved with care, leaping between compartment roofs. The wet surface made their landings unstable and caused them to shudder, especially Quentin carrying Albie. However, their caution and determination drove them forward, leap by leap, edging closer toward the train's front.

"I know there's an emergency call button at the front. These buttons are scattered around the compartments, but I'm unsure exactly where. However, I know for sure there's one at the front. If the conductors or staff were still there, they would have pressed it unless they were hostages or gone. That's their modus operandi—taking hostages."

Quentin explained while vaulting across to another compartment.

"What do you think the hijacker wants?"

Aiko asked, keeping pace behind him.

"No idea. They usually cause chaos or destruction, taking over trains recently, but their motives are a mystery."

Quentin responded, contemplating their predicament.

Aiko mulled over Quentin's words, thoughts swirling. Why was he following someone he barely knew? He pushed those thoughts aside, focusing on the immediate task.

"Did you see a girl following the hooded person?"

Quentin asked, watching his steps carefully as he waited for Aiko to catch up.

"No, I didn't notice. Why? Could she be involved?"

Aiko thought of as his attention divided between the current situation and thoughts of Albie's safety.

"I don't think so. She was walking close yet seemed distant. I doubt she's part of this. Let's keep going; we're almost there."

Quentin urged, picking up the pace. Albie seemed somewhat cheerful, his mouth agape, absorbing the exhilaration of their adventure, akin to an endless roller coaster ride.

With each leap, the distance grew smaller, but the sun's rays failed to evaporate the persistent wetness. The cold breeze clung to the moisture, making everything damp. Aiko followed Quentin, striving to catch up. During another jump, Aiko's foot slipped, sliding him down the train's side. As he desperately sought something to hold onto, he gripped a corner of the roof, his fingers slipping on the water puddles, rendering his grip futile. Panic surged through him, nerves ablaze, and muscles froze. He couldn't hold on much longer.

A sudden hand seized Aiko's arm, pulling him back up.

"Aiko, pull yourself up!"

Quentin strained, trying to assist Aiko. But even Quentin's strength might not be enough. Quentin had to set down Albie to focus on helping Aiko.

"I'm sorry, Albie, I need both hands."

Quentin said, grasping Aiko's arms and struggling against the slippery conditions. The misty water covered them, making their grip tenuous.

Albie sat frozen, watching Quentin struggle to save Aiko, feeling utterly helpless. His gaze fixated on Quentin, scrutinizing every detail of his tense face. Suddenly, Quentin's features reminded Albie of someone familiar, a boy with silky, medium-length black hair and piercing green eyes. Someone from his distant memory. Albie's pulse quickened, memories rushing in, and without hesitation, he lunged toward Quentin with all the force he could muster.

Quentin was taken aback by Albie's sudden action. Without a moment to process, he sensed the sheer concern in Albie's tight embrace, spurring him into a surge of determination. He grasped Aiko's arms with strength, straining every muscle to hoist him upward.

"ARRRRGH!"

Quentin's guttural grunt echoed their collective effort. Aiko pushed himself, too, their combined strength gradually lifting him upward. Inch by painstaking inch, they hauled Aiko onto the roof, each movement a Herculean feat. Finally, Aiko lay sprawled on the roof, motionless, having been pulled clear.

Exhausted, Quentin sank to a seated position, shielding his face with his arms, his breaths ragged. Beside him, Albie slumped with closed eyes, his head buried in his arms as he drew in a long breath. A moment of reprieve washed over them, and Aiko, catching his breath, exchanged a silent, grateful nod with Quentin.

The metallic clanking reverberated, growing louder with each passing second. Suddenly, a subtle yet unmistakable pushback nudged them, prompting a panicked glance forward. A silent exchange of dread passed between Aiko and Quentin, a shared realization dawning upon them.

Reacting swiftly, Quentin seized Albie, who clung to his back with an unyielding grip, while Aiko sprang into action, darting toward another compartment. The train surged forward, its speed escalating dangerously. Quentin scanned ahead, noting the proximity of the first two compartments, precariously linked to the central operations hub. He spotted a tunnel looming ominously, threatening to propel them off the compartment roof as the train barreled ahead.

"We're nearing a tunnel—get ready to jump!"

Quentin barked, taking the lead. He hurled himself downward, barely avoiding a collision upon landing. Aiko followed suit, but his trajectory unfortunately met with a wall, eliciting a swift "Ouch" from him.

As the train gained velocity, the world outside blurred into a dizzying rush. The wind howled, whipping their faces, while the landscape whizzed past in a frenzied blur. Suddenly, the daylight vanished, plunging them into an inky darkness. All that remained was the relentless clatter of metal colliding, echoing endlessly in the abyss.

Aiko and Quentin, still catching their breaths, peered through the window of the door, the pane offering a fleeting glimpse into Quentin's harrowing suspicions. The view revealed an interior akin to where they were earlier, but this area was interconnected with the train's central operating hub. The sight that met their eyes was grim: individuals, handcuffed or bound to poles, some roped together, all subjected to

44

captivity against their will. Among them was a mother cradling a child in her arms, both confined in a manner that defied their innocence. Quentin recognized the girl he had mentioned earlier, tied and seated with an inscrutable expression etched on her face.

"That's the girl I mentioned."

Quentin murmured, trying to make himself heard over the relentless din of metal clanking. Aiko leaned closer, his gaze flickering between the girl and a figure shrouded in a hood.

"And there's the guy with the hood."

Aiko noted quietly, his attention momentarily drawn to a new arrival. Another individual, adorned in a mask and a bulletproof vest, emerged, engaging in conversation with the hooded figure. The masked person's eyes were the only visible feature, darkly lined with makeup. They conversed, but their words were lost in the tumultuous clamor of the train. The hooded figure wielded a pistol, manipulating it with an unsettling fluidity, while the other person held a rifle, its barrel steady yet pointed ominously at the captives.

The tension crackled between Quentin and Aiko as they weighed their options. Quentin positioned himself against the opposite wall, adopting a stance of readiness.

"We need to stop them."

Quentin mumbled urgently to Aiko.

"We'll get ourselves killed!"

Aiko's protest came in a panicked whisper.

"There's no other choice. Some of those hostages are the personnel who can operate this train."

Quentin started to consider their option. His eyes darted from the dark void outside, swallowed by the tunnel's oppressive darkness, to the windowed door, where a red cylinder marked "Fire Extinguisher" caught his attention. His gaze widened with realization.

"I have a plan. Once that guy exits, we strike. I'll grab the fire extinguisher nearby. I'll distract or disarm the hooded figure. You free the captives with his gun. We need those personnel."

Quentin explained, his eyes filled with determination as he looked at Aiko, seeking solidarity.

"I can't; I refuse!"

Aiko was caught off guard, his hand trembling uncontrollably. He attempted to steady himself, pressing his palm to his side to quell the shakes, but his fear was palpable.

45

Quentin, with his other arm, grabbed Aiko by the shoulder.

"Aiko, you must shoot at the handcuffs; I'll be too busy controlling the guy. Get the handcuffs off the personnel to get more people to tackle the hijackers!"

Quentin tightened his grip on Aiko's shoulder.

"Aiko, we're out of options. You just need to shoot at the handcuffs. I'll handle the guy. Free the personnel so we can outnumber them!"

Albie's eyes flitted between Quentin and Aiko; his anxiety was visible as he started trembling.

"Guys."

Quentin said, closing his eyes to ease the tension.

"We have no choice. We need to act, or none of us will make it out. Aiko, you've survived the most hostile zone. You've faced danger before. Aiko, you managed to get here from the most hostile area and even take care of Albie. If you can do all that, I need you to believe in yourself."

Quentin released his grip on Aiko's shoulder, allowing him to absorb his words. Aiko glanced at Albie, a boy he'd cared for, feeling strongly connected despite their differences. Quentin, older and confident, stood nearby, exuding reassurance.

With his hands clenched, Aiko rose to his feet, nodding at Quentin. Quentin gently set Albie down.

"Albie, we need you to stay here until it's safe. Promise you won't go in?"

Quentin's voice was both firm and kind.

Albie, still shaken but comforted by Quentin's demeanor, managed to give a small smile as a response. Aiko was surprised by Albie's compliance but said nothing, silently acknowledging him before refocusing on the task.

"The door is locked from out here, so I'll have to break the window; when I do that, you follow behind me; I'll charge at him and grab his gun till he lets go. I took martial arts when I was little; I have ways of putting him down."

While getting his elbow ready, Quentin charged up his arm for a decisive blow.

"On three."

Quentin announced firmly, his stance resolute. The man with the mask moved back to the adjacent compartment.

"One."

Quentin tensed, his eyes fixed on the unfolding scene.

"Two."

Albie, hiding behind cover, shut his eyes tightly, blocking the tension.

As the masked man closed the compartment leading to the train's operation area, the hooded figure remained turned away from the hostages. Aiko, hidden beside Quentin, felt his hands quiver, thoughts of uncertainty flooding his mind. What if this plan failed? What if he couldn't make a difference?

"Three!"

Quentin bellowed.

With swift determination, Quentin shattered the window with a powerful elbow thrust. He swiftly reached for the door handle, wrenching it open for their charge. The hooded figure turned, caught off guard by the commotion. Quentin led the charge, with Aiko closely following.

Seizing a fire extinguisher nearby, Quentin hurled it at the hooded figure, sending them staggering backward. Seizing the opportunity, Quentin darted forward, grabbing the extinguisher back. With relentless force, he hammered at the hooded figure's hand, causing them to release the pistol. Quentin pinned the hooded figure by pushing down the figure's arms to prevent them from moving and using his legs to restrain the figure's legs.

Aiko picked up the pistol and struggled to steady his aim, panic clouding his thoughts. His breaths came in heavy gasps, his whole-body trembling. His gaze flickered to the pistol.

"AIKO, I CAN'T HOLD HIM FOR MUCH LONGER!"

Quentin's desperate plea echoed. Suddenly, the hooded figure headbutted Quentin with brutal force, causing him to stagger and release his grip. The figure rose menacingly, fixing a chilling gaze upon Quentin. Vicious kicks sent Quentin reeling, each blow sapping the air from his lungs.

Realizing he had delayed too long, Aiko's eyes locked with the hooded figures. Aiko raised the pistol, finger poised on the trigger. But his relentless tremors thwarted any steadiness. His mind raced: "I can't... I can't afford another mistake!" A crippling fear surged through him, his heart pounding so violently it threatened to betray him. He aimed at the hooded figure, frozen by indecision, as Quentin's breaths slowed until they were no more.

"Shoot the damn gun!"

The sudden voice shattered the tension. The girl, having managed to unlock one side of her cuffs, grabbed the gun away from Aiko and-

She shot the hooded figure's legs. The figure dropped to the floor, moaning from the anguish.

"Why didn't you shoot at him? You'd be dead if you stood there."

Her words clawed at Aiko's senses as she freed herself from the cuffs, her fingers revealing a bobby pin. She stormed toward him, and Aiko remained motionless as a statue in the chaos that unfolded. In the distance, Albie cowered, unable to shield himself from the unfolding scene.

Struggling to his feet, Quentin shielded his bruised belly with one arm. The girl approached him, offering a hand and then lifting him up. Quentin winced, gasping in pain, his words labored.

"It wasn't his fault... it was my idea. He choked."

Guilt stained his voice. He looked at the girl, then turned to Aiko.

"I should've known you weren't ready."

Aiko remained resolutely still, refusing to budge. Quentin hurried to the hooded figure's side, examining the wound on the leg. His fingers checked for a pulse at the figure's neck, a tense moment that stretched the air with anticipation.

Quentin assessed the hooded figure's condition and announced.

"He's still breathing."

Aiko crumbled, his hands shielding his face as he whispered a mantra of denial: "Not again, not again, not again."

Overhearing Aiko's words, Quentin rushed back to him. Meanwhile, the girl began releasing restrained passengers and personnel.

Quentin's words hung heavy in the tense air, laden with guilt and regret.

"You can't blame yourself; it was my fault for putting you and your brother in this situation. Forgive me."

Quentin bowed his head, a gesture of contrition and responsibility. Meanwhile, Aiko remained shrouded, his hands still shielding his face. His tremors persisted, each shudder a testament to the turmoil raging within. His racing heart threatened to suffocate him, each breath becoming more labored and strained.

With no immediate words to console Aiko, Quentin rose from his spot, his next objective clear: to retrieve Albie from his place of refuge. As Quentin moved away, Aiko was engulfed in a sudden deluge of memories. Images and emotions flooded his mind, fragmented recollections weaving in and out like elusive shadows. Among them, a figure with black hair emerged, a name escaping his lips in a hushed whisper: "Anbu..."

"Stop whimpering!"

The girl's sharp command pierced through the chaos, addressing Aiko. The passengers and personnel remained shaken, trying to recover from the ordeal. Just as she was about to speak further, a sudden movement caught her eye.

In a chilling moment, a silhouette appeared at the door's window leading to the train's operation area—the unmistakable shape of a barrel. Reacting swiftly, the girl instinctively ducked for cover.

The deafening gunshot echoed through the compartment, plunging everyone into a state of instant panic. Instinctively, they ducked for cover. In response, the girl, fueled by fury, retaliated, firing back at the assailant. But amidst the chaos, the harsh darkness from the outside, and the light inside not highlighting her target, her shots missed, the masked figure darting away. Undeterred, she sprang to her feet and gave chase.

Aiko, shaken by the sudden gunfire, slowly rose, his eyes following the path where the girl had gone. Quentin, leading Albie by the hand, re-entered the compartment after hearing the shots.

"Albie, stay here. These people will keep you safe. We'll be right back."

Quentin urged, but Albie, consumed by fear, remained frozen, his response lost in the turmoil. Quentin acknowledged Albie's silence and ran after the girl in pursuit of the masked assailant.

Amidst the chaos, Aiko remained motionless, a silent spectator to the turmoil unfolding. His gaze fixed on the ground, Albie glanced at Aiko, their eyes meeting despite the cover of Aiko's mask. Neither moved, locked in a moment of shared apprehension and uncertainty.

# Chapter Four: Turbulent Ride Part 2

The masked figure maneuvered through the operation area, panels flickering in a dazzling array of lights as gears clashed and metal resounded. Rifle shots echoed as the figure returned fire, the girl carefully taking cover behind nearby panels. Her own shots missed their mark, and she swiftly assessed her remaining bullets.

"Three left."

She murmured, glancing around to see if the figure persisted. The door's solid thud indicated their retreat. Leaning back, she gripped her ammo cartridge and pistol, collecting herself in a moment of respite.

"Hey."

A sudden voice jolted the girl, causing her to instantly point her pistol at the speaker.

"WOAH, IT'S ME!"

Quentin raised his arms, stepping back to give her space. She lowered her weapon, frustration evident in her palm against her face.

"What are you doing here? I didn't ask for your help."

She said, reloading her pistol and checking its function.

"HEY, we're the ones who rescued you!"

Quentin's arms swung up before dropping into fists.

"Firstly, you and the kid were almost goners. Secondly, I didn't need your help. You made things worse for me."

She rose, eyeing the direction the hijacker had gone.

"Besides, weren't you heavily injured? You need rest. I don't need you."

"It's fine; I've taken way worse punishment before."

Quentin retorted, meeting her gaze. She closed her eyes, pressing forward without further acknowledgment.

"Whatever."

She muttered as she stealthily approached the central control room, where the masked figure had headed. Quentin followed, his arm guarding his belly against the pain. Each step felt like a jolt, a persistent reminder of the blow he'd sustained. His thoughts drifted

50

to Aiko, wondering if he was safe, but he couldn't divert his attention from the immediate situation. Observing the girl's precise movements, he pondered why she was trailing them, her intentions shrouded in mystery. Questions piled up, yet he couldn't find any conclusive answers.

"What's your name?"

Quentin asked, and she turned her head a bit softly.

"Suki."

"Ok. Suki, why were you following him?"

Quentin asked. Cautiously follows her.

"He and his partner are part of The Excesses organization; I was going to ask for answers from one of them quietly until he started waving his pistol around and eventually caught on to the fact that I was following him. And I ended up captured like the rest of the people."

"What answers for? You have a death wish or something?"

"Maybe we don't have time to discuss my actions."

As they reached the door, they both positioned themselves at its side. Suki pressed her ear against the wall, straining to catch any sound amid the train's rattling and clanking metal. She tested the door handle cautiously, revealing it was slightly ajar.

"He's hiding in here, waiting."

She whispered to Quentin, who peered over her shoulder to confirm the door's slight opening.

"It's a trap. He's cornered but likely waiting for one of us to enter and spring it."

Quentin murmured in return.

The two exchanged a quick glance, their eyes briefly locking in a moment of shared apprehension. Quentin hadn't paid much attention to her appearance before, but now, in the heat of the situation, he noticed her stylish, messy black hair and sapphire eyes. Her attire, a jacket adorned with numerous pins and badges, spoke of a mix of nature and gloom. But amidst the chaos, their interaction felt oddly synchronized.

"Hello, are you even listening?"

Her whispered inquiry snapped Quentin back to the task at hand.

"Oh, sorry, I won't be charging in first again."

Quentin replied, refocusing his attention on their strategy.

"Then how are we going to get in?"

She prodded, a note of urgency in her voice.

As Quentin thought, she made her focus to Aiko. He looked away momentarily.

"He's not doing well; let's leave him for now. Another mistake is the last thing I need."

She stressed.

"We must act quickly."

Quentin's gaze shifted around the room, finally landing on the fire extinguisher. A plan began to form in his mind.

"I've got an idea. I'll toss the fire extinguisher inside. He'll be ready for anyone to charge in. That's when we strike."

Quentin explained.

"And I'll end him as well if he doesn't answer any question I have. His accomplice is unconscious; I need answers."

She said, her tone resolute.

"No, you won't."

Quentin responded firmly, noticing the intensity in her eyes.

"Is there more to this? I don't even know what answers you're seeking. We need to secure the room first."

The tension between them simmered, the unspoken questions hanging like an invisible barrier. Their faces showed determination and a sense of unease as they prepared to confront the figure lurking behind the door.

Quickly, Quentin seized the fire extinguisher, darting back to her side. They exchanged a determined nod, signaling their readiness. Quentin crouched, stealthily maneuvering around her, inching toward the door, readying the extinguisher for a throw. She pressed against the door, providing just enough space for Quentin to launch the projectile. Quentin silently counted down with his fingers, mimicking the countdown with his lips.

Each finger counted down by Quentin heightened the sense of anticipation. Finally, as his last finger dropped, Quentin propelled the extinguisher with all his might toward the door. Simultaneously, she pressed the door, ensuring the extinguisher cleared the threshold. The room was engulfed in a cacophony of sound.

Gunfire erupted within the compartment.

The sudden onslaught echoed throughout the train, sending shivers down the passengers' spines in nearby compartments. Panic ensued as people sought cover. Torn between protecting Albie and the commotion, Aiko glanced anxiously between the chaos and his brother. His heart raced wildly, uncertain of his next move amid the chaos and danger.

The bullet impact exploded the fire extinguisher, releasing a dense cloud of foam and carbon dioxide into the air, engulfing Quentin and Suki. Quentin was hit directly by the cloud, his vision obscured. He coughed uncontrollably, but despite the toxic fumes, he pressed on.

Suki, covering her mouth to shield herself from the toxic cloud, charged at the figure. Seizing the opportunity, Quentin followed suit, plunging into chaos despite the burning sensation in his lungs. His vision blurred with each step, his heart pounding furiously against his chest.

Suki threw herself at the masked figure, catching them off guard and restricting his movements. Quentin rushed to assist her, tackling the figure to neutralize the threat. He struggled to pin down the figure while Suki slowly raised her arm, revealing a gun she had concealed. Quentin noticed this in a fraction of a second.

"NO!"

Quentin lunged towards her, swiftly disarming her. She coughed violently from the smoke, her breaths shallow and strained.

"WHAT ARE YOU DOING?!"

She erupted at Quentin, her voice fraught with urgency.

"I SAID YOU'RE NOT GONNA KILL HIM!"

Quentin exerted pressure to keep her arm away from the figure.

"I DON'T CARE WHAT YOU SAID! HE WAS WILLING TO KILL US ALL. YOU HAVE NO IDEA WHAT YOU'RE DOING!"

She struggled against Quentin's grip, her movements frenzied.

"IT DOESN'T MATTER; YOU'RE GONNA PULL THE TRIGGER REGARDLESS OF WHEN YOU'RE SATISFIED!"

Quentin maintained his hold on her arm, trying to restrain her without causing harm.

"YOU DON'T UNDERSTAND—"

She began, but her words were cut short as she noticed movement from the corner of her eye. The masked figure had risen and was aiming his rifle at them. Quentin reacted swiftly, his heart racing as he and Suki dodged just in time to narrowly avoid the barrage of bullets fired by the masked figure. Dust and particles clouded their vision, shrouding the chaos in the compartment.

Suki and Quentin charged at the figure together, attempting to restrain him against the control panel. His eyes scanned the controls, and he broke free from their grasp with a sudden surge of strength. He took aim at the control panel, firing a hail of bullets that tore through the metal, revealing the circuits beneath.

As the dust settled, the masked figure noticed an "Emergency Exit" sign and swiftly approached it. With weakened arms, he struggled to open the door. A powerful gust of wind surged in as the door opened, sucking the dust out of the area. The figure jumped through the door, vanishing into the tunnel's darkness.

Quentin and Suki realized the figure had escaped. The force of the wind threatened to pull Suki away. Quentin rushed towards her, desperately grabbing her arm. Despite his efforts, the wind was too powerful, dragging them closer to the exit.

"HOLD ON!"

Quentin gasped, his fingers slipping.

"AHHHHH!"

Suki's cry spurred Quentin to muster every ounce of strength, but it wasn't enough. His grip was slipping, his feet losing purchase.

"I CAN'T HOLD ON FOR—"

Quentin's voice was desperate, but his efforts were futile. His feet slipped away, inch by inch. Quentin clenched his eyes shut, his heart pounding in his chest. He refused to give up, but sheer willpower alone might not be enough.

An arm appeared out of nowhere, wrapping tightly around Quentin's body. A surge of relief washed over him. He turned to see Aiko, pulling him back with determination. Together, Aiko and Quentin struggled against the wind, finally rescuing Suki. Moments later, the train operator rushed in, shutting the door tightly behind them.

Exhausted and gasping for air, Quentin, Aiko, and Suki collapsed, the adrenaline draining from their bodies. Quentin cast a grateful glance at Aiko, who sat by the control panel, nodding in acknowledgment. Then he gestured towards Aiko and Suki, silently indicating Aiko's help.

"Thanks."

Suki muttered, her lips tight with reluctance to express gratitude. Quentin spotted sparks igniting from the control panels. Rushing over, he inspected the damage, his heart sinking at the sight of bullet-riddled mechanisms. Aiko, Suki, and the train operator examined the damaged panels, their expressions grim.

"Can't you still operate this train?"

Quentin turned to the trainer operator, desperation seeping into his voice.

The train operators wore a resigned expression, shaking their heads.

"We can't. The panels are completely busted."

One of them admitted, pointing at the damaged controls. Their hopes were further dashed when another pointed to the train map, showing the imminent arrival at their destination.

"Republic of Melancholia—5 Minutes to Destination," the display read. Dread filled the compartment as the realization sank in. The train was about to emerge from the tunnels, taking them closer to their fate.

Quentin's heart thudded against his chest like a drumbeat of impending disaster.

"We're going too fast."

He murmured, his voice barely audible over the train's relentless roar.

The personnel's frantic voice cut through the urgency.

"Wait! There's an emergency switch to stop the train! Our track ends at Evergreen Hub Station; we will crash if we don't stop early!"

A glimmer of salvation lay behind a glass enclosure—the emergency switch, a dark red beacon amidst the flashing panels. It pulsed like a lifeline, waiting for someone to snatch it from the jaws of calamity.

The train surged out of the dark tunnel, thrusting into a landscape of luminous cityscape. The Evergreen Hub Station stood proud and ominously ahead, tall buildings jutting into the sky like sentinels guarding a metropolis. Miniature flags danced atop wires, creating an illusion of celebration amidst chaos. The buildings, adorned in earthy tones, cast long shadows in the fading light.

A collective gasp reverberated as the gravity of the situation sank in.

"We're heading straight for Evergreen Hub Station! We're going too fast!"

The train operator's voice trembled with urgency. They activated the radio to contact Evergreen Hub Station and report the emergency.

The passengers, their faces a tapestry of concern, turned to behold the impending collision. The looming station, a beautiful but dangerous mirage, grew more prominent by the second. Panic rippled through the compartment, a palpable fear that threatened to overwhelm them all.

Albie entered the room, his gaze darting between the frantic passengers. Aiko caught sight of him and tensed, his shivering escalating, but he clenched his fists, determined to contribute. Without waiting for any response, Aiko dashed towards the emergency stop switch, slamming his fist against the glass with all his might. He grappled with the switch, struggling to pull it up, feeling a daunting resistance. His heart raced, amplifying his pain yet fueling his determination.

With both arms, Aiko strained against the unyielding switch. A surprise hand joined him, offering reinforcement.

"PULL!"

Quentin's voice strained through gasping breaths.

"The switch isn't budging!"

Aiko and Quentin exerted themselves, their muscles straining against the uncooperative mechanism.

"1:15 to Evergreen Hub Station."

Suki jumped in, adding her strength to the struggle. The switch resisted, seemingly pulling back against their efforts. Quentin's breaths grew more labored, sweat stinging his eyes, but he refused to close them. Suki strained, losing her grip gradually. Aiko's sweat dripped under his mask; determination etched on his face as he continued pulling. Albie dashed behind Aiko, gripping his body to add force to the pull. Aiko acknowledged Albie's help and, with one final push, let out a guttural scream.

"AAAARRRGHHH!"

Aiko's cry echoed just as the switch was yanked down. Emergency lights flared red, illuminating the compartment with a warning. The train's systems initiated the stop sequence. Gears clashed against the train wheels, grinding them to a halt. The sudden jolt sent everyone flying, crashing into one another. The train slowed, but its initial speed was too intense. Fires erupted outside, and the wheels and front of the train billowed smoke.

"50 seconds to Evergreen Hub station."

The screen rattled violently.

"EVERYONE MOVE BACK!"

The train operator shouted. They all rushed to the adjacent compartment, but Quentin hesitated when he saw Aiko still gripping the switch.

"AIKO! GET BACK!"

Quentin tugged at Aiko, urging him to retreat.

"I can't!"

Aiko resisted, his hands firmly clasped around the switch. Quentin realized Aiko was wrestling with it, struggling to keep it down and maintain the stop sequence.

"Take Albie with you, Quentin! I'll stay here; I can make the train stop completely!"

Aiko's voice cut through the chaos.

"NO, I'M NOT LEAVING YOU, AIKO!"

Quentin protested.

"Just go!"

Aiko's voice was firm, and he resorted to a swift kick to push Quentin away. Staggered and stunned by Aiko's action, Quentin knew arguing was futile. He grabbed Albie's hand and sprinted out to the rear compartment.

The train's shrill screeching reverberated violently around Aiko. Smoke billowed aggressively from the train's nose, obscuring Aiko's view through the windows. Relying on the screen for the destination and his strength to keep the switch down, Aiko braced himself against the intense vibrations pulsating through the room.

"30 seconds to Evergreen Hub Station."

The countdown persisted.

Heat enveloped Aiko's hands, and he glanced down to see the switch glowing red-hot. His skin sizzled from the extreme temperature. Despite the searing pain, Aiko couldn't find the strength to scream; his heartbeat slowed, and darkness crept at the edges of his vision. Suddenly smoke from the damaged control panel engulfed the space. Aiko's mask offered some reprieve from the noxious fumes, but the environment grew increasingly hostile.

"10 seconds to Evergreen Hub Station."

The toxic smoke made it nearly impossible for Aiko to see, yet he caught a fleeting glimpse of the screen through the swirling haze. His hands were now a fiery red, a liquid texture oozing from the burns, but he couldn't divert his focus from keeping the switch down, even as the train's vibrations began to subside.

The atmosphere in the compartment grew tense as the countdown echoed through the air, amplifying the impending danger with each passing second.

"3 seconds to Evergreen Hub Station, 2 seconds to Evergreen Hub Station."

Everyone scrambled to find refuge in those decisive moments, bracing for the inevitable collision. Bodies huddled against walls sought shelter behind whatever cover they could find and prepared for the imminent impact. Suki tucked herself into a corner, and Quentin held Albie protectively, a mix of anxiety and determination etched on their faces.

Aiko's struggle was palpable as he closed his eyes, summoning every ounce of strength to pull the switch down further. Smoky darkness enveloped him, a chilling reminder of the perilous situation surrounding him.

"1 second to Evergreen Hub Station. You have arrived at Evergreen Hub Station."

The train tore through the tracks with a deafening screech, its high-pitched metal grind resonating. Nearby onlookers recognized the impending danger and fled the imminent disaster.

Despite the stop sequence's efforts to halt the train's wheels, its momentum was unstoppable train collided with the wall at the end of the rails. The impact sent passengers tumbling through the compartment, crashing into different sections. The train precariously teetered; its nose perilously close to plummeting towards the streets below.

Around him, Quentin assessed the aftermath, his own body bearing bruises. He swiftly checked on Albie, relieved to find him unharmed. Casting his gaze around, he spotted Suki sprawled on the floor, sporting a few bruises and disoriented but breathing. Chaos enveloped the train car, train personnel and passengers struggled to regain their footing, were pinned by the impact, some stumbled disoriented and shaken, and still others sat in a state of shock.

With a swift assessment of the wreckage, Quentin's gaze darted, heart pounding with growing urgency, the sound reverberating through the disarray. His eyes rose when something in his mind came up.

"AIKO!"

# Chapter Five: Republic of Melancholia

The acrid tang of smoke choked the air, casting a hazy veil over the sprawling cityscape. The train's destruction had left an indelible mark, its broken nose jutting through the station wall, a surreal testament to the catastrophic impact. Evergreen Hub Station, a bustling gateway to the metropolis, stood in stunned silence, the screen above flickering with the destination: "Republic of Melancholia."

"AIKO!"

Quentin's anguished cry pierced the chaotic aftermath. His senses heightened, Quentin winced, a sharp ache pulsating through his body, remnants of the train's violent jolt. Realization dawned—he'd shielded Albie from the danger, the lingering pain a testament to the protection he'd offered. Albie lay sleeping nearby, the steady rhythm of his pulse bringing a rush of relief to Quentin's frantic mind.

Quentin scanned the scattered figures, each slowly regaining composure or seeking respite from the ordeal. With determined steps, he made his way, gently maneuvering Albie to a safer spot near the compartment door before setting off to check on Suki, who was still face down, prone on the floor.

The train wreckage and the chaos inside the compartment had taken its toll on everyone. Quentin's urgent quest to find Aiko triggered a surge of concern in Suki. She slowly rose, wincing at the bruises on her forehead.

"Are you okay?"

Quentin asked, gently turning to her to check for injuries. Her eyelids fluttered open, revealing a pair of eyes reflecting a mix of fatigue and resilience.

"Yeah, I'm fine."

She murmured, steadying herself against the wall, attempting to stand.

"Where's the boy with the mask?"

Her voice conveyed worry as she struggled to regain her footing.

"He stayed behind!"

Quentin's response was swift, offering support to help her up.

"Why did he stay behind!?"

Frustration and concern mingled in her tone, but a sudden cough interrupted her, causing her to bow her head momentarily. Sensing her discomfort, Quentin stepped back, giving her space to recover.

"He couldn't let go of the switch. He had to hold it in place so the train could stop."

Quentin explained, his face reflecting a mix of concern and regret.

"I need to get him out!"

Determination flashed in Quentin's eyes as he dashed out of the compartment, leaving her behind.

Suki saw Albie laying nearby, surrounded by people trying to recover from the tumultuous events.

"What a ride."

Observing the scene, she couldn't help but mutter to herself.

Quentin's hurried footsteps echoed through the compartment's wreckage, a mix of emotions swirling within him. Thoughts of Aiko's condition troubled him deeply. He couldn't discern Aiko's expression behind his mask, but something genuine in his voice struck Quentin. He shook off his thoughts, focusing on the task at hand. Thick smoke billowed, gradually becoming denser. Quentin's heart raced as he sprinted, covering his mouth to shield himself from the choking smoke.

Amidst the haze, a familiar blue mask emerged. Quentin made a beeline for it, swiftly reaching out and pulling Aiko's body through the smog. He fought against the acrid air, dragging Aiko away from the noxious fumes. Unrelenting coughs tore through Quentin as he struggled to pull Aiko further away, his determination overpowering his discomfort. Dropping Aiko momentarily, he doubled back to retrieve him, coughing uncontrollably.

"MOVE ASIDE!"

Quentin yelled; his voice hoarse as he tried to clear a path through his hacking coughs. He gently laid Aiko in the center of the compartment, frantically assessing his condition. As Quentin observed Aiko's masked face, he noticed the black smoke that stained part of the mask. Something wet and sticky greeted Quentin's touch as he inspected Aiko's shoulders and hands.

"His hands are bleeding. Does anyone have a tissue or a rag?"

Quentin's urgent plea reverberated through the compartment.

Suki noticed Aiko's condition, tore a piece of cloth from her shirt, and rushed over to Quentin's side.

Quentin accepted the cloth from Suki, using it to carefully wipe the blood off Aiko's hands.

Quentin grabbed something from his poncho, revealing the Skin Soothe gel he had applied to Albie earlier. He applied gel to Aiko's injured hands. The substance spread across Aiko's skin, prompting a slight reaction from Aiko as the gel alleviated some of the pain. Quentin continued to assess Aiko's hands, observing their reddened state.

"Thank you."

Quentin expressed his gratitude to Suki, who responded with a nod before stepping back.

As Quentin tended to Aiko, his mind wrestled with questions.

"The switch must have generated heat from the train overheating. You still wouldn't let go. Why did you do it?"

Quentin mused quietly to himself, opting to keep his thoughts internalized. He checked Aiko's pulse, finding reassurance in the steady rhythm of Aiko's heartbeat.

Suki approached again, but Quentin noticed her avoidance. Her demeanor reflected the gravity of what had occurred to Aiko.

A sudden burst of light erupted from the wall, carving a square shape as if it sliced through the metal like paper. The radiant flare blinded everyone in the compartment—leaving them momentarily disoriented. Gradually, a figure emerged from the luminous burst, initially shrouded in shadow and obscured by the residual brilliance.

With each heavy step, the figure advanced, revealing an imposing form clad in metallic armor. The shoulder pads and helmet were a deep navy hue, a stark contrast against the gleaming metal. Adorned with brown pouches and a blue armored collar, the figure carried an arm-mounted module. Its barrel pointed ominously at the compartment occupants, emblazoned with the name "ARC."

As the figure surveyed the scene, tension hung in the air. Quentin's eyes widened in recognition.

"FIREBIRDS."

He murmured under his breath, a name heavy with significance.

The FIREBIRDS soldier lowered the ARC and signaled.

"COAST IS CLEAR!"

His command reverberated through the compartment, prompting more figures to materialize from the light. More soldiers, all bearing bags marked with the words "Medic supply," streamed into the area, swiftly attending to the injured with practiced efficiency.

"This man! Yes, this man was one of the thugs who hijacked the train!"

The train personnel's voices pierced the air.

Their accusatory shouts echoed as they surrounded the hooded figure. The FIREBIRDS soldiers quickly encircled the man, swiftly restraining him with handcuffs before dragging him out of the compartment.

Amidst the chaos, a FIREBIRDS soldier noticed Quentin, Suki, Albie, and Aiko lying nearby.

"Are you all okay?"

The FIREBIRDS soldier approaching Aiko's motionless form.

"Yeah, we're alright. But my friend here."

Quentin gestured to Aiko,

"He suffered severe burns on his hands, and he's knocked out."

The FIREBIRDS soldier inspected Aiko's and noticed the blue mask. Recognition flickered in the FIREBIRDS soldier's eyes.

"That boy—we'll take him under our care."

The FIREBIRDS soldier declared, rising after examination.

Quentin's eyes sparked out.

"Wait, why?"

The FIREBIRDS soldier looked at Quentin's response.

"There is nothing for you to worry about. We will give him our proper care. There is a matter about the boy that must be looked at."

He felt his heart twist for a second; Quentin stood firm, determined to stay by Aiko's side.

"Hold up, if you're taking him, I'm going! He has his younger brother with him, and I'm responsible for him. Besides, I was heading to URDT anyway; I'm going with him whether you like it or not."

He straightened his stance, meeting the FIREBIRDS soldier's gaze head-on.

The FIREBIRDS soldier remained silent; his gaze fixed on Quentin. Eventually, they relented.

"Fine."

The FIREBIRDS soldier picked up Aiko and carried him out of the compartment. Meanwhile, Quentin hoisted Albie onto his back, preparing to leave. He turned to Suki.

"Do you want to come?"

He asked, hopefully.

Suki hesitated, avoiding eye contact before finally meeting Quentin's gaze.

"No, I'll stay behind...Look after them, okay?"

Quentin's eyes reflected his uncertainty, but he nodded in acknowledgment.

"I guess I'll see you around, then."

She nodded back slowly.

"Yeah, you will, I suppose."

With a slight grin, Quentin carried Albie out of the compartment. As he left, Suki watched him go, her gaze following until he disappeared into the bright light. Her eyes lowered, her head drooping slightly as the shadow swallowed her form.

Aiko's eyes slowly opened, struggling against the weight of his lids. The sounds around him were muffled at first, distant and disjointed. Albie expressing tones of concern, echoed somewhere in the haze of his consciousness. Pain throbbed through him, clouding his thoughts, and keeping him teetering on the edge of awareness. Darkness veiled his vision, leaving him in an abyss of internal musings.

Meanwhile, Quentin stirred from his slumber and saw Albie seated beside Aiko's unconscious form. His eyes fluttered open, each blink reconstructing the world around him. The glare of the light momentarily blinded him before fading into the surroundings. Albie's gaze widened as clarity seeped in. Rattling sounds from a nearby vehicle caught his attention. He turned to the window, and what he saw sparked excitement.

The skyline was a towering collage of architectural marvels, buildings scraping the sky with wires interwoven between them. Wooden structures stood in the shadow of taller edifices, adorned with names like Earl's Barn and Moxie Body Shop. The rooftops were festooned with lights and ornaments while people bustled about, each carrying their own story. Some in smart suits, others in rugged yet respectable attire. The air was filled with spices that tantalized the senses, mingling with the pungent exhaust fumes from passing vehicles.

Albie craned his neck out the window, inhaling deeply, only to feel a sudden tug at the back of his shirt, yanking him back inside.

"Hey, Albie!"

Quentin's grip tightened on Albie's shirt, pulling him back from the edge as a powerful gust of wind swept past. Another vehicle sped by, leaving Albie momentarily stunned, but he remained by the window, now cautious yet still captivated by the view.

Quentin let out a sigh of relief upon seeing Albie pull back a bit.

"You can look; just stay inside, okay?"

He stretched his arm across, cautioning Albie not to lean too far out.

"Don't lean out, alright?"

Albie's mouth was agape, caught in the intensity of the moment. He gazed at the myriad buildings, each with the city's signature red roofing, and felt the jolt as the road dipped. Looking down, he observed the bustling streets and buildings that housed numerous activities and lives.

"This is just the start."

The FIREBIRDS soldier remarked, glancing back at Albie as he drove.

"Welcome to the Republic of Melancholia. The Jewel City on planet Gaea."

Albie peered out at the breathtaking scene—the buildings, structures of concrete, metal, wood, and more, stacked together in a mesmerizing patchwork. His eyes widened, almost hurting with the intensity of his excitement, and a broad grin spread across his face. Seeing Albie's infectious enthusiasm, Quentin couldn't help but smile in return.

Amidst this architectural symphony, one building commanded attention, standing tall and proud. Its unique architecture pointed it out, capturing Quentin's gaze.

"That's the URDT. That's where we're headed."

Quentin remarked, stretching his arms back, absorbing the sights.

Albie's eyes lit up, his mouth forming a perfect 'O.' He turned and poked Aiko to get his attention, but his gesture caused no reaction. Aiko lay there, unresponsive, amidst the motion of the vehicle. Albie decided Aiko needed to rest and looked back outside.

"He's going to be okay. He will get the help he needs. And don't forget, I owe you that dessert later!"

Quentin's reassurance relieved Albie, his heart racing from the comfort. The FIREBIRDS soldier glanced at Quentin through the mirror, offering only a solemn glance.

Albie continued to peer outside, drinking in the mesmerizing surroundings as they edged closer and closer to their destination.

The URDT Building loomed with grandeur, its massive presence commanding respect. Towering walls, forming stout rectangular pillars, encircled the main structure, each side stretching almost a city block in width. These sturdy bastions cast imposing shadows, accentuating the building's formidable strength. Albie's gaze swept across the expanse of the URDT, the monumental walls stretching endlessly, punctuated only by tall columns interlocking. The building's architecture appeared like a fortress, and its exterior was designed in the shape of a trapezoid. As they drew nearer, the details of the URDT became more apparent.

The fortress-like appearance was amplified by cannons mounted on the walls, adding to its defensive semblance. Its walls boasted a robust texture, a blend of cement and metal, giving the impression of impenetrable layers of protection.

As they approached, Albie noticed the accumulation of dark orange dirt at the base of the walls, tiny particles scattered along the ground. His eyes blinked against the dust, then shifted upward, contrasting the disarray below with the pristine, unblemished expanse towering above. The dichotomy between the ground's unkempt state and the spotless heights above left a lasting impression.

Albie continued to gaze at the marvelous structure, and Quentin did the same. His hands covered his chin, and he closed his eyes.

"I made it, Dad."

He said to himself.

They drove slowly until they suddenly stopped. Albie looked around, spotting vehicles with URDT logos, personal vehicles, and a gathering of around 200 people. He observed the expressions on many faces, noticing their gaze following something. His eyes drifted over to a wall divided by a line. Albie wondered at its purpose, but his eyebrows rose as he admired the wall's sheer size.

The FIREBIRDS soldier noticed Albie's expression and realized that Albie had never been here before or in the city. He adjusted his mirror to focus on Albie's face.

"Want to see something cool?"

The FIREBIRDS soldier asked, making a gesture that caught Albie's attention. Quentin noticed, too, and paid attention as well. They both looked at the FIREBIRDS soldier, who turned his face toward the front and raised his hand with his fingers spread for a countdown.

Albie leaned forward in curiosity about the FIREBIRDS soldier's actions. Quentin joined in as well. The FIREBIRDS soldier closed each of his fingers, signaling a countdown. Slowly, each finger dropped until the last one; Albie and Quentin's eyes followed the FIREBIRDS soldier's hand.

The vehicle jerked with a massive thud, sending shockwaves through Albie's heart. A slow, unsettling vibration filled the cabin. Quentin sensed the shakiness, his gaze darting around outside. A strange sound, like metal sliding against metal, grabbed their attention as they all turned to face it. The corner lights flickered red, spinning in an eerie dance. The imposing wall ahead began to split open, sliding to the sides with grating metallic creaks. A dark atmospheric space, a vacuum pulling in the air with a vortex-like force. Another heavy thud reverberated, intensifying the tension. Quentin glanced sideways, noticing everything rising.

"Why's everything going up?"

Quentin's thoughts raced. He cautiously looked ahead and realized the unsettling truth.

"Wait, are we going down?"

"Enjoy the ride, boys."

The FIREBIRDS soldier relaxed, kicking his feet up. Quentin's realization struck hard. This was no ordinary entrance.

"Albie, we're going down!"

Quentin's urgent words broke through Albie's marveling gaze. His head spun with the surroundings, still astounded by what he witnessed. The platform they had stopped on held everything in place, people nearby gripping the rails tightly as vehicles remained parked. Everyone checked behind them, sensing something unusual. As they descended, the area beyond their illuminated spot became darker, plunging into an abyss. The escalator mechanism hummed and ground like a moving train, a testament to the architectural marvel. Albie and Quentin marveled at the ride's design, eliciting a grin from the FIREBIRDS soldier.

The grinding noise was nearly muted, the floor absorbing the harsh sounds. Gradually, the grinding died down, replaced by the distant sounds of sparking machinery, vehicle engines, and faint voices. Darkness surrendered to growing red lights, illuminating their descent. Albie and Quentin's hearts raced with anticipation as they hurtled toward the unknown at the end of the tunnel.

As the light intensified, it momentarily blinded them. The sounds intensified, pulling them out of the darkness. Albie and Quentin's eyes widened in awe. The FIREBIRDS soldier's hands gripped the steering wheel, his feet lowering to a rest.

"Welcome to URDT."

The light flooded the space, revealing a bustling scene below. Vehicles weaved through the area as soldiers marched in disciplined packs. Albie and Quentin stood in awe, their mouths agape as they absorbed the sights within URDT. Amidst the activity, they heard a distant boom, not the sound of an explosion, but something more mechanical. More vehicles emerged, each with unique designs. Airplanes were docked, hoisted by cranes, bearing a prominent label: "E-11," designed akin to tilt-rotor helicopters. Various aerial vehicles were stationed, ranging from fighter jets to helicopters. As they descended to the main floor, the bustling hub appeared more transparent. They drove slowly until they suddenly stopped. One of the sentries handed their driver a card with instructions, leaving the other sentries to do their security work.

Albie and Quentin were entranced until the FIREBIRD soldier interrupted.

"I just need to park this vehicle."

They navigated past groups of FIREBIRDS troopers engaged in drills, their chants resonating through space. "Valor Unto the Skies, Grounded in Courage, 'til our last breath!" Quentin's heart raced at the fervent speech, a surge of excitement coursing through him. The FIREBIRDS soldier followed the instructions he got earlier. They drove to their designated parking area among various military vehicles.

Once parked, the FIREBIRDS soldier and Quentin rushed to Aiko's side. The FIREBIRDS soldier knelt by Aiko, closely examining him, checking for any sign of life.

"He's still breathing. I'm going to have you wait here while I make some calls about your friend."

The FIREBIRDS soldier stepped out of the vehicle and away from the boys, then swiftly accessed his ARC, deftly manipulating the interface until he reached the communication system. With a decisive press, he activated the COMMS and replied to an urgent message:

"I need medical help down here, over. Also, I may have found the boys URDT is looking for."

The FIREBIRDS soldier looked towards the colossal building structure perched in the distance, surveying the entire scene. His device responded:

"From reports of the boys sighted at the compartment loading station near the Inhabitant Zone?"

"And seen on the train as well."

"Understood, Joule. The Premier will take it from here. He is specifically seeking the boy with the blue mask."

"And his companions?"

"They can wait at the main office; there's is enough security there to watch over them. We're sending a medical team right away. You are needed somewhere else; we are increasing security."

"Understood."

Joule finished his chat and walked back towards Quentin. Which Quentin glanced towards Joule's name tag, which has his name imprinted on it: "Joule Riday."

"So, your name is Joule?"

Quentin strolled over, curious.

"Joule Riday."

He displayed his dog tag, revealing his name, unclasping it from around his neck. His cobalt eyes lingered on Quentin.

"And what's your name?"

Joule turning the conversation back to Quentin.

"I'm Quentin Reily."

Joule's reaction to Quentin's name prompted a pause. Softly to himself, he whispered.

"Reily."

"Huh."

Quentin caught the quiet mutter.

"Oh, it's nothing. Your last name just sounds familiar to someone. What's your business here at URDT, apart from taking care of this boy's brother?"

Joule adjusted, carrying Aiko securely as Quentin signaled Albie to join them. They navigated the open space, surrounded by bustling personnel, soldiers engaged in training exercises, and intermittent announcements echoing throughout the complex.

"I came here to sign up for the FIREBIRDS Program."

"Oh, really? That's awesome! It's always nice seeing the younger generation signing up for a cause. Especially now, with the ever-growing conflict with The Excesses."

"So, those guys back on the train were part of The Excesses?"

Joule took a moment to consider before fixing his eyes on Quentin.

"Well, most of these attacks, like what you experienced, are linked to that organization. Many of these incidents share similar patterns: two hijackers together, targeting populated areas, to provoke the URDT."

Quentin glanced downward, contemplating his words. Meanwhile, Albie wandered about, awestruck by the vast openness of the area.

"So, who managed to bring down the troublemakers?"

Joule adjusted his helmet.

Quentin paused for a moment, reflecting on the situation.

"Aiko over there managed to stop the train from a worse impact."

"I see. Then how did you all take down Mr. Hoodie?"

Quentin paused for a moment, reflecting on the situation.

"Suki, a girl I met on the train, shot Mr. Hoodie's legs. Suki and I tried to stop the other hijacker, but he escaped using the emergency doors and vanished into the tunnels."

Joule paused, too, but he pressed on.

"I mean, he was able to stop The Excesses goons from causing more harm."

Quentin squinted, covering his face with his hands.

"It was my fault for putting him in that position. I should have thought about how he feels first. He couldn't bring himself to even pick up a gun..."

"Hey, it's okay!"

Joule interrupted, trying to reassure Quentin.

"Whatever happened, happened. You and your friends did the unbelievable. Stopping thugs from hijacking a train is something many people can't even do. He couldn't do what you can, but here he is. He managed to stop the train. Sometimes, you need to have more faith in yourself and others. You've got to stop doubting yourself, okay?"

Quentin paused momentarily, slowly gaining a slight grin as he looked at Albie, returning the smile.

"Well, I've got to take him over to the clinic. The place where you can sign up is at the main office."

"And where's the main office?"

Joule pointed to the middle, indicating a gate labeled: "Hub."

"See that gate over there? Head over there; a map will show you everything you need to know. The main office will have a recruitment application or be able to assist if you have any questions. And also due to the recent terrorism and the hijacking that have been happening, I'm afraid you're going to have to wait there. We got all eyes around this base and high patrolling; I am needed somewhere else. URDT headquarters is the last thing someone would mess up with; there's nothing to worry much about here. It is required for anyone visiting the URDT to get a security check; it should not take much of your time."

"Alright, I appreciate the help and the ride."

Quentin acknowledged.

"What you all did was heroic. Well, I'll see you once you become one of us. Don't worry; Aiko will get help and return in a few hours. You can wait at the office until he is done."

Joule saluted Quentin with a mini salute.

"See ya, Quentin, and you too, buddy."

Albie noticed the salute and waved in return. As Joule carried Aiko away, walking to the hurried medical team as he placed Aiko on the stretcher, Albie's eyes dropped, and his hands came together. Quentin noticed and placed his hands on Albie's shoulders.

"Hey, don't worry. Aiko will be alright. He will be checked, and he'll return better than ever! Let's take a walk."

Albie nodded, and Quentin extended his hand for Albie to grab. They walked toward the gate Joule had mentioned.

"I still owe you dessert, Albie. So, let's check if there's a food court later."

Albie's face brightened up; Quentin was spooked for a second but laughed.

In the towering heights of the building, a chamber overlooked the sprawling activity below. Soft rays of daylight filtered through the room, offering fleeting glimpses of its interior. A solitary figure stood within, peering at the bustling soldiers and civilians lost in contemplation. Unperturbed by a knock, the figure remained motionless, neither acknowledging nor turning towards the door.

As the door creaked open, a silhouette entered, marked by a name tag reading: "Kenryoku Takako."

"Mr. Acheron, there's someone you need to meet."

Kenryoku announced, his voice reverberating in the dimly lit room.

Acheron's gaze remained fixed on the stretcher below where Joule and the team carefully transported Aiko. His attention was riveted on Aiko's mask, his scrutiny intense. Slowly, he pivoted toward Kenryoku, a shard of light illuminating his features, gradually revealing a mask—identical to Aiko's mask—a deep, enigmatic blue. He only stared at Kenryoku; nothing but air filled the room.

# Chapter Six: I know you inside out

In a dream, Aiko couldn't see. His eyes were blocked by the mask he wore; blue all around him is what he sees. His hearing regains slowly in seconds, and he begins to hear air. The vision slowly shows the sky, a green texture that reveals the tall structure of the tree, creating a green ambiance from the transparent light. His heart pulses in harmony, hearing the leaves blow by a gust of wind.

His hands grasp the planet's dirt, feeling the softness of the ground, the planet's flying creature chirping evermore across the distance. Aiko began to hear footsteps from a distance; he couldn't get up from the ground; his eyes darted at the sky, only relying on the sound around him. The footsteps began to get louder and louder, trying to get closer, but Aiko was content with what was approaching him. A dark figure appeared before him; the shadow covered his appearance due to the harsh sunlight. He crouches down to Aiko, Aiko waiting to see the person's face. Slowly, his appearance reveals his dark, silky hair, his dark green jacket pops out from the sunlight, and his face slowly emerges, showing his colorful green eyes.

"Aiko"

***

"AAAHH"

Aiko gasped heavily; his heart pumped with a powerful force. Aiko regained his breath and slowly looked around him. His examination of the area around him shows it is grey with a white texture surrounding him, producing blue neon light with a mix of yellow. He looks around him at what he is on. Covering himself in a white blanket, he moves his arm to reveal a small attachment line connected to him. He traces the wire from his arm to a mini bag attached to a wheel staff. He could see the clear liquid deplete slowly but didn't know what it was; he couldn't think of anything. He looked at his hands, seeing his hands covered by layer upon layer of safe bandages hugging around his hands. He couldn't put down his fingers completely; the restriction he felt and the numbness from the fire still lingered with him.

He promptly puts his hands down and looks at his attire. His clothing is white, and his heart races until he looks to his side and sees a mini desk with his ordinary clothes there. His green, dark jacket is there. His green jacket... Aiko touched his blue mask, sighing in relief; he lay to look at the ceiling. The ceiling was completely white, and his eyes could only stare; he thought about what he had dreamed. He lets go again, another big sigh.

"I don't know this place..."

A knock at the door catches Aiko by surprise; he only looks out of the corner of his eye. The door opens and reveals a lady wearing a nurse uniform, with the URDT logo imprinted on her shoulder and side. She walks into the room, going to him. She checks on the bag and examines Aiko intently; she writes something on her keypad. Like she is checking off a list, she looks at Aiko back and forth. She covers her keypad with both of her arms, looking toward Aiko.

"Aiko Ashin. There is someone you need to meet."

Aiko only stared; he didn't come up with a response. His thoughts ran around, and he realized that he was at the URDT. He remembered saying that he wanted to travel to URDT; something was telling him to go there for a reason. Aiko couldn't think why he wanted to go to URDT; he needed answers.

"Rest for a while. The bandages around your hands will dissolve over time, healing your hands. Rest for a while. I'll unhook you when you're awake."

The nurse walked out, closing the door. Silence crept into the room; his ears could hear the deadness. The white and gray around him made him uncomfortable. He couldn't stand this, the feelings he was getting. He looked up at the ceiling and closed his eyes once more.

***

"Aiko Ashin. There is someone you need to meet."

The nurse was back and repeated the summons.

Aiko walked out of his room, wearing his hospital garment, and leaving the clothes he was wearing on the train. The nurse, closing the door behind them, walked ahead of Aiko. The light outside the door reveals hallways and structures like a hospital, walls reflecting the light, blinding him. He looked at both sides of the hallways, seeing how the light made everything around him feel small, making the hallways feel endless. Aiko looks to the nurse, who is patiently waiting.

"This way, please."

She said she walked to the left side of where Aiko was staring. She began to walk, and Aiko slowly walked behind her. She grabbed something from her uniform pouch and gave it to Aiko.

"Here, this is a visitor tag. Giving you permission to walk here freely."

Aiko looked at the tag, seeing only his name appear. His face wasn't indicated on it, nor was his location or origins. He began to think about what Quentin had said to him earlier on his trip.

*"It's called a PSC, for Personalized Score and Credits. It's quite intricate. The system evaluates how much you contribute to society, mostly gauging your value to the Republic of Melancholia and then*

*designing this system, replacing the old paper currency with instantaneous credit transfers. It covers all activities, including the educational system, rewarding academic excellence, contributions, skills, and achievements. Your score also affects your social reputation."*

Aiko grappled with conflicting emotions as he followed the nurse through the labyrinthine halls. A sense of unease loomed within him; he felt like an outsider in this unfamiliar place. Questions swirled in his mind—why was he receiving treatment without any identifying PSC? The weight of these inquiries made him dizzy, yet he pushed those thoughts aside, focusing on his current path with the nurse.

As they stepped out of the corridor labeled "PATIENT ROOMS," shadows danced against darker hues, painting a grayscale ambiance. They traversed several corridors until emerging into a bustling lobby. Aiko's gaze flitted across the assembly of people, workers, and soldiers—clad in deep navy attire, their arm-mounted "ARC" modules glinting under the lights. Quentin's words about URDT and the FIREBIRDS resonated in Aiko's mind, clarifying his surroundings.

Ascending an escalator, Aiko scanned the surroundings: tables filled with people, a basketball court, and the tempting aroma of food teasing his senses. His stomach grumbled, enticed by the scent of spices and fried delicacies, yet the mask covering his face thwarted any indulgence. Amidst these distractions, thoughts of Quentin and the recent encounter tugged at him—why had he followed a stranger like Quentin? And Albie...where was he? Memories of their journey to this place surfaced, a sudden pause in Aiko's racing heart as he recalled Albie's abrupt kick, sending him reeling against the wall.

Despite his efforts to divert his thoughts, Albie's presence lingered, flooding Aiko's mind. Echoes of a dream haunted him: Albie's voice, their shared moments, and an uttered name—"Anbu." Aiko muttered the word softly to himself, closing his eyes as if trying to summon a connection from within the depths of his memories.

Aiko ventured forth, his steps echoing against the floor as he navigated through the dimly lit corridor. His eyes swept over the nurse's face, urging him to hasten his pace. They forged ahead, heading for an entrance adorned with the inscription: "Chief of Staff Offices." Darkened windows concealed any view inside, creating mystery throughout the space. Sparse lighting barely pierced the shadows, casting offices as intertwining corridors within the building's labyrinthine interior.

Passing offices marked with names he didn't bother to read, Aiko followed the nurse until she halted by a specific door, the label reading: "Kenryoku Takako: Vice Commander."

"He's expecting you."

She stated before she walked away, vanishing from Aiko's sight. A tremor coursed through him, his hands trembling as he gripped the icy doorknob. Seeking answers about Kenryoku Takako's intentions and his own purpose here, Aiko grappled with the chill of the knob, wishing to shake off this disconcerting feeling.

Breathing in deeply, Aiko steadied himself briefly before turning the doorknob. Darkness enveloped the room, offering little visibility save for the faint glimmer from the windows. Slowly stepping forward, he discerned a desk in the room's vague outlines. However, something on the wall caught his attention—a framed picture. Intrigued, he approached, yearning to decipher the identity of the person within.

As he drew nearer to the picture, his heart raced, and his breath caught in his throat at the voice that called his name.

"Aiko Ashin..."

Aiko's breath hitched as the figure's voice cut through the darkness. He stumbled back slightly, his eyes straining to make out the contours of the seated figure.

"Have a seat, young boy."

The voice commanded. As his eyes adjusted to the gloom, a chair materialized within Aiko's sight, and with a mix of trepidation and curiosity, he complied, his fingers fumbling nervously against each other, occasionally picking at the skin around his fingertips, a nervous tic that betrayed his anxiety.

The room remained shrouded in obscurity until the figure extended a hand to a lamp, casting a harsh, bright light that illuminated Aiko and parts of the surrounding area, finally revealing the figure's appearance. Kenryoku Takako, clad in a dark navy-blue shirt emblazoned with the URDT logo and an overcoat blending seamlessly with the shadowy ambiance. Various badges adorned his attire, and his name badge was clearly displayed. His well-trimmed dark blond hair and beard contrasted sharply with his intense brown eyes that seemed to absorb rather than reflect light.

Aiko observed him intently, uncertain what to say or how to respond. He felt a jumble of emotions, unable to articulate a coherent thought.

"I can see that you are fine and well. Are you feeling anxious?"

Kenryoku's voice cut through the silence, his penetrating gaze seemingly dissecting Aiko's emotions.

The room remained tense as Kenryoku shifted his posture, producing a file that bore Aiko's name and details. Aiko's eyes darted down for a moment, drawn to his hands; he watched as his bandage slowly dissolved. He could see his hands through the transparent bandage that remained, revealing inadvertently healing tissue marred by lingering burn scars. He nervously pressed his fingers together, inadvertently highlighting the scars, before swiftly concealing his hands within his pocket.

"Well, let us begin, shall we?"

Kenryoku straightened, his attention directed to the dossier in front of him. Aiko sat in silence, bracing himself for Kenryoku's following words.

"Do you know why you're here?"

Kenryoku's sonorous voice held a gentle undertone, an unsettling contrast that sent a chill down Aiko's spine. He remained mute, grappling with unspoken thoughts and unanswered questions.

Kenryoku seemed to recognize Aiko's reluctance.

"Silence won't help you, but I can understand your hesitation. You probably have countless questions swirling in your mind. I can provide answers."

The air seemed to grow heavier as the weight of the unknown bore down upon Aiko, leaving him torn between the urge to speak and the instinct to stay guarded.

Kenryoku's lips tightened imperceptibly as he scrutinized Aiko's reaction. Despite Aiko's attempt to remain composed, his nervous energy reverberated through the room, evident in the subtle vibrations of his feet.

"Aiko Ashin, age: 16, date of birth: April 24, 2117. Origin: Unknown. ID: Unknown. Height: 5'7". Parents/Guardian: Inoue Ashin."

The words struck Aiko like a bolt of lightning. In an instant, his eyes widened, a scream echoing through his mind. He shot up from his seat, heart pounding furiously, breaths ragged. Kenryoku remained composed, observing Aiko's every move with a keen eye. He gestured calmly for Aiko to sit back down.

"Easy, take a seat."

Kenryoku's voice was measured, but the intensity lingered. Aiko's mind raced, a whirlwind of thoughts and emotions consuming him. As he slowly eased back into the chair, attempting to steady his breath, Kenryoku continued, acknowledging the evident effect the name had on Aiko.

"You're from the Inhabitant Zone, yet here you are in the Republic of Melancholia, the Jewel City of Humanity. We've been monitoring you closely. And you've brought your little companion along."

The beads of sweat dripped from Aiko's bound hands, an uncomfortable reminder of his constrained state. Despite his efforts not to feel intimidated, the intensity of Kenryoku's words loomed heavily. How did they know about his and Albie's journey here?

"We received reports of a boy with a blue mask."

Kenryoku pointed directly at Aiko, his tone holding a weight that Aiko could only absorb.

"And another child wearing a hat. They were spotted near a factory not far from Harmony Fall Station. A guard attempted to halt them, but they slipped away."

As Kenryoku closed the folder, leaning in closer to Aiko, the tension in the room heightened. Aiko's heart raced faster than ever, the drumming sound reverberating in his ears. Every second stretched into an eternity, each passing moment an agonizing wait for this overwhelming sensation to cease.

"Not only did you illegally enter and cross the Inhabitant Zone, but you and your companion breached the Embankment Fence, breaking the law without even carrying a PSC."

Kenryoku paused, considering his words carefully before adding, almost as an afterthought.

"Without Inoue's help, you could not have entered. As a result, your foster carer would've been detained because of your actions."

Aiko clenched his fists tighter, a surge of emotions threatening to erupt. Kenryoku's words struck a nerve, shaking Aiko to his core. He was lost in a whirlwind of emotions, unable to find the words to respond, unsure if he even wanted to.

Suddenly, Aiko blurted out.

"What happened to Inoue? Where is she? Is she in prison for helping me?!"

Kenryoku ignored Aiko's outburst.

"Instead of sending you straight to jail, I've decided to give you an opportunity."

Kenryoku continued, observing Aiko's surprised expression and the flurry of emotions coursing through him. Aiko's heart thundered in his chest, the stakes higher than ever.

"Despite the breach, your actions on that train were heroic. You didn't just stop the train; you prevented further damage and potential disaster. Eyewitnesses reported seeing a boy in a blue mask entering the conductor's area and never returning. They noted your decision to stay behind, realizing the emergency stop switch was malfunctioning. You had to manually hold it down to ensure the train came to a halt. It was a perilous situation, a hair's breadth away from risking your life. You might just have some sort of miraculous luck shining upon you."

Kenryoku leaned back, his hand rubbing his beard thoughtfully, allowing Aiko a moment to absorb his words and the weight of the situation.

"There is someone you need to meet; follow me."

Aiko's curiosity was piqued. He didn't know what to expect or who he needed to meet.

Aiko followed Kenryoku; they reached an elevator, and Kenryoku poked at the button of the elevator pad. Showing the numerous levels the building has, he clicked on an upper-level button. The elevator ascended, pinging as they passed each floor. Aiko felt cold; he thought it was his nerves, but he realized the elevator itself was getting colder.

76

His and Kenryoku's breath was noticeable, but Kenryoku ignored it like it was nothing. The elevator stopped at the floor Kenryoku pressed. It opened widely to a dark corridor, with mini lights spotting around. They stepped out.

Aiko glanced around nervously, unease amplified by the chilling air enveloping the corridor. Shadows danced at the edges of his vision, adding to the eerie atmosphere. Kenryoku's inscrutable demeanor did little to assuage Aiko's rising anxiety.

As they neared a pair of imposing doors, Kenryoku turned to Aiko, the weight of expectation hanging between them. Aiko's fingers traced nervous patterns on his jacket, his breath shallow in the tension-filled silence. He met Kenryoku's gaze, searching for any hint or reassurance, but the Vice Commander remained cryptic.

Aiko hesitated before the doors, feeling a surge of trepidation coursing through him. He could see a sign reading, "Jabez Acheron: Premier." He glanced back at Kenryoku, hoping for guidance or a signal, but Kenryoku's demeanor remained impassive. With a subtle nudge, Kenryoku urged Aiko to step forward.

Aiko's apprehension and curiosity swirled as he reached for the handles, the doors feeling heavier than expected. As they creaked open, Aiko hesitated, peering into the dimly lit room. The space seemed to hold its breath, casting eerie shadows on the polished floors.

Kenryoku's voice cut through the silence, breaking Aiko's trance.

"He's waiting for you."

He repeated, his voice carrying a subtle urgency.

With a deep breath, Aiko stepped over the threshold, the doors closing quietly behind him. The room ahead held an indiscernible figure shrouded in the room's shadows. Aiko swallowed hard, summoning his courage to face whoever awaited him in the darkness.

As he entered, the room appeared shrouded in shadows, revealing only vague shapes—a desk, a chair nearly bumped into. A gleam of light caught his eye, emanating from a partially drawn curtain. Curiosity drew him closer, his fingers tracing the source of the light until he tugged the curtain aside, revealing a breathtaking aerial view of the bustling facility below. The sight of FIREBIRDS soldiers, mechanics, and various activities there took his breath away. He quickly closed the curtain, suddenly feeling exposed at the height.

Turning away from the window, he noticed a set of shelves faintly illuminated by the outside light. Pictures and medals lined the shelves, catching Aiko's attention. Among them was a torn photograph of a man and a woman. Aiko studied it intently, trying to discern their faces, but the damage to the photo obscured their features. He placed it back on the shelf, curious about the people in the picture.

His gaze shifted, landing on a large closet with a locked keypad. Before he could explore further, a voice disrupted his thoughts.

"Aiko?"

The tension in the room was palpable as Aiko turned to see Acheron behind him, initially indistinct in the shadows. As Acheron approached, the light from the curtain revealed more details—an armor-like attire, sturdy boots, and an overcoat that partially concealed the figure's form.

Aiko involuntarily stepped back as Acheron looked at him. A mask, eerily similar to Aiko's, covered the Acheron's features. Acheron's hair peeked out from the sides, adding to the enigmatic air. It was an unsettling mirror image of Aiko's own mask, albeit darker in hue. But what struck Aiko most was the prominent crack across the mask's surface from the right eye.

Acheron loomed over Aiko, casting a long shadow. Aiko's heart raced as he struggled to find words. When he finally spoke, his voice trembled with curiosity and unease.

"Where did you get that mask?"

Acheron remained silent, their presence causing a knot to form in Aiko's stomach. He steadied himself and mustered the courage to press further.

"Who are you?"

Acheron took a few deliberate steps closer, their movements calculated and deliberate. Aiko's breath caught in his throat as Acheron spoke softly, yet the weight of the words felt immense.

"I... am your father... you don't know me, Aiko. But you are my lost son!"

The atmosphere in the room thickened with tension as Aiko staggered back, his world spiraling into confusion. His heart raced, beating a frenetic rhythm, while his mind wrestled with conflicting emotions. A surge of frustration gripped Aiko, and his trembling hands clenched into tight fists, manifesting his inner turmoil.

Without hesitation, Aiko lunged towards Acheron, fueled by a desperate surge of adrenaline. Acheron, composed and unmoved, intercepted Aiko's attack, firmly preventing him from making contact. Aiko's attempts to strike were futile, his desperation manifesting in a piercing scream, a raw and desperate plea for clarity.

"NO, NO, NO! YOU'RE NOT MY FATHER! WHO ARE YOU!"

"You don't know me... Aiko. But I am your father!"

Trying to assert authority, Acheron responded firmly.

"YOU'RE NOT MY FATHER! WHO ARE YOU!"

"SETTLE DOWN!"

Acheron, no longer able to withstand Aiko's relentless assault, forcefully pushed him away. Aiko collapsed to his knees, his body shuddering with intense emotions. Silence engulfed the room, Acheron remaining shrouded in darkness as the light illuminated only Aiko.

"Where did you get this mask?"

Acheron got closer. Aiko was still shaking on the floor. Acheron stood above Aiko, looking down on him. Aiko's mind raced, and his body felt cold from sensing Acheron present. He took small breaths and processed an answer.

"I've had since I was little… I don't know who gave it to me; all I know is I had it when I was small."

Acheron continued to look down upon him with no movement. Aiko slowly looked up at Acheron, seeing his presence, which was already shocking to him. Aiko made up his mind with a question, trying to approach Acheron's authority.

"Where were you?... Where were you when I was alone?"

Acheron continued to look down on him.

"Where were you when I needed YOU!"

Aiko grasped his voice to send his final word to strike Acheron. Acheron stepped back a bit, allowing Aiko to get up. Acheron still stared at him.

"Take off your mask…"

Aiko got up slowly, still in shock. His feelings were charged with confusion and anger. Aiko didn't want to listen to Acheron; Aiko wanted to know who Acheron was. He refused to believe Acheron is his father but still listened to what Acheron have to say. Aiko reached behind his head, grabbing a strap attached to his mask. The revealing bit of his face. Acheron strolls towards him, towering over Aiko. Acheron grasps Aiko's mask firmly and starts to inspect it. Scrutinizing the top layer cover of the mask, feeling the texture, looking all around. Acheron now pays attention to Aiko's face, seeing what he needed to see. Acheron stepped over to his desk and sat silently. Aiko slowly walked to the desk and faced Acheron. Acheron continues looking at Aiko's mask, pressing his thumb on its face. His silence was felt by Aiko. Aiko wiped his face a bit; the harsh darkness around the room conceals Aiko's face. Aiko only looked at Acheron's mask and noticed how similar his own mask was to Acheron's.

"I haven't seen these masks for a long time…"

Aiko stared intently at Acheron.

"I remember she used to wear this mask. Before…."

Aiko's hands were on Acheron's desk. Acheron slowly handed back the mask to Aiko. Acheron now looked at Aiko. Acheron's silence creeped in on Aiko, and Aiko's anger ebbed.

"You are indeed my lost child; I never thought you existed until now..."

Aiko continued to gaze and, for a moment, put his head down.

"I didn't want to have this meeting; I didn't want to believe that my son was alive—"

"Then what do you want from me? Why have this meeting? Where were you when I needed you?"

Aiko's breathing grew heavy, making up the sound of the office.

Acheron got up and walked over to the locked closet. He signaled Aiko to come over. Aiko didn't like it, but Acheron insisted. Aiko was next to his father. He felt angered by his question not being answered.

"You didn't answer my question."

"I'm here with higher authority than you; you are not allowed to ask questions while I'm speaking. You're under my watch while in this room."

His father proclaimed that Aiko could only watch if he restrained his anger.

His father began pressing on the keypad, unlocking the sealed door. Opening the door revealed something metallic inside that was larger than himself. Aiko only made the shape and the color of the lights shown from the outside.

Aiko stepped back a bit, taking in the picture before him. A metallic suit, with plates covering the torso, it had navy blue shoulder pads and smaller pads overlapped three times on the sides. It had a helmet in navy blue sporting circular silver tubes with markings on them. The helmet had a jaw-like appearance, both sides divided by a plate, giving it an eerie appearance.

"This is the Melancholic Knight. Humanity's last hope."

Acheron proclaimed, gazing at its stature. As Aiko continued to gaze as well. Suddenly he felt woozy for a moment and stumbled. Acheron took notice.

"You felt that, didn't you? The energy of the suit radiates to you; your mask... You felt its power and presence when you walked here and at times before."

Aiko's mind began to whirl, he put his hand on his forehead. Aiko remembered what he said to Quentin. That he felt the need to go to the URDT Was the suit calling him? Was his father calling him? He felt like he was going to vomit.

"I can't believe you haven't experienced this. The energy. You don't know the ancestry of your birth from..."

Aiko slowly looked up at Acheron; hearing the word ancestry got Aiko's attention.

"What ancestry!"

"You really don't know, do you?"

Acheron mumbled. He looked to his side before looking at Aiko. He began to point to his own mask and to Aiko's.

"My mask…. your mask…. We are from the same race. The race is known as Harmonians. We do not know about the unknown alien race, but they left their history and technology to the people, thus why we call ourselves Harmonians. We are different from the rest of these people."

Aiko contemplated his father's words. His confused thinking slowly died down.

"You're experiencing energy from your mask; you and it are connected to the Synara. The Synara allows you to see many memories of yourself, your feelings."

Aiko remembered the dream of seeing the boy with green eyes. Anbu. He thought it was real, but it shook him when he woke to find it was a dream.

"The suit becomes radiant in your presence. It was designed to be wielded by Harmonians like us."

Aiko got up, looked at the suit, and turned to his side to give his father a glare.

"Why should I wear the suit? There is nothing inside of me that desires to wear it. I have gotten nothing but anger from you; you can wear the suit yourself."

"I need you."

His father only looked upon the suit; he took steps back.

"My time is up; wearing the suit would only destroy me. My body's condition is already damaged."

Aiko thought about his sentence: "The suit only destroys me." He felt something cold from that.

"You are a pure Harmonian. Many would like to wear this suit, giving them immense strength and a sense of themselves, but it will only lead them to their demise. They aren't strong enough mentally, unlike Harmonians."

Acheron said.

"Why does anyone need to wear the suit?"

His father walked up slowly, meeting Aiko's eyes.

"There is an ever-growing threat by the organization known as The Excesses. They've been attacking our nation. Harassment and sabotage like you experienced. Our manpower is stretched short; some are spread to defend our allied nations. We need more troops at outposts to check for excess activity and preserve order. We're losing our soldiers from these attacks; we can't afford to lose more. Our attention is protecting what humanity we have left on this new planet we call home."

Aiko processed his father's words and thought about them for a moment. He began to think about what he had told Quentin about Albie and why he had traveled to the Republic of Melancholia. He began to remember a woman who wore simple farming clothes; the image he remembered was hard to process; he started to reflect upon Kenryoku's words: "*Without Inoue's help, you could not have entered. As a result, your foster carer would've been detained because of your actions.*"

He remembered his foster carer; the memory pained him. He had left with Albie to go to the Republic of Melancholia to find answers.

"I'll…think about it…."

His father only gazed upon him; the silence filled the room, clearing Aiko's words up.

"I'll have someone escort you out of here; just wait outside."

Aiko didn't nod or speak, his mind echoing those words. He simply walked toward the door.

"Before you go."

Aiko paused, reluctant to turn around.

"You mustn't breathe a word of our discussion, your involvement in this work. The Melancholic Knight's existence is not to be uttered for the safety of the people and your own."

Aiko turned around slightly, seeking clarification.

"And if I do…"

His father met his gaze, leaning forward ever so slightly.

"There are only consequences, for all our sakes."

Aiko felt a jolt of anxiety. Consequences? Whose life was at stake—his or his father's? The weight of uncertainty pressed on him, compelling him to exit immediately. His father leaned back, fixing his gaze on where Aiko had stood.

# Chapter Seven: Unfamiliar home

Albie sat leisurely at the food court tables, savoring each bite of the delectable cotta dessert. Across from him, Quentin meticulously examined the registration form, an extra slip clutched in his hand. As he began filling in the details, he smoothly transcribed his full name, "Quentin Reily." and his place of origin, "Sanguine Provence." The ease in his writing halted abruptly when he reached the section for parents or guardians.

A sudden chill ran down Quentin's spine as he encountered his father's name. Gripping the pen tighter, his gaze fixed on the inked letters. Sensing Quentin's unease, Albie observed him attentively from across the table.

Quentin closed his eyes, taking a moment to reflect on the turbulent emotions stirred by his father's name. The silence was broken by the soft sound of Albie's plate moving across the table. Albie placed the remnants of his cotta dessert in front of Quentin. Quentin's eyes flickered open, and he looked up to find Albie offering a comforting grin.

"Thanks, I'm all good."

Quentin assured, declining the leftover treat.

Resuming his task, Quentin continued to fill out the form. As he wrote his father's name and completed the remaining sections, Albie reclaimed the cotta dessert and indulged in the sweet conclusion.

The duo returned to the office, where Quentin confidently submitted his registration to the front office lady. Her stern expression softened as she reviewed the paperwork.

"You'll be expected to return tomorrow for a full orientation of the FIREBIRDS program. The time to be here is at 8:30 am—be here ready to shine."

She handed back the application.

"Everything looks good. You need to turn this in when you report."

She instructed, her tone becoming encouraging.

Quentin nodded appreciatively.

"Thank you very much!"

Eager to leave, Quentin signaled Albie to follow him, but the front office attendant halted them.

"Wait, here's a napkin for your little brother."

Quentin noticed the Cotta dessert mustache still adorning Albie's mouth. The unexpected sight drew a chuckle from both of them, lightening the atmosphere and leaving a memorable impression on the threshold of their new adventure.

"Thanks. He isn't my... brother."

Quentin said with a subtle pause.

Quentin wiped the cotta desert off Albie's face, and Albie responded with a wide grin. Quentin reciprocated with a grin of his own. As they strolled away from the main office, entering the expansive open lobby of the URDT, Quentin took a moment to absorb his surroundings. His eyes betrayed a sincerity, a recognition of the world enveloping him. In a quiet voice, he muttered, "Tomorrow will be the day."

Turning around, Quentin noticed a figure approaching. Clad in a blue mask, the figure drew closer, revealing a stature shorter than Quentin's. Excitement bubbled within him.

"AIKO!"

Quentin rushed toward Aiko, enveloping him in a massive hug. Aiko's arms shot out awkwardly, caught off guard by Quentin's sudden embrace. Albie lingered in the background, and as Quentin's eyes swept the area, he noticed Aiko's arms not reaching around to reciprocate. Quentin let go and stepped back.

"Oh, my bad. The injury must still bother you."

Quentin remarked, recognizing Aiko's discomfort. Aiko's arms slowly relaxed.

"So, how are you feeling?"

Quentin breaking the silence. Aiko stood in silence, flexing his injured hands. He turned his gaze upward, observing the darkness above and the brightness below. After a moment, Aiko collected his thoughts.

"Cold."

He walked past Quentin and Albie, heading towards the facility's exit. Quentin and Albie exchanged glances, Quentin lowering his eyebrows as he signaled Albie to join him.

"Hey, Aiko, wait up!"

From a distance within the office, the father observed his son. He watched as Aiko distanced himself, moving away. The father's gaze lingered on the diminishing figures, tiny specks crossing the distance. Just as he remained contemplative, a knock on the door interrupted his focus.

"Come in."

The door opened to reveal Kenryoku Takako.

"So, how did it go?"

The father's attention remained fixed on Aiko, who was now accompanied by a boy with blond hair and a younger child. He watched as they entered a massive escalator, ascending and eventually disappearing from his sight.

"He said he'll think about it."

The father replied, his eyes still on the fading scene.

Kenryoku approached the seat and sat down, grabbing a cigarette and lighter from the desk.

"So, you're going to let him think? What if he leaves?"

The father closed the curtains, returned to his desk, and took a seat.

"Don't worry, he'll be back. You can be sure of it."

Jabez reassured.

"And if he doesn't?"

Kenryoku exhaled a stream of smoke, coughing slightly.

"We must send troops to go after him if he doesn't return."

Kenryoku, affected by the smoke, rested his head for a moment.

"You can't wear that suit, Jabez."

Jabez, still gazing at Kenryoku, his emotionless mask belying the conclusion of his thoughts, responded.

"I know, but I don't want that boy wearing the suit. I don't want him."

"Think about what you're saying. That boy may be our only chance to regain humanity's dream."

"Or our doom."

Jabez countered, leaning his chair back as he processed the surroundings.

"Did he have any requests?"

Kenryoku pressed down his lit cigarette on the ashtray.

"I believe he'll ask to find-"

"Inoue Ashin, I assume. What are you thinking?"

"I would have to arrange a council meeting about the boy's demands and reintroducing The Melancholic Knight back to the military. But society cannot know that. They will fall into riots because of what Melancholic Knight's sin brought us."

Kenryoku spun his new cigarette, the smoke swirling around it.

"You gotta hate having the pressure weigh on you. You know this boy can help end The Excesses. Finding a pure Harmonian like him is nothing but an old prophesy from a bygone era. Even if some of the old knights still exist, they are overextended to wear the suit. Their bodies are damaged like yours."

"But mine is worse."

Jabez got up and walked toward a picture of a man and a woman. He looked down, lost in thought.

"I want every record of what we know about this boy. I want to know his origin, his foster carer, everything we know about him."

Turning around to face Kenryoku, who was listening attentively, Jabez continued.

"I want to know why he was hidden from me."

"As you wish."

Kenryoku replied, leaving the office.

Silence enveloped the room as Jabez stared at the photo of the man and the woman. His gaze shifted to the torn corner of the picture, and the room filled with an eerie stillness.

***

Aiko walked ahead, exiting the URDT entrance, with Quentin and Albie trailing behind. The headaches from the suit and his memories lingered, causing Aiko to stumble. Quentin hurried to his side.

"Hey, Aiko, you good?"

Aiko glanced at him without speaking, walking towards the block of cities ahead. Concern filled Quentin and Albie's expressions as they followed suit.

"Aiko, you need to talk to me. Are you okay? What happened over there?"

"I don't want to talk about it."

Aiko replied, still looking forward.

"Don't be like this. I'm sorry if you're still hurt from earlier today or having a bad experience here, but please just talk to me, and I'll try my best to help you."

Aiko stopped suddenly and turned around towards Quentin and Albie. They halted, awaiting what Aiko would say next.

"You want to help? Take Albie with you. I want to be left alone."

Aiko turned back and walked into the busy crowd. Quentin looked down at Albie, who was behind him, glared at Aiko, and then followed Aiko into the crowd.

Aiko continued walking, lost in thought. The sun dipped into a crisp orange on the horizon. His mind replayed his father's words: *"I didn't want to have this meeting; I didn't want to believe that my son was alive. I... am your father."*

The sentence echoed like a broken record. He bumped into people, causing a chain reaction of collisions. Many people glared at him, but he didn't have the mental capacity to register their faces, only seeing his father's eyes behind the mask, acting like a silhouette.

His mind raced with images of his father, the suit, and the URDT facility. Disappointment and anger welled up inside him. He struggled to believe in his father's existence. Aiko walked until he found a bench, sat down, and covered his face with his hands, curling his fingers. The words repeated in his mind: *"I didn't want to believe that my son was alive."*

"Where were you? When I needed you."

Whispering to himself, Aiko positioned his arms on his lap, still covering his face. The bustling road filled with vehicles and people seemed distant to him. Voices echoed, and the sounds of cars became muffled as he closed his eyes, plunging himself into darkness and quiet. In the solitude, he sat, detached from reality.

As the roads quieted and the sun neared its end, Aiko felt the silence surrounding him until he heard approaching footsteps. Refusing to look, he remained motionless. The figure sat beside him, maintaining silence. Aiko resisted the urge to move or look until he took a small peek from the corner of his eye. It was Quentin sitting beside him with Albie resting nearby. Quentin avoided staring at Aiko, giving him his personal space.

Aiko collected his thoughts, breathing slowly. Gradually, he shifted his position, glancing around. The vastness of the Republic of Melancholia struck him, and he realized he had been wandering through unfamiliar areas. Observing the emptiness and reduced crowd, he looked forward while Quentin remained still.

"Look, I don't know what you're experiencing or what happened there. I just want to let you know that I'm here."

Quentin spoke, his gaze fixed ahead, respecting Aiko's need for space.

Aiko slowly turned his head, not fully facing Quentin. Quentin continued.

"It's okay that you don't want to share anything that bothers you, but bottling is not good. Just talk when you need to."

Fully turning his head towards Quentin, Aiko met his green eyes. A resemblance to the boy with black hair and green eyes lit up inside Aiko, filling the void with acknowledgment. Their silence spoke volumes, forging a connection in that quiet moment.

Footsteps echoed, this time in Quentin's direction. He turned to his side, his eyes lighting up as he saw Suki. She wore a skirt, and a jacket adorned with numerous pins and badges and had a messy hairstyle with attached clips. Aiko also took notice of her.

"It's you!"

Quentin exclaimed.

Getting up, Quentin walked towards her while Aiko remained seated, still reflecting on Quentin's words.

"I didn't expect to see you again."

Suki remarked.

"Cool it. It's only been a day since we met. Doesn't exactly make us 'friends.' I was only concerned about the morning accident. I'm still not going to forgive you for ruining my shot."

She retorted.

Quentin stepped back, defending his actions.

"Whoa, I did you a favor. I wasn't going to let you kill him!"

"And what happened? He jumped out of the train. Not to mention, he probably is still alive and going to hunt us down!"

"Also, not to mention that I saved you twice from attempted murder and kept you from flying out!"

Quentin remarked.

"Anyways, these guys never caught your name."

Quentin interjected.

"It's Suki Kimani."

Suki noticed over Quentin's shoulder that Aiko was still seated.

"How's he doing?"

Quentin looked over but turned around quickly.

"He's still healing."

As they conversed, shadows indicated that the sun was setting. Quentin returned to Aiko, allowing him space to answer Suki's question.

"Do you guys have a place to stay at?"

Aiko remained still, and silence lingered until he replied.

"No...."

Quentin looked up at the skies, sighing deeply. Suki noticed the boys' tiredness. She closed her eyes and shook her head, murmuring, "I don't want to go back." She looked at the boys again, repeating the line before taking another look and breathing deeply.

"I know a place."

She declared.

Both Aiko and Quentin looked back at her.

"It's pretty far from the outskirts of the Republic of Melancholia, but we'll make it there after sunset."

Suki began to walk back south in the direction she had come from. Aiko and Quentin exchanged glances before following her with Albie.

They ascended the steep stairs, the towering building looming over them. The building's lights reflected off its surfaces, and people hurriedly passed by. Albie rested his face on Quentin's back, enjoying a piggyback ride. Suki walked just a short distance ahead of them, while Aiko ascended the stairs next to Quentin.

Quentin turned to his side, not fully facing Aiko but wanting to ask him something. After a moment, he mustered the courage to inquire.

"I know I'm prying, but I wanted to know more about Albie. Did he ever talk?"

Aiko sighed deeply.

"He is my foster brother. I don't know where he came from. He just appeared in my life when I was little. He didn't speak then, either."

Quentin wanted to delve further into Aiko's past but sensed the exhaustion in Aiko's response. Ignoring the lingering questions in his head, he spoke again after a brief pause.

"When I look closely at you and Albie, you two don't share any similarities, but you and Albie are like brothers."

89

"I can guarantee you that we're not brothers. He's someone I take care of."

Quentin's eyes dimmed, and he looked forward, silent for a few moments before finally asking.

"Then why do you have him if he's not your brother?"

Aiko's thoughts and memories kicked in, and he pondered for a split second. At that moment, his attention shifted to an older woman with gentle wrinkles. Her dark gray eyes expressed wisdom, and she wore old fashioned clothes that hinted at her age.

*"Promise me! To never look back."*

The sudden quiver in Aiko's breath sent a chill down his spine. Aiko looked at Albie for a moment before turning forward.

"Because I have to."

Aiko sped up the stairs even faster, catching Quentin off guard. The weight of those words lingered in Quentin's mind: "Because I have to."

He thought about it, closed his eyes, and nodded, contemplating Aiko's situation deeply.

They walked out of the city landscape. The further they traveled, the less urban it became. Open vegetation surrounded them, with trees lining both sides of the dirt road they walked on. Suki remained ahead, the others following. They gazed at the sun setting, and the city's skyline slowly illuminated with lights. Passing a few rundown houses, they could still see signs of life. Small native creatures, no bigger than a person's palm, clicked their miniature wings together, creating a buzzing sound that echoed through the tall grasses.

As the sun fully set, light posts along the dirt road flickered to life, providing enough illumination to see without revealing what lay ahead. Aiko's stomach growled, catching Quentin's attention.

"Are we close yet?"

Quentin asked Suki.

"We're almost there; it's just down this route."

Suki responded back. Aiko lagged behind, his breathing steady but strained. He hurried to catch up with Quentin; they both looked at the starlit sky, watching as more stars appeared. Quentin was lost in thought and bumped into Suki.

"Hey, watch it!"

"Oh, my bad!"

She glanced back at Quentin, a hint of anger fading quickly.

"We're here."

Aiko and Quentin gazed at the house—a two-story structure made of weathered wood. A dim yellow light post near the door offered a faint glow, and lights behind the curtains hinted at a welcoming interior. The roof, lava red against the dark sky, had a small window on top, revealing nothing but darkness. Quentin scrutinized the exterior.

"Is this your home?"

He asked.

Suki replied.

"It was."

Turning her back on the house, she walked toward them, avoiding eye contact.

"Tell them that your friends with me, and they'll let you in."

She instructed Quentin.

"Wait, you're not going inside?"

Quentin questioned.

Still avoiding eye contact.

"I don't want to be here. But you need a place to stay. I'll be fine on my own."

Suki stated.

"Wait! Why are you leaving?"

Quentin pressed.

"I told you I don't want to be here; I have other issues I must take care of."

"Is there something wrong? That doesn't mean you can leave on your own again."

Quentin insisted.

He followed her back towards the direction they came from before she stopped abruptly and turned around.

"I said I don't want to be here!"

Aiko, unfazed, looked behind him at them. She turned back around and walked away until the door opened.

"What's with all this ruckus?"

A woman exclaimed, stepping outside with a broom. The light cast a shadow over her appearance as she slowly walked outside her door.

"Show yourself!"

The woman smacked the broom shaft on her palm, demanding their presence. Quentin didn't have time to argue with Suki; he ran to the front.

"I'm sorry, ma'am, for disturbing you this late. My name is Quentin Reily; that boy over there with the blue mask is Aiko Ashin, and this kiddo is his brother, Albie Ashin."

Aiko looked up upon hearing "brother."

Gripping his hands briefly before letting go.

"We're friends with—"

"Suki?"

The woman dropped her broom and rushed towards Suki. Quentin was momentarily flustered.

"Suki Kimani..."

He turned to see the woman pass him and Aiko, reaching Suki. She was slightly taller than Suki. The woman gently wiped her hair back from her eyes and examined Suki for a moment. The woman put her hand on her mouth.

"It's really you!"

Suki remained silent, refusing to speak or answer any questions.

"Yume! Who's that out there?"

An elderly couple stepped outside the door. The woman, Mio, wore a cooking apron with a green sweater, black pants, and dark slip-on shoes, with messy hair like Suki. The elderly man, Jito, well-groomed, wore a brown shirt suited for suits, black pants, and dark slip-on shoes.

Quentin looked back and forth between the elderly couple and the woman, realizing something.

"You must be Suki's mother."

Quentin said. The woman turned to look at the boys.

"Yes, we haven't seen her for a while. She left home for a good time until now. You and the boys must have found and returned her to us."

"Actually, it was her idea to bring us here."

"Ooh, very thoughtful of her. My name is Yume Kimani. These are my parents. Would you care to join us for dinner?"

"Actually, we would like to eat something."

"Well, come in. We just need to set up the table and the rest."

Yume walked back into the house with the elderly couple. Quentin approached Suki.

"Come on, what's wrong with spending family time? You could've told us if you were shy about visiting your family."

Suki blushed slowly, avoiding eye contact with Quentin.

"That's not what it's all about."

She walked past him into the house. Quentin watched her go, trying to process what she had said. He was tired from carrying Albie the entire time. Walking back, he turned his head to Aiko.

"Coming in?"

Aiko didn't respond immediately; he looked around the house, examining it.

"Yeah."

Quentin walked in, leaving Aiko alone outside. After a moment of contemplation, Aiko finally entered the house.

Inside, bright orange light illuminated the ceiling. A mini living room was at the far back behind the kitchen, next to the table where dinner was being prepared. The living room revealed dark but notable stairs leading upstairs. The home was small but roomy enough for people to move freely. Quentin sat with a sleeping Albie in a big chair, resting his head on his arms.

Yume and Mio began arranging napkins, bowls, and spoons on the table. Nine chairs surrounded the square table, and Aiko wondered who else was there.

"Boe and Kaito! Come down here for dinner! And help, too!"

Aiko shivered slightly at Suki's mother's yell but found it comforting. Two boys, very young, around 5 and 4 years old, came down. They looked like twins, but their apparel was noticeably different. Boe wore a sizeable grey shirt, shorts, and slip-on shoes. Kaito wore a purple short-sleeved shirt, brown shorts, and similar black slip-on shoes. Both boys had combed and yet messy hair. Both boys made small talk with Albie, expressing their interest. Albie's eyes glowed in excitement upon talking to the boys.

"Okay, Mom."

Kaito responded, walking down to help Mio. Boe went over to the kitchen to assist Jito. Aiko looked around, taking in the scene, his heart feeling warm until he shook off those emotions.

"Young man, care to sit down?"

Mio invited.

Her sincere smile prompted Aiko to take a seat next to Quentin. Jito poured something from a pot, and the enticing aroma filled the air—a spicy kick with the scent of potatoes. Albie woke up from his nap, sensing the smell, too. Jito poured the food into bowls, with Suki sitting across from Quentin, her head nodding down without moving her lips. Boe and Kaito, having finished helping, sat next to Aiko, who didn't mind their presence.

Yume sat in the middle of the table where she could see everyone. Mio sat next to Suki, opposite Aiko and Quentin. Jito began passing down the bowls. Upon inspecting the bowl, Quentin noticed that it contained a soup with a very organic texture. Slices of potatoes floated on the liquid, and the fragrance of the soup filled the air. The spices swirled around, enticing Albie and Quentin, making their mouths water. They immediately dove into the soup, Albie repeatedly spooning the liquid into his mouth and Quentin enjoying the plant textures combined with the juice.

"Wow, this is amazing!"

Quentin exclaimed.

The spices embraced Quentin's palate, the flavor of the broth warming his body. Albie's mouth was covered in the broth as he slurped it eagerly.

"What's in this anyway?"

Quentin asked as he continued to consume the soup.

Jito finally sat down, preparing himself to enjoy the soup.

"I gathered the fruits and vegetables we planted. This is a Nectar fruit. You're already enjoying spice pods and roots from the nectar tree that gathered enough juice with mineral water inside. With a bit of salt and lime, you present this soup."

"I haven't tried anything like this before."

"Well, I'm happy that you're enjoying it."

Albie pushed the bowl out, grabbing Jito's attention.

"I see someone is ready for round two. I'll get you some more."

Jito poured more into Albie's bowl, and Albie immediately grabbed it back, slurping the soup even faster.

"Wow, someone is really enjoying my dish more than you. Say, what's your name again?"

Quentin wiped his mouth with a napkin.

"I'm Quentin Reily. This is Albie Ashin, and my friend next to me is Aiko Ashin."

"Those are lovely names."

Mio remarked.

Aiko looked to his side, observing the two kids roughhousing around but not bothering him. He sighed internally but chose not to express it.

"And these are my boys, Boe and Kaito. No playing around at the table!"

Jito scolded.

The boys settled down, grabbing their spoons and enjoying the soup. Aiko chuckled a little in his mind but didn't show it.

"So, where are you guys from?"

Jito asked.

"Well, I'm from the Sanguine Nation."

Quentin replied, cleaning his area.

"And what about you, son?"

Aiko remained silent, having heard Jito's question but choosing not to speak.

"Forgive him; he's pretty worn out and tired. He and his brother are from outside of the nations."

Quentin explained.

Jito, Mio, and Yume's eyes widened at this revelation—outside the nation.

"You mean outside of the Republic of Melancholia? Not just outside like here, but far away."

Jito clarified.

Quentin recalled what Aiko had mentioned earlier when they first met. He gathered his thoughts.

"That's what I'm told, yes."

"Well, that's enough for me to let someone like you and your brother stay with us. It must be hard traveling here and finding food around."

95

Jito empathized.

Yume observed Aiko, who sat still without touching his soup. She felt the urge to say something to him but held back, allowing Aiko to settle in.

"Where are y'all from?"

Quentin continued slurping his soup. Yume decided to speak up.

"We are all from the Phlegmatic Nation. We are farmers who traveled here for trades and a better lifestyle."

Suki remained silent throughout dinner, gazing only at the table. Quentin occasionally glanced at Suki but refrained from seeking her attention.

"We were originally going to live in a better area in the nation, but with a sudden event that happened in our—"

"Don't tell him."

Suki interrupted, her fingers forming a fist, veins popping out as she squeezed her hands.

"We were going to get a better home, but my husband—"

Suki slammed the table, capturing everyone's attention."

"Stop talking about HIM! I don't care about him. He's GONE!"

Yume stood up to confront her.

"Why can't I talk about him?! It's all in the past! Why are you still angry at me?"

"You keep mentioning how much he used to love you. He didn't love you, me, or any of us!"

"Suki dear, I don't miss him, and I know I still have feelings for him, but I wanted to mention it to them."

"They don't need to know! No one cares about him. I don't care about him, and I don't care about how you feel about him."

Yume's eyes widened, taking a step back. Suki scanned the table while Jito and Mio looked down together. Boe and Kaito silently stared at the table, and Albie recoiled from the sudden uproar. Quentin, shocked, remained composed, and Aiko, though still, observed the situation from the corner of his eye.

"It was a mistake returning here."

Suki declared, storming out of the home.

"Suki, wait!"

Yume called out, but her plea was ignored. Yume slowly sat down, placing her hand on her forehead. Quentin shifted his gaze from where Suki had gone to look at Yume, his eyes softening.

"I'm sorry for you and your friends to experience this. It's been a while since she returned home. She hasn't been able to move on."

Quentin said, choosing his words carefully.

"It's okay."

"What was she referring to?"

Aiko asked.

Yume paused, and a heavy silence filled the once-happy table with emptiness.

"Her father. My husband."

Yume finally revealed.

Aiko listened to Yume's words, feeling mixed emotions as anger bubbled within him, mirroring Suki's sentiments. However, he chose to keep his feelings to himself, not wanting to burden others.

"He left our family, engaging in activities we didn't support. Leaving me and the kids alone with no support. I convinced my parents to stay with us, helping us stay together. Unfortunately, I didn't try my hardest to bring Suki together. She felt betrayed when her father left. Everything they did together didn't matter to him. Now, it doesn't matter to her. I guess she left us because she wants to forget her past and forget about us."

Yume sighed, the weight of the past heavy in the air.

Aiko reflected on Yume's words. Betrayed. Aiko began to sympathize with Suki, feeling the weight of resentment towards someone who wasn't there for them and ultimately forgot about them.

"She disappeared on us for a while until she met you fellows. I'm grateful that she still has a heart for caring about people. I don't blame you if she's hasty and harsh. Everything nowadays isn't the same anymore..."

"Everything nowadays isn't the same anymore."

Aiko repeated the sentence, contemplating the profound truth in those words.

Quentin stood up and gently held his plate.

"I'll talk to her later, just to check on her. Do you need help with the plates and cleaning?"

He offered.

Yume grinned upon hearing Quentin's words.

"I'd like that. Thank you very much, Quentin."

Quentin observed Aiko, deep in contemplation, his untouched supper languishing before him, utensils pristine and unused. With a subtle sound, Quentin drew Aiko's attention back to the immediate world, signaling him to join in the post-dinner cleanup. Aiko rose, engaging in the rhythm of tidying up. Everyone swiftly collected plates and converged at the sink, where Yume and Quentin awaited the cleansing ritual.

After the rest diligently scrubbed the table and floor, Quentin conversed with Yume while Jito and Mio found solace in the living room. Boe and Kaito proudly showcased their artistic creations to an elated Albie. Aiko, leaning against the wall, cast his gaze upon Albie and then to the rest, his eyes resting for a fleeting moment.

The ambiance resonated with the sounds of nature, creating a backdrop for Aiko's reflections. Anbu's voice echoed in the recesses of his mind, entwined with the delicate peak of Inoue's words, forming an ethereal symphony. A vivid memory manifested before him—the image of a younger Albie playfully tugging at his shirt. Aiko's heart stirred, and a sense of normalcy, elusive yet undeniable, enveloped him. He saw Albie's involvement with Yume sons made him happier. Aiko looked down, only thinking...

Opening his eyes, Aiko felt a genuine warmth emanating from his core, an inexplicable connection to the ordinary. Leaning back, he closed his eyes again, surrendering to the comforting embrace of the present moment. The collective hum of voices, the soothing sounds of nature, and the distant echoes of familial voices coalesced into a harmonious melody, granting Aiko a fleeting reprieve from the weight of his journey.

Quentin concluded his assistance to Yume, stepping outside into the fantastic night to seek Suki. Following the dirt trail she had led them on, guided by the light posts illuminating his way. Houses with warm lights emanating from their windows dotted the outskirts, testifying to the community still thriving in this quiet corner of the nation. As Quentin continued, he momentarily felt a sense of disorientation but spotted another route on his left. The light posts beckoned him, and he dutifully followed.

The path led him through a symphony of nocturnal sounds, the occasional rustle of leaves, and the distant chirping of crickets accompanying him. The rhythm of water, faint and distant, began to reach his ears. Guided solely by the intermittent glow of the light posts, Quentin pressed forward until the surroundings became more apparent.

Before him, a bridge emerged from the darkness, its silhouette defined against the night. The steep hillside obscured parts of the scene, and with the minimal illumination, it challenged Quentin to discern the details. Climbing the stairs toward the bridge, he saw a figure seated on the railing—Suki. Her hands firmly gripped the railing as she stared into the abyss below, where the river flowed with an echoing resonance.

Approaching cautiously, Quentin sensed the weight in the air. The ambient sounds of flowing water created a backdrop to Suki's contemplative state. Quentin waited for a moment before softly addressing her.

"Suki."

He spoke, his voice matching the hushed atmosphere.

"I always visit this bridge when I feel like this. Staring at the currents moving through the stream, away to somewhere else. Far away from where I am, forgetting where it came from because of constant movement. Doesn't need to remember where it came from."

Quentin approached her, giving her the space she seemed to need.

"I hope you don't mind me being here with you. Is that fine with you?"

Silence, except for the soothing sounds of the water. Quentin, respecting the quiet, tried to choose his words carefully.

"Is this where you went to after the train accident?"

For a moment, she said nothing, allowing her thoughts to settle.

"Yeah... thinking about what I was doing."

Quentin took a step closer, attempting to listen and understand.

"I was really gone for a while from them. I can't let it go. And I won't, not until I can feel satisfied."

"Suki..."

He uttered softly, acknowledging the depth of her emotions.

"Quentin, you don't understand. How much it hurts. Letting something go, something I can't do. I won't forgive myself or my family. Even after all this time, my mom still thinks about him. I only remember my father through the lens of bad memories. I really hate him. For leaving me..."

Quentin inched a bit closer, offering his support.

"I'm here for you."

She turned to him, her eyes revealing a mixture of pain and vulnerability.

"I won't leave you..."

Closing her eyes, she turned back to the water, then slowly gazed up at the skies, revealing the stars. Moments of silence with the sound of the water and wind spreading around their ears.

99

"That means a lot, but it doesn't mean we're a couple or a thing, okay?"

She clarified.

Quentin chuckled.

"What are you and Aiko going to do here?"

She asked.

Quentin unfolded a paper to reveal the extra registration form from his poncho.

"Signing up for the FIREBIRDS Program."

Quentin replied, holding out the form.

Suki's eyes widened.

"Why would you sign up for the program? Do you not understand the responsibility it takes? The danger and struggle to maintain your role?!"

Quentin chuckled again.

"Yeah, I know, but it won't stop me."

"But why sign up?"

Suki thought about it in her mind, bringing it up to Quentin who walked over to the railing, gazing at the moving water below.

"I wanted to be a FIREBIRDS like my father ever since I was young. He always told me about his journey and missions, making me proud. He was amazing to me, teaching me to stay strong. You continue to push even when you feel alone in a fight."

Suki listened intently to Quentin's words as he shared his admiration for his father.

"He was someone I looked up to, too, and I want to be like him. I know our fathers are different, but I want to give you this form. You don't have to fight alone; I'm asking if you want to join me?"

Suki looked at the form, her brows raised.

"You got another form just in case we ever meet again?"

Quentin blushed but tried to hide it.

"No, no, no."

He stammered.

"Just in case the registration process didn't work out, and I would have to do the process again."

Suki's eyes darted at Quentin, grinning a little.

"Sureee..."

Quentin sighed.

"Do you want to join me? I really like your headfirst spirit and want to help you."

Suki thought for a moment, looking at Quentin holding the form. She gently took it from his hand.

"I'll think about it."

"Well, you have until morning; that's when the enlisting is done. Sorry if I gave it to you too late; I didn't know how to approach this."

"It's fine. I have time to think."

Suki replied.

Quentin shivered, feeling the cold in the air.

"I think we should go back; it's getting colder outside."

Suki gazed at the stream momentarily, closed her eyes, and stepped off the bridge railing.

"Okay."

From a distant entrance along Quentin's route, Aiko concealed himself behind a wall. His gaze remained fixed on Quentin and Suki, silently observing their interaction.

# Chapter Eight: Decision Weighs Your Outcome

The night skies cleared the surroundings clouds from the numerous stars casting far across the galaxy. The moon's glow through the window provided the only light in the room where Aiko was sleeping. Boxes and other objects were scattered across from him, resting near the moonlight reflection. With his mask on, Aiko only stared at the light he could see. He continued to stare and stare, refusing to blink his eyes.

*"His hands are bleeding. Does anyone have a tissue or a rag?"*

His consciousness still hears voices when he has passed out.

*"Aiko Ashin, age: 16, date of birth: April 24, 2117. Origin: Unknown. ID: Unknown. Height: 5'7". Parents/Guardian: Inoue Ashin."*

Aiko continued to shake aggressively.

*"There is someone you need to meet; follow me."*

*"I... am your father..."*

*"YOU'RE NOT MY FATHER! WHO ARE YOU!"*

*"Where were you when I needed YOU!"*

*"I didn't want to have this meeting; I didn't want to believe that my son was alive—"*

*"The suit radiates your presence. It was designed to be wielded by Harmonians like you."*

*"This is the Melancholic Knight. Humanity's last hope."*

*"Why should I wear it? There is nothing inside of me that desires to wear it. I have nothing but anger from you; why should I wear it when you can wear it yourself."*

*"I need you."*

*"Promise me!"*

Aiko then pictured Albie from their journey to get here, seeing his face in anger. The kick he gave to him is still felt. Aiko couldn't close his eyes anymore.

*"I need you."*

His father's voice echoed throughout many pictures of the people. Seeing Quentin, Suki, his father, Kenryoku, Inoue's faded image, Albie, and Anbu's picture, Aiko got up fast, breathing heavily. He looked out the window, staring at it increasingly.

Yume, walking from the upstairs hallway, heard sounds above her. She was carrying the bowl of soup with her from supper. She got up to Aiko's room, where she heard the sounds, noticing the window was open, releasing slow wind to engulf the area. She went over and looked outside, only to see Aiko staring at the skies with his arms wrapped around his legs. His bandages are gone, revealing healed scars and burns. She slowly climbed out the window and walked on the roof to where Aiko was.

"So that's where I heard the noises from."

She sat just close enough so he could see her.

"I noticed earlier that you weren't touching your supper at all. I wonder if you didn't want to take off your mask. Quentin said that you weren't feeling bright today."

Aiko listened to her. He still looked at the stars but leaned his head to his side, showing that he was listening.

"Do you care to talk about what you're thinking? You're not sleeping; everyone here is already passed out. If it's the attic you're staying in, then my apologies; there was no room I could comfortably place you in. Forgive me."

"How is Albie?"

Yume's expression changes, and she redirects her attention.

"Your little brother? He is doing well. Immediately after you left to check on Quentin and Suki, he slept on the couch fast. I guess he is tired like you, too. He is sleeping with the younger brothers of Suki; he will be fine."

Aiko nods, looking away from the sky. Yume looked over to his hands and saw his hands. She grabbed his hands for closer inspection.

"What happens to your hands? Are you feeling well?"

"Yes."

"Are you not, okay? Just tell me how you are really feeling. I'm not going to leave until you tell me."

Aiko starts to move his head slowly to his side, now directly looking at Yume's face. He sees her eyes down, her eyebrows lowered, and her breathing slow. He feels a small surge of guilt swallowing him up, but he can't show it physically, so he closes his eyes and opens them.

"I was in an accident; I got my hand burned. Quentin and Suki were there to"

"WHAT!"

Yume interjected.

"But they're fine. Albie was there, too."

"WHAT!"

Yume interrupted again.

"Can I finish? They are all fine; I was the only one who got badly hurt, but it doesn't matter."

"Yes, it does matter! Did you do something reckless to cause yourself to get into an accident?"

Aiko pressed his hands together, pondering her question."

"A little... I did it to save them."

Aiko returns to look at the dark skies again.

"I've been given the offer to work for the URDT. I don't know how long I'll be gone or if I'll return."

Yume listens intently to Aiko's words.

"I was wondering if you could take Albie in for me?"

Yume looked away from Aiko, looking at the ground below them.

"I can take care of him; he'll be fine while you're gone, but..."

Aiko turned his direction towards her.

"But I want you to promise me you'll return here, not only to be there for him but also to be safe."

Aiko couldn't think of any answers; he didn't know how to answer her question.

"I don't know; that's why I am asking you. Albie looks happy here, but I can't take care of him. I need to go; leaving him here is for the best."

"Leaving and not returning is how you'll take care of him. I will take care of him, but can you take care of yourself? Are you going to return?

Aiko wanted to say something but was reminded of his father's words: *"You mustn't breathe a word of our discussion, your involvement in this work. There are only consequences, for all our sakes."*

Aiko's silence was accompanied by the wind and the trees brushing against one another.

104

"I'll be gone by morning; I'll join Quentin so your worries can end here."

Yume got a bit closer to him.

"I don't know where you and Albie came from; traveling here wasn't easy. I am willing to take care of Albie; I just want you to know that you have a place here to stay; you're not alone."

Yume slowly hands over the soup to Aiko. He notices her gesture of placing the soup in front of him, allowing him to think about whether to take it or not. He thinks for a moment and looks at her. He grabs the soup, feeling the warmth and the scent of the spices swelling up.

"Just come back here. You may think he doesn't care about you, but he does. Don't push yourself away from him or others. Also, be careful; the soup is a bit hot."

Yume got up and walked over to the window, going in.

"Get some sleep, please; you need it."

Her presence left Aiko silent; her voice filled his mind.

"Take care of yourself."

Bringing him small fragments of memories of a familiar voice to him.

"*TAKE CARE OF YOURSELF!*"

"Inoue..."

Aiko gasped for a moment, looking at the soup. He lifted his mask up, placing it on top of his head. He took sips from the soup, sighing softly from the taste. He looked towards the skies again.

# Chapter Nine: URDT

Quentin's eyes slowly opened, his ears absorbing the persistent vibrations of the buzzing sound. Sensing it nearby, he reached over to the source, discovering it to be a watch. Slipping it onto his wrist, he rose from the floor and surveyed his makeshift sleeping quarters. The sleeping bag cocooned his surroundings, the room feeling somewhat cramped. Stretching languidly, he gathered his clothes and poncho, making his way to the bathroom for a quick refresh.

Navigating the space with deliberate quietness, Quentin descended the stairs, gravitating towards the door. He noticed Yume was already up, immersed in early morning tasks in the kitchen while cradling a bag.

"Heading out?"

Her voice, subdued and resembling dust settling in the air, cut through the morning hush.

"Yeah, I have to attend an event over at the URDT."

Quentin spoke, gradually improving the clarity of his voice as he approached Yume. "Sorry, I forgot to mention it yesterday. I was pretty worn out from that day."

"Don't worry about it. If the nap helps you recover, that's all that matters. But I'm glad you mentioned it. Is Aiko going with you?"

Quentin's eyes lowered upon Yume response, closing his mouth slowly, glancing to his side.

"I'm not sure. He's been through a lot. I asked Suki if she wanted to accompany me. Is that okay with you?"

"It's fine. She's grown up, and I can't watch over her as much anymore. Seeing her back brought me hope that she might have returned to her younger self. It's new to me to see her with you and Aiko. She never helped anyone. Just promise me you'll watch over her. I hope she finds something new in her life and grows. Promise me."

Yume said, her gaze fixed on Quentin, direct but gentle.

Quentin's mind quieted down, and he sighed softly.

"I promise... I just hope."

Quentin made his way out of the door, pushing it open before glancing back at Yume. Her brightened grin imparted a sense of hope as he stepped outside. Encouraged by her silent gesture, he walked away, leaving Yume's smile to fade slowly as she gazed upstairs, lost in thoughts of Suki and Aiko.

Following the path Suki had guided them on the day before, Quentin was surrounded by dense, cloudy fog. He occasionally looked back, hoping to catch sight of Suki and Aiko running toward him. Only the wind echoed in his ears as the fog shifted its appearance around him. Closing his eyes, he continued walking. The sky hinted at the approaching dawn, the blue gradually asserting itself.

Walking away from home, the shrinking silhouette marked the distance he covered. Consulting his watch, Quentin realized time was slipping away, with only 45 minutes left to reach URDT.

"QUENTIN!"

The voice, initially faint, gained clarity as it called his name. Turning around, Quentin saw a figure running towards him. Adjusting his course towards the approaching figure, the fog made it challenging to identify until the person drew near.

"QUENTIN! DON'T LEAVE!"

The voice grew recognizable, and Suki's appearance gradually came into focus. Quentin's eyes lit up.

"SUKI!"

He ran towards her as if reunited after an eternity. However, as he looked closer, he noticed Suki's raised arm, her hand clenched into a fist. The aggressive tone in her voice and the intensity of her expression—raised eyebrows and tightly sealed lips—signaled anger. Quentin halted abruptly, realizing her emotion, and stepped back.

"WHY ARE YOU ANGRY AT ME?"

Quentin yelled; his voice tinged with frantic confusion.

She sprinted towards him with such speed that his sentence was cut short, and she tackled him to the ground, creating a small explosion of dust around them. Quentin found himself on the ground, looking up at Suki, who gasped upon realizing her position. Swiftly getting up, she stepped back, leaving Quentin to cough from the dust he had inhaled.

"What was that for?"

Quentin asked, still recovering from the unexpected tackle.

Suki collected her thoughts and kicked more dust towards him.

"That. Was."

She said, kicking each time she completed a word,

107

"For."

Another kick.

"Leaving."

And yet another kick

"Me!"

Quentin coughed even more, prompting him to get up and dust himself off.

"I didn't know if you would get up on time."

Quentin defended.

Suki strolled; her movements are now more passive.

"Well, how am I supposed to know when to wake up? You didn't even specify the time. You said I have till this morning."

Quentin's expression changed quickly as she quoted back his words.

"Oh... my bad. Hey, at least you're here."

He added hopefully.

She stared at Quentin, slowly lifting her arm and delivering a soft punch to his shoulder.

"Ow."

Quentin murmured, rubbing the spot where she had hit him.

"Is he coming?"

Suki asked, relaxing her arms. Quentin looked down, scanning over her.

"I don't know. I never mentioned him about joining me, or at least I don't think he intends to join us."

Quentin responded, his words trailing off as he heard footsteps approaching. Another figure emerged from the fog, wearing a blue mask.

"Aiko?"

Quentin called out. Suki turned to see Aiko standing before them, panting softly from the run.

"It was for you, but once she saw us leaving, she made more for us."

Aiko held out a bag, explaining.

Quentin and Suki accepted the bags from Aiko, and Suki curiously reached inside, revealing a snack. Her eyes widened as she gasped softly.

"This is what I used to eat when I was little. Nectar Seed Gummies. I'm surprised that she can make them again."

"Are they good?"

Aiko asked, opening his own bag. Suki looked at him as if he didn't understand.

"Yes, they are. You gotta try them. They're the best."

Quentin's grin widened as he observed Suki and Aiko exchanging small talk. He sighed softly, checking his watch, which prompted a change in his expression.

"Okay, we've got to go now!"

He declared, urging them to move.

Quentin ushered Suki and Aiko, and together, they ran into the enveloping, foggy cloud, gradually disappearing from sight. Back at the house, Yume stood on the porch, watching them vanish as they continued running. She looked down momentarily, her mind replaying Aiko's words from the previous night.

*"I don't know; that's how I am asking you. Albie looks happy here; I can't take care of him. I need to go; leaving him here is for the best."*

Her expression shifted, eyebrows furrowing. Looking back up, she gazed at the thickening fog.

"Please return, Aiko."

She whispered, lost in contemplation as she stared at where they had disappeared.

***

The city's buildings soared high, and shops opened windows and doors as many people navigated the bustling streets. Aiko stood by the station railing, observing the metro train gliding along the tracks. The train moved gracefully past pedestrians, but Aiko's focus shifted between the moving train and the path they had taken. Lost in thought, he heard footsteps approaching from his left but remained unmoved.

"So, you're coming with us?"

Suki's voice reached him, leaning over the railing but not turning her face towards him.

Aiko glanced at Suki, acknowledging her presence without a direct response, his thoughts lingering on the decision he needed to make.

"I can say the same thing to you."

Aiko responded, glancing at the ground. Suki snickered briefly but composed herself.

"So, how do you feel now? From yesterday…"

She spoke. Aiko's mouth remained shut, his mind barricading against a flood of images, voices, and memories. Emotionally constrained, he struggled to articulate his feelings, choosing to keep them closed off entirely.

"I see… well, I wanted to make this up to you. For what I said to you yesterday."

Suki reached into her bag, pulling out something to hand to Aiko. He examined the bag he had given them, realizing it contained the snack she liked.

"I get what you're feeling, except I shout with it. But I know that yesterday I pressured you. It was my bad. And I know you didn't have a choice; I chose based on my feelings. I'm sorry."

Aiko held the snack in both hands, its homemade scent wafting with sweet and flourishing notes.

"By the way, you better finish them. I really love them."

Suki added, playfully bumping his shoulder. Aiko, seemingly unfazed, allowed her a small smile. She walked away, leaving him to absorb the thoughtful gift. Glancing behind him, Aiko watched her retreat and then turned his attention back to the snack, tightly squeezing it before carefully placing it in his jacket pocket.

Quentin stood at the front of the metro train, gazing at the URDT Fortress, the wind gently brushing against him. Footsteps approached from behind, prompting him to turn around and find Suki walking towards him. Looking forward as the train moves.

"How is he?"

Suki asked, and Quentin maintained eye contact as she positioned herself on the other side of the railing.

"Fine. He really likes to look at everything. I can't tell if he is alive behind his mask or if he can even breathe."

Quentin chuckled, then shifted his gaze back to the URDT, lost in his thoughts.

"There is a part of me that feels guilty. I can't expect anyone to be like me; he is different from me and you. I can't get over that from yesterday."

Quentin admitted.

Suki looked to her side.

"He is definitely different from the people I know. But he is not so much different. I was like him once in some ways, just trying to figure out how to deal with my emotions.

Seeing him here with us means something; he still cares. He's still with you, so that should mean something to you."

Quentin turned to Suki, finding her words insightful.

"Yeah… I hope he finds what he's looking for. So, what made you want to join me?"

Suki looked down, observing the disappearing road devoured by the train's pace.

"I don't know, really. Maybe my consciousness told me so. Maybe I want to find more meaning in life. This is probably an excuse for me to leave my family behind again. I guess I want to be with others."

"Others who?"

Quentin asked, looking at her from the corner of his eye.

"I guess I'm saying that hanging out with people is nice. I've never met or seen anyone like you, especially Aiko. It was a nice change of pace. Living in this world isn't worthwhile..."

"Glad you came."

Quentin replied.

Suki returned her attention to Quentin.

"It'll be an experience for all of us."

They both gazed at the URDT base, watching as it gradually gained light from the sun. The horizon embraced the sun, glowing on the Republic of Melancholia. After disembarking from the metro train, they hiked towards the entrance of URDT. Joining the assembly of people their age, tall and slender figures, both male and female, stood scattered across the vast space. Thousands waited patiently, maintaining their distance from one another. They waited for the light to turn green, signaling the floor beneath them to descend.

***

In the initial darkness, the surroundings were obscure, but as the floor descended, lights illuminated the scene. The spotlight from the ceiling of the URDT headquarters proudly shone down on the floor, where numerous FIREBIRDS troops formed a perimeter. More young individuals stood within the spotlight, waiting with anticipation. A stage adorned with a microphone hinted at forthcoming announcements. Aerial vehicles gracefully docked and departed from their bays above, while ground vehicles moved purposefully to various locations, setting off to nearby destinations. The atmosphere buzzed with excitement and uncertainty, a prelude to the unfolding events.

After stepping off the escalator, Quentin sprinted toward a person in a URDT uniform, carrying stacks of papers received from recruits. His agility caught the attention of the uniformed woman, causing her to step back slightly upon his arrival. He halted just before taking another step.

"You're late."

She declared.

"I know; we were staying at a place far away. It was taxing on us to get here on time."

Quentin explained.

She glared at him but shook off her expression.

"Well, you're here, and that's what matters. Anyways, do you have the registration forms on hand?"

"Yes, we do."

Quentin replied, reaching for his poncho, pulling out a folded form, and handing it over to her. He turned around to check if Suki had her form. She slowly lifted her hand, revealing that she also held the form, passing it to the lady. The woman examined the forms and scrutinized each of them. Her gaze lingered on Aiko for a moment, the mask seeming to pique her interest.

"I see... you all can go in."

They exchanged glances, Quentin and Suki briefly looking back at Aiko before focusing on their path. Passing the lady, she turned back to Aiko, reaching for her earpiece and pressing a button to communicate with someone.

Quentin and Suki hurried toward the center where recruits gathered. They glanced at each other, pondering the same question: Why wasn't Aiko asked for the form? Quentin hadn't even given Aiko a form. Suki's mind puzzled over why Aiko was present without a form. The unanswered questions lingered as they pressed on, knowing they needed to reach their orientation in time.

The air within the URDT headquarters hung heavy with an unusual stillness. All vehicles, from flying crafts to landing vehicles, froze in their movements. The crowd, covered by thousands of recruits, displayed diverse clothing from different nations. Some, like Quentin, wore ponchos, while others adorned masks to shield themselves from toxic substances in their native regions. The recruits stood tall; eyes fixated on the platform ahead.

Quentin and Suki maneuvered to spots next to each other, with Aiko silently following suit behind them. As they settled, an unexplained silence permeated the atmosphere, causing confusion among the assembled recruits. The ambient sounds slowly crept into the stillness. Some began to exchange puzzled glances.

"It's 8:36. They should've started when we got here..."

Quentin observed, checking his watch.

"Maybe they were waiting for us or the others that got here late, too."

Suki suggested in a hushed tone.

Quentin surveyed the area, realizing that everyone seemed equally bewildered. Aiko, however, remained fixated on the top of the facility's roof, his gaze lingering on the part of the building where he had been the day before—his father's office. His mind wrestled with echoes of his father's voice, a haunting presence piercing his thoughts.

"Screw this; why did I bother to sign up if URDT can't even properly set up orientation! I'm out! This is a waste of time!"

A male recruit, positioned far to Quentin's right, stormed out of the area. Passing by others, he garnered looks from some while others exchanged glances, seemingly sharing the same sentiment with the departing recruit.

Out of nowhere, a line shot from above, the spotlight obscuring its origin. All eyes turned upward, and a dark figure materialized in the light. The shadowy outline gave the mechanical figure a striking appearance as it descended like a meteor, swooping near the departing male recruit.

As the figure turned, its armor became visible, resembling that of the FIREBIRDS but with distinctive features. Sharp-edged armor plating adorned its chest, accompanied by pouches and stripes underneath. Emblem of a shark with menacing teeth adorned the helmet and chest, while a mask with intricate armor pieces extended from beneath the ears to below the lips, featuring a V-shaped visor.

The sudden appearance of the figure left everyone in shock. Swiftly, the figure executed a leg sweep, knocking the recruit down. With remarkable speed, the figure activated a wrist module, shooting a cable that entwined the recruit completely. The intention behind this display remained unclear, but a chill permeated the air.

Turning attention to the surroundings, the figure surveyed the shocked crowd. The cable was released with another touch to the wrist module, setting the recruit free, who remained motionless.

"Waste of time, you say?"

The figure spoke, a male voice immobilizing everyone in their positions.

"Then why are you all here then?"

All the recruits exchanged glances, with Quentin and Suki looking back. Aiko processed the words.

"Then why are you all here, then?"

Which caused him to look down and contemplate the recruits.

113

"I'm here for the payment!"

A male recruit from the back of the crowd declared.

"Yeah, same!"

Chimed in a female recruit.

"URDT's throwing around rewards and cash like candy for people our age to sign up—I'm in on that!"

Another recruit added. The revelation disgusted Quentin, making him turn away from the crowd, appalled that people his age were joining solely for monetary gain. Suki's expression remained unfazed as she observed the crowd of recruits circling around the figure. Aiko looked on, staying still and seemingly uninterested in the conversation but attentively noting the unfolding situation.

"So, for the rewards then…"

The figure began popping his fingers as he looked around.

"How about this? Everyone will get their cash credit if you can take me down."

Recruits looked at each other, with uncertainty spreading among them. Some huddled together, contemplating the idea of taking on the challenge. The crowd circled around the figure while Quentin and Suki remained at a safe distance, keen on witnessing the conflict. Aiko followed suit, watching from a distance. Suki surveyed her surroundings, noting that the FIREBIRDS remained motionless, not intervening to assist the figure becoming surrounded.

"Why aren't they helping?"

Suki questioned, her concern evident.

"Something is up his sleeve, and they seem aware of his plan. This is only going to get intense…"

Quentin observed, realizing the unusual behavior of the FIREBIRDS.

The figure stood surrounded, locking eyes with every recruit, the tension palpable. Though someone seemed eager to charge, they held their ground, awaiting the opportune moment. The figure remained vigilant, scanning for any signs of attack. Suddenly, a recruit charged at full force, catching the figure's attention. Calmly waiting until the attacker was close enough, the figure used the palm of his hand to strike the recruit's face, forcing him to stumble backward, stunned.

The crowd recoiled at the defensive move, and the figure gestured, inviting further attacks. Hesitation spread among the recruits while some began to plot behind the nervous crowd. Undeterred, recruits took turns charging at the figure, attempting double-team maneuvers, only to be effortlessly countered. The figure demonstrated

114

astonishing skill, tripping legs and using hands like blades to incapacitate his opponents. Surprisingly, he even used one of the recruits to shield against ongoing attacks.

Witnessing the figure skillfully put down every attacker, Quentin recognized that this individual was a force to be reckoned with, regardless of his identity. The FIREBIRDS' indifference further heightened the mystery surrounding the situation.

In the crowd, a lone recruit strolled towards the figure, passing others in awe of the ongoing performance. Suddenly, he dashed towards the figure, catching the attention of the mysterious combatant. Just as the figure prepared for the attack, two arms came from behind, holding him in place. Another recruit, almost as tall as the figure, had grabbed and immobilized him. The initial attacker landed a series of blows, focusing on the exposed body parts of the figure's armor. Sucker punches and elbow hits were strategically delivered to stun the figure.

Caught in the moment, Quentin found himself rooting for the two recruits despite knowing their motivations were driven by the reward. Seeing two individuals taking control of the battle stirred excitement among the crowd, and others started cheering for the brave duo.

Sensing the change in the crowd's mood, the figure lifted his leg when he noticed the attacking recruit preparing for another blow. Waiting for the opportune moment, he swiftly kicked the assailant to the ground. Observing the sudden counterattack, the other recruit became the figure's new focus. The figure weighed himself down, gradually causing the recruit to release his grip and tire out. With a quick 360-degree turn, the figure landed a series of non-lethal blows. Overwhelmed, the recruit used his arms to block the attacks but found himself unable to withstand the onslaught.

Using his wrist module, the figure employed a grapple to tie the recruit's legs, causing him to fall. With full force, the figure kicked the fallen recruit towards his initial attacker. The figure then pointed at both boys with his module.

"Humph."

The figure chuckled to himself, a wry smile playing on his lips, as the two recruits exchanged glances, silently acknowledging the unexpected turn of events. The crowd's shock only intensified as they witnessed the figure effortlessly thwarting those who dared challenge him, even while physically restrained.

"You almost had me there, but it wasn't enough. You both let your guard down, and I seized the opportunity to strike back."

Remarked Ryne Maverick, addressing the two recruits with admiration and amusement.

"What are your names?"

Maverick looked towards them. The recruiters, regaining their composure, rose to their feet. One snapped into a sharp salute, catching the other off guard.

"Odie Ulysses, sir!"

Odie, sporting black-framed glasses that contrasted with his dark blonde hair, which was slightly shaggy but neatly combed, stood clad in a camouflage jacket with a scarf draped around his neck. His attire was complete with jeans and tennis shoes.

"And you?"

Maverick turning his attention to the other recruit.

"Jerome Aguilar, sir!"

Nearly matching Maverick's height, Jerome had olive skin tone and deep brown eyes. A hint of a mini beard adorned his chin while his impeccably combed hair reflected the light. He was dressed in a smart tee with a collar and tan pants, complemented by sturdy boots.

"Good! I like that energy! Join the rest of the recruits."

Maverick declared with a nod of approval, his voice resonating with authority.

Lowering his ARC, Ryne shifted his attention to everyone present.

"My name is Ryne Maverick, and I am the leading commander of the 31st battalion of the URDT."

A hush fell over the crowd as they listened intently to Ryne's words. With purpose, he made his way towards the platform, leaving everyone in awe of the skilled commander who had just revealed his identity.

"You are all here for many reasons, and I am here to tell you that you will receive your credits eventually by becoming part of URDT. URDT stands for United, Resolution, Defense, Tranquility. We are looking for dedicated individuals to help serve their nation, be protectors, and uphold the laws we've created. In the following 10 weeks, you all will undergo rigorous training, proving yourselves worthy to bear the URDT name. My fellow commanders and I will watch and mold each of you into powerful individuals capable of taking on any challenge!"

Ryne Maverick declared. Beside him stood three captains, Maverick walking beside them.

"Allow me to introduce Captain Curtis Ayabusa, our hand-to-hand combat specialist. He'll be your guide in the art of personal confrontation warfare."

In his thirties, Captain Ayabusa wore navy armor plating on his chest reminiscent of the FIREBIRDS. Beneath, a light green muscle shirt peeked out. Straps secured his armor, and a large knife was holstered. His limbs bore the distinct markings of the FIREBIRDS, with customized alterations enhancing his knee armor for extra durability. Beneath a military cap adorned with the URDT logo, his dark skin framed a pair of intense black eyes, above which sat a well-groomed mustache connecting to a neatly trimmed beard. He idly stroked it with gloved hands, his name badge proudly displaying: "Captain Curtis Ayabusa."

Turning to the next captain, he continued.

"And here we have Dahlia Mackenzie, your key to survival in the perils ahead. She's an expert in infiltration warfare and will assist you in adapting to your surroundings."

Standing beside Ayabusa was Captain Dahlia Mackenzie, a woman of similar age. She sported attire akin to the FIREBIRDS, with lighter armor affording her greater mobility. Despite her petite stature, her presence commanded attention. A mini-torn scout scarf adorned her, cascading down her sides. With porcelain white skin and wavy blonde hair framing cornflower-blue eyes, she exuded a sense of confidence. Her name badge bore the inscription: "Captain Dahlia Mackenzie."

Moving on, Maverick gestured to the last captain.

"And finally, meet Captain Cade Valente, our Weapon Proficiency Master. He's the finest sharpshooter the URDT has ever known and will teach you how to wield the ARC module—Automatic, Resourceful, Convenience—which encompasses all you'll need to learn."

At Maverick's cue, Valente swiftly aimed his ARC toward the sky, unleashing rapid-fire shots. The precision of his bullets was such that they seemed to blur, leaving observers unable to even blink. Taking aim at a recruit, Valente fired a cable-like grapple that swiftly snatched the recruit's drink before retracting back to him. He offered it to Maverick, who declined with a shake of his head. Valente then proceeded to reload his ARC with battery-like cartridges stored beneath it.

"For those aspiring to become sniper specialists, Captain Valente is your go-to instructor."

Odie's excitement was palpable as he nudged Jerome's shoulder, eliciting an annoyed glance from Jerome.

"Once the basics are complete and if you succeed, you will face the FIREBIRDS initiative. More details will be provided later. You will be assigned to your squadron when the time comes. We are focusing on individual evaluation and training to determine your abilities. You will have a place to stay, share bathrooms, and wake up early. There is a lot of work to be done!"

Ryne continued, emphasizing the intense nature of their upcoming training.

Ryne paused momentarily, his gaze shifting to Aiko and seeing the mask that stood out in the crowd. He sensed a resemblance to Aiko's father but quickly refocused.

"URDT is counting on you all to do your part, serving not only here but everyone around you."

117

Motivation rippled through the crowd. Some pressed their hands together, while others looked away from Ryne. The expressions of those present revealed amazement and respect for his authority.

"We will now give you a tour around the facility, helping you become familiar with your new home. But before I send you away, you need to take the pledge. Dedicate yourself, your service, and your honor to humanity."

Ryne swiftly moved his legs together, standing in a rigid pose.

"Repeat after me: 'Valor unto the Skies.'"

He commanded.

He put his arms behind his back, continuing.

"Grounded in Courage."

Tucking his head down, he concluded.

"'Till our last breath!'"

Recruiters exchanged glances, unsure whether to follow suit.

"Valor Unto the Skies, Grounded in Courage, till our last breath!"

Echoed Quentin, standing proudly in the exact pose Ryne had demonstrated.

Suki, grinning at Quentin, joined in, following his lead. Soon, a ripple effect took hold, and all the other recruits followed suit.

"Valor Unto the Skies, Grounded in Courage, till our last breath."

"Valor Unto the Skies, Grounded in Courage, till our last breath."

"Valor Unto the Skies, Grounded in Courage, till our last breath."

The chant echoed, a symphony of voices in harmony. Ryne remained still as the powerful words reverberated around him. Not participating in the pose, Aiko gazed at the building's top, lost in thoughts about finding his father. Walking towards the entrance, Quentin noticed Aiko's departure and followed him.

Ryne's eyes tracked Aiko's movements toward the office. He considered approaching and preventing him for a moment, but a sense of restraint held him back. The sight of Aiko's mask triggered images of Jabez's mask, raising more questions about Aiko's identity. Ryne chose to wait, letting the uncertainty linger.

Entering the facility's corridors, Aiko was surrounded by the dense metal texture, illuminated by blinding lights. Walking towards the elevator, his mind echoed his father's words, "Melancholic Knight and Son," like a broken record that couldn't be fixed.

"Aiko, wait up!"

Quentin called out, dashing towards him. Aiko turned around, feeling a slight jolt in his heart at the sight of Quentin following him.

"Where are you going?"

Quentin asked, his expression growing concerned.

Aiko looked at Quentin, noticing the downturn in his expression.

"I, uh, I'm heading off somewhere. I got this job offer, but I can't say if I'll return to be with you and everyone else. It's kind of uncertain."

"A job here? You didn't want to tell me earlier?"

Quentin questioned.

"I didn't know how to approach it; just so much was happening in my head. I just can't take it."

Aiko replied, his eyes reflecting the internal struggle.

Moving closer, Quentin reassured him.

"Hey, you know you can open up to me, right? I won't judge. You've always been mysterious, Aiko. Can you at least share if we'll get to see you again?"

"I- I hope."

Aiko hesitated, his words stumbling. Thoughts of his father lingered in his mind, making him more hesitant.

"I already told Suki's mother about this; she'll take care of Albie for me. While I can sustain myself. This is an opportunity for me, and I don't know how I can live with myself if I can't be something to Albie. I want to do better for myself."

Quentin placed his hand on Aiko's shoulder, offering reassurance.

"That's reassuring, plus we're here together. If you see me and Suki, come find us. You're not alone here. It will be amazing working here; just provide for Albie's well-being and for yourself, too."

Quentin's gentle pat on Aiko's shoulder felt comforting, warming his body with the reassurances Quentin offered.

"I guess this is goodbye for now. Unless we cross paths later or in the future. Take care of yourself."

Quentin said, removing his hand from Aiko's shoulder.

119

Aiko nodded in response, feeling a mixture of gratitude and uncertainty. Quentin offered a grin, a parting smile etched in Aiko's memory. As Quentin made his way out of the facility, Aiko could only watch as he disappeared. The door closed behind Quentin, marking the end of their current chapter.

Lost in contemplation, Aiko wondered if he would ever see Quentin, Suki, and the others again. His emotions and thoughts swirled within him as he directed himself towards the elevator, determined to seek answers from his father.

# Chapter Ten: The Melancholic Knight Oath

As Quentin walked out of the facility corridor, he was somewhat optimistic after encountering Aiko. Although some of him entertained the possibility of crossing paths with Aiko, he couldn't summon much excitement. Hearing Aiko's voice failed to elicit happiness; he mused that Aiko was consistently like that, but there seemed to be more to Aiko's words and the person behind his mask.

Upon exiting, the scene unfolded with recruits meeting one another, exchanging names, sharing their origins, and forming alliances. Spotting Suki in the distance, Quentin hurriedly sprinted towards her, weaving through the recruits until an obstacle blocked his way.

Ryne Maverick's imposing mask confronted Quentin, sending chills down his spine as he came face to face with him. The unexpected encounter left Quentin focused on reaching Suki.

"Running without paying attention to your surroundings?"

Ryne remarked, arms behind his back, his presence firmly opposing Quentin's.

"I wasn't mindful of where I was going, Commander Maverick."

Quentin replied, attempting to maintain composure and show respect to Ryne.

"It's Commander Maverick. That's how you address me."

Ryne asserted.

"Yes, Commander Maverick."

"SPEAK UP!"

Maverick's raised volume demanded attention from the surroundings, showcasing his commanding presence.

"YES, COMMANDER MAVERICK!"

Pleased with the acknowledgment, Maverick walked a bit closer to Quentin.

"What is your name, son?"

Quentin's body surged with adrenaline; his mouth seemed paralyzed, rendering him unable to speak or move. He was cautious not to say anything that might provoke another outburst from Maverick.

"His name is Quentin, Commander Maverick."

A voice interjected, breaking the tension.

Quentin detected a voice that seemed vaguely familiar, resonating with recent memories. He turned around and recognized the face—Joule.

"Ah, Joule. You know this boy."

Maverick remarked as Joule approached, standing alongside Quentin.

"Yes, sir, his name is Quentin Reily."

"Quentin Reily... Reily."

Maverick repeated, briefly looking down before refocusing on Quentin.

"What's your father's name?"

Maverick prompting Quentin to wonder about the relevance and connection.

Puzzled but composed, Quentin closed his thoughts and replied.

"Hudson Reily."

Maverick stepped back, and Quentin braced himself for what might follow.

"Hudson Reily. You must be his son, then. I expect great things from you in the coming time."

Placing his hands on Quentin's shoulders to convey a gesture of respect, Maverick walked away, leaving Quentin somewhat surprised. He had anticipated more from Maverick, but the encounter turned unexpectedly.

"I got your back, Quentin."

Joule reassured, patting Quentin on the back.

Quentin's thoughts and emotions momentarily vanished, though they lingered in his mind.

"Hey, Joule, I didn't expect to see you."

"I'm stationed here momentarily. It has been a while since I received an assignment, but I am waiting for a call from the higher-ups to give me something to do. I realized that today was the orientation for the recruits, so I assumed you would be here, too. So, what do you think?"

"I'm a bit anxious and lost, but I'll make it through."

Quentin admitted.

Recalling Maverick's words.

*"Hudson Reily. You must be his son, then. I expect great things from you in the coming time."*

"Don't let the commander get to you; he's just like that. He seriously hates waking up in the morning, but that's his job."

"Is he your commander or...?"

"Used to be. I was moved to the 42nd Battalion due to the dwindling numbers of FIREBIRDS we've been getting. Ryne is one of the best commanders you'll ever see. Once you get through your basic training, he'll train you."

"Well, I've got to train my hardest then. So, he knows my father too?"

Joule paused; hearing Quentin's words softened a bit.

"Yeah, he does. Well, everyone does, as a matter of fact. Your father was one of the best of the best here. Everyone respected him, including me. I talked to your dad once."

Quentin's face brightened, his heart swelling with a feeling he had never experienced.

"You talked to him! What did he say?"

Joule's expression sobered.

"Save me a drink when I get back... that's what your dad said before he went MIA."

Quentin's face remained stoic; his eyebrows and expression faded slowly, his heart sinking.

"Quentin, your dad was amazing! Seeing you here, your father would be proud of you. Just train your hardest in the upcoming training. They'll be testing your stamina, teamwork, and discipline. Especially discipline. Each week will focus on those requirements, but I believe you'll make it there."

Joule extended his hand to Quentin, who reciprocated with a handshake, symbolizing the formation of a brotherhood. Quentin grinned at Joule's encouraging words, and Joule returned the gesture.

"Now, if you'll excuse me, I was supposed to head off to the weaponry specialist, Cade Valentine. You'll meet him in the following weeks. I've got to get my ARC checked on. I'll be seeing you around, Quentin."

Joule darted away from Quentin, who waved to him as he departed. Quentin's thoughts lingered on how everyone knew his father's name. He pondered if his father was legendary and questioned whether he could live up to his legacy.

"Somebody got in trouble."

123

Suki remarked, smirking toward him.

"No, I was just introducing myself to him."

Quentin clarified.

"Well, it makes it look like you actually did something wrong."

Suki teased.

Quentin looked down slightly, expressing his concern.

"I hope not."

Suki surveyed their surroundings, sensing that something was amiss.

"Where's Aiko?"

Quentin remembered Aiko's words: "Got this job offer; can't really say if I'll make it back to be with you and everyone else. It's kind of uncertain."

"He got a job here. We'll probably not see him for a while."

Quentin explained.

"Oh, he's a strange boy."

"Yeah, but a diligent one." Quentin added, reflecting on Aiko's unique qualities.

***

Aiko waited patiently for the elevator to reach the designated floor, sensing a noticeable drop in temperature around him. As he ascended, he observed each floor number pass by until the final level, where his father resided. Stepping out into the ominous corridor, a familiar chill ran down his spine, reminiscent of his last visit. His body felt weary, and his mind raced with doubts about the reasons behind his actions. Why was he here? Why was he heeding his father's call? Did he indeed seek answers? Despite these uncertainties, he pressed forward, knocking on the door and awaiting a response. However, silence prevailed.

Opening the door cautiously, the dimly lit office revealed itself—the same coldness. A dark figure stood near the window, holding the curtain. Yet, he couldn't remain silent any longer.

"I got notice of your arrival from one of our agents upfront. I am glad you made it here."

Acheron said, facing Aiko. His imposing presence made Aiko want to retreat, but he held his ground.

"Have you made up your mind?"

**124**

His father leered, his voice hinting at the gravity of Aiko's decision.

Aiko contemplated the weight of his decision, pondering the implications of becoming a Melancholic Knight. Questions about finding answers, learning more about his father, locating his people, earning credits to support himself and Albie, and ultimately, finding Inoue flooded his mind. The internal struggle almost drove him to reject the offer, to run away from the uncertainties. However, he recognized that fleeing wouldn't resolve his issues; he couldn't escape from himself and the responsibilities ahead.

With a determined yet uneasy tone, he uttered.

"Yes... I'll join."

His father, a stoic figure, remained silent, offering no immediate response.

"Unexpected. I thought you would say no. But my mind needs to be revised. Well, you must decide your course of action. We'll head to a council meeting called LYN. They will decide if you can become a Melancholic Knight."

Aiko was left perplexed, trying to decipher the meaning behind his father's words. What did he mean by his misguided? Did he doubt Aiko's capabilities?

"What is LYN?"

Aiko questioned as he waited at the door.

"League, Yielding, Network."

His father explained.

"You've never heard of the organization, and you never will speak of it to anyone besides me and the associate you'll get to know."

Aiko's father swiftly grabbed a card from his desk, collecting essentials in a quick motion. As Aiko observed, he suddenly felt a touch behind his ankle, catching him off guard and causing him to trip. Startled, Aiko turned to see a hairy creature walking on four legs and possessing a curious face. The creature had a long snout pointed at Aiko's face, and he crawled back, uncertain about this unknown creature, feeling a surge of adrenaline.

"Yasuka! Down!"

Aiko's father commanded, bringing the creature to sit. It stared intently at Aiko with its eyes, each displaying assorted colors—dark emerald, green on the left and sapphire blue on the right, lightened in hue. A leash and collar were attached, and Aiko's father gained control over the creature. Looking down at Aiko, he remarked.

"What, you've never seen a dog before?"

Aiko's mask revealed no expression, but his shoulder and leg positions betrayed his fear. He slowly got up and looked back at the dog, whose fur was adorned with white, brown, and black merle-colored spots.

"Dog?"

Aiko questioned.

His father, wearing a mask of confusion, stared at Aiko, realizing the gap in understanding.

"Yes, a DOG, specifically an Australian Shepherd. But I'm sure you've never heard of Australian Shepherd either."

"I don't know that too."

A sigh escaped Aiko's father.

"It's an animal found back on Earth, where you were born. But that's a story for another time. We need to go already."

Aiko's father briskly dismissed his questions, leading the way out of the room. Aiko followed suit, trailing behind him towards the elevator. As they descended, Aiko felt nervous energy standing beside his father, his dog, Yasuka, sitting by his side. The rhythmic sounds of passing floors became a familiar backdrop to Aiko.

The elevator paused, and the doors slid open to reveal an unfamiliar woman. She wore a modest uniform with the URDT logo, her long, curled hair cascading to her shoulders. Her gait sounded distinctive due to the metallic foot on one side, and her height exceeded Aiko's. Brown eyes and light skin completed her appearance.

"Good morning, Mr. Acheron."

She greeted, acknowledging Aiko with a friendly nod. She crouched down to pet Yasuka.

"And you too, Yasuka! Good morning to you too, Akarui."

She said, addressing the dog and Yasuka back to her.

Making her way to Aiko, she noticed his mask and couldn't help but glance between him and his father.

"Is this your—"

"Son... Yes. Aiko, this is Akarui Fenimore, Tactical Operation Captain. She helps in giving direction in the field and intel. Get to know her well; you'll need her very much."

Aiko's father stated.

Akarui's question about Aiko's identity was swiftly answered by his father. Though stunned, she regained her composure and greeted him.

"You must be Aiko Ashin... nice to meet you."

She extended her hand, prompting a hesitant Aiko to reciprocate with a firm handshake. The contrasting temperatures of their hands softened Aiko.

As the elevator reached the last level, Acheron inserted his card into the pad, unlocking the door and revealing a corridor with scattered mini lights in a distinct pattern. Acheron, accompanied by Yasuka, stepped out first, followed by Akarui. Alone in the elevator, Aiko scrutinized the area, feeling a disconcerting connection to his father's office.

Stepping into the corridor, Aiko noticed the limited illumination, with only sporadic lights revealing portions of the surface area. The eerie darkness unsettled him. Ambient sounds of staccato clicks, reminiscent of miniature switches and relays engaging, filled the air. Accompanied by gentle electronic chirps and beeps, these sounds signaled successful self-checks and the establishment of connections. A symphony of technology coming to life unfolded before Aiko's senses. By their left, another door was sealed off, camouflaging with the wall.

He followed his father and Akarui, gradually falling behind as the electronic symphony resonated around him.

Akarui noticed Aiko's uneasiness and worried about his well-being. Still unsettled by the eerie environment, Aiko tried to brush it off, but Akarui understood.

"Are you okay?"

"Yeah... just—"

"I know, this area is eerie. Also, it is restricted and only accessible to people like your father and me. I wanted to check on you. I have never seen another individual who has a mask like your father's before. Your father never mentioned having a son..."

Aiko's heart sank at the revelation. His father had never mentioned having a son, and the weight of this newfound information left him struggling to process it.

"I didn't know that I had a father too..."

"I can see how both of you are related now. But he is more of a troglodyte. You're just shy."

"No, not really. I am just nervous..."

"It's alright. This meeting should be eloquent if everything goes as planned."

As they walked together, Aiko observed a series of black boxes producing the sounds he had heard earlier. Acheron waited for them, using the same card to unlock the door ahead. Opening it revealed Kenryoku standing, staring upwards at something.

"Are they up?"

Acheron approaching Kenryoku.

"They're powering up right now..."

Kenryoku responded, indicating a significant development about to unfold.

Kenryoku stood before the images of LYN, encased in a sleek, concrete structure that defied the passage of time, cables connected from the floor to the walls. Lycoris, Yvette, and Nicodemus were displayed on the monitors, towering above in their machine-like structures. As Acheron, Aiko, and Akarui entered, the door closed behind them, and the room resonated with the sound of something powering up.

A rhythmic pulsing began, reminiscent of the steady beat of a primordial heart. The ancient yet vibrant sound carried with it the essence of ages long gone. Metal gears, worn by the passage of time, interlocked with a subtle clink, setting in motion a cascade of mechanisms.

"Premier Jabez Acheron. You have summoned us?"

Lycoris' voice, distorted and mixed with digital mess, echoed through the room, raising Aiko's anxiety.

"What is the meeting about? Waking us like this must be damn important!"

Nicodemus' deep, distorted voice added urgency to the atmosphere.

"Premier Jabez Acheron, Kenryoku Takako, Akarui Fenimore, and—"

Yvette paused, noticing Aiko standing among them. The machinery hummed, and exhaust left as the monitors processed information.

"Aiko Ashin."

Yvette continued, surprising Aiko with the monitor's ability to discover his name.

"They are AI, remnants of the higher-ups of URDT. They are our surveillance, monitoring our safety for The Republic of Melancholia."

Akarui explained to Aiko.

"They were my and Jabez's comrades during the fall of Earth. Our first line of defense, detecting anything that threatens us."

Kenryoku stood beside Aiko, and Akarui leaned in, emphasizing the importance of the monitors. Jabez walked up and stood before the monitors.

"This is Aiko Ashin. Jabez, who is he?"

Lycoris examining Aiko.

"He is my lost son. His last name is from his foster mother. He hasn't adapted my last name."

Jabez's revelation lingered in the air, unveiling a layer of his past that Aiko had yet to uncover. The room buzzed with questions, and Yvette directed her attention to Aiko, asking about his last name.

"You wear a blue mask; are you, boy, part descendant of the Harmonians?"

Yvette asked, catching Aiko off guard. Jabez gave him a pointed stare, urging him to respond. Feeling a touch on his shoulder, Aiko glanced over to see Akarui offering support. Encouraged, he mustered the courage to speak.

"Yes..."

"That mask, did you steal it?"

Lycoris questioned.

"WHAT NO, I had this mask when I opened my eyes."

Aiko clarified.

"Who is your mother, Aiko?"

Lycoris intervened.

"Where were you during the fall of Earth?"

Nicodemus chimed in.

Aiko stammered, unable to provide coherent answers.

"ENOUGH!"

Jabez's yell echoed through the room, cutting through the questions and bringing silence, except for the ambient hum of machinery.

"We are here to discuss Aiko's enlistment as a Melancholic Knight."

Jabez declared.

"Melancholic Knight, Jabez?"

Yvette questioned.

"The Melancholic Knight Program was discontinued after the Fall of Earth, made by the agreement of the nations besides the Republic of Melancholia. Records show the project was canceled due to the failure to protect the people."

Lycoris stated, presenting visual documentation and images of protests. Aiko's eyes widened as he learned about the existence of Melancholic Knights in the past.

"Not to mention, the resources became more limited after each Melancholic Knight fell one after another. Reinstating the program for a mere boy is senseless."

Nicodemus said.

"Yet the leap in warfare The Melancholic Knight Program has done. Giving us victories over the Nekrothians. We were able to win battle after battle!"

Jabez proclaimed.

"What use is the boy in the suit, Jabez? There are no Nekrothians or any sense of their return. We don't need to pull more resources."

Yvette argued.

Aiko struggled to understand the references to Nekrothians and the Melancholic Knight Program. The words bombarded him, leaving him standing amid their discussion.

"I know the Nekrothians were last seen nearly two decades ago. The program must be reinstated. The ever-growing threat of The Excesses has become more prominent. They are tearing our government apart and destroying everything we've done on this planet to start over. We don't have enough FIREBIRDS, enforcers, and numbers to operate the URDT. Our forces are protecting areas in Sanguine Provence, Phlegmatic Federal, and more numbers near the inhabitant zone. More numbers near the inhabitant zone watching over The Imperium of the Choleric moves."

Jabez argued.

"You realize, Jabez, that our treaty with The Imperium of the Choleric has remained intact. The use of our Synacore would not be allowed. Only in an act of threat or alliance against the Nekrothians is it used."

Lycoris provided context, introducing another unknown term, Synacore, leaving Aiko with numerous unanswered questions.

"What are the Harmonians? Synacore? Who am I?"

Aiko's questions hung in the air, drawing everyone's attention, and even Jabez took a step back from the center of the discussion.

"Aiko Ashin? You don't know your people's origins, or did Mr. Acheron leave them out?"

Yvette pondered, observing Aiko's eagerness as he moved closer.

"Harmonians are unknown but ancient beings that traveled from far beyond galaxies. Little is known about them; we only know that they are travelers."

Lycoris provided a brief explanation.

"They traveled to Earth, leaving us with energy buried underneath the Earth's core. Humanity discovery was made, and the people who discovered it decided to take the name Harmonains themselves. Creating a nation and your people, Aiko."

Nicodemus added.

"The ancient Harmonian energy that was buried is known as Synara. The energy that is amplified by an individual's biological energy. Synara can grow stronger through the individual's connection to others, nature, and themselves."

Jabez explained, shedding light on the mysterious origins of Aiko's people and the significance of Synara.

"That energy is flowing in you right now, Aiko Ashin. You just don't feel it yet. The energy is connected to the Synacore."

Yvette explained.

"There are three Synacore that the ancient Harmonians left us. We had them until the invasion of the race that we recognize as the Nekrothians."

Nicodemus added.

"And who are the Nekrothians?"

Aiko's question echoed in the area, Akarui ready a response.

"Same with the ancient Harmonians; little is known about them. They invaded our home planet. Their motive is centered around the Synacores."

"Your people, Aiko, had the three Synacore. The nation of the world formed the United. Resolution. Defense. Tranquility to combat the Nekrothians. The Harmonians gave us one Synacore, giving us an edge against the threats and forming an alliance with the Harmonians. The creation of the FIREBIRDS program was the first measure of defense that worked for a while..." Lycoris provided further context, outlining the historical events that led to the creation of defenses against the Nekrothians.

"The Nekrothians would make their own soldiers but worse than anything we faced... Armageddons.' They were powerful versions of the Nekrothians, able to wipe out civilizations within days... one that was made. That one died by two nukes. The downside of the Armageddons is the amount of resources the Nekrothians used on the Armageddons."

Akarui explained somberly.

"This is where your father, Jabez Acheron, was made from the creation of the Melancholic Knights. Your people, Aiko, died to serve as crusaders against the growing numbers. Each of the Melancholic Knights could take down numbers of Nekrothians; it would be only a limited time before they brought out the second Armageddon but stronger."

Nicodemus elaborated.

"Your father, with the full support of the Harmonians, was able to kill the second Armageddon. But the result was our planet becoming inhabitable, leaving your father in the condition he's in. The Melancholic Knight was originally called Metalstrike, but since the failure of protecting Earth, the name was changed by humanity. The Melancholic Knight became a burden to anyone that wears it, carrying the hopelessness and depression from their action. But maybe you will bring honor to the name."

Kenryoku added, approaching Aiko.

Aiko turned to see his father against the wall, staring. As Jabez walked towards Aiko, grabbing his arms and squeezing, adrenaline coursed through him. Jabez's revelation left Aiko cold and silent. Kenryoku stepped in, putting his hand on Jabez's shoulders and creating distance.

"Your people, Aiko, are gone... your mother is gone... The Nekrothians attacked them."

Jabez disclosed, staring directly at Aiko with a chilling intensity. Kenryoku stepped in again, reassuring Aiko.

"He's right. You are what remains of your people, Aiko."

"This is where we are: The Nekrothians stole one of the Synacore from the Harmonians. URDT has the second Synacore. And The Imperium of the Choleric has the final Synacore.

Akarui explained.

"Who is The Imperium of Choleric?"

Aiko softly asked.

"We don't talk about them."

Kenryoku interjected, with Akarui backing him up.

Lycoris provided context, steering the conversation back to Aiko.

"Another nation that rivals our own. It's best to disclose information to you."

"This is what history has gathered. Humanity is rebuilding; everything is returning to the way everything was back on Earth. Earth is now taken over by the Nekrothians, terraforming it to their liking. We're on this new planet: Gaea..."

"Not for long."

Jabez intervened.

"The Excesses organization is threatening everything we are building. With growing numbers of attacks throughout our nation."

"The recent one happened yesterday, with Aiko being a casualty of the hijacking. His heroic action was memorable, stopping the train from causing catastrophic damage to the train and the surroundings. Pulling the switch to get a full stop of the train resulted in his hands suffering heavy-degree burns."

Kenryoku added, grabbing Aiko's arms and revealing the remnants of healed scars on his hands.

"With this boy's help, not only did he manage to stop the train, but a few of his friends helped capture one of the two suspects who were the ones that started the hijacking, associating with The Excesses. We are still trying to find their names, but later, they will be examined more in the following days."

Kenryoku explained, stepping back from Aiko and standing aside with Akarui.

Jabez looked at Aiko and then shifted his attention towards the three monitors.

"With your permission, LYN., I would like to reinstate the Melancholic Knight Program for Aiko only. He will be trained and wear the suit when he is ready. He'll be given a prototype suit to adapt to. Extensive training will be given to him."

"Do you realize that if the public and the other nations find out about the program, you will face many disapprovals and a loss of trust in the URDT?"

Lycoris responded.

"Yes, I am prepared for the consequences. It is for the safety of the people to be protected by any means."

Jabez asserted.

The three monitors turned to each other, and a quiet moment passed.

"It is decided—"

"WAIT!"

Aiko spoke out loud.

"I'll become a Melancholic Knight if you swear to me to find someone for me!"

133

Aiko declared, capturing everyone's attention. Kenryoku nodded, indicating he anticipated Aiko's request. Akarui's expression showed excitement, and Jabez maintained a silent demeanor. The monitors processed Aiko's words.

"And who is the person that you want us to find?"

Yvette asked.

Aiko stared intensely at them.

"Inoue Ashin!"

A quiet moment followed as the monitors exchanged glances, deciding their response.

"It's a deal. Your service to become a Melancholic Knight will cover enough. In return, we will find your significant other."

Yvette responded.

Kenryoku leaned towards Jabez, whispering.

"Are you sure you want his guardian to be found? She broke the Embankment Fence."

"What choice do we have? This boy will only serve if his request is made. Little does he know the weight of being a Melancholic Knight isn't going to be easy..."

Jabez remarked, acknowledging the challenges that lay ahead for Aiko.

Jabez remained still, his gaze fixed on Aiko. Kenryoku returned his attention to the situation.

"It is settled."

Lycoris responded.

"Is it good to let the boy wear the suit, Kenryoku?"

Akarui leaned towards Kenryoku.

"He's barely a boy."

Kenryoku replied.

"A boy that is needed. We need him for our operation. He has committed himself by choice. He has nothing to lose."

"Aiko Ashin."

Yvette proclaimed, capturing everyone's attention. All eyes turned towards Aiko.

"You are sworn to obey the commands of your leaders, you are owned by the URDT, to protect the people of this nation."

Yvette declared. Aiko's heart pounded furiously; every word felt like a drop of rain to him, cleansing him into a new person. He awaited each word with determination. Suddenly, something summoned above him. A thorn-like item rested, and Aiko looked at it curiously.

"You must give a part of your blood to show your commitment is real."

Yvette explained.

Aiko hesitated but complied, poking his index finger, and a droplet of blood sprouted out, falling into a drain and being collected by a vial.

"It is settled."

In unison, LYN spoke together.

"Aiko Ashin, you are, at this moment, The Melancholic Knight."

# ACT 2: How To Continue

# Chapter Eleven: Dust and Echoes Part 1

*March 12, 2125*

T he melodic chirping of native birds echoed above, their harmonious notes dancing through the skies. The gentle rustling of leaves brushing against each other added a soft, calming undertone to the serene atmosphere. Lying down, Aiko gazed upward, observing the leaves of the straight trees casting transparent shadows in the warm sunlight. Staring at the sky brought a profound sense of tranquility to his body and stillness to his mind.

The quiet ambiance was abruptly shattered by the distinct sound of approaching footsteps, the breaking of sticks underfoot as an alarm for someone drawing near. As the intruder loomed above him, a silhouette obscured his view. The figure, clad in a green jacket paired with a muscle shirt, thin black pants, and plant-based straw shoes, leaned in, revealing a face framed by long hair tied into a mini ponytail and captivating green eyes. This person, slightly older than him, bore an air of familiarity.

"Aiko. Aikooo, Aiko."

The figure called out.

Aiko acknowledged the address but chose not to respond.

"Aiko."

The figure persisted, lightly kicking him.

"Hmph."

Aiko grunted, shifting slightly from the gentle kick.

"Come on, Inoue wants you back at home. Get up."

The figure urged.

"I don't care."

Aiko replied, leaning against the ground.

"I know you don't care, but she does. Please don't make it harder for her to come to fetch you herself or for me to drag you back home."

The figure reasoned.

"I told you, Anbu, that's not my home."

"Well, it's a temporary home for both of us."

Anbu accidentally dropped something onto Aiko, who quickly caught it, revealing a soft-textured fruit. Aiko squeezed it, causing orange juice to spill out. Opening his mask slightly, he licked the juice, relishing the taste.

"Come on, I'm done collecting the berries here. I'll give you more if you don't tell Inoue about it."

Anbu proposed.

Aiko contemplated the offer, examining the berry before reluctantly agreeing.

"Fine..."

Getting up from the ground, Aiko stretched his arms and legs. Anbu said.

"Dust yourself off; you look like a dirty rag."

Aiko, realizing the state of his clothes—tan pants, a dark navy-blue shirt, and slip-on shoes—brushed himself off. Anbu pulled a mini wagon containing a bunch of berries, prompting Aiko to follow.

"She doesn't like it when you venture away. Going too far out will get you lost."

Anbu warned.

Ignoring the advice, Aiko grabbed another berry, listening as Anbu continued.

"Well, that's what she thinks. I've often been far from her sight, and nothing has happened to me."

"Yet."

Anbu added.

Aiko, still dismissive, retorted.

"Pfft, like what? The Plume Chickens?"

"Don't be naive, Aiko. There's a reason Inoue specifically instructed us not to cross over the fence. Creatures have been hunting our Plume Chicken lately. Without the chickens, we won't have much trade or supplies."

Aiko remained nonchalant, stated.

"Hmm, I don't mind that. I have me and berries."

141

Anbu turned around, witnessing Aiko with two berries in one hand while grabbing another from the wagon. Anbu warned.

"Hey, don't get too many berries. Don't stuff them in your mouth again. I had to pull on your stomach the last time; you spit one berry so far."

Anbu chuckled at the memory, but Aiko was chastised and pressed his lips tightly. Anbu continued

"I think you can help yourself. You could've helped me earlier. Collecting these berries wasn't fun. Eating fast will make your stomach dizzy; those berries pack a load once you let them settle in."

Aiko sighed, conceding.

"Oh well..."

Anbu uttered a warning as he looked forward along the path, flanked by towering bark trees with shells as rugged and sturdy as the boys' resolve. Massive in stature, these trees loomed over them, casting a shadow on the ground covered with decomposed dead twigs and berries from the trees. In the distance, a vague fog obscured their vision, while in the mid-range, more of the ground became discernible. They walked a distance from where Aiko had laid, crossing a mini wooden bridge that wiggled with each step, its planks creaking and threatening to give way. The liquid underneath, dark brownish red, flowed against the rocks.

"Watch your step."

Anbu cautioned, and Aiko, acknowledging his words, still managed to break a bit of the plank from the bridge, momentarily getting his foot stuck.

"Got that."

Aiko responded.

"Oh yeah, I got more letters."

Aiko's head turns up, about to speak.

"And if you're going to ask, no. There is no news of our guardian looking for us."

Aiko's head slowly turned down from the response, feeling cold.

As they continued their journey, they encountered another settler—a figure with a mask around their mouth, a long hat to shield from the sun, and bare feet adorned with torn clothing. A wave from the settler prompted reciprocal waves from Aiko and Anbu. The settler led a creature with mid-length fur, pig-like ears, dark eyes, and hind legs with hoof-like structures. Together, they moved along their respective paths.

Upon reaching a mini gate, a lady outside on the porch was sweeping the floor. Dressed in farming clothes with socks on, her slightly wrinkled face wore a modest expression. A mini blanket shielded her head from the sun. The home bore the marks of history, with decaying wood, a roof weathered by time, and a porch creaking with every step. Acting as a makeshift door, a used blanket hung in place, blocking off the sun and providing shade. The front yard boasted a variety of vegetation, including turnip-like vegetables with a soft texture and long, oval-shaped fruits pressing firmly against the ground. The area was open enough to allow a view of everything, though the surrounding trees made it difficult to see beyond their immediate vicinity. Anbu opened the gate while Aiko pushed the wagon further into the entrance, catching the attention of Inoue, who noticed Aiko's presence and exclaimed.

"Aiko, where have you been?"

Aiko anticipated Inoue's response, offering only a brief explanation.

"Out somewhere."

"In a place where I can't see you? You're well aware of the dangers of wandering outside our designated area."

Inoue admonished.

"I wasn't even gone that long, just 15 minutes."

Aiko retorted.

"Actually, it's been an hour..."

Anbu interjected, closing the gate behind him as Aiko settled the wagon.

Inoue put away her broom and walked down the porch to confront Aiko. Amusement flickered on her face as she lowered her gaze. She inspected Aiko's mask and head with both hands, finding dirt on his mask, hair, and around his ears. Stepping back, she assessed his clothing, now stained and dirty.

"Come on, Aiko, what were you doing that got your clothes so dirty? You know it's difficult enough to clean them with our limited supplies."

She chided.

"Hold up, here are some letters."

Upon seeing the letters, she grabbed them and put them in her back pocket.

"He was just lying on the ground the whole time; probably a gust of wind carried dirt onto him."

Anbu offered.

143

"Probably sleeping on the ground again. Anbu, dear, can you open the gate for the chickens while I get Aiko cleaned up?"

Inoue requested.

"Yes, ma'am."

Anbu strolled over to the chicken pen, a tiny abode crafted for the feathered residents. As he opened the gate, many chickens appeared, standing tall enough to reach half of Anbu's legs. These unique chickens showed off their three heads, carrying wings adorned with little feathers featuring a circle-like pattern. The wings broke into a narrow and straight pattern, revealing skin with feathers only covering their exposed parts. Their pointy-tailed elegance was matched by stubby yet purposeful legs as they gracefully made their way to the fields, snacking on ticks or grubs that clung to the vegetation.

Inoue, satisfied with Anbu's compliance, redirected her attention to Aiko. Grabbing his arm, she pulled him inside their home. The small living room, adorned with a few scratches, boasted furnishings made entirely from the surrounding wood. The well-worn table held a picture of Inoue carrying Aiko as a baby with his mask on while Anbu stood on her other side, indicating he was a few years older than Aiko. Inoue then led Aiko down a hallway from the living room to a cramped bathroom. The room featured a slightly broken mirror, a clean bucket, worn-down curtains, and walls that creaked in response to the howling wind outside.

Rummaging through a cabinet near the cracked mirror, Inoue retrieved a rough paper that softened upon contact with water. She wiped off the dust and scratches from Aiko's mask, her expression mild and downcast.

"You're ten years old, Aiko. I shouldn't be cleaning you up like this."

Inoue remarked.

"Then why are you cleaning me up? I can do it myself without your help."

Aiko countered.

"Okay, so you didn't do it before you got here?"

Inoue retorted, turning Aiko toward the slightly broken mirror. His clothing, hair, and mask were covered in dust and scratches.

"I thought I did dust myself."

Inoue sighed as she cleaned Aiko's torso, her frustration evident.

"I've caught you exploring outside too much. This is the third time Anbu has had to come to get you. I specifically said you could be outside for 15 minutes or less, but you're gone for a whole day. I need your help around the house."

144

"You've got Anbu to ask for help. I'm not useful around here."

Aiko again countered.

Inoue continued dusting and picking off specks from his clothing, insisting.

"There. Look at yourself now."

Aiko examined himself in the mirror, noticing that his once-dusty mask now appeared very blue and that his clothing stood out.

"See, you look modest. Calling yourself useless here is ridiculous."

Inoue affirmed, standing behind him to clean whatever was on his shoulders and back.

"I am. Much of the work I do is hard. Anbu makes everything look easier."

Aiko admitted.

"Now, now. Don't start comparing yourself to him. He may be older than you, but that doesn't mean you don't do anything unique. You want to know what makes you stand out?"

"My mask?"

Aiko guessed.

"Yeah, that too, but what makes you special to me is that you are stubborn."

Aiko looked back at Inoue, sensing the odd response.

"Wow, thanks..."

"You are very stubborn, but simultaneously, you are willing to listen."

Inoue grabbed his shoulders, turning him around to face her.

"You could've stayed where you were earlier, ignored Anbu, ignored me, but you listened."

Aiko looked down a bit.

"I have nowhere else to go. I'm stuck here with you and Anbu. I don't have a choice but to find a home. I don't know who I am. You never told me where I came from..."

Inoue also looked down.

"Yes, I still need to shed light on that. I won't tell you."

"Why not?"

"When you're ready. Like I said, you're stubborn. But I want you to be ready when the time comes for you to get the answers you want. You are willing to listen. Now, saying that you're ready to listen isn't the same as being willing to listen. I want you to embrace what I will say, listening is the best you can do."

"But—"

Aiko shook his head. Inoue acknowledged his frustration, patting his shoulders.

"Just hang on; I'm trying to provide you and Anbu with the best I can do. Living here stinks, but we just must continue working, Aiko. I need your help and his. With enough trading from farming with the locals, we can finally move out of here. Go to the Republic of Melancholia, find a new home, new people, a new life."

"That's what you want. I want to know about myself."

Aiko replied.

"You will! And that is the beauty of it. You don't know it yet, but once you're out in the real world, you'll learn more than just about yourself. But for now, I need your support to try my best. Try your best to help, and eventually, you will get what you want, Aiko."

Aiko remained still, looking down and refusing to make eye contact.

"Okay..."

Inoue understood his tone and rubbed his shoulders.

"Inoue! Someone is here to see you!"

Anbu called urgently.

Inoue patted Aiko once on the shoulder and made her way to Anbu. Aiko stayed still, reflecting on what Inoue had said. He still didn't understand why she refused to answer his question. When would he be ready? Aiko walked out of the door to find Inoue talking to someone. He moved slowly behind her to avoid attracting attention, peeking to the side to see a figure obscured by the harsh reflection of the sun. Aiko listened in to their discussion.

"Are you Inoue Ashin?"

The figure asked.

"Yes, sir. What is it that you want?"

Inoue replied.

"I was told by the locals that you run a daycare here."

"Well, not necessarily, but it's a foster home for kids lost during the fall of Earth. I also run a farm. But what do you want, sir?"

The figure turned to his side, paying attention to Inoue.

"I want to leave him in your care."

He extended his hand, revealing a kid who looked younger than Aiko. Wearing worn-out clothes, broken-down shoes, and layered-cut hair, he moved around restlessly.

"I can no longer take care of him."

The figure brought the kid, Albie, forward, and Inoue stepped back hesitantly as he was presented.

"His name is Albie. He has a severe condition, is nonverbal, and has difficulty expressing himself."

The figure handed over a document to Inoue, who initially hesitated but eventually grabbed it. She read the notes: "First name Albie, Age: 5, Guardian: ------, Condition: Unknown." Her gaze lowered increasingly, reflecting a mix of concern and understanding.

"You never saw me; I need to go somewhere. I can't take care of him any longer. Here for the trouble."

The figure handed an envelope to Inoue, revealing credits that slightly raised her facial expression. Inoue was about to speak, but she noticed the figure dashing away from them, walking out the gate and disappearing along the route. Inoue looked down, finding Albie curiously looking around the house. She carried him, inspecting him. Aiko, from the side, observed Albie, his heart slowing down. Anbu walked in, sharing the same mixed emotions with them. A heavy silence lingered, enveloping the room.

***

*April 18, 2134*

"We're losing him!"

"His blood loss is becoming more significant!"

"The suit's synara energy is dropping!"

Vague, echoey voices filled the air, difficult to discern. The visor glitched out of control, displaying images of men and women in white coats. Aiko felt a strong, pulling motion as if a weight were being lifted from him. His eyes were slightly open but resisted opening fully. His body felt limp, his arm like jelly, and his leg uncomfortably twisted. Every part of him hurt, and his brain throbbed in pain. Amidst the chaos of blinking lights and indistinct voices, he longed to rest, closing his eyes.

Life support machines were strapped to Aiko, wires connecting the devices to his arms, torso, and legs. His helmet displayed more static. Doctors and nurses rushed in, carrying Aiko to a designated spot. Engineers, not in their usual uniforms, entered and observed

**147**

Aiko's suit with a broken chest plate. Quickly grabbing their tool bags, they began repairing whatever damage they could find. Doctors and nurses closely examined the extent of the damage sustained by Aiko, noting liquid oozing from various parts of his body.

"Quickly! Stitch up his wound—"

A splash of blood gushed onto the doctors, the suit opening to reveal that Aiko's condition was worse than they had imagined. The engineers swiftly closed the suit and used metal parts to cover the exposed areas of Aiko's flesh wound. Delicately welding each part, they did not cause any further harm to him. Aiko mumbled softly; his words caught by the attentive doctors. As his soft moans grew louder, one doctor stepped back, blood dripping from Aiko's wounds and touching the boots of the medical team.

"You guys continue stitching up the parts where it's exposed. The rest of you, follow me."

The doctors and nurses left the room, leaving the engineers shocked at the extent of Aiko's injuries. They continued to weld the areas where Aiko was leaking while he mumbled.

Aiko's eyes flickered back and forth, the persistent beeping ringing in his ears. The red light from his visor flashed incessantly, blinding him repeatedly. Opening his eyes increasingly, he thought about his dreams—no, memories. The suit continued to shake him, and his mask was covered in his own blood. He breathed heavily, feeling his chest compressed as if something heavy had smashed into him. His mind felt shaky, recalling the sound of a homing rocket whistling towards him. The violent shake brought more pain, and he heard his blood flowing down to the ground.

A figure welding him up caught his attention, but he couldn't open his lips. The visor of his mask started to cry, small liquid flowing down. The liquid hardened, radiating up as dust, confusing Aiko. Images popped into his head—faces of Quentin, Suki, Albie, Yume, Boe, Kaito, and their grandparents. He thought about the peaceful times he spent with them, even if only for a day. Closing his eyes upon thinking about them, images of Kenryoku and Akarui, hearing their voices, straightened him. Their orders matched the persistent beeping, which seemed unending.

Jabez's face appeared in his mind, causing his brain to hurt even more. He tried to grip his hand but failed. Then, he remembered Inoue and Anbu, calming himself down. The serenity he felt being with them slowly eased his pain. He closed his eyes, the beeping fading away, his brain shutting off, and his eyes settling down. Every sound, every sensation disappeared.

148

# Chapter Twelve: Permanent Agony

*May 6, 2134*

Whispers of dust and echoes softly signal their presence, whistling from the air that carries them aloft. Within the void, these remnants of sound and particulate matter fade, giving way to a voice that begins to swell. Its murmurs weave back and forth, growing into a chorus of voices from around, their origins indistinct and muddled. Then, as suddenly as they appeared, the voices vanished, leaving behind the dust and echoes. An enveloping silence prevails, so absolute that not even the subtlest heartbeat or whisper of thought disturbs its dominion.

For a fleeting moment, a screen flickers to life, its glow heralding the return of a slow, rhythmic heartbeat.

Once more, the screen illuminates, this time its light lingering a few seconds longer. The voices resurface, among them one voice distinctly piercing the cacophony.

"Continue the progress."

The command, icy and imperious, claws at the mind, its departure as swift as its arrival.

The air seems to escape in a sigh, its departure barely felt against the skin. A sensation of heavy compression tightens, unyielding.

The voices, now clear and recognizable, cut through the stillness.

"Synara levels are not yet visible."

"Target the center and the torso, then connect to the limbs."

A visceral crunchiness permeates the body as if being pierced from within.

"Reinforce the torso!"

The impact of each directive lands, not with harshness, but as a numb, felt force. The compression intensifies, squeezing tighter.

*Gasp*

Aiko's soft breathing breaks the silence, his senses dulled to the world around him—sightless, numb, unknowing. Another wave of compression overtakes him, plunging him into darkness.

"His life signs are stabilizing?!"

As the voices fade again, the mystery of Aiko's condition lingers, shrouded in the dust and echoes of an enigmatic realm.

The cadence of Aiko's heartbeat intensified, becoming the dominant force within his sensory world. It was all he could discern—the steady thumps echoing in his ears, each breath he took stretching out longer and more pronounced than the last. With his eyes sealed shut by an overwhelming numbness and the darkness enveloping him, his own vital signs became the soundtrack to his isolation. Yet, amidst this auditory solitude, voices pierced through once more.

"Congratulations, everyone, for your service."

"Thank you for your work, Rebuen Malik."

"I don't approve of this order from Acheron."

"You've done your part, Malik."

The air was suddenly ripe with the sound of jubilation: voices cheering, the explosive pop of bottles, fueling the crescendo of Aiko's heartbeat and breathing. The applause seemed distant, as if muffled by a barrier, with only the subtle vibrations reaching him. Gradually, the clamor diminished, and the applause faded into silence, leaving behind a solitary voice that lingered just a moment longer before dissolving into the void.

"Mr. Acheron will be pleased."

With the voice gone, the steady rhythm of Aiko's heartbeat and his breathing resumed as his only companions in the silence.

Unexpectedly, another heartbeat infiltrated Aiko's auditory landscape, synchronizing with his yet distinctly more forceful. It grew louder, an invasive echo overshadowing Aiko's own rhythmic pulse. The sound of drilling pierced the silence; a corner of the screen, barely within his perception, flushed red, its glow intensifying subtly. This foreign heartbeat was louder and heavier, accelerating, engulfing the space around him.

Aiko's body began to tremble, an inexplicable movement stirring within him. An alien and invigorating sensation coursed through his veins, starting from his spine, spreading to his torso and limbs, and converging at numerous points. This electrifying feeling surged upwards, culminating in a powerful pulse that struck his brain.

"AAAAAAAAHHHHHHHH!"

Aiko's eyes flutter open, his vision initially shrouded in darkness before the visor gradually brightens, revealing a world rendered in stark clarity through its enhanced optics. He squints, attempting to discern the specifics of his surroundings, but finds his movements constrained; his head is immobilized, forced to stare straight ahead. As he focuses intently, a liquid trickles down from his mask, caressing his neck before vanishing into thin air. The more he tries to narrow his gaze, the more this mysterious fluid seems to seep from his mask.

150

Intriguingly, the visor is in sync with Aiko's eye movements, the display panning to whatever his gaze settles upon. Tightening his eyes further, he commands the visor to zoom in, enhancing his view of the environment. This action elicits a sharp intake of breath from Aiko, his body instinctively trying to move, only to be met with an alarming realization: his arm is immobilized. Despite his efforts to shift it into view, he encounters resistance, feeling as though something is lodged within his very flesh, binding him.

A similar experiment with his legs yields the same unsettling discovery—restraints, not just external but penetrating deep, brushing against bone. Panic starts to set in, his breathing grows erratic, and his heart thunders in his chest. Attempts to arch his back are futile, the same invisible shackles holding him in place. The fear and frustration crescendo, culminating in a primal scream that tears from his throat.

"AAAAAAAAAHHHHHHHH!"

His breaths grow ragged, matching the intensity of his struggles against the bindings that grow ever tighter with each movement. As he grinds his teeth in desperation, the liquid from his mask flows more freely, cascading down his neck as if his mask itself were weeping. Suddenly, his visor melts, flickering ominously before plunging his world into darkness again. Electrical sparks dance across his suit, growing in intensity and frequency, mirroring the chaos unfolding within Aiko.

A door slides open before him, bathing the room in light and revealing a figure standing in the doorway. Despite his best efforts, Aiko finds himself unable to break free from his restraints, the numbness spreading as the bindings tighten around his limbs. The figure strides purposefully towards him, eventually breaking into a sprint and swiftly navigating the system adjacent to Aiko. With deft movements, they punch in a code and retrieve a syringe, swiftly administering it to Aiko's exposed skin near his torso. A wave of dizziness washes over him, but he manages to calm himself, lowering his head to get a better look at the person who has entered the room.

"Calm down, please!"

The voice is distinctly feminine, and as Aiko's vision clears, he notices the woman's features more distinctly. Her hair is cropped short but frames her neck elegantly, while a red scarf conceals the lower portion of her face. Clad in a rubber suit that hugs her form from neck to toe, she sports navy shoulder pads and leggings with a primarily blue hue that contrasts against the darker secondary shades. Her hands are encased in dark gray gloves, and her eyes gleam a striking gold behind round glasses; she peers at him with intensity. Aiko feels a flutter in his chest upon seeing her, a sense of reassurance despite his predicament. She is around his age, albeit slightly older.

"You need to stop shaking! Your system and body core aren't fully stable yet!"

Her hands pressed against Aiko's chest as if assessing something, her tone firm yet concerned. Aiko trembles even more at her words, attempting to respond but finding his throat clogged by the liquid from his mask, rendering his voice raspy and ineffectual.

151

He wonders about her mention of his system and body core, a notion that resonates with the sensation of being restrained. His body feels oddly refreshed after a lengthy period of unconsciousness. He longs to inquire further but struggles to form coherent words.

"Rest your voice; you've been unconscious for quite some time after the incident."

Incident? Memories of his mission to locate Jax Maddox flood back, the sensation of a heavy impact to his torso fading into the recesses of his mind.

"My name is Saskia Collier, and I'm your new armor smith."

Armor smith? The realization dawns on Aiko, prompting him to flex his hand, only to feel a subtle resistance, as if something metallic grinds against his fingers. Clenching his fist, he senses a metal scrape against his skin, prompting him to reach out tentatively, catching Saskia's attention.

Aiko meets Saskia's gaze, confirming his interest with a nod. She retrieves a small mirror from her pocket, wiping it clean with her scarf before offering it to him. However, her hesitation doesn't go unnoticed as she pauses, her gaze briefly drifting downward.

"You're certain you want to see yourself? It's... different from what you remember."

She cautions, her tone carrying a hint of concern.

Aiko's desperate attempt to move all his limbs prompts Saskia to turn her pocket mirror towards him, momentarily halting his struggles. As the initial brightness of the reflection subsides, his eyes widen in disbelief. He had been wondering about the source of his immobilization, and now it became painfully clear.

His arms and legs are extended, encased in a formidable suit of armor. Tubes snake around his limbs, serving as the conduits for whatever mechanism binds him. The torso is heavily armored, with plates overlapping and compressing around his body. Part of his skin is exposed, covered only by a layer of black material, beneath which two lights emit a soft blue glow. His pelvis is shielded by additional layers of armor extending entirely around his waist. Starting in navy hues, the armor gradually transitions into a light brown, with navy plating extending down to his thighs. He realizes the tightness around his knees is due to the lights emanating from within, accompanied by navy plating resembling fins protruding from the sides. Even his feet are encased in heavy shoes, every inch covered to ensure protection.

Looking at his shoulders, Aiko observes navy pauldrons, with each successive layer overlapping the previous one. His arms seem shorter within the armor, but he can feel the suit enveloping them. Gazing over Saskia, he realizes he towers over her, his increased height momentarily unsettling him. The mirror reveals his hands, now grey and textured with additional layers of armor, confirming that his entire body is ensconced in its protective shell.

Turning his attention to the helmet, he notes the navy and light brown armor forming a sharp parallelogram on both sides, with extensions resembling elongated right triangles connecting to the jawline. Behind the jaw armor, he notices gray circular tubes, from which steam unexpectedly emits, sending a shock through him.

Before Saskia can help, Acheron interrupts firmly, his voice muffled by the mask.

"That won't be necessary."

A voice slices through Aiko's thoughts, igniting a spark of anger within him. He turns his gaze past Saskia, spotting a figure clad in a long coat and armor akin to his own—the unmistakable presence of Jabez Acheron. With purposeful strides, Jabez approaches, circling around Saskia as if assessing the situation before him.

"I presume you are Saskia, our recruit. What are you doing here? You don't start your job until next week."

Jabez marched in, his tone calm and authoritative.

"I heard a disturbance coming from the corridor, finding him in a state of panic. He is awake, sir.

Saskia responds, her voice tinged with urgency.

Jabez observes Aiko in his new suit, acknowledging the situation with a nod.

"I see. His assimilation isn't completed yet."

Assimilation? Aiko wonders, puzzled by the term and growing increasingly frustrated with being spoken about as though he were merely an object.

Saskia explains her actions, detailing how she had intervened to alleviate the strain on Aiko's body. Jabez, however, dismisses her concerns with a nonchalant demeanor.

"This is normal. Reacting to having a bolt of metal forced into you is normal."

He asserts, his voice tinged with a hint of indifference.

Aiko's agitation mounts. His muscles tense as he leans towards Jabez, and his arm trembles as he attempts to break free from the restraints.

"Yes, Aiko, shake more. You're doing yourself a favor. Get used to the suit and familiarize yourself with your new perspective."

Jabez taunts, his words laced with cold indifference.

Struggling to articulate his thoughts through his raspy voice, Aiko asks a question.

"What... did... you... do... to me?"

Jabez meets Aiko's gaze with a steely glare, his demeanor unwavering.

"What do you think I did to you? I saved you. During the mission we sent you on, you were ambushed by The Excesses organization. Everything went according to our plan, but they somehow knew of our intentions. You followed Akarui's instructions, and I can only assume they knew of your presence beforehand."

Turning back to face Aiko, Jabez strides towards him with deliberate steps, his presence commanding. Saskia watches silently, observing the tense exchange unfold before her.

As Jabez's words wash over him, Aiko's glare intensifies, but he remains silent, his head bowed in defiance and resignation. Jabez's impassioned explanation rings in his ears, each word a reminder of the precarious thread that now binds him to this existence.

"You barely escaped with your life, surviving close combat with Jax and taking a direct shot from a rocket. Armor-piercing caliber to revise that. I was given a choice to either cancel the program and let you die out or try to piece together whatever remained of you. You should be grateful that you are still breathing! You mad at me for what?! That you're alive! That you can get mad at me for saving you! That suit is the only reason why you're breathing. Remember what I told you during our first meeting when I showed you this suit? The suit that I wore is passed down to you because you almost went to heaven."

Aiko's fists clench reflexively, his anger simmering beneath the surface. Yet, despite his resentment, he cannot deny the truth in Jabez's words—the suit, this armor, is his lifeline, the only thing keeping him tethered to the world of the living.

Jabez's gaze burns into him, and Aiko meets it with an unyielding stare, refusing to show any sign of weakness. With a dismissive gesture, Jabez turns away to head out of the room. He paused before he left.

"After evaluating your training, vitals, and progress, I saw that you were, in a sense, ready to wear the suit. Only because I still need you. Our agreement is not over until your services are completed. And in return, we will find your caretaker. You're forgetting that you made a deal, Aiko Ashin. You gave your blood, your devotion. Until you die, your service is therefore not completed. For now... Saskia. Your presence here must be accounted for, but you shouldn't be here. Leave now."

Acheron left, with Saskia silent throughout the exchange. She nods in acknowledgment, her expression a mix of concern and understanding. Without a word, she turns on her heel and exits the room, leaving Aiko alone with his thoughts and the weight of his newfound purpose.

Aiko sits in silence, the only sound is his heartbeat echoing in the cold, empty room. He recalls memories of Anbu and Inoue, bowing his head in resignation as the operating machine compresses and restrains his suit further. Acceptance settles over him, and he allows the darkness to envelop him.

***

Meanwhile, Jabez strides purposefully down the corridor, his shadowy figure stark against the sterile white surroundings. He heads towards the elevator, ready to descend to his next destination. Suddenly, he hears the distinct sound of a set of footsteps approaching, heels clicking in tandem with metallic stomps, growing louder with each passing moment. He turns to see Akarui hurrying towards him, her breaths coming in short gasps as she slows to a stop beside him.

"You're always late to our meetings."

Jabez remarks, his tone tinged with a hint of amusement.

"Forgive me, Acheron. Scheduling my therapy sessions and rushing to appointments can be tiresome."

Akarui replies, her words punctuated by labored breaths.

"At least you made it."

Jabez acknowledges, and they both stand silently as the elevator descends, each lost in their own thoughts.

Akarui considers speaking but remains silent. Her gaze flickers towards Jabez just as he stumbles back against the elevator wall, his expression betraying a hint of surprise.

"Acheron, are you okay?"

Akarui's concern cuts through the silence, drawing Jabez's attention.

"Yes. Forgot my medication."

Jabez replies tersely, a hint of irritation in his tone.

"Have you been taking them lately?"

Akarui probes gently, her concern evident.

Jabez's silence hangs heavy in the air, speaking volumes to Akarui's intuition.

"I know pills are scary, but you should be taking them regularly."

She urges, her voice soft but firm.

"I know I should."

Jabez concedes after a long pause, his tone resigned.

Akarui waits for a moment before continuing, her words thoughtful yet cautious.

"I understand, but just take them once in a while."

As the elevator continues its descent, Akarui breaks the silence again, voicing the thought she had previously contemplated.

"How's Aiko?"

She gazed at Jabez, her concern for the young man evident in her tone.

Jabez hesitates, taking a moment to gather his thoughts before responding.

"We had a chat; it didn't go well."

"Jabez, he's—"

Akarui starts, her voice trailing off as she struggles to find the right words.

"Barely a boy, I remember what you told me."

Jabez interrupts, his tone firm.

"He's old enough to take responsibility. He already showed it when he agreed to become the Melancholic Knight. He agreed to serve and be useful to the URDT until he dies."

Akarui's eyes widen slightly at his words, a mixture of shock and concern flickering across her features.

"He's your son... Did you forget that?"

She presses, her voice tinged with a hint of reproach.

"Acheron, have you considered what he will experience? You could be scarring him for life."

"Just like our meeting on our first day, I gave him two choices: flight or fight."

Jabez continues, his voice heavy with the weight of his words.

"Running away from his choices, the choices that led him here, determined from his past to now. His actions and thoughts weigh into his decision-making process. Choosing survival in our world, in what's left of our species. He decided to fight. Fighting me and our actions, knowing that he has no choice. Because his decision was already determined."

Akarui listens quietly, her gaze lowered as Jabez pours out his thoughts.

"I was chosen to fight long ago when our world was dying. They needed men, not boys, and we had to grow up. All my comrades aren't here. Their choices were determined for them, and my choices were limited. I had to make a difficult choice—letting Aiko perish or still using his ability. He should be grateful to be alive; wearing the suit will extend his abilities further, but he will develop a rebellious mindset. He had that since the start but can't neglect our order and duty. It's just a matter of time before he snaps."

Before Akarui can respond, the elevator rings, signaling they have reached their destination.

"We're here; let's go."

Jabez states, his tone final.

Akarui pauses for a moment, then, with a silent nod, she follows Jabez as he strides purposefully towards the LYN lair. Her eyes lowered, and she walked alongside him, observing his straightened posture and determined gait.

As they approach, Kenryoku awaits them by the entrance, his presence a silent acknowledgment of their arrival.

"They are all waiting for you, sir."

Kenryoku informs Jabez.

"Okay, let's not keep them waiting anymore, shall we?"

Jabez responds, his gaze fixed ahead.

Acknowledging Jabez's words with a nod, Kenryoku opens the chamber doors, revealing the center stage where the AI LYN and its monitors—Lycoris, Yvette, and Nicodemus—are powered up and ready to report in.

"Sire, the nation leaders have been 'eagerly' waiting for your presence, Acheron."

Lycoris chimes in smoothly.

"Put them through."

Jabez commands, striding confidently up to the stage. He signals Nicodemus to initiate the virtual meeting, and holograms begin to materialize from the ground.

Six holograms take the form of two soft yellows with hints of orange, representing the Sanguine Provence; three shining with purple hues, signifying the Phlegmatic Federal; and one revealing only red, representing The Imperium of the Choleric.

The leader of the Sanguine Provence appears first, adorned in a large hat and a mask that conceals his mouth and throat. He wears a brown suit with a purple tie and a white vest, giving off an air of authority. His green eyes betray his age, showing wrinkles. Beside him stands a younger individual, dressed similarly in a green tie and back-combed hair, sharing the same green eyes.

In the middle of the Phlegmatic holograms stands an elderly woman in a purple dress, her hair combed down to cover her ears, with a scarf indicating the alliance between the Phlegmatic and Sanguine factions. Flanking her are two assistants, their heads adorned with machinery chips as they await any directives, their high-tech typewriters ready.

The hologram representing The Imperium of the Choleric remains anonymous, refusing to reveal its identity.

"Premier Jabez Acheron! Your attention and presence have been requested since last week! You received timely notice of our meeting, and only now have you decided to answer our call!"

The leader of the Sanguine Province accuses, his voice tinged with impatience.

"We've been aware of activities you've been taking."

The Sanguine leader's muffled and rough voice says, necessitating translation by the assistants flanking him.

"What have I been persecuted for?"

Jabez responds, his gaze steady as he meets the Phlegmatic leader's eyes.

The Phlegmatic leader wastes no time in addressing the matter at hand.

"There were activities from the south near the Phlegmatic territory. Reports of explosions and fires were witnessed at an abandoned Refugee Point."

With a signal to her assistant, the Phlegmatic leader triggers the display of an image depicting a helicopter with a rope dangling down, obscuring a covered object.

"I heard the news shortly after the incident—only twenty minutes later. There were helicopters near our area. Our security took pictures of the helicopter, pinpointing the logo URDT on the vessel."

"Mr. Acheron, what we want to know is what that covered object is?"

The Phlegmatic leader presses, her tone demanding an explanation.

Jabez studies the image before him, his expression unreadable for a moment.

"It is an ARC bomb that was recovered from The Excesses. They were reconfiguring a stolen ARC system into a bomb."

He finally responds.

"We received word from our intel that one of the Excess leaders was holed up in the abandoned facility. We could gather from our FIREBIRDS Squadrons, led by my commander Akarui Fenimore, spearheading the operation, that The Excesses were using the facility as a bomb factory. Unfortunately, the team was ambushed, resulting in the bomb detonating prematurely."

"I see. What is the leader's name and origin? If you have conclusive data on that."

The Sanguine Leader's voice comes through muffled by his mask, prompting the translator to relay the inquiry with hand gestures to accompany the translation.

"We identified one of the leaders as Jax Maddox. He was an ex-ordinance specialist here at the URDT. He must have left our organization and joined The Excesses as they were beginning their activities."

Jabez responds, his tone measured and factual.

"While we may not have photographs of the bombs, we have gathered evidence of his involvement and other new technologies they were producing."

With a signal to Nicodemus, Jabez instructs the submission of the evidence to the holograms, allowing the leaders to witness the damning proof. The images revealed Jax Maddox clad in a giant, heavy mechanized suit, attacking the camera's operator. The leaders exchange looks while the assistants of the Phlegmatic faction intensify their typing in response to the visual evidence.

"We now realize that The Excesses have been working on new projects of their own, utilizing heavy suits of armor. Upon examination, we discovered that they have managed to steal a valuable ARC, modifying it to make it even deadlier."

Jabez explains, his voice tinged with concern.

"The recent events, such as the organized hijacking of railway systems and disturbing the peace we as a nation have built, indicate that they are becoming increasingly hostile and unpredictable. They have been labeled our highest priority to locate and dismantle the organization."

"Are these the reasons why each of the nations is sending you more metal plating and bits of Synacore energy from our nation, Acheron?"

The Imperium of the Choleric inquires, their voice altered but stable.

Jabez turns his attention to the hologram representing The Imperium.

"Your resources align with our agendas, supporting our men and women of the URDT in finding and neutralizing the threat."

He replies evenly.

"I'm not questioning your agendas; I'm only curious about the resources you're pouring into funding. What does it mean for us?"

The Imperium persists, their tone firm but not hostile.

Akarui and Kenryoku exchange concerned glances while Jabez remains composed.

"We provided you with funds to support your nation, The Imperium of the Choleric. We never inquire about the activities of your nation, nor do we question our own actions."

Jabez asserts calmly.

The Imperium falls silent, contemplating Jabez's words before speaking again.

"There is no need to be hostile, Acheron. My curiosity is simply heightened due to the recent events involving The Excesses. But if you're hiding something from the nations, expect consequences."

"Noted."

Jabez responds curtly, his expression unreadable.

He stares at the holographic screen until the Phlegmatic leader's intervention breaks the tension.

"We are not here to discuss issues between you two but to learn about the events that transpired earlier. I found the evidence truthful; wouldn't you agree, Sanguine?"

The Phlegmatic leader interjects, directing the conversation back to the matter.

The Sanguine leader nods in agreement, placing his hands over his heart in a gesture of understanding.

"But Imperium of Choleric, regardless of their concerns, is correct. Our trade with your nation and funding of the URDT must be utilized properly and not squandered. Our resources are becoming scarcer, and we don't want conflicts, Acheron. However, if necessary, we will cut our trading and sanction your nation if anything illegal or rule-breaking occurs."

The Phlegmatic leader proclaims firmly, emphasizing the importance of responsible resource management.

"I understand, madam. We will continue to pursue the organization and ensure that they are brought to justice. We will keep a close eye on any activities and report back."

Jabez responds respectfully, acknowledging the Phlegmatic leader's concerns.

With that, the Phlegmatic leader nods in approval and exits the hologram, followed by the Sanguine leader. Only The Imperium of the Choleric, their presence lingering momentarily before they depart, leaving Jabez alone on the stage.

Akarui approaches him, but she is halted by Kenryoku's gesture and a subtle shake of his head. Jabez isn't in the mood for company as he remains deep in thought, absorbing the silence around him.

# Chapter Thirteen: Cadets

*May 7, 2134*

T he sky was a canvas of unblemished blue, its vastness stretching as far as the eye could see. This serene expanse was abruptly shattered by the piercing echo of projectiles slicing through the air at breakneck speeds. One after another, these missiles rained down upon the earth, stirring clouds of dust from the once peaceful and clean roads. These roads now mirrored the chaotic trajectory of the rockets that had launched them into turmoil.

Amidst this chaos, a solitary figure was seen sprinting toward a building, desperate for the sanctuary it promised from the deadly rain. With agility born of necessity, the figure executed a forward leap, seamlessly transitioning into a tucked roll, narrowly evading an explosion from a nearby projectile. Finding refuge near a window, the figure paused to survey the surroundings. The attire was unmistakably that of the FIREBIRDS. Yet, the color scheme was unique—pristine white armor accented with navy on the shoulder, knee pads, and the helmet, marking a distinct identity.

Across the street, the figure's gaze intensified, searching.

"SUKI, ARE YOU THERE?"

The urgency in Quentin's voice cut through the din of battle.

"Yeah, Quentin, I'm in position!"

Suki's response crackled over the comm link, her voice a beacon of reliability amidst the havoc.

Quentin, pressing a button on the ARC, glanced over to see Suki donned in similar armor, signaling him with a wave—a moment of normalcy before she tensed, noticing another projectile zeroing in on her position.

"SUKI, we'll meet in the middle of the buildings on the floor. I'll secure the objective and wait for the others."

Quentin declared his plan set amidst the unpredictable chaos.

"Whatever you say, Quentin."

Suki replied, her tone a mix of resignation and trust, knowing well the stakes of their mission.

Their exchange was a brief respite, a moment of human connection in the face of relentless adversity, as they prepared to navigate the dangers ahead.

Nodding to each other in silent agreement, they lunged towards the upstairs of the building. Quentin advanced cautiously, his ARC poised and ready, scanning each corner as he ascended. Moving in harmony, his footsteps echoed softly on the stairs. Glancing down, the ARC's screen displayed a timer reading "5:22." Gritting his teeth, Quentin quickened his pace into a sprint. He rechecked the ARC, this time accessing a map of his surroundings. It highlighted Suki and two others whose signals were faint and elusive. Midway up the floor, Quentin's advance was abruptly halted by a forceful tackle.

The weight pressing down on him was immense. Struggling, Quentin managed to glimpse his assailant—another young man of Quentin's age, clad in similar armor but distinguished by red accents on the shoulder pads, knees, and helmet. The assailant, a fellow cadet, exerted his strength, pinning Quentin down. Quentin repelled the cadet with a swift kick, gaining precious seconds to dash towards a nearby window. As he approached, he saw the cadet charging, firing shots that morphed into projectiles resembling tiny plastic balls. Quentin dodged left, seeking cover from the barrage.

About to retaliate, Quentin realized his ARC had been disabled, the cadet brandishing a cartridge with a smirk. Quentin was left defenseless as the cadet aimed, ready to fire.

Suddenly, a miniature projectile whizzed from nowhere, striking the cadet squarely in the chest. The impact stunned the assailant's suit, granting Quentin a fleeting opportunity. He drew his knife, sliding into a kick that toppled the cadet before stabbing into the leg armor, effectively immobilizing him. Quentin then dragged the incapacitated cadet to the side of the wall, ensuring he was no longer a threat.

"If this hadn't been a simulation, you'd be dead by now."

A voice remarking Quentin through his comms, retrieving the cartridge from the cadet. He inserted it beneath his ARC, efficiently reloading. With a confident press, his ARC was back online.

"I appreciate the scouting, Odie."

Quentin said, his gaze shifting to the rooftop of the building. There, a silhouette emerged, and a modified sniper rifle, the ARC, was welded into its design. Odie saluted Quentin and communicated through the ARC.

"My pleasure. Is Suki with you?"

"No, we agreed to meet on this level. She should be here any moment—"

"You know, I can hear you both. You left the comm line open to everyone, Quentin."

Suki's voice interrupted, a hint of amusement in her tone. Spotting her signal, Quentin waved back in acknowledgment.

"Alright, are we all here now?"

"Not exactly."

Odie chimed in, gesturing downwards. Quentin peered through the window, his expression falling as he brought a hand to his face in dismay.

"Oh no."

From the ground level, a figure in heavier armor, reminiscent of the FIREBIRDS but sturdier, charged forward. With an ARC modified to include a minigun, this new adversary began to fire upon unsuspecting cadets who scrambled to respond to the unexpected assault.

"HE'S HERE, TAKE COVER!"

A cadet's warning cry cut through the chaos as he retreated from the heavy FIREBIRDS assailant. Beside him, another cadet absorbed the brunt of the attack, multiple pellets striking his chest and stunning him completely.

"Don't worry, Quentin, I'm already in route to the objective."

"NO, Jerome! We're supposed to stay together as a unit. I wanted us all to rendezvous at a higher level."

"Sorry, Quentin, but I didn't fancy being rescued by Odie. Besides, this way, I control the ground level. And by 'I,' I mean just me. I've got the fight here."

Jerome declared, confidently activating his ARC and striding forward.

"Dang it, Jerome!"

Quentin exclaimed in frustration.

"Hey, Quentin, don't feel too bad about Jerome opting out of a rescue. He's probably just jealous."

Odie quipped, barely suppressing his laughter from his vantage point.

"I, for one, could've made it there in time if you, Quentin, had held your ground."

Suki added, her tone challenging.

"No, you wouldn't have."

Odie and Jerome countered simultaneously, their voices overlapping.

"FOCUS!"

Quentin's command snapped everyone back to the urgency of their situation. Peering out from the side of the window, he noticed a light blinking red repeatedly ahead.

"We need to move in unison. Suki and I will approach the adjacent buildings on the same level. Odie, with the high ground, will guide us with updates. Jerome…"

Quentin's voice trailed off, indicating a strategic pause as he contemplated Jerome's role in their rapidly unfolding plan.

"Yeeeesssss."

Jerome drawled, drawing another exasperated hand-to-face gesture from Quentin.

"Just keep up."

Quentin sighed, a mix of resignation and determination in his voice.

"You got it, boss man."

Jerome replied, his tone a blend of jest and acknowledgment.

"Okay, on MARK."

Each team member gripped their ARC tightly, anticipation and adrenaline surging through them as they prepared for Quentin's signal. The air was thick with tension, and their collective heartbeats were almost audible in the silence that enveloped them.

"1."

"2."

"3."

"MARK!"

On cue, they all burst into action, propelled by the urgency of their mission. Quentin and Suki dashed across the building, heading straight for the nearest window. They raised their arms instinctively to shield themselves as they leaped, the glass shattering upon impact. Midair, they both activated their ARCs, navigating swiftly to the equipment section to deploy their grapples. With a flick of their wrists, a long cable tipped with mini thorn-like hooks shot out, anchoring securely into the cement wall. Clinging tightly to their lifelines, they ascended the wall with practiced grace.

Meanwhile, Odie executed precisely timed jumps across the rooftops, his movements a blur of efficiency and skill. Jerome took a different approach, his path leading him across the open streets below. He moved with a deliberate swagger, taunting the air confidently, his voice echoing between the buildings.

Above them all, an observation window appeared against the backdrop of the open sky, a silent monitor overseeing the unfolding drama below.

\*\*\*

Inside the observation room, the tension was apparent, mirrored by the viewers' focused intensity on the monitor screens. Displayed prominently were the names of the cadets under scrutiny: Quentin Reily, Suki Kimani, Odie Ulysses, and Jerome Aguilar, collectively designated as BLUE TEAM. Three captains stood in the dimly lit room; their eyes locked on the ongoing exercise.

"You've taught them well, Dahlia. They're moving faster than before. Their leaps and strides have improved significantly."

One captain, identified as Curtis, remarked, his tone a mix of admiration and analytical detachment.

Dahlia, a figure of authority and experience, responded with a nod.

"If that's how you want to phrase it, Curtis. I've honed their endurance and taught them to seize every opportunity. As the battlefield becomes more treacherous, finding shortcuts to survival becomes crucial. Take Suki Kimani's movements, for example."

The monitor shifted focus to a camera attached to Suki's helmet, providing a first-person view of her actions. The footage showed her leaping from a window and rapidly deploying her grapple hook. She sprinted along the side of a wall before crashing through another window to dodge incoming fire.

"Although she narrowly avoided getting hit, she still needs to work on refining her stride a bit more."

Dahlia critiqued, her eyes never leaving the screen, capturing every detail of Suki's maneuver.

At that moment, the door to the observation room slid open quietly, and Captain Ryne Maverick entered. The change in the room's atmosphere was immediate, with the other captains turning to acknowledge his presence with a series of respectful nods. Maverick's arrival signaled a shift in focus, his reputation and command authority imposing a silent reverence. His keen eyes quickly moved to the screens, assessing the situation with a practiced gaze that missed nothing.

"Glad you could make it, Maverick. You've arrived just in time for the most exciting part."

Curtis greeted Maverick as he entered the room.

"Am I?"

Maverick responded with characteristic calmness, joining Dahlia near the monitors.

"What are we looking at?"

She prepares to explain with attention immediately drawn to the screens displaying the ongoing assessment.

165

"Their fourth test assessment. They're attempting to breach the other team's defenses, RED TEAM, and secure the Command Post."

Dahlia explained, gesturing towards the action unfolding on the monitors.

"Are the members of RED TEAM also cadets?"

Maverick asked, her gaze fixed on the intense skirmish.

"Yes, they're volunteers who've already passed their assessments. Despite their dwindling numbers, they're proving quite formidable."

Dahlia confirmed.

"And who comprises BLUE TEAM?"

Maverick continued her line of questioning.

"The squad is led by Quentin Reily, who excels in strategic command but struggles in close combat. He seems to harbor some self-doubt."

Dahlia observed.

"Reily... I recall our first meeting. He possesses potential but lacks assertiveness. His involvement in the Evergreen Hub Station Train hijacking incident showcased his dedication, although he failed to stand up to a confrontation. Perhaps he doubts himself."

Maverick reflected.

"And what about her?"

Shifting her focus to Suki Kimani's actions on the screen.

"Suki Kimani, skilled in agility and traversing terrain, follows Quentin's lead closely. However, she appears to be holding back, showing restraint in her approach. She complements Quentin well but is more aggressive in her tactics."

Dahlia explained as they watched Suki take down a member of RED TEAM and immobilize him with precise shots to the chest.

"I see..."

Maverick murmured, absorbing the information.

"Then there's Odie Ulysses, a passionate birdwatcher with hobbies in hiking and photography. His enthusiasm translates into natural skill, as seen in his timely intervention to save Quentin from a potentially dangerous confrontation. Despite his prowess, his penchant for humor often earns him the title of jokester among his peers."

Dahlia concluded, painting a vivid picture of Odie's character and abilities.

"I suppose you taught him how to aim like that, Cade?"

Maverick redirected his attention to Cade Valentine, who closely observed Odie's precise marksmanship on the monitor.

"Most definitely. His eyes are trained to lock onto his targets, taking them down with precision regardless of angles or obstacles. He exceeds my expectations; he's much better suited to solo operations. He should have remained in my battalion."

Cade remarked, his gaze lingering on the screen displaying Odie's progress.

Maverick noticed Cade's subtle questioning and responded.

"It wasn't my decision to transfer Odie Ulysses to my battalion initially; it came from higher up. With my battalion's numbers dwindling, there was a need for reinforcements."

"I hope he doesn't become too reliant on his squadron leader's orders. His talent could be utilized more effectively if he were given greater autonomy."

Cade added, his concern evident in his tone.

Maverick remained silent, acknowledging Cade's banter before refocusing on the monitor. Meanwhile, Dahlia prepared to provide insights on the remaining members of BLUE TEAM.

"Lastly, we have Jerome Aguilar, a heavy-class cadet recently transferred from Curtis' battalion. He's not particularly vocal, which might explain his shaky adjustment to the squad dynamics."

Dahlia began, her gaze shifting to the monitor displaying Jerome's actions.

"Additionally, Jerome and Odie are close friends with a shared history, which might account for their lively conversations."

Curtis added, scrutinizing the screen showcasing Jerome's movements.

Jerome's camera perspective revealed him trailing behind his teammates before coming under fire from three cadets. Using a broken vehicle door as cover, Jerome swiftly maneuvered, surprising his adversaries with a duck-and-roll tactic before eliminating them with expert marksmanship. The display of skill and tactical ingenuity elicited nods of approval from the observing captains.

"I can see where he got that from, Curtis."

Maverick remarked, acknowledging Curtis's influence on Jerome's tactical decisions.

"I'm glad someone prioritizes a more personal approach, unlike others."

Curtis responded, focusing on Quentin, who maintained distance while aiming his ARC at another cadet.

Maverick scrutinized Odie and Jerome closely.

"Is this the formation they're following?"

His eyes widen, seeking clarification.

"Well, that's what Quentin ordered. He believes that by spreading out, you'll force the enemies to split their attention."

Curtis explained, gesturing towards the monitor displaying the team's movements.

"This is nonsense. They should operate as a cohesive unit, not as lone wolves. They'll get picked off one by one."

Maverick interjected, her gaze shifting back to Quentin's precarious position.

***

As Odie noticed Jerome falling behind, Odie urged Quentin to pull back.

"Quentin! Jerome isn't catching up; we need to pull back."

Odie's urgent voice crackled over the communication link.

Hearing the plea, Quentin paused to look back towards the window. He glanced briefly at Jerome, then at the objective ahead, before reaching for his ARC.

"Negative, we're getting close to the post. We need to push!"

Quentin insisted, his voice firm with determination.

"No, Quentin. We can't!"

Odie's urgency was evident as he pleaded with his teammate.

"Forget about me, Odie. I'll catch up."

Jerome reassured, his resolve unwavering despite the danger.

The sound of pellets whizzing past Jerome intensified, the threat palpable in the air. Odie hesitated momentarily, torn between his loyalty to his squad and the instinct to protect his friend. But with a deep breath, he pushed forward, focusing on the objective ahead.

As they neared the target, Odie peered through his scope at the tower housing the RED TEAM. He reached for his ARC, ready to act.

"Quentin! There are multiple targets surrounding the post. Can I take them out?"

Odie's voice crackled over the communication link, his eagerness evident.

"Stand down, Odie. You'll blow our element of surprise once we move in."

Quentin's command was decisive, emphasizing the importance of maintaining the element of surprise.

"Quentin! I'll make it easier for us all to take them down. I can take them all."

Odie persisted; his determination clear.

"You can't, Odie. Once you take one down, they'll be alerted, and they'll be scanning the area. Stay back and wait for assistance."

Quentin reasoned, his tone leaving no room for argument.

Odie's hands trembled as he gripped his rifle, the weight of the impending confrontation settling heavily upon him. With a determined breath, he steadied himself and resumed his position, focusing intently on the cadets stationed at the tower.

Meanwhile, Quentin and Suki navigated through the building, leaping from window to window with practiced agility. However, Suki's progress was abruptly halted when she locked eyes with a cadet who began firing pellets at her. Despite her best efforts to evade, one struck her leg, sending a sharp jolt of pain through her body. With no time to spare, she sought refuge behind a nearby desk, her heart pounding in her chest.

Frantically, Suki reached for her ARC, her fingers trembling as she attempted to call out for Quentin's assistance.

"QUENTIN, I'M DOWN! PLEASE, I NEED ASSISTANCE!"

She pleaded, her voice strained with urgency.

But as she glanced at her ARC screen, panic surged as she realized the communication signal was offline. Desperation gripped her as she watched Quentin continue his daring leaps across the buildings, unaware of her distress.

"QUENTIN! DON'T LEAVE ME!"

Suki's voice echoed in the empty room, filled with fear and desperation as she faced being left behind, alone and vulnerable.

As Quentin dashed across the windows, his movements swift and agile, he narrowly dodged oncoming pellets, his heart pounding with adrenaline-fueled urgency. With each glance at his ARC, he saw their objective drawing closer, fueling his determination to press on. Suddenly, he noticed that the barrage of pellets had ceased, a momentary respite that spurred him to sprint even faster across the buildings.

As he leaped from window to window, his gaze drifted to the side, catching sight of the flickering light from the command post. Realizing their proximity to the objective,

Quentin's focus sharpened, his mind racing with the next steps of their mission. With a quick glance at his ARC, he activated the communication function, reaching out to his comrades urgently.

"I'm close to the objective. Suki, are you with me?"

He called out, his voice carrying a mix of determination and concern as he awaited her response.

As Quentin's attempts to communicate with his comrades were met with nothing but static, a sense of unease crept over him. He scanned his surroundings, searching for any sign of Suki, Odie, or Jerome, but their absence only heightened his apprehension. With his heart pounding in his chest, Quentin hesitated momentarily, torn between the urge to backtrack and the pressing need to press forward.

Ultimately, fueled by determination and a sense of duty, Quentin chose to push onward. With a swift motion, he propelled himself out of the window, his grapple hook shooting out and anchoring onto the side of the building. The force of his ascent was exhilarating, the wind whipping past him as he soared through the air.

Upon reaching the next window, Quentin crashed through with calculated precision, his focus unwavering as he sprinted up the stairs toward the command post. However, his advance was met with fierce resistance as enemy forces unleashed a barrage of fire upon him.

Taking cover behind a nearby table, Quentin frantically reached for his ARC, only to realize he was utterly alone. With no reinforcements to rely on, he knew that he had to rely on his own skills and instincts to prevail.

Gritting his teeth, Quentin assessed his surroundings, quickly formulating a plan of attack. With swift and decisive movements, he launched himself out of the window again, using his grapple hook to maneuver from one window to the next.

In a flurry of action, Quentin dispatched each cadet with precise shots from his ARC, his movements fluid and calculated. With the final Cadet subdued, Quentin wasted no time activating the command post, his eyes trained on the fading light as he completed his mission objective.

However, as Quentin turned to leave, he was taken aback to see the simulation lights flicker back to life.

"Quentin Reily, report down at the streets."

The announcement pierced through the tension, singling out Quentin Reily. Without hesitation, he leaped out of the window, descending gracefully to the street below.

As he landed, Quentin was immediately confronted by Captain Maverick, who wasted no time in delivering a stern reprimand. The force of Maverick's push knocked Quentin to the ground, leaving him shaken both physically and emotionally.

"Only you reached the objective; your squadron needed to be more organized. You and your team disobeyed orders and left your comrades behind."

Maverick's voice cut through the air like ice, his gaze unwavering as he addressed Quentin.

Quentin met Maverick's cold stare with a sense of resignation, his heart heavy with guilt. His gaze drifted beyond Maverick, revealing Jerome supporting the unconscious Odie, his cadet armor showing signs of damage. Suki, limping slightly, cast Quentin a disapproving glance, her expression reflecting her disappointment.

For a moment, Quentin closed his eyes, grappling with the weight of his failures.

"NOW!"

Maverick's command snapped everyone to attention, prompting them to follow him out of the simulation, each burdened by their own thoughts and emotions.

Quentin waited near the interview doors, where he could subtly hear the voices of the commanders. He couldn't discern their exact words but sensed it wasn't good.

"Jerome Aguilar, you're not only the anchor of this squad; you must act like it. Disobeying Quentin's orders leaves not only your comrades but yourself vulnerable as well. You and Quentin aren't fighting these battles alone."

Curtis said, standing near his desk and speaking down to Jerome, who had his arms crossed.

"Quentin isn't the leader I can work with, sir."

Jerome replied.

"Why not, Jerome? There will always be changes in our organization, especially now that we're losing recruits at an alarming rate."

"Quentin doesn't understand my class and specialty. I can't run or glide across the skies like the others. You know that sir, don't you?"

"Yes, I understand you're not accustomed to this new squad, and I know you miss your old one. But you must adapt, even if you feel incompatible."

"My responsibilities are demanding, sir. You taught me to stand my ground and confront my adversaries. Quentin doesn't understand me; he's too inflexible."

In the next room labeled "Captain Cade Valente":

"How many targets did you eliminate before the ambush?"

"Only 12, and that was before I had to assist Quentin."

Cade sat, looking at folders, revealing information about Quentin, Suki, and Jerome.

171

"Do you remember the 'One and Done' motto, Odie?"

"Very much so, finishing everything in one shot. I wish he'd allow me to advance instead of sidelining me as a cameraman for them."

"I understand, Odie. Moving you out of your original squad from my battalion hampers your skills as a sniper. But there's little I can do within my power to bring you back. What are your thoughts on this squad?"

"Jerome and I go way back; we're practically brothers. I can't say the same for Quentin. I'd refer to him as an older stepbrother who only expects me to listen and follow but restricts my development in my skill."

In the next room labeled "Captain Dahlia Mackenzie":

"I know that you and Quentin are quite close, Suki."

"We're not engaged in any relationship."

"I'm not accusing you of anything. Being attached to someone will only, in essence, slow you down."

"He doesn't slow me down; he redirects me on the path."

"Is he a good friend to you?"

"Yeah, I just wish he wouldn't dive headfirst into situations."

"Like he did in the simulation test?"

"I tried to call him before the ARC communication line got cut off. I tried to catch up, but he only ended up running right ahead to the objective."

"I was monitoring him, Suki; he glanced back twice, then went alone."

"He pulled back the same stunt during the train incident but with another of his comrades. He expects us to follow him, and I can do that. But I can't do anything if they don't have confidence in themselves or in me to listen. I just want to know if we can do it together."

Quentin sat against the wall, his back supported by it, and closed his eyes as the voices from the rooms continued to seep into him.

***

As the night settled early, the lights of the URDT illuminated the surrounding area. Quentin and the others walked silently across the corridor, passing a sign that read "Bunker." Each of them avoided eye contact, lost in their own thoughts. Upon reaching their bunker, they dispersed to their individual rooms, each marked with their names on the door. Quentin lingered, watching his comrades enter their rooms before finally entering his own. He collapsed onto his bed, laying back while staring up at the ceiling. Illuminated only by the faint glow from the window, he couldn't help but notice the decorations adorning his walls. There was a portrait of him and the other squad members, their smiles frozen in time. Another photo captured Quentin and Suki during their orientation at the URDT. Suki is holding the camera out with Aiko in the background, lost in thought and not facing the camera. Quentin whispered to himself, pondering Aiko's absence.

"I wonder where you've been... it's not the same."

He reached for another photo hidden behind the portrait, revealing two pictures of himself, Aiko, and Suki with her family. Another showed Quentin as a toddler, his mother standing alone beside him. With a heavy heart, he gently stroked the photo, bowing his head in sorrow.

Leaving his room, he made his way quietly across the dormitory towards the space between two rooms. Voices emanated from the room to his left, and reading the name on the door, he found himself outside "Odie Ulysses" room.

"You took a lot of hits, Jerome. Nothing new for you to bear, eh?"

"Not really. I just wish something new would happen, either tomorrow or right now. Taking hits is all I know, Odie."

"How's your family?"

"They're doing great... Just great..."

"..."

"You haven't told them about being transferred from Curtis' battalion?"

"No, I haven't. I didn't want to disappoint my father again."

"What was he disappointed about this time?"

"With me not wanting to take over our family business near the Sanguine nation. He believed I wasn't cut out to join the URDT. He needs to understand the rigorous process of registration, not just for the FIREBIRDS. All the training we've undergone in these past months... And he still insists that I return. He's growing older and more aggressive about it by the day."

"And your mother?"

"She doesn't care. She only cared when I was young. I was told that if I didn't work hard for someone, I'd be left behind and disowned. It's funny to think about how weak I was back then. I couldn't even lift a single-pound sack of plum seeds. And here I am! Carrying a heavy mounted minigun on my ARC."

"Doesn't sound that bad."

"You don't even know, man. You're like carrying a stick in my perspective. I bet you couldn't even lift a sack of plums!"

Odie chuckled at that response, reclining on his bed while playing with a Rubik's cube.

"You may be right, but I don't need to be this big and spongy fellow. I'm already compatible with all the tasks I'm given."

"Given..."

Jerome emphasized the word.

"Don't give me that 'na na na.' You practically had everything handed to you from a young age. I remember you flexing your Fighting Falcon model. Those are considered vintage by now."

"Back when Earth was a thing."

They both paused for a moment, sharing the silence.

"How long do you plan to stay in this squad, Odie?"

"Forever, I suppose... I just don't understand. Or I don't understand Quentin's approach most of the time. I'm supposed to be scouting, but he doesn't let me advance ahead and do more."

"And he expects me to keep up with you when my equipment is so heavy. I can't fly like the rest of you. He can't keep subjecting us to this simulation test over and over again. I'm tired of taking the hits, man. I just want to pass this final test and become a FIREBIRDS."

"I hear you. You and I will try to get out of this squad if we fail another test. Don't get me wrong; Quentin is a cool guy; I just wish he was more attentive to us than to himself."

Quentin shook his head on hearing the negative comments. He walked across to another door with the name "Suki Kimani." He knocked gently on the door.

"What is it?"

Suki answered, still in her cadet armor.

"You haven't changed yet?"

Quentin asked.

"I'm too tired to change. Does it bother you or something?"

"No, not really."

"Or is there something bothering you right now?"

Quentin sighed, nodding at her response. Suki leaned against the side of the door, lost in thought for a moment before motioning for him to come in. As Quentin entered, he took in the sight of her dorm: clothes stacked haphazardly and familiar photos hanging on the walls. One showed Suki as a child with her family, including a torn image of her father, whose resemblance to Suki was striking.

"Was it the test or our discussion with the guys in the captain's office? I could tell she thinks we're in a relationship, and I said definitely no."

"Oh, oh."

Quentin responded, feeling a bit taken aback by the revelation but quickly refocusing on his thoughts.

"No, it's the evaluation, Suki. Be honest with me. Am I that bad as a leader?"

Suki sat on her bed, leaning back and staring at the ceiling.

"No... Well, that's what I think, but I can't speak for the guys."

"Yeah, I know."

"They barely arrived before the simulation tests began. We've already done the test four times, Quentin. I'll be honest with you, I'm tired of it. I want to pass."

"I know! I want to pass, too, but it's difficult to keep an eye on everyone!"

"Were you? You left us all behind. You left Jerome behind, even though he weighs as much as a truck. Odie would've been with us. It's our job to scout, but we must stick together when we're this close to winning. But Quentin, you left me behind."

Suki lamented, putting her hands on her face.

"You should already know I don't want to be alone again. I hate it! I hate being left behind and alone."

"Suki... I—"

Quentin started, but he didn't finish his sentence. He simply acknowledged her words, stood up, and walked out the door.

"Sorry for bothering you."

He said softly as he closed the door, leaving Suki alone in her room. She nodded in response, feeling the weight of the silence.

She made her way to the portrait of her and Quentin from their orientation, grabbing another picture—this time of her, Quentin, and Aiko together. Looking back at the door where Quentin had left, she thought about how that experience might have stressed him out and forced him to leave. She stroked the picture gently, letting out a deep sigh that filled her empty room.

# Chapter Fourteen: Taking the Initiative

Quentin walked endlessly through the corridors of the bunker area, leaving nothing but silence in his wake. His gaze remained fixed on the ground as he turned each corner, his eyes the only part of him engaged with his surroundings, disconnecting himself from reality. As he passed by two male and female cadets, they briefly placed their arms on his shoulders in acknowledgment. Quentin acknowledged their presence fleetingly but didn't make complete contact. He continued until he heard voices ahead, and as he walked, the light from an open sliding door became visible, revealing cadets celebrating, dancing, and passing drinks to each other.

"FIREBIRDS FOR LIFE!"

They cheered, raising their glasses to a toast. One of them was roughhousing with another in pure excitement. Quentin slowed his pace upon hearing them, letting out a small gasp before hastening away from the room. Voices echoed in his mind—Odie and Jerome's remarks on his leadership, Suki's faith in him, and her belief in his personal growth. He made his way out of the area and into an elevator. He watched the numbers ascend; each click of the level hitting echoing in the silence around him. The silence enveloped him until the elevator finally stopped. The doors opened, and he heard a mix of regular and mechanical footsteps. Quentin glanced at the newcomer, revealing a woman whose name badge read: "Akarui Fenimore." She approached him as she entered the elevator.

"Can you press floor 50? Please."

Akarui requested.

Acknowledging her request, Quentin pressed the button, and the elevator door closed. They both listened to the elevator's sound as it continued to rise. Quentin remained silent; his gaze fixed on the ground. Akarui, glancing at him from the corner of her eye, observed his appearance.

"Are you a cadet?"

She wondered.

Quentin was caught off guard.

"Yes."

"Which battalion are you in?"

"31st, ma'am."

"Ah, the Maverick kiddos."

"Your leader has put you all through a serious training regimen. I bet the workload put numerous strains on you."

Quentin looked up slightly at her response.

"It really was a strain."

"What's your position or ranking?"

Furthermore, she continued.

"So far, I'm a squadron leader, trying to work my way up."

Quentin answered.

"Did you work your way there, or were you just chosen?"

She probed.

"Both; I can't say for sure. I really did work my best, waking up every morning to meet standards that my teammates wouldn't do. It's like a fight to wake up and face the same battle every day, and it really doesn't end. Or if it does end, was it worth it?"

Quentin reflected. Akarui lowered her expression, turning her attention toward him.

"I heard there are already final tests to become a FIREBIRDS Have you attempted it?"

Quentin didn't want to respond to the question but gestured in a way that showed he wasn't comfortable talking about it. She nodded in acknowledgment and backed off.

"You're right; it is always a fight to wake up and fight the same war. Everyone, including you, is in this war. Some of us are fighting to get to work on time, passing a test, being the best to others, or putting a smile on the days that our battle has really consumed us."

Akarui remarked. Quentin looked towards her response; his interest piqued.

"You sort of, not sure, but remind me of a... dedicated individual I work with. He wakes up extremely early, undergoes a mandatory regime of physical labor, gets evaluations of himself, and repeats the same orders he is given. It's like he's hypnotized and catatonic, just going through the motions as if he's dead from doing the work. But at the end of the day, I understand that behind the look, there is a battle he is going through."

Akarui continued, entirely giving her eye contact to Quentin.

"And he still continues to fight, even to the point where he's ready to give up."

178

She added, making Quentin grin a little, showing his gratitude for her response. The elevator door opened, prompting Akarui's attention.

"I better get going. I do hope whatever you're going through, you continue to fight."

She said, offering a grin before walking off. Quentin returned the grin but then turned his attention to the floor. Akarui looked back at him, seeing his reflection shining back at her.

Quentin left the elevator after reaching his floor, heading straight for the railing where a sign read: "Airport Shuttle." He observed the different flying vehicles docked nearby, his gaze falling to the ground below where he used to walk. Maverick's voice filled him with excitement, recalling memories of Suki, Odie, and Jerome training under the best captain in the URDT. Still, simultaneously, he remembered Aiko's hesitation on the train, Suki's inability to fully connect with him, and her masked emotions as she walked away, saying their goodbyes.

Footsteps approached from a distance, drawing Quentin's attention. He turned to see Maverick approaching, causing his heart to pound with apprehension. He quickly saluted him.

"Relax, I'm off duty."

Maverick said as he returned the salute, leaning against the railing beside Quentin.

Quentin slowly relaxed and turned his attention back to the ground, gripping the railing tightly.

"What are you doing up here?"

Maverick asked. Quentin hesitated before forcing his mouth to move.

"Nothing. I just wanted to clear my head, I guess."

"You know the docking area is off-limits, but I'll let it slide. And from your look, you need some rest."

Maverick observed. Quentin tightened his lips.

"I don't think I need it, sir."

"Why not?"

Maverick asked.

"It makes me more restless from thinking. It's become a habit for me to overthink things overnight. I can't rest until I understand myself."

Quentin explained while Maverick looked at Quentin, his expression serious.

179

"Being a leader or taking the lead will always be stressful. I pushed you for a reason, Quentin. Why do you think I did that?"

Quentin paused, wanting to respond correctly for the first time.

"To punish me?"

Maverick shook his head.

"Because you are the leader. A leader! You are the leader of your team; you are responsible to your comrades and yourself. Leaders need to master taking hits, scouting, advancing, and communicating. I pushed you down to remind you of who you are; I know you don't think you're tough enough or fit for this role."

Quentin looked at Maverick as he continued speaking.

"How do I know I am good enough?"

He asked.

"You just ignore that, don't you? Leaders like us must maintain integrity; we stand tall even when our legs give out."

Maverick replied.

"It's hard. The weight of carrying this burden is…"

Quentin trailed off while Maverick prepared to speak.

"A lot. Life doesn't get easier as you continue. As a leader, you will see many things that you stand for, what everyone thinks of you, but it's about remaining still, even if we're the only ones standing."

"I wonder if my comrades think the same. Or even care about my place in this."

Quentin said. Maverick adjusted his position and turned his attention to Quentin.

"When I started out in my squadron, a man thought the same as you. He was someone I once feared when he saw me. He was given a role that stressed the living daylights out of him, managing his own team members. Later, as he learned more about his place and his members, he took the initiative to break his comfort zone. He led into battles, even if no one wanted to follow. He always reassured them that they would make it if they followed. He passed the test and got promoted, and I watched him become a changed man. I eventually found confidence in him. So, Quentin, you just need to let go of what is and what will happen. You don't know it, but your squad needs you more than you need yourself to pull each other together. Take the initiative to find strengths within yourself and show them. You don't know how capable you are."

Quentin looked away but with a full grin.

"I'll give you some quick advice."

Maverick said, getting close to him and whispering something. Quentin's eyes shined as the lights from the docks shone ever brighter on him.

***

Later that night, Quentin walked back to his quarters, making his way to his desk. He grabbed files for each of his teammates: Jerome Aguilar, Odie Ulysses, and Suki Kimani. He glanced back up at the photos and portraits on the wall, smiling as he read over the files. The window reflected the night, growing lighter and lighter as time passed.

The following day, Suki woke up to the sound of buzzing alarms. She dressed, stretched, and walked out of her dorm to find her cadet armor on the floor. Jerome and Odie emerged from their dorms, also preparing themselves. The door to their bunker opened, revealing Quentin in his cadet armor.

"C'mon, let's try this again."

Quentin with a small smile expressing. Suki, Odie, and Jerome looked at each other in confusion as they waited in the elevator. With each floor level hit, their destination grew closer. Odie played with his Rubik's Cube, Jerome messed with his ARC, and Suki pressed her hands together. Quentin leaned back in the elevator, pondering over the previous night's events.

"What makes you think this test will be different, Quentin?"

Odie broke the silence.

"It is going to be different; I went over last night."

Quentin replied confidently.

"Are you sure it's going to be different? Are we supposed to just follow your lead?" Jerome asked, turning to Quentin. Suki noticed his attention and observed Quentin's resilience.

"No."

Quentin responded, causing everyone to turn to him in confusion, sharing the same bewilderment from earlier.

"Because the approach we are taking is going to be fun. Here's what's going to happen."

***

Back at the observation, all the captains awaited their arrival.

"I'm expecting the same result or a different outcome that leads to the same results."

181

Cade mumbled out loud.

"You don't know; every day is different."

Curtis shared his thoughts.

"You both don't know what will happen, but Curtis is right. Every day is a new day."

Dahlia responded.

Maverick waited near the sideline, ready to see them in action. Once the elevator slid open, they all came charging out, sprinting together in unison.

"Go ahead, Jerome, do your thing!"

Quentin encouraged.

"With pleasure!"

Jerome sprinted ahead of them, putting his arms up as a shield. Quentin, Suki, and Odie followed closely behind. Pellets rained down on Jerome, striking his arms, but he pushed on. Voices from the previous day echoed in Jerome's mind.

*"Even if you don't like your squad and following orders isn't your thing, you still are the anchor. You must be resilient and take the punch from anyone! Even if your teammate does it to you, you will brush it off and push through!*

Curtis had said, patting Jerome on the shoulder during his evaluation.

Jerome continued to push forward as pellets poured down on them.

"Okay, everyone, pick your target!"

Quentin urged his comrades to shoot. Each of them looked up and down, meeting the eyes of the RED TEAM cadets. Suki and Quentin aimed their ARCs at the cadets, taking some out. Quentin adjusted his aim while Odie, with his rifle, targeted the cadets on the second floor. They pushed forward towards the middle, the objective being further away but managing to stick together.

"Their formation is impressive; it's reckless, but they're sprinting behind Jerome as a shield."

Curtis noted, nodding in approval.

"They're taking turns and firing at different targets. Each of them is taking hits for one another, making sure they stick together."

Dahlia added.

"This is still early; they need to figure out a way of passing the main defense of the command post, with swarms of cadets taking the ground battle and sky to themselves."

Maverick remarked.

Jerome took hits, feeling the impact already affecting him, but he turned his head to Quentin, giving him acknowledgment.

"Okay, everyone, head down to the building!"

Quentin commanded. They all nodded, making their way towards the building. The RED TEAM focused their fire on where they entered, awaiting their move. Suddenly, smoke filled the area, and pellets flew out of the building, hitting the unfortunate cadets. Odie, with his rifle, gunned down the cadets, his helmet equipped with a goggle-like visor that allowed him to see through the smoke and detect heat signatures.

"Good job, Odie! Suki and I will go together, and you and Jerome will cover each other on the other side, firing. Are we good with that!?"

Quentin asked. They all nodded in response to Quentin's plan. Jerome led the charge, with Odie following closely behind. They burst out of the building onto the street, where cadets began to fire. With Odie's precise shots hitting the cadets with sharp accuracy, Jerome fired back with his modified minigun, prompting them to stand down and retreat.

"Okay, Jerome, I'll give you covering fire up here. I won't go higher until we make it close to the command post!"

Odie shouted.

"You got it, Odie! You got my back, man!"

Jerome responded back.

"Always!"

Odie cheered.

"WHOOO!"

Jerome let out a roar and charged out into the street while Odie grabbed onto the third floor of the building. Quickly gunning down cadets, Odie continued to aim and shoot at each one, a voice recalling him.

*"Regardless that I can't take you off this squad; I know it is part of the soldier to adapt. Adapting to our order and situation will enhance our learning curve and skills. This is what it means to be a scout; everything changes, but we adapt to what we are given. Even if breaking order or listening order is enough to win the battles we are fighting."*

Odie remembering Cade Valente's response from his office. Odie sprinted over windows in front of him while shooting at the cadets. Cade watched from the monitors, nodding his head in approval.

Meanwhile, Quentin and Suki moved up the stairs together, watching each corner they turned and having each other's backs. Suki looked at Quentin with a little grin while Quentin focused on the stairs he had taken. Reaching the floor he wanted, he looked behind to see Suki following suit, reaching for his ARC.

"Okay, how are we all feeling?"

Quentin asked.

"Great! Taking the hits like you said, Quentin."

Suki yelled.

"You're doing great. Take cover in the buildings. Odie should be covering you."

Quentin instructed.

"I am Quentin. There are a lot of targets for me to take down, and there are more in your direction. Can I get them for you?"

Odie asked.

"Light them up, Odie. Good job, everyone, we're going to make it."

Quentin praised. Quentin looked at Suki as she waited near the wall, peeking over the windows.

"Suki, you got my back?"

Quentin asked.

Suki hesitated for a moment before opening her mouth a little.

"If you don't—"

"I won't."

Quentin finished her sentence, his eyes lowered to show his understanding. Suki nodded to him approvingly, and Quentin reached back for his ARC.

"Okay, on my go, prepare for Operation Dancing Skies."

"1."

"2."

"3."

Suki was in position, ready to sprint; Odie aimed his rifle at the unknown dangers, Jerome took cover behind building walls, and Quentin stood in his ready stance.

"GO!"

Quentin and Suki ran together out of the window in front of them; Jerome ran out onto the street while Odie followed behind his comrades, shooting at whatever targets appeared. Jerome mowed down the cadets, forcing the RED TEAM to take cover. Quentin and Suki jumped from the window onto the next building, moving together and shooting back in different firing directions.

"They seem to be following the same formation they did yesterday."

Dahlia said.

"Same formation, same failure."

Cade remarked, nodding in agreement. Maverick looked at the monitor, focusing on Quentin specifically.

Quentin and Suki ran together, grabbing onto the side of the windows. Once they saw cadets on each side surrounding them, Quentin returned to his ARC.

"Operation Dancing Skies, GO."

Quentin jumped out of the building, positioning himself above the street below. He grappled across to the next building, and the cadets below started shooting at him until Jerome provided covering fire. Once Quentin reached the other side, he signaled Suki to do the same. Suki jumped out of the building, grappled onto the side, and Quentin managed to hold her grappling hook, which got her across to the other side. They both entered the window and repeated the process.

"What are they doing?!"

Curtis exclaimed.

"They're nearly getting shot at."

Maverick observed.

"Wait, they are drawing fire so Jerome can fire back, getting the cadets off their back. That was the issue they were having yesterday. They couldn't operate as a group and cover each other effectively. Whatever Quentin thinks, it's reckless, but he is taking away the burden Jerome is facing on the ground. Suki is taking Quentin's lead by protecting his back. On top of all that, Odie has everyone's eyes and hearts, allowing him to make calls to Quentin more effectively."

Dahlia explained.

"Hah, Odie is getting more cadets than last time!"

Cade shouted out in excitement. Maverick continued monitoring Quentin closely.

Quentin and Suki jumped out of the window and grappled back while grabbing each other's hooks, giving each other momentum to get to one side or another. Odie gunned down the cadets from the floor and inside the building while Jerome continued to shoot at each cadet he saw, taking cover inside buildings. The cadets looked back and forth, visibly confused about where to aim, while getting shot at from multiple directions. Quentin and Suki both noticed they were close to the command post. Quentin ducked down near the window while Suki fired back at the ground and areas where she saw cadets.

"We're drawing near the objective. Jerome, you will be a gentleman and welcome yourself in the buildings?"

Quentin said.

"With pleasure!"

Jerome replied, peeking out the window to see the entrance of the command building.

Jerome sprinted out of the building and charged into the entrance. The cadets formed a defense, shooting all their pellets, only to be met with Jerome's minigun shooting back and unexpected sniper shots from Odie, who used the smoke and chaos to his advantage.

"Suki."

Quentin called, getting her attention. Suki looked back at Quentin.

"Follow my lead."

"All the way through, Quentin."

Suki replied. Both nodded in acknowledgment. They ran together out the window. Quentin looked at the distance to the command post and then back to Suki.

"Suki, I'll grapple with you. Swing me to the building. I'll get you once you grab onto the side of the building."

"Yes, Quentin!"

Suki agreed eagerly, taking the lead and then jumping out with great force. Her distance was halfway near the building. Quentin followed along, grappling far enough where she could grab his grapple and throw him further. Quentin got close enough to the command post, meeting gunfire from the ground. The cadets were getting shot by Odie, who was nearing a sniping position in the command building. Quentin grappled the side of the building, looking back to see Suki far behind. He quickly got inside the building, noticing Suki's struggle.

*"Do you think Quentin will be there for you, Suki? Will he be there to save you in moments of stress, when you lose control of yourself, when you are in desperate times?"*

Dahlia's voice echoed in Suki's mind during her evaluation. Suki remembered hesitating but stared back at Dahlia.

186

"He will."

Suki affirmed. A grapple shot out of nowhere towards her above. Suki grappled onto it, and Quentin held her with all his force. Hearing footsteps approaching from the stairs, Quentin instructed.

"Suki, grapple to the floor below me, please!"

Suki nodded, and Quentin swung her back where she could grapple to the floor below him. Reaching out the window, Suki caught three cadets off guard and took them out with precise agility. She walked up to see Quentin leaning on the side of the wall, breathing heavily. Suki put her hand on his shoulder, grinning at him, and Quentin smiled back. They heard another heavy footstep and looked back to see Jerome stretching while walking up. Jerome nodded to Quentin with a little grin. They all moved up, taking out each cadet that stood in their way. Once they reached the command post entrance, Quentin returned to his ARC.

"Are there a lot of targets defending the post, Odie?"

Quentin asked.

"Oh yeah, there are a lot. There might be more defending. I can't get an angle on them."

Odie replied.

"Well, once we breach, give them a surprise party, Odie."

Quentin ordered.

"I've been waiting to hear that, Quentin."

Jerome said, following Quentin's lead. Suki joined them as they leaned against the wall, waiting for Quentin's word. Once Quentin kicked the door, a voice called to him.

*"Always take the charge, lead your comrades to the fight. You weren't alone in this fight. Stand firm to confront."*

Maverick said, patting his shoulder as Quentin let go of the railings. He watched as Maverick walked away, and Quentin shouted after him.

*"Who was the man you looked up to?"*

Maverick turned around. pausing for a moment.

*"Your father, Quentin. Your father."*

He said, giving a mini salute to Quentin. Quentin's eyes widened from the revelation. His determination was boosted by talking to Maverick.

187

Breaching into the door, they were met by multiple cadets already shooting. Quentin and Suki ducked down while Jerome provided covering fire. The cadets each took cover, but unexpected pellets came out of nowhere, realizing that Odie was sniping the cadets from the windows.

"They're covered; get them!"

Jerome shouted at Suki and Quentin. Both nodded at each other, moving to opposite sides and shooting pellets at the cadets in cover. Once the final two were down, Odie communicated to them.

"They're all down; go for it!"

In the distance, Odie howled in celebration, Jerome kneeled and put his hands on his face, and Suki waited as Quentin sprinted towards the command post machinery. With his ARC, he connected to the post and deactivated it. The red light turned to green, emitting a loud sound, signaling them all that they had done it. Jerome grinned and laughed in relief; Odie shouted in celebration in the distance. Dahlia, Curtis, and Cade nodded and applauded in the observation room. Maverick looked at the monitor, shaking his head to approve the results.

Suki walked up slowly to Quentin, hugging him tightly and catching Quentin off guard.

"Ooohhh!"

Jerome exclaimed, taking notice.

"What? What happened?"

Odie asked over the communication.

Quentin grinned a little but blushed a bit. Both Suki and Quentin adjusted their positions, ignoring what happened.

"It's nothing; WE DID IT!"

Quentin shouted back over the communication.

Suki, Quentin, and Jerome grappled down to join Odie. They all jumped in celebration, shooting pellets towards the sky with joy, shouting together:

"FIREBIRDS FOR LIFE!"

# Chapter Fifteen: The Excesses

The streets teem with people from diverse backgrounds, many accompanied by cattle-like creatures that resemble cows. They carry goods and make deliveries along the bustling thoroughfares. Parents stroll with their children, visiting various vendors to collect goods or simply allowing their curiosity to guide them. From a nearby corner, two masked individuals clutching bags observe the scene. One of them prepares to dart towards a vendor, bag in hand, but is halted by their companion. With a nod, the friend directs their attention to the intended target, revealing the presence of children and parents. The individual pauses, stepping back, and peers down to discover something has fallen from their bag—a cube-shaped object with a timer set for one minute. A child from the vendor notices the dropped item and rushes over. The friend signals for a retreat to the alley, prompting the individual to prepare to flee until interrupted.

"Hey, sir, you dropped this."

A voice calls out, interrupting their escape.

The person pivoted to find a child holding the object, their fingers poised on the button, initiating the countdown. Acting swiftly, the individual retrieved the object from the child's grasp, offering a nod of gratitude. With the object secured, they hurried away, promptly deactivating the countdown, leaving the bewildered child in their wake.

The two individuals continued to navigate the labyrinthine alleys of the Republic of Melancholia, passing by outdated vehicles, cattle being herded, meandering in the streets, and hurried commuters in route to work. Eventually, they reached a warehouse nestled amidst the bustling thoroughfares, identified by a sign reading: "Republic of Melancholia Meat Manufacture." The warehouse loomed overhead as they approached, delivering a swift knock on the door. It creaked open slightly, concealing the identity of the individual within.

"Who sent you?"

The guard doorman behind the door responded in a deep, resonant tone. The two figures exchanged a glance before one of them stepped forward.

"The Excesses, codename Romeo and Juliet."

They stated. Showing their badges with the names imprinted on their outfits.

"Ah, Romeo and Juliet have finally returned."

The guard doorman chuckled for a bit after hearing the response, letting Romeo and Juliet in. Stepping inside, they were met with the sprawling interior of the factory. Four floors loomed above, filled with workers in uniform going about their tasks—some cutting meat, others taking breaks, and a few disappearing behind curtains, their activities obscured from view. Ignoring the stares of the meat workers, Romeo and Juliet made their way towards the back curtains.

As they approached, two guards emerged, eyeing them suspiciously and noting the full bag they carried. The guards seized them both without hesitation, dragging them behind the curtains into a room where two men sat at a table.

"I'm telling you, when I spotted that metallic knight crusader, I knew it had to be the Melancholic Knight! Nerdhard."

One of the seated men exclaimed.

A fist slammed down on the table, revealing a muscular figure clad in a black muscle shirt. His scarred skin was marred by fresh stitches, and there were burn marks around his neck. With a bald head and piercing yellow eyes, he exuded an intimidating presence—Jax Maddox.

"Your actions are nothing short of amusing, Jax. I'm sorry, but this is just another failed attempt to prove yourself."

Spoke the slender figure across from him. Adorned in a heavy trench coat over a white-collar shirt and black pants with horizontal white stripes, he wore heavy black boots and sported a short haircut, his green eyes piercing through the haze of cigarette smoke as he regarded Jax with an air of amusement.

"Failure!? I was inches away from success! You shouldn't have interfered with our arrangement!"

Jax retorted, his frustration evident.

"It appeared to me that you were already struggling, treating the experimental ARC and the suit as mere toys, much like our crusader. It seemed more like a childish game than a serious endeavor. I had to intervene before our leader took notice. Thanks to your recklessness, URDT is now aware of the suit and the stolen ARC, jeopardizing our operation and The Excesses' as well."

The slender figure responded coolly.

"Our operation, or should I say your operation. You should be grateful that Mr. Mortis is still willing to proceed with your endeavors."

He added, a hint of sarcasm lacing his words.

"Of course, unlike you, I am not grateful for your brute force tactics. I have other activities underway that can yield far greater benefits. Your reckless plans jeopardize my operation and The Excesses' as well."

190

He concluded disdainfully. Jax Maddox leaned back, crossing his arms to display his frustration, while Nerdhard observed Jax's apparent anger with a hint of approval.

"Don't be so quick to anger, Jax. Your efforts were not only futile but unnecessary. It wasn't you who revealed the appearance of The Melancholic Knight; it was one of our spies who did the job for us."

Nerdhard remarked calmly, unperturbed by Jax's demeanor. Jax cracked his neck, the sound reverberating throughout the room, a physical manifestation of his agitation.

"You should consider yourself fortunate that I've been instructed to protect you by Mr. Mortis's orders. Otherwise, you'd be feeling the same pain I endured around my neck. Only this time, my hands would be wrapped around yours."

Jax threatened, his voice laced with menace.

"I'm grateful for your protection, though I must say, it's more sensational than I anticipated. With you safeguarding me, I can focus on my work without distraction."

Nerdhard replied, a hint of sarcasm tingeing his words. As the conversation unfolded, two guards entered the room, addressing Nerdhard.

"Mr. Wyatt."

One of them spoke out. Nerdhard turned to face them, displaying the wrinkles accumulated from years of smoking. The guards, dressed in suits and bulletproof vests, held rifles and wore gas masks obscuring their faces. Their weapons were pointed at the two masked individuals who were now kneeling on the ground, their bags full of explosives.

"Why do you still carry those bombs? You were supposed to deliver them to their designated location!"

Nerdhard demanded, his tone stern. The guards wasted no time kicking Romeo and Juliet to the ground, then forcing them back onto their knees as they looked up at Nerdhard. Jax observed from a distance, folding his arms with a sense of detachment.

"Sir, we encountered some complications..."

Juliet attempted to explain.

"What sort of complications? There shouldn't be any. The only complication here is why you both disobeyed orders—"

Nerdhard began but was interrupted by the voice of one of the masked individuals.

"There are civilians!"

Juliet exclaimed.

Nerdhard's gaze shifted to Juliet speaking out, curiously studying their masked visage.

"Civilians?"

He echoed, his tone betraying a hint of concern. Nerdhard slapped himself in disarray, a gesture of frustration and confusion.

"We were not informed that our target would be a local vendor frequented by families. There are innocent people involved! I instructed my partner to disengage from the attack. I am uncomfortable targeting places that draw attention to us and put innocents at risk, sir! I demand an explanation for why we were ordered to conduct this act!"

Juliet exclaimed, his voice filled with a mix of defiance and concern. Nerdhard stared intently at Juliet, his partner shifting uncomfortably but remaining silent with his mask covering his expression. After a moment of silence, Nerdhard stretched his back and approached Juliet.

"Get up... GET UP."

He commanded. The two guards seized Juliet and forcefully directed them toward a seat near Jax Maddox's location. Juliet complied, feeling the tense atmosphere enveloping them as they sat beside Jax. Nerdhard approached them slowly.

"Why did you join The Excesses, then?"

He continued to talk, his voice laced with curiosity and accusation.

Juliet's blend of confusion and fear opened his mouth to respond.

"To fight against the unjust power of the URDT, sir."

They answered tentatively.

"Yes, joining our organization means committing yourself to the cause. It means obeying any order we give, even if it means carrying out acts you may find morally questionable. But consider this: the URDT continues to implement oppressive policies and exploit other nations for financial gain. They are growing in power, and soon, they will become unstoppable."

Nerdhard explained, his presence looming over Juliet, invading their personal space.

"Even if you believe that committing acts of terrorism is wrong, it doesn't change the fact that the URDT will continue to operate unchecked, hiding their true intentions from the people. We are fighting against a formidable foe—a lion that preys on the weak, a lion that dominates our jungle, a lion that will stop at nothing to maintain its power."

He continued, his words heavy with intensity. Juliet felt the weight of Nerdhard's gaze, their eyes darting nervously between him, Jax, and their partner. As Nerdhard walked away, grabbing a piece of meat and placing it on the table, Jax and Juliet exchanged surprised glances.

"Here. Cook it."

Nerdhard commanded abruptly, shifting the focus of the tense moment to a mundane task. Nerdhard clasped his hands together, which heightened Juliet's confusion and unease.

"This... this, sir?"

Juliet stammered, unsure of what Nerdhard was asking of them.

"Just do as I tell you."

Nerdhard replied firmly, his tone leaving no room for argument.

Reluctantly, Juliet rose from their seat and retrieved the meat, making their way to the nearby stove. They ignited the fire and began cooking, feeling the weight of everyone's eyes on them as they worked. Nerdhard leaned back against the wall, observing the scene with detachment.

"What's your name?"

Nerdhard said after the moment, breaking the silence.

"Theodore, sir."

Juliet replied, his voice tinged with nervousness. Speaking as Theodore rather than his codename now.

"Theodore, a nice name. Do you have anyone significant in your life?"

"Just my family."

Theodore answered.

"A family! Then why did you join the organization, Theodore, if you have a family to provide for?"

"Because I can't provide for my family's needs. The job market in the Republic of Melancholia is unfair. Qualifying for a position with the URDT isn't feasible for me and my family, and—"

Theodore began but was swiftly cut off by Nerdhard.

"Don't say anything more. We all find ourselves in similar circumstances. I understand why you chose not to attack a local business that serves many families, yes?"

Nerdhard interjected, his tone softening slightly.

193

Theodore nodded in response, flipping the meat over on the stove.

"Well, I hope this meat you're cooking can help alleviate some of your stress. It's sourced from cattle on ranches east of Melancholia. We've infused it with a plant scent that aids in digestion and promotes a sense of calm. It's a creation of mine, developed when Mr. Mortis was still young and ambitious. No one has tried it yet, but I want you to be the first. Give me your critique of my creation."

Nerdhard explained, a hint of pride in his voice.

Theodore nodded again, grabbed a plate, and transferred the cooked meat onto it. The aroma filled the room, enticing everyone present.

"I can smell it from over here; it smells damn good."

Jax remarked, his expression softening slightly. The two guards lifted their masks, drawn in by the enticing scent wafting from the meat. Theodore grabbed a knife and fork, eagerly cutting into the meat, then took off his mask and took a bite. The texture was chewy, but a warm sensation filled his mouth as the plant scent coated his throat, offering soothing relief.

"Wow, this is delicious, sir."

Theodore exclaimed, his eyes lighting up with delight.

"You think so? It took numerous attempts to achieve the exact reaction I was aiming for."

Nerdhard replied, a hint of satisfaction in his voice.

"Really, sir? I'm thoroughly enjoying this; it's exactly what I needed."

Theodore responded genuinely.

"No, no, you haven't experienced the full effect yet. It's going to be quite the experience."

Nerdhard chuckled, eliciting confused looks from everyone in the room. As Theodore savored the flavor of the meat, his initial happiness slowly gave way to a distant look in his eyes. Sensing the shift in Theodore's demeanor, Jax moved away slightly, observing the scene with caution. Theodore's partner glanced at him, his masked identity concealing any discernible expression. Nerdhard approached Theodore, his gaze penetrating as he addressed him.

"I can provide you with more supplies of this meat if you're willing to deliver the bombs to their designated location."

Nerdhard offered, his tone betraying a sense of urgency.

Theodore's eyebrows furrowed, and he dropped his fork and knife, his arms resting heavily on the table as he stared into the distance. His mind wandered to images of his family—his two children playing happily, their modest home a symbol of their simple joy. But the photos soon darkened, morphing into scenes of financial struggles, marital discord, and the heartbreaking sight of his children witnessing their parents' conflicts. Theodore's tears began to fall, each drop a testament to his pain and despair.

"I can only imagine the pain you've endured, Theodore. You must have worked tirelessly to provide for your family and yourself. Joining this cause must have tested the morals you once held dear."

Nerdhard remarked, his voice tinged with sympathy. Theodore's anguished cries pierced the air, catching everyone in the room off guard except for Nerdhard, who placed a comforting hand on his shoulder.

"MAKE IT STOP, MAKE IT STOP!"

Theodore pleaded desperately.

"As you wish..."

Nerdhard responded calmly. Theodore's cries grew louder, causing the two guards and Jax to back away in shock. Nerdhard rubbed his shoulder reassuringly before retrieving something from his side and holding it behind Theodore's head.

*BANG

Theodore's head slumped forward onto the table, his lifeless body now at rest. Shock and disbelief filled the room as everyone processed what had just occurred. Nerdhard stood there holding a Glock, his expression unreadable.

"You two, get his body out of here. Notify his family that he was killed during a gunfire exchange at the local establishment."

Nerdhard commanded, his voice eerily calm.

"Yes, sir..."

The two guards replied in unison, moving to obey his orders. They dragged Theodore's body away, leaving a somber silence in their wake. The remaining individuals watched in horror, feeling a surge of emotions coursing through them but unable to move or speak.

"I forgot to mention that the plant is called Stupor Lotus, and it is found near the outskirts of the east of Melancholia. It contains active components that affect a person's hippocampus neurotransmitters, modulating long-term memories. It targets their worst memories and causes them to relive the pain in their past."

Nerdhard explained calmly as if discussing the weather.

He dumped Theodore's plate of meat into the trash, eliciting a tense reaction from Jax. Unable to contain his anger any longer, Jax marched up to Nerdhard and grabbed him by the shirt.

"What is wrong with you? His actions were disappointing, but killing a man with purpose crosses a line, Nerdhard!"

Jax shouted, his voice filled with rage.

"Why are you suddenly empathetic now, Jax? We crossed the line long ago when we started targeting high-profile areas. We've been crossing the line every day by disrupting people's lives. This is the attention we need to break people's trust in and protect the URDT. We must force them to relinquish their power and allow for a better government to emerge. Everything has a price, including democracy."

Nerdhard retorted calmly. Jax's grip tightened around Nerdhard's throat, choking him intensely before releasing him with a breath. Nerdhard fell to the ground, gasping for air.

"Don't expect to achieve freedom through these actions, Nerdhard."

Jax warned sternly.

"I will achieve freedom through my actions. They will be forced to give up. By providing the meat to the store, we'll make the locals blame the URDT for the operation. We are merely the disruptors; the URDT control our daily lives and dictate what we should have. That's why you cannot fail to deliver the bombs to this local business."

Nerdhard asserted, focusing on the remaining individual.

"So, I don't care if the local target is filled with people; it engages in illegal activities just like us. This is how we survive: we do what we must. Don't be swayed by their facade; they are only an obstacle standing in the way of forcing the URDT to surrender."

Nerdhard concluded, his words carrying a chilling determination. Nerdhard approached Romeo slowly, the weight of his presence looming over them. Romeo could only watch as Nerdhard's arm swung, the Glock following the motion menacingly.

"You have a second chance to prove yourself to The Excesses, or you'll have your final meal with me... Do you understand?"

Nerdhard's voice was low and commanding. Romeo nodded quickly, his heart pounding as they affirmed their understanding. Nerdhard turned and walked out of the curtains, leaving Jax and Romeo alone to process the events unfolding.

# Chapter Sixteen: Dust and Echoes Part 2

*April 13, 2125*

The day was as clear as flowing water, reflecting the dense colors of the skies, white with a pinch of blueness filling the void above. The wind blew against the trees, causing the branches to dance, dropping trapezoid-shaped leaves, and guiding them with the wind to their unknown destinations. The leaves levitated down, floating away from the skies, eventually landing near a person's shoes. Sitting on the porch stair, Aiko grabbed the leaves and inspected them closely. Ignoring the sounds around him, he let the void envelop him.

A tiny, subtle footstep approached him, but it wasn't enough to capture his attention. Leaning out the door, Anbu revealed himself, calling out to Aiko, yet his voice wasn't enough to draw Aiko's focus.

"Aiko! Inoue needs our help with Albie!"

"ANBU, COME HERE NOW!"

Hearing Inoue's distress, Anbu was prompted into action before glancing at Aiko, who seemed lost in his own space. He rushed past the living room and reached the kitchen, where he found Inoue struggling to restrain Albie, who was thrashing about frantically, attempting sudden movements to hit or kick Inoue.

"Quick, Anbu, grab his legs and hold him still."

Inoue urged. Nodding in response, Anbu reached over to Albie, managing to seize his left leg, but Albie's right leg struck Anbu in the stomach with impactful force, causing him to kneel and cough for a moment.

"SWEETY, ARE YOU ALRIGHT?"

Inoue exclaimed.

"Yes, just let me."

Anbu responded, using all his strength to grab Albie's legs and restrain his movements.

"GEEZ, Albie is overly aggressive for a five-year-old! Or I've gotten weaker."

Inoue remarked.

"Don't say that Inoue. You still carry more water gallons than I can."

Anbu straightened his back to show his strengths.

"That's only when I've had my tea and daily yoga. It's just been tiring managing the trades and—ARGH!"

Inoue's frustration peaked as she struggled to hold down Albie, attempting to place a thermometer close to his mouth, only to be met with more force pushing against her.

"Where's Aiko? I asked for the boy's help minutes ago!"

Inoue exclaimed.

"He's not listening; he's just dozing off."

Anbu replied.

"What's wrong with him? I need help to get Albie to settle down. I must check his temperature."

Inoue said, her frustration evident as she struggled to restrain Albie, her hand with the thermometer poised near his mouth, yet still met with resistance.

"Is that why Albie is acting up?"

Anbu asked, narrowly avoiding another one of Albie's kicks.

"I think so. It's hard when you have a boy who can't speak or even have cognitive understanding. That's probably why he's acting up like this."

Inoue remarked.

"We're not even helping since we're just restraining him at this point."

Anbu observed.

"Okay, hold him still!"

Inoue instructed. Carefully she inserted the thermometer into Albie's mouth, her hand closing tightly against his lips while Anbu held tightly onto his legs. They waited in tense silence until the results were ready. Inoue retrieved the thermometer, but as she did, she collapsed to the ground.

"INOUE!"

Anbu cried out in alarm, releasing Albie's legs, causing Albie to retreat to another room and peek at them.

"I'm fine. Is Albie, okay?"

Inoue managed to ask as she gasped for breath.

Anbu looked behind him to see Albie shaking in the corner.

"Yeah, he's just spooked."

Inoue leaned against the cabinet wall, still gasping and breathing heavily momentarily.

"These past weeks haven't been easy for any of us, but I appreciate your help, Anbu."

She said, putting her hand on his shoulder. Anbu nodded slowly in response.

"Having another kid to take care of, different from us, is something else."

Inoue remarked, looking over at Anbu and signaling for Albie to come over.

"It's okay, sweetie! It's over; you can come out."

Inoue reassured him. Albie's response prompted him to retreat to the dark room, leaving Inoue with a small sigh.

"Anbu, can you do me a favor? Take Albie for a walk later and have Aiko accompany you?"

She requested.

"I—I will."

Anbu replied.

"Thank you... I'll prepare supper and medication to soothe him. I just need a break, but later, take them out, dear."

Inoue said, expressing her gratitude before turning her attention to attending to Albie's needs. Inoue got up and walked into the living room, noticing Aiko still sitting where he was. Letting out a sigh, she lay down on the couch.

As the sun set, Anbu grabbed his bag and slipped on his straw-link sandals. Walking out of his room, he glanced at the other bed, feeling a pang of sincerity. He made his way out quietly.

"Hey, Anbu."

Inoue greeted as he entered the room.

"I thought you were sleeping, Inoue?"

"I was until I realized what time it was. I'm just glad you listened earlier. Can you also take our Thicket Colt out from the backyard?"

She asked as she got up and began to stretch.

"You mean Olive? Is the colt doing well?"

Anbu wondered.

"Yes, he is. He can help make the transportation of plume fruit easier. Now you don't have to carry it with Aiko. Speaking of which, go get them out."

Inoue explained. Anbu nodded in response, ensuring her request was met. He went to where Albie was sitting on the couch next to Inoue, then went to the backyard to retrieve the colt. The animal resembled a horse but had more fur and a long tail that swished around to rid itself of insects. Its fur was dark, not quite pitch black, but expressive nonetheless. Its eyes were brown and keen, with two horns pointing towards the sky.

Meanwhile, Aiko stood near the side of the porch stairs, gazing at the sky until he heard multiple footsteps approaching. He turned to see Anbu leading the colt with Albie riding on its back.

"Come on, Aiko, let's go for a walk."

Anbu suggested. Aiko looked down momentarily, then glanced at Albie, which Anbu noticed.

"Okay, if that kid is sitting with you."

Aiko finally agreed, nodding a little.

"That's fine."

Anbu replied, leading them to the front yard, where the plume chickens watched quickly, and the vegetables swayed with the wind. Inoue walked out onto the front porch to see them depart, carrying a small smile. From a distance to the left side of Inoue, multiple figures watched in silence. As the colt paced itself slowly, walking on the soft ground surface, Anbu held Albie in front of him, showing him the reins of the colt.

"Hold it like this, and we can stay slow, okay?"

Anbu explained while Albie looked down at the colt's head, observing the reins and leads.

"He doesn't understand anything you're talking about."

Aiko remarked.

"You don't know that, Aiko. Many living things do understand what's around them. It doesn't make them dumb because they can't speak."

Anbu countered.

"He doesn't even care."

Aiko retorted.

"And you?"

Anbu's question made Aiko fall silent, and he looked at the serene beauty of nature around them as they passed tall trees and alien vegetation.

"I don't understand why you don't help Inoue and me around here. You used to be happy and cheery, willing to help early in the morning. Now you're just gazing at leaves and the skies."

Aiko expressed in frustration. Aiko looked at the sky before responding.

"Well, I don't understand why we must care for the boy."

"Don't say anything about him. You shouldn't be talking since we're practically taken care of by our caretaker."

Aiko retorted.

"Well, Anbu, it's already enough stress as it is with Inoue trying to balance her trading, feeding the animals, and taking care of you and me. She isn't her young self anymore. She shouldn't force herself to care for someone who will cause her to get more stressed and worried."

Aiko continued, expressing his frustration. Anbu let out a sigh.

"First, Aiko, I am taking that step of being independent. I'm doing the work she can't do anymore. I'm doing everything possible to ensure she doesn't get up and work. But she does everything she can to take care of us. We're parentless, Aiko. She's all we've got."

Aiko scoffed momentarily while Anbu looked at Albie, who grinned while riding on the colt.

"I know he just came out of nowhere. He needs our help. Why can't you just understand that, Aiko? Why can't you just help? Sitting outside and waiting for something to happen isn't a hobby."

Anbu pleaded.

"No, it's not. It's just something I like. It makes me zone out, forget where I am."

Aiko replied, causing Anbu to sigh again.

"Just help us, Aiko. We need you."

"I won't. We've been working our whole lives, Anbu. That's all we do. We wait for anyone to pick us up or for our 'supposed' parents to pick us up. When that doesn't happen, we return to work and repeat the cycle. I'm tired of this life, tired of working for something we're forced to do."

Aiko stated firmly.

"Inoue isn't forcing you, Aiko. She needs your help. And in return, we get care and love, like a mom and dad would give. It's about working to keep what we have. I just wish you could see it that way, Aiko. Eventually, you'll be older, and there'll be a lot of responsibility we don't want, but we keep what we have, so our humanity remains with us. And hey, you might have to take care of Albie for us, too."

Anbu reasoned.

"What! No. I don't like him. I don't see myself like you."

Aiko protested.

"You won't; you'll be you. Just remember to hold onto hope. It will carry you out from where you're at."

Anbu advised. Aiko continued to look off into the distance, observing the passing scenery of distant mountains, tall trees casting shadows, rivers flowing down, and the wind blowing fast.

"Okay, let's head back. Inoue made us some supper."

Anbu suggested. Albie's stomach growled in response.

"I see someone is already hungry. Let's go."

Anbu chuckled. Upon arriving back, they noticed multiple figures surrounding the front porch. Anbu's heart pounded, urging him to lead the horse quickly back to their home.

"What's wrong, Anbu?"

Aiko asked, noticing Anbu's unease.

"There are men in front of our house. Surrounding Inoue!"

Anbu exclaimed. Upon closer examination, they noticed the men wore clothing that covered every part of their bodies, concealing their mouths and heads and showing only their eyes. One stood out, looking at Anbu but then focusing on Aiko specifically. His apparel was dark blue, with his eyes a dark tan. They all appeared to have traditionally made metal armor that protected their chests, knees, arms, and legs, each carrying a katana or a mini blade. The men turned their attention to the boys.

"WAIT. Leave them out of it. It's about me, isn't it?"

Anbu demanded.

"Yes."

The fighter with dark tan eyes replied.

"We only came to seek trading. We require supplies that can last us, and in return, we will grant you protection."

The man explained.

"Protection from what!?"

Anbu shouted, getting the man's attention.

"From wildlife and the URDT, especially the URDT, they have been known to scout areas such as yours, locating any living beings outside the Inhabitant zone."

The man elaborated.

"I thought they didn't care about us?"

Anbu questioned.

"They do now. With the recent actions of The Imperium of the Choleric making moves around here, it has bothered the URDT to the point where they want to scout and find their suspicions of resolve about the Choleric surprise attack."

The man explained further.

"They're not at war. 'The Treaty of No Killing Beings' was created to prevent nations from killing each other."

Anbu interjected.

"That was during the Nekrothian War back on Earth. We only have each other. We are barely surviving, while the ones in power remain untouched. That's why you will trade with us, guaranteeing our protection for you and them."

The man countered, pointing specifically at Aiko. He walked up slowly to Aiko, standing taller than him, and placed his arms on Aiko's and Albie's chests.

"We will trade, but our resources are scarce, and other traders are coming to us. We couldn't provide you with everything you need, sir."

Anbu explained.

"Well, I expect you to get to work. These supplies are needed immediately. We will be back. Our protection is needed, especially for the boys you care for. If our demands aren't met, there will be consequences. You'll have four weeks to prepare."

The man declared sternly. Inoue tried to speak but almost collapsed, causing her to cough. The fighter only looked at her, his eyes lowering for a bit, then glanced at Aiko, exchanging a glare. They all left on Thicket Colts.

Once they left, Anbu rushed to Inoue, helping her up.

"Are you okay!?"

"Yes, dears, I'm alright. We need to get to work."

Inoue replied weakly.

"We don't have to work for them."

Aiko protested. Aiko's words hung heavily in the air as he expressed his frustration. Anbu's patience waned as he tried to maintain composure.

"Don't start, Aiko. We talked about this."

Anbu interjected firmly.

"I'm sorry, Anbu. I won't—"

Aiko began to respond, but Anbu cut him off.

"Just stop, Aiko! Go wait out here if you can't help yourself. Come here, Albie, let's get some rest."

Anbu directed, leading Albie inside. Aiko could only glare from behind his mask as he went out to the front porch, where he continued to gaze at the sky while lying down. Inoue sighed again, feeling the weight of the situation. Albie walked over near Anbu, and together, they stepped inside, leaving Aiko alone with his thoughts.

The sound of machinery echoed faintly in the distance as Aiko drifted into a restless sleep, the void of his mind offering no solace. Suddenly, a shock jolted through his body, forcing him awake with a gasp.

***

*GASP*

Aiko breathed heavily, his vision still obscured by the visor of his surroundings. He found himself in the same room, suspended in place, restrained, and unable to move freely. Panic set in as he struggled against his restraints, feeling the familiar sensation of confinement and claustrophobia.

The sliding door opened, revealing the same woman he had encountered before. Her suit name tag identified her as "Saskia Collier."

"Morning, or almost afternoon. You're finally awake."

Saskia greeted as Aiko's eyes adjusted to the light. Aiko's gaze focused through the visor, zooming in where he wanted to see closer, momentarily startling him.

"Whoa! Take it easy! You've been resting for 2 weeks. I couldn't check on you due to Premier Acheron's orders. He wanted you to get adjusted to the suit calibration. So that is what we're going to focus on today. Let me tighten up some of your body parts so you can walk comfortably."

204

Saskia explained, placing her notepad on the desk and grabbing a wrench. She began tightening areas around Aiko's suit, causing him to shake a little from the sensation of screws meeting his skin and flesh.

"OOPS, I'm sorry! I forgot that this suit... is part of you."

Saskia apologized.

"What do you mean?"

Aiko questioned; his voice soft but audible.

"You can talk now. Your throat must have healed and strengthened up with the suit. The Melancholic Knight has many systems, all connected everywhere in your body. For example, spine integration is the main component of supporting your body and suit. There is also a heating system for you, regulating your body. I can go on, but I don't want to bore you."

Saskia explained. As Saskia continued to tweak his suit, Aiko felt it tighten and become less loose.

"Okay, I think we're ready to start. I'm going to lift you down. Once you feel your legs, you must be still. You must get used to these adjustments."

Saskia instructed. Saskia approached the wall, revealing a switch to set Aiko down. Once Aiko's feet touched the ground, he felt a sense of instability, nearly stumbling. Saskia quickly caught his attention.

"Easy."

She said, holding his chest piece and wrapping her arm around his back for support. Aiko's heart pounded, but he felt relief once he lifted his back.

"Good. I need to check your calibration matrix, so watch. Look up."

Saskia directed, retrieving a pen with a light attached from her suit pocket and turning it on.

"Look up."

She repeated, prompting Aiko to move his neck upward despite the heaviness of the suit.

"Now, look down."

She instructed, guiding him through the motions. Saskia observed Aiko's calibration percentage from the monitor near him as he followed her instructions.

"Okay, now look right."

Saskia directed, and Aiko complied, feeling some freedom around his neck.

"Now, look left."

She continued, and Aiko finally turned his head to the left, focusing on the light.

"Great. It may seem a bit silly that I made you look, but we're taking it slow and steady for you to get used to the suit for a while."

Saskia explained, her words stirring questions in Aiko's mind about what she meant by "for a while" in the suit. Nevertheless, he continued to listen intently.

"Now, let's take nice baby steps, not long strides."

Saskia instructed as Aiko felt the force against his legs, urging him to put his weight down. He struggled to move, but Saskia got behind him to support his walking. Each step sounded heavy and carried the weight of the suit. Aiko took soft breaths with each step, and once he made it across the room, he sighed in relief.

"Wonderful. You can walk around this room while I'm checking off some things."

Saskia encouraged. Aiko began to walk around, his gaze shifting back to where he had been hanging, noticing the hook that held him. He examined his body, noting the height difference between him and Saskia. Looking at his hand, he saw the metal plating covering even his fingers, but beneath it, he could see the black surface layer providing protection for his skin, gripping tightly. He then glanced at his arms, noticing a part that seemed to conceal something, prompting him to investigate further.

"Whoa, don't touch that."

Saskia exclaimed, rushing over to Aiko and grabbing his arm, panting from handling his heavy arms.

"Those are your gauntlets, hiding a blade."

She explained to Aiko, who looked at her in visible confusion.

"There's a lot to explain. Just don't touch it; it shoots out and cuts like butter."

Saskia warned before retreating to her desk to continue her work. As Aiko examined the texture of his gauntlet and the intricate work around his arm, he couldn't help but wonder why the gauntlet made his bones and body feel heavy and connected.

"What's in them?"

Aiko questioned.

"I'll let Premier Acheron explain."

Saskia replied.

"Acheron?! What's he going to do now?"

206

Aiko's voice betrayed his apprehension.

"He summoned me to see if you're well-conditioned and ready for your training in your new suit. But I came a bit earlier to check on you. I don't know what he will put you through, but from your tone, you hate it. He's your father, Aiko."

Saskia added softly.

"Not to me..."

Aiko muttered, his resentment evident. The door slid open, revealing Akarui walking in and approaching Aiko.

"Can he?"

Akarui questioned softly.

"Yes. He can hear you and talk."

Saskia confirmed, adjusting a bit of the suit armor around Aiko's knee while Akarui examined the suit.

"So, this is the suit he wore. It must be constraining your muscles and chest, Aiko."

Akarui commented.

"I don't feel much now."

Aiko replied quietly. Akarui sighed, her hand resting in her pockets as she contemplated Aiko in his suit. She then turned to Saskia.

"Is he ready?"

She continued to examine.

"Yes."

Saskia affirmed.

"Come, Aiko, and you too, Saskia, if you wish to see Aiko in action."

Akarui beckoned, gesturing for them to follow her. Akarui took the lead, with Saskia walking beside her and Aiko following. The echo of Aiko's footsteps resonated in the corridor, his breathing becoming slightly louder with each step. They walked through the corridors of URDT, white light reflecting off the walls as they made their way to the elevator. The hallway was devoid of personnel or engineers.

"Why is no one here, personnel or engineers?"

Saskia queried.

207

"Because we need it that way."

Akarui replied, her attention focused on her ARC device as she adjusted the knobs.

"How come no one should know about the Melancholic Knight's existence besides me?"

Saskia pressed further.

"First, we need the Melancholic Knight's existence to remain unknown. We were required to disband the Melancholic Knight program due to the defeated results URDT encountered during the Nekrothian war. After the fall of Earth, many officials and governments didn't want to allocate any more resources to the program, focusing their attention on rebuilding and reforming their government for the overall survival of humanity. Second, you are the only person we were able to hire. Many other armor smiths are focused elsewhere in the nations. Plus, you and he share a similar age."

Akarui explained.

"Wait, really?" Saskia whispered, leaning in closer to Akarui's ear.

"Is he older than me?"

She eagerly question.

"Maybe."

Akarui replied with a slight grin, causing Saskia's mouth to widen before she closed it upon realizing that Aiko was behind them.

They continued to the elevator, pressing the button for their destination. Aiko's towering presence filled the small space, his height nearly reaching the ceiling. The elevator descended, taking them away from the populated areas of the URDT.

Upon reaching their floor, they walked up to a sign labeled: "Exercise Drill." Akarui turned towards Aiko, catching him off guard.

"Aiko, we need you to be down there."

She instructed, pointing to indicate the direction. Aiko stepped forward to the window to see the vast expanse below, the window spanning an area like a football field. He gazed out, his eyes adjusting to the brightness.

"We'll be watching you from up on the observation deck. Instructions will be given once you're settled in. Okay?"

Akarui explained. Aiko didn't respond; he focused solely on the empty space before him. He noticed the elevator waiting for him and began to walk towards it while Saskia and Akarui headed to the observation room. Akarui activated the monitors and cleared the workspace.

"What made you want to see Aiko in action?"

Akarui asked.

"Because you asked me if I wanted to go?"

Akarui chuckled.

"Well, yeah, but asking you."

Saskia replied while leaning back and placing her hand behind him as she looked up.

"I guess to see how he'll do. It's just that…"

Saskia paused, catching Akarui's attention, though she hadn't looked at him directly.

"The suit isn't ready…"

Akarui leaned back as well from her response, stumbling a bit.

"His suit calibration is clear to go, but his Synara level is low. Extremely low! Akarui, I couldn't say no to Premier Acheron. He isn't—"

"Ready, I already know. Since the start of his commitment, I was worried about what would happen to Aiko. He made his allegiance to the URDT an oath to the Melancholic Knight. He can't leave, escape, or fight against it."

"Deal with the devil."

Saskia muttered, nodding to herself. Akarui nodded in agreement.

"Except the deal is supposed to benefit both the URDT, mainly his father, and Aiko. Aiko serving grants him citizenship, PSC, passing it to his close relatives for care. He added that he would become the Melancholic Knight if the URDT finds his caretaker."

"What happened to his caretaker?"

"I don't know much; they separated from the Embarkment Fence. URDT is still looking for his caretaker, I think…" Akarui trailed off, closing her lips and herself off from the response.

"He wasn't well from the start."

Saskia observed.

"He wasn't ready; I fear for him."

Akarui admitted.

The door opened, revealing Kenryoku Takako and Jabez Acheron walking in. Akarui and Saskia assumed a pose to welcome them.

209

"At ease. We're here to see him finally! Right, Acheron?"

Takako stated as he moved to the middle, where the command controls and monitors for his viewing were located.

"Is he checked?"

Acheron stood in front of them.

"Yes—Yes, Premier Acheron. I checked his calibration, motor function, and nervous system connections."

Saskia replied, her voice wavering slightly under Acheron's gaze but quickly regained her composure.

"What are his synara levels? You have it on your ARC.

Acheron pressed his tone firmly.

"Yes, Premiere. His levels are…."

Saskia trailed off, glancing at her ARC display, which showed Aiko's exoskeleton inside the suit, with various colors coordinating with different functional parts of his suit. Next to it was a circle labeled "Extent" surrounding a smaller circle labeled "Synara Sync Levels." with a small circle beeping monotonously, indicating his levels were low.

"Are low, Premier Acheron."

Saskia confirmed. A tense silence filled the room, with Acheron's stern demeanor casting a pall over the atmosphere. He clenched his fist slightly until his dog, Yasuka, started putting her paws on his leg, easing his tension.

"Let's begin."

Acheron declared, his voice cutting through the silence. Both Akarui and Saskia exchanged somber glances, their expressions reflecting concern.

# Chapter Seventeen: Learning never hurts this much

Aiko tightened his grip, slowly acclimating to his surroundings within the suit. He twisted his neck, feeling the heavy weight threatening to pull him down as if gravity had intensified its hold on him. His eyes struggled against the bright light, momentarily burning his vision, but the visor of his suit adjusted to brightness, providing a cooling relief.

"Aiko Ashin! The URDT is here to evaluate your condition as The Melancholic Knight. Considering the deal we made; your service is still needed. You have been given a second chance to prove your worth and honor to the URDT."

Kenryoku's voice reverberated through the simulation room, surrounding Aiko intensely.

"This is the Melancholic Knight suit, passed down from your father and now to you. It is what remains of the Melancholic Knight race and your legacy, Aiko. While your training and assessment have shown promise, they also revealed unpreparedness. Your unfortunate accident has forced our hand. We must evaluate whether you are fit to serve us or if this project is a failure. Instead of nullifying our agreement, we wish to see how much you have learned from your training. Specifically, Jabez wants to assess your synara levels. This will determine your synchronization with the suit. In other words, if you are perfectly connected to it."

Kenryoku explained, his words hanging heavy in the air. Aiko remained silent, his visor zooming in on the observation area to give him a clear view. He locked eyes with Jabez, their gazes piercing each other. Aiko could still hear Jabez's words as if he were being asked to forgive him for what he had done, yet he also heard echoes from the past, soothing his anger. Jabez noticed a spike in Aiko's synara level and continued to observe closely.

"We will evaluate your reflexes and agility. Understand that this suit is new to you. The prototype was light and quick, but this suit will put more strain on you."

Akarui said, noting Aiko's condition in the suit.

"You are barely able to walk but remember what was taught to you."

Aiko muttered quietly. Suddenly, a large pole appeared horizontally from the side, faster than the blink of an eye, sending Aiko flying back against the wall.

"Wait, we didn't give him a head start or any warm-up?"

Akarui exclaimed, her concern evident.

"There is no need for that. He well knows the warm-up he's done in the past. He should expect the unexpected with that suit; he should have already adapted to it. I need to know."

Jabez asserted, his tone firm, emphasizing the need for Aiko to demonstrate his readiness. Akarui wanted to speak out more, but Kenryoku raised his hand, silencing her. She stepped back, turning her head to Saskia, who shared her disbelief.

"Remember, expect the unexpected, Aiko. You should already have that in mind from your accident."

Acheron reminded him sternly. Aiko got back up, still feeling the suit's weight but now able to move more freely. He looked up to see them peering down at him, prompting him to survey his surroundings. Determined, he rushed to the middle, his heavy boots crashing as he sprinted.

In a swift 3.4 seconds, he reached the center, his cape gliding in motion as he turned to face the room's corners. He observed, his senses honed, ignoring his breathing and thoughts, focusing only on the void and the particles touching the surface.

Meanwhile, Jabez continued to observe the monitor, noting Aiko's synara levels were still low but slightly higher than before.

Suddenly, a horizontal pillar came hurtling toward Aiko from behind. He executed a backflip with lightning reflexes, narrowly avoiding the pillar but still getting grazed by a part of his suit. Another pillar followed, prompting him to perform a quick dodge. Jabez nodded to Kenryoku and then pointed upward, signaling for the obstacles to be increased.

More pillars emerged from all directions, overwhelming Aiko. However, his consciousness remained calm, and he reacted naturally as if outside the suit. With swift movements, he ducked, performed high-skilled rolls, and timed his dodges perfectly, avoiding the pillars from different elevations that came at him from all directions.

Meanwhile, Jabez continued to observe the monitor, noting Aiko's synara levels were still low but slightly higher than before.

"He's performing well, just barely in the suit, and he's already pulling off these maneuvers."

Kenryoku remarked, nodding toward Jabez, who silently observed Aiko's sync levels. Akarui sat near the command module, focusing on the monitors displaying Aiko's movements. Saskia observed from behind Akarui, her hand covering her mouth in awe.

"Saskia."

Suddenly, Acheron's voice broke the silence, causing Saskia to freeze momentarily.

"Yes, Premier?"

Saskia responded, turning to face him.

"Do you understand how the suit operates?"

Acheron asked her. Saskia hesitated before replying.

"Not completely, sir, just the basic mechanisms."

"Take a look at his sync level."

Acheron ordered.

Saskia approached the monitor displaying Aiko's sync levels, observing the pulsing circle indicating his synchronization with the suit. With every action Aiko performed, the levels fluctuated.

"A user controls their level of thinking, breathing, and focus. It's something we do naturally, but not for him. Do you think you could manage that?"

Acheron asked. Saskia shook her head.

"No, Premier. I am not particularly adept at acrobatics or combat, sir."

"Just be aware. I want that suit to be 100% functional and combat-ready for anything. Aiko must have every vital aspect of the suit working seamlessly with him. Understood?"

Acheron emphasized.

"Yes, Premier!"

Saskia replied, nodding in understanding.

As Aiko continued to dodge the pillars, he began to feel dizziness creeping in. Glitches from his mind and visor erupted, displaying fragmented memories of a forest area from Aiko's dreams. He saw his fist covered in blood and heard his own screams echoing through his consciousness. Lost in these visions, Aiko's focus wavered, and he failed to notice an incoming pillar, which struck him in the back and sent him flying.

The sudden event caught Kenryoku off guard, his expression showing evident surprise. Akarui's face mirrored shock as she observed Aiko, surveying the situation with concern. Saskia followed suit, equally taken aback. Meanwhile, Jabez remained unfazed, closely monitoring Aiko's sync levels as they dropped significantly.

"Aiko! Are you okay?"

Akarui viewing Aiko, her voice tinged with concern.

"Yes, just—"

Aiko began, but Jabez cut him off abruptly.

"Your sync level dropped, Aiko. What's the problem?"

Jabez's tone was stern, leaving Aiko momentarily speechless in response to his harsh words.

"Sir, let me talk—"

Akarui interjected, but Jabez silenced her firmly.

"Hold it, Akarui. We are here to assess his performance; sync level is our top priority. Failure is not an option you want to entertain."

Jabez stepped away from the communication, casting a meaningful glance in Akarui's direction.

"Send in the drones."

He ordered, prompting Akarui to return to the control modules and press the necessary buttons. Aiko struggled to focus as his vision blurred and his hearing distorted. The voices from his memories echoed loudly in his mind, drowning out the sounds of the present. But Akarui's urgent calls broke through the haze, snapping him back to reality.

"Aiko..."

"Aiko..."

"AIKO!"

With renewed determination, Aiko refocused just in time to see six drones hovering above him, armed with weapons aimed directly at him. Bullets rained down, forcing Aiko to dodge and evade with lightning speed. Despite feeling the weight of the suit and the pain from a bullet hitting his left knee, he continued to sprint, his movements fluid and agile.

As Aiko dodged the barrage of bullets, Saskia's concern grew evident. She turned to Jabez, seeking answers about the nature of the ammunition being fired at Aiko.

"Wait, what's in those bullets, sir?"

She delves, her worried voice tinged. Jabez remained composed, dismissing her concerns with a casual wave of his hand.

"Nothing to worry about, just minor pinches for him."

He replied nonchalantly. Kenryoku chimed in, offering his own insight into the situation.

"A Melancholic Knight is strong enough to withstand almost anything thrown at it, but that doesn't make it invincible. One of the Knight's weaknesses is electricity, which can short-circuit the suit's functions momentarily, leaving the user vulnerable. The suit's outer layer is a light alloy that heightens Aiko's perception, but it's not strong enough to take kinetic force."

With this revelation, Aiko presses on, determined to overcome the obstacles.

Saskia's question hung in the air, prompting Kenryoku to respond pragmatically.

"This suit is one of a kind and differs from all the other Melancholic Knights back on Earth. Carrying the genes of Armageddon and its need for its alloy does improve the user's ability and perception. However, the downside is that electricity can disrupt the suit function and the genes that enhance the user. The suit has only just been deployed and is still in its initial stages of service. Modifying it to resist electricity would require extensive resources and time, both of which are in short supply on this planet. We simply don't have the luxury to make such modifications. If you're eager to make changes, feel free to try, but be prepared for your challenges. Gaea resources are limited, and the cost of maintaining the Melancholic Knight program is already a contentious issue."

Saskia listened with a heavy heart, realizing their limitations in improving Aiko's suit. Meanwhile, Akarui remained silent, focusing solely on observing Aiko's performance.

As Aiko continued to evade the drones' attacks with impressive agility, his heart pounded in sync with his exertion. With each move, he pushed himself further, his determination unwavering.

Then, to everyone's surprise except for Jabez's, Aiko performed a series of acrobatic maneuvers that defied the suit's weight. He executed backflips and spin jumps with ease, effortlessly navigating the room. As he recalled his encounter with Jax, Aiko improvised a move he remembered, sprinting towards the wall and performing a mini wall run to avoid the incoming shots.

Saskia watched in amazement as Aiko executed the move flawlessly, leaving his footprints on the wall as he sprinted across it.

"He can wall run?! Despite the increased weight of the suit?"

Saskia was surprised by Aiko's movement.

As Aiko struggled to maintain his balance on the wall, the shots from the drones relentlessly pummeled him from all directions. Each impact sent jolts of pain through his body, disrupting his concentration and leaving him disoriented.

Akarui watched with concern as Aiko endured the barrage of bullets, her protests falling on deaf ears as Kenryoku and Jabez exchanged words about his performance.

"These aren't ordinary bullets."

She argued, her voice tinged with frustration.

"He doesn't have his gauntlet to defend himself, and these shots are more powerful than he's used to. He needs to be able to defend himself before he can focus on striking back."

Jabez's response was firm, emphasizing the importance of Aiko learning to take hits and retaliate effectively. Akarui's expression grew somber as his words sank in, realizing the weight of the situation.

Meanwhile, Aiko's gaze locked with Jabez's, memories of their previous encounter flooding his mind. His breathing grew labored, his body feeling heavier with each passing moment as the bullets continued to rain down on him. The echoes of Jabez's words reverberated in his mind, fueling his growing sense of dread and helplessness.

Despite his efforts to push through the pain and disorientation, Aiko found himself struggling to maintain his focus, his mind clouded by doubt and fear.

*"Where were you when I needed you!?"*

Aiko thought about when Acheron and he exchanged stares. As Aiko's adrenaline surged, he launched towards the observation window where Jabez and the others stood, his determination burning brightly in his eyes. Saskia's voice rang out in alarm as she observed his approach, while Jabez remained unmoved, his expression unchanged.

With a mighty leap, Aiko landed against the window with enough force to shatter it, sending a spider web of cracks across the window. His gaze locked fiercely with Jabez's, a silent challenge passing between them.

In a swift and fluid motion, Aiko launched himself from the window towards the swarm of drones that pursued him. He grabbed hold of each drone with precision and strength, hurling them away with incredible force. As he fought, he noticed a canister among the wreckage labeled "Caution: Smoke Grenade."

With a determined grip, Aiko seized the canister and used it to trigger an explosion, engulfing the drones in a cloud of smoke and debris. The observation room fell into tense silence as they waited for the smoke to clear, the monitors displaying Aiko's vitals and sync levels.

As the smoke dissipated, revealing the wreckage of the drones scattered across the floor, Aiko knelt heavily, his body shaking from exertion. Akarui and Saskia breathed a sigh of relief, relieved to see him victorious.

"He managed to take down all the drones."

Akarui remarked, her voice tinged with admiration.

"I expected him to cause more damage, but he showed remarkable control."

Saskia leaned closer to Akarui, her eyes scanning Aiko's vitals on the monitor. Kenryoku observed stoically, crossing his arms as he awaited the subsequent developments.

216

Akarui's gaze fell to Aiko's jaw piece, noticing something amiss.

As Jabez signaled Kenryoku to zoom in on the monitor, they observed Aiko's cracked jaw piece, from which steam was escaping.

Akarui's expression darkened as she realized the implications.

"His helmet is exposed to the outside air."

She explained.

"His focus relies on his synara energy, and the steam you see is his energy leaking out. It will disrupt his concentration."

Saskia's eyes widened in understanding.

"I see..."

Meanwhile, Aiko's breathing grew more labored as he looked up at Jabez, who remained impassive, his gaze fixed on Aiko.

"Unleash his gauntlet."

Jabez commanded, and Akarui quickly complied, activating the mechanism. Aiko felt a heavy shake as the gauntlet released its sharp blades, known as the Valor Edge. The weight of the blades caused Aiko's arms to drop momentarily, but he quickly regained control.

"These are the Valor Edge."

Akarui said.

"They will be your weapons from now on. Since you have shown the capability to take hits and evade, you must harness your energy and adrenaline with these blades."

Akarui spoke over the communication to Aiko, who looked at each blade before him, noting symbols on each one. On his left is the word "Truth" and on his right is "Justice."

"I think that concludes this session—"

"Hold."

Jabez interrupted Akarui, preventing her from ending the communication. He glanced over at Kenryoku.

"Have the runner and shooter been checked?"

"Yes, Premier."

Akarui's eyebrows raised, hearing unfamiliar terms.

217

"Wait, what are 'runner' and 'shooter'?"

She asked Jabez. Jabez remained still, walking towards Kenryoku's side and reaching for another module.

"While Aiko's calibration for the suit proved successful, Jabez and I have been discussing other possibilities."

Kenryoku explained.

"What possibilities?"

Akarui's confusion lingered as she glanced between Kenryoku and Jabez, who was busy messaging on his ARC.

The door near Aiko opened, revealing people in lab coats guiding others and a large, covered object. Two smaller covered objects were being pulled alongside it.

"Aiko's synara energy is why he's here. Without his energy powering him up, his results have made us consider other options."

Kenryoku continued.

"Perhaps even bringing people back from the dead. Jabez and I have attempted many times to revive the deceased, but it hasn't been possible. There have been exceptions, though. With significant resources from LYN, we've resurrected some of our old friends."

"What old friends?"

Akarui gaze fixed on the figure as the lab coats removed the cover, revealing a sizeable, mechanized suit with navy coloring on the shoulders and a black overall. Its helmet bore similarities to Aiko's but with additional attachments. The suit's legs and arms were more significant than Aiko's chest piece, and it carried a heavy backpack with various attachments.

"Deagmund!?"

Akarui exclaimed as the other covered object unfolded. It revealed a slim figure adorned with more armor around its legs and arms, sharing the same color scheme as its counterpart. The figure resembled Aiko but emitted a vibrant red glow.

"Ernaline..."

Akarui's eyes widened in shock, and she turned towards Jabez.

"If you're worried, yes, they're fine."

Jabez assured her.

"It's not about that, Acheron! It's about what I'm not aware of! You're experimenting with them!? Why?"

Akarui's voice was filled with concern and disbelief.

"Their minds are stable. LYN insists that they are ready."

Jabez responded calmly.

"You're using dead soldiers, Acheron."

Akarui retorted, her tone accusing.

"They were my comrades, Akarui. Don't you think I know that what I am doing is cruel? I remember them very well. I remember Deagmund's desire to continue fighting, even if he lost his legs. Ernaline was always loyal to the URDT and to me. Search parties found their remains intact. Preserving them was the only way I could honor them."

Jabez explained.

"And you're using them."

Akarui said, her voice trembling with emotion.

"They are still Melancholic Knights loyal to the URDT. They swore an oath just like that kid. I know them well, and they still want to continue the fight. Now, they can help him, so he doesn't meet the same fate."

Jabez concluded.

"Acheron..."

Akarui whispered to herself, sinking into her seat. While remaining in the background, Saskia was only confused, trying to understand the exchange between the two.

Aiko stared in confusion as both figures locked eyes with him. Once the scientists left, Deagmund extended its arms and fired upon Aiko, shooting a railgun-like weapon. Aiko blocked the hit with his blade, but the impact sent him flying back. Shocked by the unexpected attack, Aiko felt the impact reverberate as he tried to return. His heightened hearing forced him to look up, locking eyes with Ernaline, who delivered an uppercut kick. Aiko blocked the attack, but Ernaline's speed kept him on his toes while Deagmund continued to fire precise shots, blocking any escape routes.

"You didn't even tell him about them."

Akarui voiced her frustration over the situation.

"He doesn't need to know everything, and he saw them unveil their presence. He should already be ready for anything."

Jabez replied calmly.

219

As Ernaline's speed continued to challenge Aiko and Deagmund's precise targeting, it blocked any escape.

"Do they have a program installed? Deagmund's targeting is exact."

Saskia pointed out.

"Yes. While their minds are suppressed and dulled for now, the programs installed in their heads allow them to enhance their skills. Their training is paying off now because they were once Melancholic Knights. It's only a matter of whether Aiko can overcome their attacks..."

Kenryoku acknowledged. Jabez continued to observe Aiko's sync level, noting its peaks and valleys. Aiko, meanwhile, persisted in blocking and dodging, feeling his heart pounding harder with each passing moment. Despite the increasing warmth within his suit, he knew he couldn't afford to stop. As he evaded Ernaline's attacks again, he felt his focus waver, his mind slowing down under the strain. Despite stumbling briefly, he kept moving, dodging Deagmund's railgun shots.

"Not to mention, Aiko's focus is already breaking down from the damage he caused to himself."

Kenryoku commented.

Feeling trapped, Aiko realized that no matter what he did, he was at risk of being caught off guard. Nevertheless, he continued to dodge and analyze Ernaline's attacks. He noticed a pattern in her kicks—up and sideways—and schemed an idea. Timing his kick to coincide with hers, Aiko's greater weight and power forced her to kick back. Seizing the opportunity, he grabbed her arms and swung her around, hurling her into the air.

Ernaline responded swiftly, revealing whip-like chains as she descended. The chains' barb pierced and adhered to Aiko's arms and helmet, making it difficult for him to break free. She attempted to pull him toward Deagmund, who was taking aim at Aiko. Sensing the danger, Aiko countered by pulling Ernaline toward him, resisting her efforts to drag him into Deagmund's firing line. Despite her retaliatory kicks and whip attacks, Aiko persisted in his efforts to gain control of the situation.

Aiko continued to feel the warmth around him, but also inside of him, rising higher and higher. He felt the punches becoming numb from the constant strikes on his gauntlet continued to rattle. He focused on his gauntlet, realizing he could use the blade. After another kick, he prepared a blade to catch her off guard but was met with another whip attack around his arm. Using his strength, he sent her flying to the wall, where she landed on her feet.

Aiko locked eyes with Deagmund, both assessing each other's distance. Deagmund assumed a ready position, launching missiles towards Aiko. Aiko prepared for the explosion, his unfocused gaze reflecting the diminishing energy leaving his body with each passing second. Standing poised, he sidestepped, cleanly evading the missiles. His visor adjusted, coordinating with his eyes to track the trajectory of each rocket.

Deagmund toggled a switch on his gun and unleashed a barrage of bullets towards Aiko. A surge of warmth coursed through Aiko's body, channeling the energy through his arms. As the bullets closed in, Aiko's arms initially moved slowly but accelerated out of control. He instinctively blocked each bullet, his movements precise yet driven by raw instinct.

Saskia and Akarui marveled at Aiko's incredible speed in deflecting bullets traveling at high velocity. Jabez remained unfazed by Aiko's actions.

"That's insane. How is he able to control his arms like that?"

Saskia pondered as she monitored.

"He doesn't. He allows his energy and instinct to take control. It's a miracle that he manages to match the speed of the bullets, even as his synara energy diminishes. It's only a matter of time before he realizes..."

As Aiko's control over his arm waned, he shifted it around, heating up with each movement. Sensing the rising temperature within him and his arm beginning to overheat, Aiko struggled against Deagmund's relentless assault while Ernaline watched from a distance. Gradually, Aiko's defensive maneuvers slowed, his arms losing their speed. The barrage of bullets ceased, leaving Deagmund standing with his machine gun trained on Aiko.

Aiko sank to one knee; his body began to shut down. Steam billowed from his shoulder armor and helmet vents, his suit's lights flickering weakly.

"He can overheat himself."

Acheron concluded.

Aiko felt the heat engulfing him, constricting his throat. The synara energy from his mask dripped off and evaporated, making it difficult for him to breathe even with the mask. Voices echoed in his mind: "*Hold on to hope...*"

"Not again..."

Aiko said to himself softly. Deagmund and Ernaline studied Aiko's motionless body as it knelt.

"They're going to attack him again! Acheron, please shut them down!"

Akarui pleaded.

"He's done enough for this test run; please shut them down!"

221

Acheron remained still, looking at Aiko. Akarui wanted to run up and take away the Acheron's control module but hesitated. Saskia could only stand back and let the event unfold. Kenryoku stood by Acheron, awaiting orders. Deagmund powered up his machine gun, and Ernaline prepared to leap toward Aiko. Acheron continued to look, Akarui's voice echoing as she pleaded. He looked at Aiko's sync level, seeing a recent peak to the ideal level. He paused and looked down.

Seeing a woman in his head holding a baby, the woman's face was hard to see, but he realized who she was. Holding the baby with Aiko's mask. Acheron's eyes widened.

Deagmund and Ernaline were about to resume their attack until their black-colored own steam sprouted and poured from their backs.

"Acheron, you shut—"

"No, their power source ran out as well. Their source of power runs through a battery-like core that needs to be recharged. It's the cheapest but still costly source we could obtain to bring these guys up online."

Akarui looked over at Acheron, seeing his fingers looming over the button, seeing: "Shut Off."

"I see what I wanted. Saskia repair—

"Kenryoku!"

"What is it?"

Kenryoku's ARC plays the message from communication.

"We have new intel on The Excesses Operation. We request Acheron's presence."

Kenryoku, looking over to Acheron too, took notice.

"He'll be there in a bit; you will speak to me on this matter."

Shutting off his ARC.

"I'll check on this matter."

Kenryoku walks out from the observation, and Acheron turns around.

"Make sure his armor is repaired, Saskia."

Leaving Akarui and Saskia alone. They both look at each other, then at Aiko on the monitor. Akarui lets out a sigh.

"He wasn't ready. I wasn't ready."

Saskia wanted to speak but let her thoughts close, leaving Akarui alone with her thoughts.

222

# Chapter Eighteen: Feet onto action

Kenryoku and Acheron paced each other as they walked down the Military Command Center corridors, with a station worker following suit.

"When was this report?"

Kenryoku asked, facing forward but speaking to anyone willing to respond.

"Just a while ago. The Excesses members captured by the Maverick Battalion have revealed the location of one of their bases in the middle of the city."

The worker replied.

"Are these rumors true?"

Kenryoku asked.

"We're unsure whether or not they are telling the truth. It's only from their tone that we sense any sincerity."

The worker admitted.

"Who broke their will? Was it Maverick?"

Kenryoku asked, chuckling slightly.

"Well, actually, it was Captain Valentine."

The worker answered.

"How come we didn't obtain this information faster? We could've had days to prepare for this."

Kenryoku pressed.

"Sir, these members are deeply committed to their cause. They refused to reveal anything at first, only murmuring.

"I can't go back."

The worker explained.

Kenryoku paused for a moment, deep in thought.

"Well, next time, break them harder."

Kenryoku ordered.

"Yes, sir!"

The worker nodded. They all rushed to the operations center, where a large monitor displayed a series of rows with data from various districts. They watched over the operation, checking systems throughout the city.

"Everyone, report!"

Kenryoku's voice resonated through the room.

"We rerouted traffic from the supposed coordinates."

One woman reported.

"Most of the roads near the location are experiencing heavy traffic due to the evacuation orders, but the civilians are leaving the area."

A man added, clicking through his modules.

"Very well."

Kenryoku said, feeling pleased with their work.

"Sir, what about the recent bomb attack in the market area?"

Another woman voiced her concern.

"What about it? Send medical treatment and spare a few FIREBIRDS. We'll be playing into their hands if we focus all our attention on that. If this location houses The Excesses' operations, their organization will decline. Which battalions are available for this strike force attack?"

"Captain Curtis's Battalion is monitoring the city from the north district of the Republic of Melancholia: New Arcadia. Captain Dahlia's Battalion is conducting a regional expedition around Sanguine Province for a joint exercise with the local forces. And Captain Cade Valentine is on standby but stationed at the Embarkment Fence, overseeing The Imperium of Choleric."

The worker replied.

"What if we use—"

"We're not using The Melancholic Knight now."

Acheron interrupting Kenryoku response.

"His sync level is nearing the standard I'm looking for, but he isn't ready. His results against the Runner and Gunner weren't great. Order Captain Maverick to send in a strike force and use the best FIREBIRDS he has. Caution him that whatever happens is to be kept secret. Destroy the base by any means necessary."

Kenryoku commanded.

"Can we use Runner and Gunner, then?"

"Their cores are still recharging from their battle."

"Understood. You heard him, everyone!"

Acheron redirected Kenryoku's orders to the workers in the operations room, signaling Maverick Battalion.

***

Voices echoed between the walls, and pictures of Quentin, Suki, Odie, and Jerome celebrating with their certificates were reflected on them. Next to the image was a second certificate: "Certificate of Honor, presented by URDT to FIREBIRDS: Quentin Reily."

"No, no, I'm good. I appreciate your care, Yume. I just haven't been blessed with time to talk with anyone outside of the URDT jurisdiction."

Quentin, talking while listening with his earbuds wirelessly connected to his ARC. Yume appeared on the monitor of his ARC.

"Suki? Yeah, she's doing great. She's changed from when I met her; she was hotheaded, but now she's less so. Not to mention, with our new comrades, it's working out for us."

"......"

"So, how's Albie?...... That's good. Learning sign language, I see... Surprised that someone hadn't taught him where he came from, not even Aiko..."

"......"

"No..."

Quentin looked up and saw a picture of him, Suki, and Aiko together.

"I haven't seen him... He told me, too, that I wouldn't see him around. But I didn't expect it to be this long without even a glimpse of him. I've practically been everywhere in the building, but there's no sign of him... He made a promise?"

"......"

"To visit you and Albie... How long has that promise been? ......wow..."

Quentin's ARC shook rapidly, indicating another phone call, this time showing: "Mom."

"Yume, it was great talking to you. I got a call from my mother; I haven't spoken to her for a while now... Tell Albie and your kiddos I said hi... I'll still look around for Aiko if he pops up randomly... and yeah, I'll tell Suki you said hi... Take care... Bye-bye."

Quentin rolled his head around, looking down as he prepared to talk to his mother. He sighed softly.

"Hello?"

A murmured scream unleashed from his earbuds, prompting Quentin to take them off to avoid hurting his ears.

"Yes... Yes... and yes... You've described everything I did these past weeks. Minus being hijacked by an evil organization."

Another murmured scream forced him to pull his earbuds out again.

"I know, I know, I know. No... I'm doing what I want... Following Dad's footsteps."

He sighed.

"I knew you would be like this. Yes, I know what I'm getting into and what I'll face."

More unintelligible screams followed.

"I've become a FIREBIRDS... Mhm... I did it, Mom... I did it for him."

Quentin put his hand on his face.

"It's fine... you were worried about my safety... No... I won't end up like him. Just don't think about that, Mom... Talk to you soon then."

Quentin ended the call, leaving the silence in the room to surround him. A door beside him slid open, revealing Odie leaning against it, trying to fix his position. Quentin was stunned.

"Were you listening?!"

"Noooo. No, I wasn't... only the part about your mom."

"What the hell, man?"

Quentin put both hands on his face. Odie raised his hands to clarify his reason.

"Ay, listen. If it makes you feel any better, I always listen through the wall to Jerome. He calls his parents often at night, not out of curiosity but because of how loud he talks, like geez. It makes me want to eavesdrop on conversations if they're that loud. So, there's nothing to feel embarrassed about when talking to our parents, Quentin."

"It's just... it's been a while since—"

227

Quentin coughed to regain his thoughts.

"So, what is it? Not about my mom's conversation."

"We got our first new assignment from Captain Maverick; this one is serious. It's from the higher-ups!"

Quentin's face lit up with a mix of anxiety and excitement, feeling a surge of adrenaline.

"Gear up."

Quentin ordered.

Suki began putting on her gear, wrapping a dog tag around her neck. She tied her hair into a ponytail, fixing it while gazing at the mirror. As she prepared to wrap her hair, an image of a hand emerged out of nowhere, followed by a head leaning next to hers. She turned, showing her side and revealing a scar. Startled, Suki saw the image of a man with the same hair color as hers. She freaked out, causing her to hit the wall and drop a picture of her, Quentin, and Aiko. Regaining her composure, she continued preparing herself.

Quentin, Suki, Odie, Jerome, and selected troopers from Maverick Battalion gathered at the place where they had been introduced to the URDT.

"I selected each of you for an important mission. We have intel that The Excesses are active at the Republic of Melancholia Meat Factory. We don't know if the captured members are telling the truth, but our friend Captain Valentine, with his 'persuasive manner,' forced them to confess. Still, we have only a vague idea of the building's layout and no idea who is in there, so we are going in blind. Quentin's squadron will go with me while another group follows behind, watching our backs as we penetrate deeper into the factory. Odie will oversee us from a nearby rooftop, keeping an eye on the main entrance."

"More watching… yup…"

Odie muttered to himself.

"The URDT kindly loaned us some drones for this operation. We will use them to scout into the factory and stop whatever activity. Any questions?"

Quentin wanted to raise his hands up but lowered them immediately. Only Suki caught Quentin's movement.

"Good, let's get moving ladies. Valor Unto the Skies."

"Grounded in Courage."

Everyone saying the following line beside Maverick.

"Till our last breath!"

228

With everyone yelling together.

"Okay, head to the Humvee now!"

Quentin's squadron takes one Humvee. As Quentin is about to get in, he looks at the other squadron. Hearing...

"Here he is! One of us!"

Joule ran up to Quentin. Quentin didn't know how to react due to his mixed feelings. Joule grabbed his torso and swung him around.

"You made it!"

"Yeah…"

Quentin chuckled. Quentin stretched himself from the unexpected.

"So, you got this assignment. That must mean that Maverick was impressed by your results. I wish I had been there when you did it. It's insane how we met. You were just a little boy, and now you're already my equal. You know what that means??"

"What?"

Joule put his hand on his shoulder.

"My brother..."

Quentin only chuckled but ended immediately.

"Don't worry if you're nervous; that's normal. We all have to take that leap of faith; you'll get used to it. Well, better get going. We'll see you there at the destination."

Joule saluted him and left, leaving Quentin alone. Quentin turned his attention to the Humvee back door and entered.

The Humvee was designed to carry heavy plating armor around the vehicle. Two large tiles are on the back of the cars, and one is tied to the steering sides. Carrying out the navy with a greyish tone around the armor pieces, navy on strong armor while the base coloring is grey. Bulletproof windows offered visibility. Jerome moved to the back of the Humvee and the main gunner seat as he moved around, checking his surroundings. Odie sat next to Maverick, the driver, while Suki and Quentin remained in the back seat. Both exchanged looks of hopefulness with one another. The Humvees take the large elevator out of the URDT headquarters and drive off to their objective.

Quentin and Suki didn't make eye contact; the bumpy road pushed them back and forth. Hearing only the road from the outside surrounding their ears. Quentin's heart pounded as they continued to reach their destination.

"You're good?"

229

Suki broke the silence. Quentin only nodded to her response.

"You're not okay."

"I am. It is our first assignment."

"I noticed that you were going to ask Maverick; why didn't you say anything?"

"I guess I hesitated. I just think that we're heading towards a trap."

"What makes you say that?"

"The lack of intel about what we're heading into and what we're going to do?"

"Maverick knows what he is doing. He'll give us orders, and we should be fine if he is with us. This is why he probably chose us for this assignment. We did surprise him and the other captains with our performance, surpassing their expectations after we couldn't pass the other test. This shouldn't be new to you, Quentin. Risking your life."

"I know."

"You and me stopping the hijacked train."

"I know…"

"You and me passing our test."

"I know…"

This time louder from Quentin.

"And-"

"I know!"

Quentin responded a bit louder.

"You and me staying together…"

Quentin put his hand on his face from his reaction.

"Forgive me."

Quentin paused for a moment, following his thoughts.

"A while ago, I spoke to my mother. It's been a while since I talked with her."

Suki only listened, looking at his face intently. Quentin trying to put his words together.

"I left home without saying goodbye to her. I remember how angry I was, packing my clothes and leaving while she slept."

Quentin continued to put his hand on his face.

"It has been a few months since we've spoken; I lost almost all of what I was carrying. My clothes got stolen, I spent most of my credits, and sometimes I got free rides. And other cases slept on the street."

"Then why did you leave?"

"I guess I miss my father too much. He went missing in action, becoming a FIREBIRDS. It meant a lot to me. I dream of finding him, but simultaneously, I'm hurting myself by doing actions I want. Placing this burden on me to achieve more and get what I want just made me more guilty. We're doing this mission; I just don't know if we're going to return safely."

"Quentin!"

Suki placed her hand on his hands, easing Quentin's emotions.

"I get it; we both left home because of something we wanted. I don't know if I can let go of my past when I reflect. Leaving my family behind because of my dad, the trauma. I-"

Suki remembered the figure behind her when she was preparing her hair. Sending chills down her spine.

"We have each other."

Quentin said, reassuring Suki.

"Here we are; we're trying our best for ourselves. Only glad I met you."

Suki's eyes were a little widened, and she offered a little grin at his response.

"WE'RE HERE!"

Odie screamed from the front.

"You don't have to yell, man."

Jerome got down from the turret and opened the back door of the Humvee. Quentin and Suki both got up, and Suki got off the Humvee.

"Oh yeah, Suki."

Suki paused.

"Your mom said hi to you."

Suki paused to send Quentin her acknowledgment. Quentin followed out of the Humvee.

They parked a distance away from the factory, Maverick pressing a tiny module on his helmet and zooming in on each entrance point of the buildings.

"Okay, everyone, set your ARC for stun. We are to abide by the order of humanity, "no killing one another." Our population is growing, but we lost 75% of our race."

Quentin's squadron and the other squadron on their ARC set their input to stun, seeing a series of types of ammo that the ARC contains.

"Odie, you're in position?"

"Aye, aye."

Maverick, with his ARC, looked up at the building roof nearby. Odie waved at him.

"Okay. We've sent in the drones and follow suit. Be prepared for anything. Let go!"

Maverick and Quentin's squadron ran together at the entrance, with the other squadron following suit. Maverick signaled Quentin and Suki to enter through the windows. He signaled Jerome to remain with him. Jerome adjusted his minigun attached to his ARC, nodding to Maverick. Maverick signaled the other squadron to join him.

"Prepare for breach…"

Maverick communicated to everyone through the ARC.

"On mark… MARK!"

Maverick broke the door, rushing in while aiming his ARC. Jerome and the other squadron followed, running behind and observing around them. Quentin and Suki grappled in through the windows.

Upon breaching, no one was visible. The drone coming in hovered all around the interior of the factory. Through the camera perspective, Acheron and Kenryoku observed what they were watching.

"No one is present. I knew those thugs weren't telling the truth."

Acheron hears Kenryoku's anger. He watched as the events played out.

"Search; there must be more than this area if The Excesses members were telling the truth."

Maverick reaching for his ARC.

"Odie, there seems to be no one here, but in any case, if our communication goes out, signal the URDT Headquarters. Worst-case scenario, send for reinforcements."

"Understood; there's no one out here for the moment, sir."

"Very well."

Maverick walked and looked around as he observed while aiming with his ARC. They all walked around the building's interior, seeing a horizontal conveyor belt with spoiled meat. Quentin kneeled, looking at some spice on the ground, touching it gently but ignorant about what it could be.

"What is it?"

Joule approaches behind him.

"A spice, possibly."

"10 credits to smell it."

Quentin immediately dropped the spice and continued to search around more.

Suki notices the curtains, opening them to reveal a table. She finds a stove and refrigerator and sees more powder like what Quentin saw. She kneels to inspect it. She gets closer, but she slips, falls off, and hits her head on the wall. Hearing a hard bang of metal, she inspects the wall, knocking on it a few times.

"Captain Maverick! Come over here."

Suki calls Maverick over the ARC.

Maverick, making his way along with Quentin and Jerome, another squadron, follows suit.

"I think there is something behind the wall."

Maverick walked up to the mystery wall. Using a knife hidden in his sleeve, he sliced the coating off the wall, revealing a hidden gate with a keypad module.

"Open it up. Everyone, aim at whatever comes out!"

Everyone takes aim at the gate, and the other squadron member, with his ARC, starts hacking the keypad module.

"Clear!"

He spoke. The gate slowly opened, revealing a dark corridor leading to a set of stairs. The corridor lights were out. The squads cautiously made their way down in formation. As they traveled down, their ARCs started acting up, and Maverick's helmet started to glitch.

"We're losing signal as we continue traveling down."

Maverick shook his head.

"What are orders?"

One of them said. The drones lost their signal and fell.

233

*** 

"What happened?"

Kenryoku proclaimed from monitoring the drone from the tactical operation room.

"We lost a signal to the drones, but we still have audio."

One of the workers checked over their module's keypads.

"That would mean that they'll lose communication with us, too."

"They must continue the mission; we can't miss any opportunity. If we get any leaders from The Excesses, it will bring a big blow to their operation and leadership."

Acheron noted to Kenryoku.

"Get into their communication."

Kenryoku ordered.

"Yes, sir!'

The workers continue to type as the monitor only displays the audio of the events unfolding.

*** 

"We must continue the mission. Besides, I got Odie to call for backup if we don't make it back. Push forward."

Quentin gulped for a bit from Maverick's response.

"Yes, sir!"

"It is getting darker; switch to night vision."

Everyone beside Maverick pulls a visor that is transparent green as glass for their right eye on the side of their helmet. They can see everything in the dark but leave their other eye exposed. Upon reaching the bottom floor, they enter a corridor. They step and splash in several puddles; the smell from the puddle starts getting to them. The aroma of rotten material reaches everyone's noses.

"DUDE! What is this smell!?"

"Just ignore it!"

Two of the squadron members barked at one another.

"Put on your mask; they won't eliminate the smell but will help you focus more easily."

Maverick ordered everyone.

"He's so lucky to have that helmet."

Joule whispered to Quentin.

"He's our captain, just the best of the best."

They continued walking down, relying on their night vision to lead them to unknown areas.

"What is this area?"

Jerome, while aiming his minigun in front of him with Maverick.

"Sewer system, probably. It reeks of it. I do recall the URDT shutdown of the sewers for certain areas in the city. The Excesses must be hiding here; they're probably surrounding us. Just be prepared."

Both tightened their focus and continued walking.

The squads could hear the sound of water dripping from the ceiling. Rat-like creatures retreated, disturbed by the squad's presence. The squads looked for anyone hiding or anything unusual. They made their way out to a more open area, sharing similar aspects to where they traveled but in a circular shape.

"It seems to continue straight, push for-"

A bullet struck Maverick in his chest armor, the impact knocking him over.

"Formation!"

Maverick screamed out. The squadrons formed around Maverick, with Jerome in the middle, covering Maverick. Out of the shadows came a man wearing tactical clothing but wearing a suit over it.

"It's The Excesses, fire!"

Joule yelled out. All of them fired upon the members who were closing them. The members wearing tactical masks all ducked and fired with their rifles.

"Don't get KILLED!"

One of the squadron members was shot around his hips, causing him to collapse.

"I'm fine! GET THEM FIREBIRDS!"

Maverick yelled.

Breaking formation, the squads charged and fired upon The Excesses members, both male and female. The members tried to fight, but they didn't stand a chance. The squads took the members swiftly and precisely.

The sounds peak from the speaker, traveling to Kenryoku and the people working them as they could only listen to the ongoing carnage. Acheron remains still.

\*\*\*

Quentin used his grapple to stab a member on its tactical chest, with Suki coming in and dropping a roundhouse kick. Jerome continues to offer protection to Maverick as he regains his energy.

"Cover fire for me!"

Jerome nodded to his response. Maverick charged at two of the members, quickly changing his ammo settings. Changing the ammo type into shotgun shell but making sure it is for stun. Maverick aimed his ARC at the member's belly and began to blast them. Instantly leaving the members unconscious. Maverick kicks another member's rifle away and applies the same punishment to him. Joule, covering the squad member that was hit, was firing as they tried to reach for a wall. Members who are female fire upon them but instantly get gunned down by Jerome, who releases raining stun upon them. The firing continued until it slowly ended when a member tackled Quentin, putting his rifle on his face. Until Suki stuns the member and pushes him off Quentin. Both breathing heavily and acknowledging.

"Everyone, sound off!"

Maverick orders while putting down a member.

"Here!"

The squads check in.

"Any casualties?"

"Just one of my teammates, sir! He got shot around his exposed hips."

Joule was carrying his teammate on his shoulders.

"Okay. We can't communicate with headquarters from here. Joule, take him out of here while we round up The Excesses members."

"Yes, sir."

Joule was carrying his comrade out of the area. Suddenly, he felt a sharp pain around his knee, causing him to yelp.

"What happened?"

Quentin, taking notice.

"It's nothing; I've been having a pain around my left knee. All from the exercises, running."

Joule laughing it off.

"Are you good?"

"Yeah, yeah! I need to—oof."

"Let me take him up; you can recover here."

"Are you sure? He is pretty heavy."

"This is what being a FIREBIRDS is about."

"That's the spirit."

Joule grins at Quentin's response.

"Maverick! Quentin is willing to take my comrade up. I sprained my knee a bit; I need to recover."

"Very well, you heard him, Quentin."

Maverick and Quentin exchanged nods. Quentin, carrying Joule's comrade on his shoulder, felt the weight but pushed through back where they came from. Everyone started rounding up the unconscious Excesses members. As Suki made her way to one body by the wall, she started hearing noises coming from the pipes. She glanced as something dropped out and made a mechanical sound from the impact. Suki looked at the mystery object and noticed it was a grenade and that the pin had been pulled out.

"TAKE COVER!"

Suki yelled before the canister exploded, shooting out smoke. Everyone turned around to see gas coming from her side. Other pipes started and shot out canisters, which exploded upon impact.

"COVER YOUR NOSE, RETREAT OUT!"

Maverick ordered. Everyone started choking and getting smoke in their noses. It was too late for the mask to filter the smoke. Upon inhaling the smoke, it traveled to Suki's mind. She started seeing memories, memories of her when she was little. Vivid but blurry of a man slapping a woman, with Suki screaming in anger. Back to reality, Suki is screaming in pain. Maverick watched as his troops got consumed by whatever they inhaled.

*** 

Back at the headquarters, the audio started cutting in and out as the connection was breaking up. Only screams and yells were heard, leaving everyone stunned to hear heavy footsteps and a vast punch out of nowhere, which Maverick. Who prompted a return kick; upon impact, he felt the heavy armor of what he hit. Looking up, he could see a heavy figure. It was hard to see fully, but Maverick knew who it was.

*** 

"Jax..."

Maverick responded.

"Hello. Maverick."

Jax pulls out a fast punch on Maverick's helmet, knocking him out instantly. Jax, in his helmet, presses a button.

"Round them up now."

***

Quentin continued to carry Joule's comrade out, making it to the stairs. Upon hearing the scream, he stopped and turned around. He wanted to return, but Joule's comrade yelped from the pain. He wants to leave his comrade and return, but he knows his comrade is severely wounded. He continued up, but hesitation filled his heart.

***

Jax looked around and only saw an unconscious body on the floor.

"See what my plan can do, Jax?"

A voice from Nerdhard through his helmet.

"No, putting our troops in danger for this doesn't work."

"It doesn't work for you. We successfully captured URDT's best. I remember Maverick; I never liked him. Can't wait to meet him finally. With them here, URDT would be forced to bring him out."

"I await his arrival then."

"You will, my friend. Now all we can do is wait."

***

Back at the headquarters, they are left with static.

"What was that...?"

Kenryoku put his hand on his mouth.

238

"Gas of some sort. This must have been one of Nerdhard's traps. Should've known from one of our own men, sadly turned against us."

"We can't leave our troops behind. We must-"

"I'm not sending him. He isn't ready."

"Sir... if I may. The result has shown Aiko's capability with the suit. You saw his sync levels reach their peak."

"But his battle against the runner and gunner proved enough."

"From his encounter with Jax, he put the guy down. I see it before my eyes."

Acheron remained silent from Kenryoku's response.

***

Quentin made his way out of the factory, laying Joule's injured comrade by the factory's wall. He checked that the journey had not disturbed the bandages applied before their journey.

"QUENTIN! Is that you?"

The voice coming out from his communication on his ARC.

"Yeah, Odie, it's me!"

Quentin looked up as Odie waved at him. Odie grappled down from the building and made his way towards Quentin.

"What happened?"

"We were ambushed. Obviously, I knew this was a trap. Oh god, SUKI!"

Quentin tries to go back but is tackled by Odie.

"What else happened? WHERE'S JEROME?"

"I DON'T KNOW!"

"WHAT DO YOU MEAN YOU DON'T KNOW!"

Quentin pushes Odie off the side.

"I don't know; we survived and stopped The Excesses. I agreed to bring one of the squad members out to safety. I wanted to go back, but..."

"DUDE, DUDE, DUDEEE!"

Odie starts kicking the factory wall.

"WHAT DO WE DO!"

Quentin's silent gaze from the ground only made Odie panic more. Quentin thought about Suki and Joule and everyone else, but he knew he couldn't give up. His eyes widen.

"Contact Command. Open frequency to anyone; we need help."

"We can't go down there ourselves!"

"BE MY GUEST, ODIE; whatever happened took down everyone. Stop making me wor-"

Quentin gasped at the thought that they were all gone. Odie runs back to the rooftop, opens his ARC, and starts finding a connection to the communication.

"IF ANYONE CAN HEAR US! WE NEED HELP. REPUBLIC MEAT FACTORY HAS EXCESSES! WE NEED HELP!"

***

The speaker in the tactical operation room exploded with Odie's voice, reaching Acheron, who was looking down.

"Send him..."

Kenryoku looks at Acheron in distress.

"But have him wear a cloak. We cannot make Aiko's appearance known to everyone. Get Akarui here now! We need to make this operation fast and swift. The nearest reinforcement is Captain Valente, but it will be a while till he can get to the location."

"Yes, Premier!"

Kenryoku reaches his ARC and contacts Saskia. Acheron looks at the void for the monitor; doubt reaches him about the future that is unclear to him.

# Chapter Nineteen: The Cloaked Metallic Crusader Returns

Darkness covered the vision; the sound of the surroundings could only provide an imaginary vision. The sound of breathing chambered in, back and forth. Aiko could only breathe, feeling the steam coming out from his mouth but covering his face due to his mask. His mask's eyes continue to drip synara energy, dropping on his chest, flowing down to his neck, or evaporating due to concentrated steam. He could recall the scratches of Ernaline's whips, the impact of Deagmund shooting at him, feeling both of their attacks rattle his bones inside. He could feel the adrenaline, remembering how much energy it took from him. The memories. The memory he recalled during the training. A fist slamming on the unknown person only makes him shiver more when thinking about it.

"Just this spot."

Saskia used a welder to stitch back the suit's armor. Music was blasting out from her headphones, but without his energy, Aiko's suit prevented his hearing. She was standing on an unstable platform, trying to balance herself as she was repairing. Aiko could feel his arms a bit loose, as if he could move them freely from his restraint. His vision opened more, seeing the same room locked in, settling his heart cold.

"And there."

Saskia lost her balance and collapsed back, where the fall would injure her severely. Saskia didn't have time to react, feeling the motion play around her. Suddenly, she felt something cold and metallic on her back. Looking around at the corner of her eyes, she saw Aiko's suit arm holding her. Seeing the rope-like restraint attachment dangling from Aiko's arm. Gently, Aiko leaned forward and placed her down, where she regained her thoughts.

"Thank you, Aiko. I didn't think much that I would fall, even though this stool was unstable."

Saskia pants as she catches her breath, the sudden shock catching her off guard.

"I would've sworn I reinforced the restraints."

She glances back at Aiko in the suit.

"But I understand how much it bothers you."

She walks over to a keypad module and presses a button. The monitor shows the restraints, which she loosens, allowing Aiko to move freely and setting him down on the floor. Aiko loses his footing, causing him to lean into the wall.

"Aiko, are you okay?!? You must be drained. Just lean back on the wall so you can catch your breath. I'm sorry. I didn't think about how much you went through."

Aiko settled himself back on the wall, but he could at least feel his body moving free. He pointed at his shoulders to signal Saskia to lower his shoulder armor.

Saskia, taking notice with her tools, lowers each of Aiko's shoulder armors down. Upon doing so, steam continues to release increasingly.

"Wow…"

Saskia said to herself.

"I guess he made you work harder."

Saskia returned to her table, cleaning her tools after repairing Aiko's suit.

"If you don't mind me asking, are you and Acheron related?"

The name Acheron only upset Aiko, but looking at her, he couldn't ignore her question. His mind wondered how he should respond.

"He's just someone else…"

Aiko is speaking but keeping his tone of voice checked.

"I know that you and he both share the same mask. I just wonder if he is your father."

"He not! -"

Aiko checked his voice, regaining his mind.

"It's okay, Aiko. You don't have to share your past with me if it bothers you. If it makes you feel better, I can share about mine. If you want."

Saskia put her tools away and took her gloves off her hands. She continued to inspect Aiko's armor on the monitor.

"Really quick, can you stand up? I just need to adjust anything."

Aiko acknowledged her words. Getting back up felt like a fight, but he made his way into the middle of the room, allowing her to check him around.

"When I was little, I wanted to go explore the world; I wanted to know what was out there. I thought about how much I could do in other places, be in other places. I lived with my mom and dad on the outskirts of the Republic of Melancholia, given the dangers of traveling since this was when humanity was settling here on this planet; my

242

father discouraged me from traveling. He made me get into other hobbies, but the ones he found interesting. He repairs old vehicles and tools he can use; that is all I knew while growing up. Fixing and welding while I look outside the windows from my desires."

Saskia gently presses Aiko's suit around as she continues to inspect.

"Was he nice?"

Aiko softens, voice piercing out.

"He was. Back then. I, too, don't want to talk much about my father, funny enough. But I keep tabs on him here and there for other reasons. My parents were divorced when I was little, just due to my father's work, which my mother disagreed with."

Saskia backed off a little, from what she was saying. Aiko gripping his hand.

"I'm sorry..."

"No, don't be!"

Saskia responded positively back to Aiko.

"I didn't mean to share my deep past; I just wanted to tell you that I sometimes feel how you feel. I want you to know that it will get better in the future. You don't know it; the future is uncertain. Just hang on."

Saskia put her hand on both Aiko's arms, feeling the thud from his armor but warmth in his heart.

The door slides open behind them.

"Saskia!"

Kenryoku with Akarui behind him.

"Is he repaired?"

"Yeah, just repaired everything in detail. What is—"

"We need him now. Our troops are taken hostage at the abandoned meat factory in the city."

"Jax Maddox is there, Aiko..."

Akarui talks after Kenryoku finishes his sentence. Aiko's heart froze; he remained still and didn't move.

"Aiko, your mission is to stop Jax Maddox and another associate, whom we discovered to be another higher-up member connected to the leader of The Excesses. Nerdhard Wyatt is one of the former scientists from the URDT who left in the past. Now we

243

know which side he joined. The capture of these two is our priority. Aiko, you must complete this mission. Swift and decisive."

Aiko remained still, and Saskia gave him his space as he processed the information.

"And put this on."

Kenryoku throws a large cloak towards Aiko.

"The cloak you wore over your prototype suit. Your identity is only known by The Excesses and us; you can't be seen by the public or our troops. It is crucial you follow your order no matter what. This mission must be completed while you're hidden. We can't have the nations get on us again. Is that understood?"

Kenryoku finishes the instruction. Aiko lowers his head down, seeing the cloak. His heart and mind proceed the flow from his suit, knowing what he must do.

"We are communicating with you through suit Aiko. Get ready to set off."

Akarui shares her orders, and she and Saskia both share glances, acknowledging each other.

"We await your departure, Aiko Ashin."

Kenryoku left the area, and Akarui was about to leave until stopping.

"Aiko."

Aiko looked up at her.

"Be careful..."

Akarui's words softened Aiko a bit, following Kenryoku out as well.

"Wait! Before I forget, I need to add these attachments to your gauntlet. They will help you scale buildings and walls, making it easier for you to travel to higher places. I just wonder if your suit weight would allow you, but better now or never!"

Saskia begins welding the grapple attachment on the side of Aiko's gauntlet.

"Premier Acheron ordered you to have these. He just wouldn't let you use them before."

Aiko wondered if his father purposely didn't let him have the grapple, making his training harder or toying with him.

"Akarui should help you learn how they used them. You're going to need them. Okay, there!"

Finishing her last touches.

"Aiko, go get them!"

Aiko didn't say anything, feeling the sudden responsibility, grabbing his cloak. He looks at the door, knowing what he must do.

"Is he ready?"

Acheron standing behind Akarui and Kenryoku. All looking at the monitor.

"He is making his departure out the E-11."

One of the workers responded.

"Is his grapple attached to his gauntlet?"

Acheron ordered.

"Yes, sir. Saskia notified me before he departed."

Akarui checking over his modules.

"Acheron, are you sure Aiko performing a skydive down to the city is a good idea? The boy sure won't handle the weight of the suit."

"He will, Akarui. Even if he fails, the suit impact will protect him. He knows he can't fail this task. He will skydive to the area near the destination, make his way to the factory, take down any members, and find Jax and Nerdhard."

"What about the other troops? Captain Maverick, sir?"

Akarui shows discernment about them.

"What about them? Maverick is a capable man; his troops are fine. They are being used as hostages; they want Aiko. They're playing a gamble with us."

Acheron walks up between Akarui and Kenryoku.

***

"Commence the jump!"

The crew operator opened the helicopter door, holding his hand out for Aiko to hold. Aiko used the cloak to cover his suit.

"Go, GO, GO!"

The crew operator pointed out the helicopter door; Aiko, jumping out from the helicopter, is met with intense wind resistance and an extremely high fall. Aiko adjusts his position to dive, and his visor pinpoints his destination. Aiko continued to descend faster than ever. Aiko looked at his gauntlet, activating the grapple attachment. In which he prepares himself to swing. Aiko flew down to the nearby building to swing down safely. Once near the building height, he timed his shot to the building. Using the momentum of his fall, he swung across. His arm felt a powerful strike when grappling; he grappled onto another building with his other arm. Continually grappling and swinging to slow his fall. Once near the ground floor, he landed roughly, bumping into a nearby car.

"He got it..."

Akarui was surprised by Aiko's action.

"Those training from the FIREBIRDS helped him from here before the suit transformation."

Kenryoku chuckled at how much training Aiko had gotten.

"Aiko, head towards the area."

Akarui's voice reached Aiko's communication. He sprinted towards the destination, performing moves by the wall. Now, running with his grapple made it easier for him to traverse the area.

***

"WHAT DO YOU MEAN, RETURN BACK TO BASE?"

Odie voices his anger as he communicates with the URDT operator.

"You are ordered to return; Valentine and his troops are making their way. That is all."

The operator ended the call. Odie rashly kicked the side of the building.

"So what?"

Quentin asked.

"They are ordering us to return to base, saying that Valente and his troops will handle it."

"BUT THEY WON'T GET HERE TILL LATER!"

"That's what I told them, useless bastards."

"We can't stand around here, Odie; we must head back inside."

"And disobey orders, getting us killed in the process."

"We need to try, Odie! We have to..."

"I know Quentin, but we can't just—"

A sudden crash was heard near them, silencing Quentin and Odie. Forcing both to get behind the building wall, Quentin had his ARC drawn while Odie had his sniper ready. Both peeked over the wall side, seeing what appeared once the dust settled.

A large figure with a navy-blue cloak covering its appearance, creating a bit of fear inside Quentin and Odie, who are both in disbelief.

"No one should be out there, correct?"

Kenryoku asking.

"No, sir, everyone in this area is evacuated."

The worker announced.

"Proceed with the operation, Aiko!"

Aiko turned his attention to the door, opening it so hard that it tore open. Walking into the factory.

Both Odie and Quentin look at each other in confusion.

"What was that thing..."

Odie stuttering.

"Whatever it was, the thing is going into the factory. For what reason, I don't know...I'm going in."

Quentin makes his way to the factory.

"WAIT, QUENTIN, we were ordered to head back, and we don't even know what that thing is?!"

Quentin stopped slowly, turning around to Odie.

"Do you want to help Jerome or head back to the base carrying the guilt of not knowing if your friend is alive or not?"

Odie was about to speak but gripped his hand into a fist, looking up at Quentin. Quentin checked on Joule's comrade, then left him where he was down by the wall, letting him rest. Quentin and Odie then both proceeded to the factory, following the figure stealthily.

Aiko continued following the tracks left behind by the Maverick's squad.

"Following the track, they were last heard from down the stairs. We won't see what is happening, nor will you hear us, as the signal disappears; just be safe, Aiko."

Akarui gives Aiko information while he is making his descent down.

247

"How long until Valente and his troops reach there?"

"In 15-10 minutes, sir!"

The worker responded to Acheron's response. Acheron continued to look at the monitor as Aiko's visor displayed the ongoing events playing out.

Aiko continued making his way down, reaching the area where Maverick and the rest were attacked.

Aiko moves his arms near his face and opens his Valor Edge as he prepares for anything. Aiko, noticing the entrance in front of him, continues, and he dashes into the unknown. Aiko's visor displays an outline around him, giving him a picture of the area he is traveling to. Quentin and Odie slowly follow Aiko, putting their masks on and running when Aiko is too far ahead.

In the Control Room, Akarui and Kenryoku discussed Aiko's situation.

"There is no ambush for him."

"They have something bigger planned; we need him to spring the trap."

***

Beneath the meat factory, Suki, feeling like she is stuck in a time paradox, continues to walk through her thoughts. Vivid images and memories appear. She sorts out seeing herself when she was little; she stares at a memory of her parents as they walk together holding hands, with her following behind them.

"I promise."

Said her dad.

A series of screams and yelps woke Suki up. Seeing herself locked in chains.

"I see someone is awake finally."

Nerdhard's voice pierced out from the darkness.

"You can't see me, but you won't care in a while."

Suki wanted to speak but didn't have the words.

"Don't speak, little lady; save your energy. You don't want to miss out on the grand show."

Nerdhard got closer to her, and Suki could now see fully.

"Hmm, you look familiar to someone..."

Suki wanted to speak now but was caught off guard when Nerdhard put a sack on her mouth. This caused her to scream in the bag but inhaled the powder from the sack. Nerdhard looked before him, seeing the masked figure with the codename Romeo.

"This is your time to prove your loyalty to The Excess. Wait with the rest of the troops until I give the words."

Romeo only nodded and faded into darkness.

"Get ready, Jax."

Nerdhard is holding Suki around her neck and standing her up.

***

Aiko continued to run through the dark corridors until a gate blocking in front of him closed.

"Break it!"

Acheron, in the communication, ordered Aiko. Aiko, with his Valor edge, stabs through the gate, making an X line. Breaking the X shape by kicking his hardest, Aiko shoots pieces out from the gate. Aiko dashes in, readying himself for what is in, and sees that it is dark but open space around him. Aiko looks intently around him, his heart pounding with his breathing as he looks around. Kenryoku, Akarui, and Acheron see what Aiko sees, all observing for anything to happen.

"THE KNIGHT IS IN THE HOUSE!!"

A voice from the microphone booms up from him, causing Aiko to be startled and look to where the sound came from. Light flares up, blinding him and revealing where he is. He is in the middle of an arena-like battle place, surrounded by walls. Above him are Jerome, Joule, and the other comrades locked in chains, Nerdhard with his microphone in his left hand while his other hand carries a knife that is on Suki's throat. Aiko's heart paused; seeing Suki was a surprise to him; he began to pant more, preparing himself to attack. The Excesses troopers stand alongside, all pointing their rifles at Aiko, with Romeo standing nearby Suki doing the same.

"Hold on, boy."

Nerdhard, taking notice of Aiko's incoming attack, pushed his dagger into Suki's throat more. Halting, Aiko's footsteps were heard above him. Seeing Jax Maddox in the same suit, holding Maverick by the sides. Kenryoku, Akarui, and the others work in shock and despair from the troops chained up, Acheron clenching his fist.

"So, the rumors were true; you do exist. Who would ever think you actually came? Of course, you came. To see these troops suffer or to save them, I beg to differ."

Aiko steps forward, catching Nerdhard's attention.

249

"Make another step, and I'll give this girl a tattoo she has for the rest of her life."

Forcing Aiko to stop and stand still.

"Aiko, stay still!"

Akarui whispers to Aiko through his helmet.

"You listened? Do you listen more when I do this?"

Nerdhard puts his dagger away and pulls out a gun. Shooting one of the comrades on the sides. Causing Joule to scream out

"YOU BASTARD!"

Everyone remained silent and defeated, Aiko's body filling with the cold.

"Knight, put your blades down NOW!"

Nerdhard demanded. Aiko, looking at his gauntlet, pulled out his Valor Edge and threw it on the ground.

"What are you doing? Don't listen to him!"

Kenryoku gets after Aiko, but Aiko ignores his voice.

"What else is he supposed to do, Kenryoku?! Let the troops all die."

Akarui retaliated back at Kenryoku.

"Now, remove that cloak you hide in. We know who you are."

"Don't listen to him!"

Kenryoku barked at Aiko to restrain himself from listening to Nerdhard's demands.

Aiko relentlessly followed through, pulling his hood down. Quentin and Odie were both far away from Aiko, seeing his appearance from the light; both looked at what was happening. Aiko removed his cloak, revealing his metallic suit. Everyone looked at him, their faces in horror but in pain from the gas.

"There you are."

Nerdhard is happy with his answer.

"So, here's what's going to happen."

Nerdhard grabbed something from his back pocket.

"These troops are experiencing the effects of a substance called Stupor Lotus. I developed it from native plants found in the Inhabitant zone. My goal was to create painful headaches for people. Instead, people experience the worst memories of their past and suffer side effects such as long-lasting cold sweats and headaches. The Excesses' goal was to blame the plant on the URDT. Now we have discovered that this substance is found in meat transported from outside of this nation. Specifically, near The Imperium of the Choleric. Therefore, people would blame them, and both nations would start to squabble again."

Nerdhard sigh.

"But that goal is discarded for a new one. For you to die..."

Aiko stepped back a bit from Nerdhard's response.

"My trusty comrade Jax begged me to say he wants to fight you again, Knight. This time, by our rules. If you refuse to fight, the Stupor Lotus will go in these troops again. I forgot to mention that this substance can cause damage to the frontal lobe of the brain. Even if you win! They will still get the substance! The best part of this is that the hero never wins. So Melancholic Knight, Valor unto the Skies!"

Jax throws Maverick to the side, his unconscious body lands by the wall.

"Grounded in Courage!"

Jax jumped down on the ground, causing a mini shock wave on the floor. Jax posed himself, ready for the instance, and stared down at Aiko.

"Till your last breath..."

Nerdhard finishes the quote while stepping back with Suki now pointing his gun at her head.

"GET IT! KILL IT!"

All The Excesses troops shouting.

Immediately, Jax, in his hulking suit, charged at Aiko at full speed, prompting Aiko to dodge. Aiko looked around, realizing that he was trapped. Jax's suit was taller than him and hulking. Aiko remembered how he couldn't defeat Jax; his body continued to run cold. Jax continued to charge at him, performing powerful hammer arm swings that damaged the floor. Aiko continued to dodge.

"Aiko, you're not a match for his raw power. You have to figure out his weakness. Our reinforcements are coming over here. You can try to stall them when they get here."

"So does the Melancholic Knight identity. He must defeat Jax now or never."

Kenryoku interrupts Akarui, who has her mouth covered by her hand as she watches Aiko defend himself. Acheron continues to watch as he focuses on his sync levels.

"YOU SHOULD NOT INTERFERE WITH OUR AFFAIR, KNIGHT! THE URDT USED ME FOR THEIR PURPOSES AND NOT FOR THE PEOPLE'S; THEY'RE ONLY USING YOU!"

Jax yelled as he continued to pull in powerful punches that Aiko parried but could feel the powerful strength from the suit. One of his punches sent Aiko flying back; being able to react, Aiko saw an incoming charge that prompted Aiko to grapple slide underneath Jax and get distance from him. Aiko continued to observe and noticed that each of his body parts had an exposed opening, giving Aiko time to think of how he would approach him. Jax slowly walks to him, cornering him. Performing power swings, Aiko continues to dodge, noticing he is faster while his moves are slow, performing ideas in his head.

Odie, with his scope, notices them fighting.

"They're fighting. And there are a lot of Excesses troops there."

Looking up, he saw Suki being held at gunpoint by Nerdhard.

"Quentin... Suki is alive, but..."

"WHAT!"

Quentin grabs Odie's sniper away from him so he can look.

"No... we gotta do something."

"What can we do, Quentin? Just walk in?!"

"Those guys are fighting; we can use that to our advantage. We try to."

"Try what!? Get ourselves killed."

"Be brave, Odie; we'll figure out something. Look around for how they get up there."

Odie and Quentin look around; Odie notices a hidden door but can't open it.

"They must have gone here, but the door is locked and can't be broken through; it is reinforced."

Odie observes the door; Quentin, looking around, notices the vents above him.

"Look, Odie! We'll use the vents; these must lead near them. Help me up."

Odie, acknowledging Quentin's order, follows through. Quentin gets up closer, grapples, and manages to fit. He then grapples Odie up.

Aiko continued to lay blows on Jax's chest, realizing it was pointless. Dodging more swings and tiring Aiko out.

"Dodge all you want; you gave in…"

Jax mocks Aiko as he continues to pursue him.

Aiko is ready for another charge; this time, Aiko uses the grapple to launch up to the ceiling and lands on top of Jax, where he lands a series of fast blows on Jax's helmet. Jax immediately grabbed him, throwing him across the wall. Hurting Aiko back in the process.

"Aiko's back is compromised."

Akarui looked over his vitals.

"C'MON BOY, FIGHT HARDER!"

Kenryoku yelling. Acheron in the back continued to observe.

Aiko regained his thoughts and saw another incoming attack. Dodging once more and aiming his attack on Jax's back arms. Piercing his exposed part severely, causing Jax to yelp from that hit.

"Lucky hit!"

Jax retaliates against Aiko. Aiko dodges more swings using his cloak to blind Jax, giving Jax a powerful roundhouse kick. Causing Jax to stumble.

"Knight, remember what I said!"

Nerdhard puts more Stupor Lotus powder on Suki, causing her to yelp. Aiko wants to move up but is forced to dodge as Jax charges him with total, powerful strikes. Aiko dodges each arm swing and again uses his cloak to blind Jax. He performs powerful punches that increase in speed as he gets an opening on the Jax expose part. These affect Jax dearly.

"You may be faster but still weak!"

Jax performed more swings, but this time predicting Aiko when he would dodge, this time kicking Aiko around his chest, throwing him at the walls once more.

Quentin hears the noise and feels the rattling from Aiko and Jax's fight.

"C'mon, Odie, this is where the sound is coming from."

Quentin listened to the sound, feeling the rattling from Aiko and Jax's fight. They observed at another vent, Quentin seeing that they were above Nerdhard and everyone else.

"Odie, can you snipe like over there?"

"I was made for this."

"Okay, aim at his hand."

Quentin gives Odie room; using the vent opening, Odie aims his rifle with his scope at Nerdhard's hands.

"Don't shoot yet; we need a clear shot when everyone is distracted."

Quentin ordered while looking closely at Suki, his heart pounding extremely hard.

Suki continued to have images spawn in her head. Seeing the man walking up to her, kneeling, and hugging her. Revealing the same man that spooked her from her illusion when fixing her hair.

"I love you, Suki! I won't leave."

"Come back, Dad. DAD!"

Suki screamed. More images appeared, with her running around rooms. Making it to the room, where she sees her father slapping a woman. Upon closer inspection, Yume gets abused by her husband. Suki felt powerless and could only cry. The next image shows the husband walking out of their house with his bag.

"Goodbye."

"NO NO NO NOOOOO, DAAAD!"

Suki's screaming slowly echoed out to her reality. Her eyes could only daze, but due to her dizziness, she could only see a mere image. Romeo got closer, observing her, until stepping back suddenly.

Aiko continues to brawl with Jax, landing a hit on an exposed area that causes Jax to yelp from pain. Returning with predicted punches to Aiko. Aiko dodges more swings from Jax, jumping on Jax and punching his helmet in fast-paced combos. Jax grabbed Aiko and threw him once more at the wall, this time pinning his right arm. Jax proceeds to punch everywhere on Aiko's suit, giving him a dent. Aiko could only breathe, and his body slowly got hotter and hotter. Quentin and Odie could only watch; Quentin felt that he should help the figure, but due to how outnumbered he and Odie were, he hesitated. Looking at Suki, he said to himself.

"I'm sorry, Suki."

"His rating is dropping..."

Akarui said softly and slowly, realizing Aiko wasn't winning.

Aiko could only think and think, the same memory appeared. A fist flew up and hit someone. Only angering Aiko, he reaches out to his other arm. Aiko wanted that memory, causing him to scream in pain mentally and physically. The Valor Blades dropped suddenly, shaking, slowly moving. Then the blade got up fast, launching into Aiko's gauntlet. Aiko, feeling the blade returning to him, surprised him. Without pausing, he quickly stabs Jax, exposing part of his suit and causing him to stagger back.

Aiko was freed, but his right arm felt loose and damaged, but he could move freely. He reached out to his blades. Realizing that his blades can return to him.

"Aiko, go get them!"

Saskia's voice told him in his mind, and he believed she might have upgraded his gauntlet. Nevertheless, did he feel the surge of confidence reach him? His shoulders and jawline piece began to release steam. Aiko's anger had reached its boiling point.

"What the?! Troops go up and investigate! Besides you and you here, I need guards."

Nerdhard ordered his troops to take the doors from the side, pointing at Romeo and the other members to remain where they were. The troops rushed from the dark area that led them out from the stairs, coming out from the hidden door Odie discovered. Upon reaching the stairs, a troop was immediately shot down by the stun ammo.

"They're here—"

Other members get gunned down. Realizing who was gunning them down, it's revealed that Cade Valente, with his modified ARC attached with a revolver-like gun, was gunning them down. Shooting precise shots at the members one after another, stunning them. Taking down 6, Cade reloaded his battery cartridge and walked forward to reach Maverick. Valente's squad followed behind him; they were met by more Excesses members who continued the firefight.

"More URDT"

Nerdhard said to himself, looking behind him. He saw the gate. Aiko and Jax stared down, but he only looked. Both he and Jax charged, creating a clash and loud metallic hit.

"NOW ODIE!"

Odie shoots Nerdhard's gun off his hand, catching him off guard. Quentin and Odie charge in and dodge as the member and the masked Romeo shoot at them. Quentin tackles masked Romeo while Odie tries to stun the other member. Nerdhard's hand was burned by the shot, so he steps back. Seeing what is happening around him, both his men are fighting, and the Valente squad is having a firefight.

"They're coming!"

The echo from the hall is complex, with bullets echoing through the area. Seeing Jax and Aiko fight. Aiko's suit began to release more steam, and with his blade, Aiko dodged more of Jax's swings. Landing a stab through Jax's arms and slices. Leaving Jax to hold his wounds. Once seeing Jax standing back, Aiko threw his blades at Jax, one at his leg and one at his helmet. Damaging his helmet and knocking him out, causing him to crash and cause a mini shock wave. Aiko got on top of him, calling his blades back; he began to punch violently at Jax's exposed face, getting blood on himself.

"Aiko did it! And Valente and his squad are there!"

Akarui yelled out, Kenryoku and Acheron listening closely to the audio.

"Seems that Jax is down..."

Kenryoku said. Acheron continued to look.

"STOP!"

Jax yelped. Aiko stopped his punches.

"You win. All I wanted... was to get my revenge on the URDT that did this to me... Hurting other people... Knight... I surrender... I beg you for mercy..."

Jax's words reached through Aiko's suit.

"What are you doing, Knight?!"

Aiko looks up to see Nerdhard's hands out.

"Who defeated him…"

Back at headquarters, Akarui and Kenryoku listen closer, Acheron following suit.

"Kill him."

Nerdhard said.

Aiko's heart stopped. Aiko's blade was crossed on Jax's throat.

Akarui and Kenryoku, sharing the same reaction to Aiko, were frozen. Acheron got closer.

"Kill him; he deserves to die, Knight. Aiding The Excesses to hurt and kill anyone that got in our way. He hurt you, didn't he? Eye for eye! He is a criminal Knight. Bring justice to your nation!"

Aiko remains frozen, and everyone in the room looks down at Aiko. Quentin and Odie looked down at him. Nerdhard grabbed something behind him, gripping it tightly.

"KILL HIM!"

Acheron continued to listen more.

Aiko, looking down at Jax, could see his face. Being devastated by Nerdhard's words, looking at him from the corner of his eye. His breathing was slow, and his face was covered in blood. Aiko tightly grips his blades closer to his throat. Until the memory returned, the fist flew down, hitting down on someone.

"STOP!"

Albie's voice from the memory appeared. Aiko remained frozen. He pulled back his blades to his gauntlet, standing up from Jax, who was breathing more and more.

"Wrong choice, KNIGHT!"

Nerdhard, out of nowhere, threw a grenade from behind his back at Aiko. Aiko, getting caught off guard, got hit by the grenade impact at his helmet, sending him down to the ground. Quentin and Odie get distracted by the explosion; Romeo punches Quentin, and Odie dodges the sudden punch from the member and makes a quick stun from his ARC. Nerdhard and Romeo make their way out behind the gate. Quentin and Odie turned their attention to Nerdhard and Romeo and began firing at them; Nerdhard threw another grenade, prompting them to move back. The grenade and the explosion caused the gate to collapse, destroying their entrance. Cade and the rest of the squad, finishing their fight, made their way out, seeing the Knight on the floor. Quentin and Odie quickly got their comrades untied. Odie cuts Jerome's chain off and checks Jerome's breathing. Quentin made his way to Joule, cutting his chain.

"MAVERICK!"

Joule is making his way to Maverick, who is still by the wall. Quentin wants to check on him but turns his attention to Suki, breathing hard.

"SUKI YOU'RE, OKAY?!"

Suki didn't say anything besides gasping.

"Is she alright?"

Maverick's words came out softly. Joule holding Maverick by the side.

"I think so. It's that powder material Nerdhard gave!"

Maverick got closer to him, checking her head with his hands.

"She is alright; she needs rest."

Quentin, easing himself, calms down and breathes slowly as he looks around. Feeling safe once more.

"Surround them!"

Cade ordered his squad as they formed around Knight and Jax. Jax was still breathing but not fighting; he just remained on the floor. One of the Cade troops looked down, seeing Aiko's helmet piece fall off.

"GET UP!"

Cade ordered the Knight to get up. Aiko slowly got up, hiding his face. Akarui and Kenryoku looked at each other. Understanding what had happened, Acheron, hitting on the module, made his way out the door, leaving both of them.

257

Aiko got up, revealing his identity and blue mask to them, causing Cade and his comrade to put their ARC down. Aiko turned around to see Quentin and others. Quentin, noticing the Knight getting up, saw Aiko's mask. Both Aiko and Quentin's hearts froze, and they exchanged looks.

"Aiko?"

Quentin said.

# Chapter Twenty: Prove your Oath

"Premier Acheron. This was due to an incident involving the discovery of The Excesses' lair. Not only did one of the leaders escape, but the URDT operation can't be trusted anymore."

The leader of Phlegmatic proclaims through her hologram. The leaders of Sanguine and Choleric have their identities disguised, aside from their voices. They surround Acheron while LYN, from above, displays images for the following discussion.

Images from the media capture a cloaked figure wandering around the city.

"While you ordered a full evacuation, some people did not listen to the orders well. You brought the Melancholic Knight program back, Acheron. Do you realize that broke the trust? Do you realize the consequences of breaking the trust within our nations and breaking a law forbidding the program to return?"

"The program proved to be a failure once the Nekrothian's Armageddons proved too much for the Knights, resulting in the demise of 75% of the human population. Resources were pulled just for the program, taking away funds and materials to continue the program. It's too costly."

The Sanguine leader, with his assistants, spoke out against Acheron.

"I understand."

Acheron announces.

"Do you? With all that was presented for today. Acheron, you are suspended from leadership at this moment. We will occupy the nation while a new leader is selected-"

"You're not..."

Acheron interrupts the Phlegmatic leader.

"Excuse me-"

"You heard me. You're not."

"What is this act, Acheron? You're doing?"

"You never heard my plea."

The rest of the leaders look at each other.

"Proceed."

The Phlegmatic leader sighed at his response.

"The following action did break our trust; I have recognized that since the beginning and followed through. These actions were required to eliminate The Excesses activities plaguing my nation. Due to our human population rising steadily, many URDT FIREBIRDS are stretched out to patrol in your nations. Even with our troops monitoring and patrolling my nation, The Excesses have broken the law that no human kills its own kind. Not risking any more innocent lives, we recently discovered my—"

Acheron paused. In the background, Akarui and Kenryoku listen.

"Son..."

Akarui said to herself while thinking about what Acheron was going to say.

"Client. Having a Harmonian mask, containing pure synara energy that saved the human from extinction. Without wasting any opportunity, I sought to make the client a deal. The deal was to acquire his service to URDT, thus initiating the Melancholic Knight program I spearheaded. In exchange for the URDT to find their significant one."

"Hmmm. Have there been programs to find his significant one?"

The Sanguine nation assistant asked.

"No. Not yet."

Akarui's eyes widened, and her hand slowly gripped into a fist from his response.

"Due to the numerous illegal crossings from our embarkment fences and the mix of identity from the process of detaining, it is tough to detect the client's significant other."

"I see."

The Phlegmatic leader rubbed her chin.

"The client has been trained through the FIREBIRDS program and The Melancholic Knight Program, learning the art of warfare. The client was prepared enough to take on one of the leaders from The Excesses."

On the monitor, it displays Jax's face with the text next to him: "Jax Maddox: Former URDT weapon master."

"We could not waste any opportunity to stop The Excesses. But our mission backfired, resulting in the client being forced to give up the prototype after it suffered major damage, and he was injured. To save his life, he was inserted into the Melancholic Knight suit. He is now adapting to it. It was that or abandon the program. We need to continue the program since The Excesses still threaten our nation."

"Is there any progress in eliminating The Excesses?"

"We made progress. Destroying their base of operation and capturing Jax Maddox in the process, with the combined efforts of the FIREBIRDS and The Melancholic Knight, we are making our nation safer once more. As we speak, Jax is getting checked by Captain Maverick, who was part of the operation. The client is being repaired as well."

"Would we know if this threat gets eliminated?"

The Choleric leader proclaimed. Everyone is paying attention to the hologram.

"Getting an answer from Jax is our hope for finding their main leader; we still don't know the leader's identity."

"Nerdhard escaped. What if he wreaks more havoc in the Phlegmatic? We would also be forced to use our nation's military to counter this threat."

"You don't have jurisdiction to cross into our nation. And our intel has more to worry about with The Imperium of the Choleric activities spending near the inhabitant zone."

"You must understand that our intention isn't a threat; surviving is key, Acheron. We send parties to trade with locals and harvest vegetation on those lands. We have no military reason to enter your nation; there is no interest in starting a war with you."

Acheron glared at the Choleric hologram.

"Case in point, the Choleric leader is right, Acheron. We can't let The Excesses activities also reach our nation, nor can we let you continue your Melancholic Knight program."

Acheron looked down from her response. Kenryoku and Akarui look at him nervously for his subsequent reaction.

"Expect the withdrawal of our troops from your nations. If I can't conduct my operation, I can't guarantee you any safety if I am not free to do my work."

"You can't!"

"I can!"

Acheron snaps back at the Phlegmatic leader, stunning everyone in the room.

"Our forces are there to protect your nation from any attack. I can easily take that away; my trust is already broken due to my plea not being considered seriously."

"OK, WAIT!"

The Phlegmatic leader and the Sanguine leader said.

"You may continue the program, but only for The Excesses. Our trade has been slow due to your lies since the beginning of the first meeting. You only have time to stop The Excesses. We need more progress, not more resources taken away. Farewell."

The Phlegmatic leader and the Sanguine leader leave the hologram.

"Let hope you can keep to your promise, Acheron."

The Imperium of the Choleric snarled at Acheron and left as well.

Acheron kneeled, starting to cough, which caused Kenryoku and Akarui to rush over.

"Are you OK? Take your pills."

"I will! I need to-"

Acheron slowly stood up and yelled with his sore throat.

"LYN, is the prototype Melancholic Knight suit modified yet?"

"Yes, it is on standby."

Lycoris responded with an image of the suit but did not reveal the suit design closely.

"WAIT, YOU'RE DOING THIS NOW?! ACHERON, I FORBID YOU!"

"You listen to me, Kenryoku! I must, and I will. You are to listen to every order I give. No matter what happens!"

Akarui stood back slowly, confused about what they were talking about.

"Akarui, head back to the simulation room. Ordered Aiko's presence to be there at once."

Acheron ordered Akarui; she didn't want to listen but knew she couldn't ignore his lead decision. She walked away, making her way to the elevator. Her face swelled up, thinking about what Acheron would do to Aiko.

***

The jail doors echo as Jax talks. Maverick, who is listening, is leaning near the jail door. Due to his injury from Jax, Maverick's helmet is still cracked, and bandages are wrapped around his chest and legs.

"You did a number on me."

"I know..."

Maverick and Jax exchange words.

"What happened to you, Jax? I remember how much potential you had. They would have given you a spot as a team leader of any FIREBIRDS."

"The Refugee Point event happened, Maverick."

262

Jax touched the bandages around his face that covered the injuries from his fight with Aiko.

"When we were forming our colonies on Gaea, I was told by the URDT higher-ups that there would be an operation near the south of the Melancholia. During The Excesses creation, a firefight took place near Refugee Point. I was ordered to give heavy artillery by one of my commanding officers. The base was far from the Refugee Point. Little did I realize that he was wrong; he had ordered those artillery to strike at the Refugee Point, believing The Excesses were hiding out there. He was wrong; innocent lives were taken, Maverick. Do you understand that?!"

Jax gets up furiously.

"I do. I remember the commander breaking the law of humans killing their own race and the backlash we received. He is in prison if you want to know."

"Maverick. I want justice! Putting someone behind bars isn't justice for the lives taken. The only reason I'm willing to tell you everything is Nerdhard's betrayal. I know that my uses of The Excesses are of no importance now; I am broken."

"And what you're doing is right. You make no difference between us and Excesses. That organization will kill innocent people; you joined that organization."

"I only joined to fight against that injustice; it still plagues the URDT Maverick. You don't know it. I want justice for the lives lost."

"You will. Not like this."

Jax represses his anger and sits back, and Maverick relaxes. He goes on his ARC, ready to tap on the record.

"Where is Nerdhard going, Jax?"

"That slime traitor. I don't know; he never shared his plans with me. We didn't see eye to eye."

"C'mon, any clue of the activities he planned?"

"Look! I can only assume he probably met our boss at their base."

"And where is their base located?"

"It varies; they start moving to different areas to get the URDT off their back. I can't tell for sure."

Maverick shook his head in disapproval.

"What is the boss's name?"

Jax got up, towering over Maverick, leaning in.

263

"Mr. Mortis."

"Mr. Mortis?"

"Even though I don't know him, Nerdhard tried to keep me from any communication with him. I'm too low ranked to talk to someone at his level. No one besides him should know about Mr. Mortis."

"And you serve a leader you don't know; he is probably no different than that URDT commander you served."

Maverick walks out.

"Wait, Maverick!"

Maverick paused.

"I want justice for people, for my action to be forgiven!"

"You will. By serving your time here. I guarantee you that is your forgiveness."

Maverick walked out, leaving Jax alone in his cell. Upon entering the elevator, he reached for his ARC. Scrolling down the names, he found Quentin's name and called him.

***

Quentin only stared at the ceiling; he continued to gaze more intently as he thought. Remembering meeting Aiko for the first time, a person who stands out from the crowd wearing his mask. Albie was with him, and it felt like years since they last saw each other. Cut to now, Quentin checking on Suki's condition turned his attention to where Valente's squad was surrounding the hospital ward. A prominent metallic figure stood up to look around. This caused the squad to raise to ARCs in confusion about the figure's identity and then pay attention to Quentin. Both locking looks, long-lost friends reunited unusually.

"Aiko."

He remembered saying and repeating the exact words while waiting alongside Suki, who was resting from her ordeal. The hospital room was like the one Aiko was in after the train incident.

Suki's mind ran around, too, seeing memories of her father's abuse.

"I promise."

Quentin said to her.

"Leave those memories behind."

Then, Suki remembered training with Quentin and his abandoning leaving her alone.

Suki gasps out loud, looking around frantically.

"Suki, it's OK!"

Quentin was taken off guard by her sudden awakening. She turned to him.

"Where are we?"

"Hospital center. Odie and I came to rescue you, and Cade brought his squad to help us. We made it."

Quentin offers her a slight grin, which she slowly grins at but slows down as he remembers.

"I hate it. The powder that bastard gave me trigger…."

Suki tried to explain but couldn't finish her sentence.

"I know, and you don't have to say more. Just rest. We're safe…"

"I was held at gunpoint, Quentin! He was talking to that… big figure… they fought with Jax guy… it hurts… my mind."

"I say rest…"

Quentin paused, thinking about seeing Aiko in the suit. He didn't want to believe it was him, but he relentlessly shared what he saw with her.

"Suki… I think I saw Aiko. I think it's Aiko."

Suki paused while stretching herself.

"That metallic being. That was fighting Jax with that hulky suit! Aiko wouldn't be able to do that."

"You were passed out; Nerdhard escaped with another of his goons making. Throwing a grenade at Aiko and Jax. Before that, Nerdhard told Aiko to kill Jax. He hesitated. He backed off, which triggered Nerdhard to throw the grenade. Tearing off the piece of Aiko's helmet, revealing his mask to us…"

"Are you sure it was him?"

"It is him. He is the only person of his kind who wears that mask. There are not many of his kind that exist. I was just shocked to see him. His suit was releasing so much steam, even around his helmet. I saw energy from his eye lens on the mask like he was crying. He didn't even kill Jax, the same way he hesitated when he was about to take one of the member's lives on the train."

Suki paused upon realization of how all this was connected.

"Where is he at now!?"

265

"I don't—"

"Quentin, report?"

Maverick's voice came out from his ARC, interrupting Quentin and Suki's conversation.

"Yes, sir?"

"Just wondering how Suki is doing."

"She's doing well now, thanks for asking."

"I just want to know how my troops are doing. I have other business, so I won't waste much of your time."

"Will do. Thanks for your concerns."

"Yeah, see ya."

Maverick call ending. Quentin was about to relax in his chair.

"MAVERICK!"

"Wha-"

Quentin and Suki are off the edge of Odie's sudden entrance from the door.

"Oh, sorry. I didn't know I was loud."

"I know, man. How's Jerome?"

"He is doing alright; he is grabbing lunch already."

"That's good to hear; what made you this loud!?"

"Oh yeah, something big is happening in the simulation room!"

Quentin's face rose in confusion alongside Suki's.

***

Within minutes, Odie, Quentin, and Suki made their way to the simulation room. Quentin showed concern to Suki, who had a bit of trouble getting to the elevator.

"Suki, you need to rest. You don't have to see him."

"I do, Quentin; a bit of me wanted to see him. I want closure because a friend we saw wasn't a memory."

Quentin only sighs. They rode the elevator to reach their destination. Each stop level they take to reach their destination is met with more personnel, FIREBIRDS, mechanics, office workers, and even cadets from the URDT crowding into the elevators, which caused most of the elevators not to work due to the amount of personnel using them.

"I guess everyone has the same idea as we did."

Odie whispered to Quentin, making sure no one around them heard him. Upon reaching their destination, everyone immediately rushes out. People crowd around, and most of them run to the windows to observe the simulation room from above. Quentin got closer, noticing that Cade Valente, Dahlia Mackenzie, and Curtis Ayabusa were in front of the crowds. Quentin was surprised by their presence.

"Hey, Quentin."

Quentin turned around and saw Joule beside him.

"So, you heard the news as well."

"About?"

Joule walks to the window.

"The Return of the Melancholic Knight!"

Quentin's eyes lowered from what he said.

"The URDT has returned an old relic warrior from during Earth's final days. Deployed to fight the Nekrothians, it's crazy that the URDT kept the Melancholic Knight a secret from us. Yet again, that's why everyone is here."

Joule points at the captain.

"You see them; they show their anger. Upset that the URDT is hiding secrets from us. Makes you wonder what else they have kept from us."

Quentin looks more closely at the captain until he sees two individuals standing near the observation room. Akarui Fenimore and Kenryoku Takoko. Akarui catches Quentin's attention.

"I know that lady."

"You do?"

"We chatted for a bit. She mentioned someone similar that went through the training but had it worse."

"You suspect it might be the person in that suit. I only heard that a Harmonian with pure synara energy can use the suit."

"How do you know all this?"

"It's old legends; we were taught about this in school. Before schools dropped that learning due to the backlash of the Melancholic Knight Program."

"Why did it get backlash?"

"Mostly blaming the Knight for failing to save Humanity and Earth. It's a long history..."

Quentin walks out to the window, looking down. He can feel a sense of distress in his body, understanding that Aiko is in the suit. Bearing that responsibility, Quentin becomes eager to see him if this event is about him.

Everyone watching from the window looks down, waiting for the Melancholic Knight.

Walking down the corridor, Aiko saw the light of the simulation room open up to him. Aiko could still feel his suit being worn out, steaming slowly out, and his mind was drained.

He closes his eyes with each step he makes when approaching the simulation room each time his mind wants to rest. His eyes felt strained from the suit visor. Aiko feels his body tired but can't leave, can't lose everything he worked for. Upon walking to the simulation, he is met with the same bright light; it was only a few hours since he was fighting to return to fight. He felt like this was tormenting him, whatever it took to stay noble in this suit. Aiko looked around, seeing everyone banging on the windows to get his attention; others watched while some booed at him.

"What. That thing is going to replace us?"

Some said, showing resentment to Aiko. Aiko felt the energy around him, surrounded by eyes that refused to look away. Aiko looked until she saw Quentin and Suki. Each of them stares intently, acknowledging that they have seen each other at least. The moment was cut short by the door in front of him sliding open. Multiple stomping is heard, and Aiko wonders if it could be Ernaline and Deagmund. This is true, walking around him and meeting back near the gate. Many people above question who those mechanical beings are, watching in envy how that machine can replace them.

Aiko heard another stomping, this time lowered. Making its approach, it revealed its identity. The suit having similar inspiration to The Melancholic Knight but coated black. Aiko noticed that the insignia on the chest piece looked like Acheron's. The shoulder armor isn't like Aiko's, but it has normal padding like the FIREBIRDS but reinforced. The helmet is the same as Aiko's.

"Aiko Ashin."

The voice boomed around, enough for everyone to hear him.

"The world now knows that the Melancholic Knight has returned. Everyone here is eager to see what the Melancholic Knight is back for. Why are you here? To prove your service and loyalty to the URDT, this battle will determine not only everyone's faith but answer if you are worthy of the suit. Are you worthy enough to protect people, everyone you know, and humanity? Our Knights are gone from the old days; I hope you can bring honor to them. I want to challenge your faith if you are indeed to be called the Melancholic Knight!"

Immediately, Acheron points at Aiko, and Deagmund starts firing at him. Due to her quick speed, Ernaline's evasive action shocks everyone. Ernaline does a high-end kick, prompting Aiko to move, but he is met with firing from Deagmund. This time, Aiko can feel the bullet hitting him.

"Whoa, that guy is speedy!"

Joule shouted while Quentin and Suki said nothing but stared. Their feelings were low as they watched someone they hadn't seen for a long-time fight for their lives.

"Saskia didn't have time to repair his armor."

Akarui thought to herself; she could only hope Aiko could hold on.

Feeling the bullets, Aiko realized that his suit was neither checked nor repaired after his battle against Jax. Realizing that he has his blade, he can finally take advantage of it. Aiko set his mind calmly, focusing on Ernaline's attacks. Aiko parried each kick with his arms while blocking off Deagmund's shooting with his right arm blade. He moves his arms so fast that it looks like a fan spinning. Everyone above was stunned by how quickly he could move and manage to defend himself from each attacker, understanding that he cannot hold on like this. Thinking about how Jax's exposed corners around Jax's suit weakened it. Forcing him to exploit weaknesses to exploit around Ernaline and Deagmund, he cut corners around Ernaline, making him believe Deagmund may have one. He focused on Ernaline's speed, understanding the power it takes. With Aiko having the plan set in motion, he made his move and leaped back to recover his energy.

Knowing that Ernaline would continue to chase him, he quickly threw his blade out to her, but Ernaline dodged the blade. Leaping on Aiko, she began to violently kick him aggressively. Everyone above was yelling like they were watching a game, seeing how intense this fight was. Having Ernaline attack him up close was what Aiko wanted, grabbing her side and squeezing the suit tightly. Using the same raw power Jax used on him, Aiko applied the same to Ernaline, understanding that her armor was light. He swung her against the wall, breaking bits of the wall in the process. Where he began to violently use hammer arm swings and punch aggressively at Ernaline's arms and legs while getting shot in the back by Deagmund. He could feel the power of the bullet really bothering him, but he knew that putting down Ernaline was enough to focus on first. He managed to disable Ernaline, who began to struggle. To add salt to the wound, Aiko, using the blade, returned to him, purposely aiming for Ernaline's chest, pinning her on the wall.

Everyone above was surprised by Aiko's sudden move. Quentin and Suki looked at each other. Odie and Jerome were taken away by Aiko's precise manner. Joule's excitement from the battle thrills him.

Akarui notes Aiko's sync level, seeing his number rise even more than from his training. She wonders why his level is increasing fast, thinking that Acheron is his main attention, knowing that both he and Acheron have tension with one another.

After finishing off Ernaline, Aiko turned his attention to Deagmund, who was pushing the attack. Shooting endlessly at Aiko, who grappled on the wall and performed a run on it. Aiko's speed was insane, running up and sprinting across like a speeding bullet; everyone was amazed by his action. Deagmund grabbed something from his backpack, attaching it to its gun. Once Aiko launched off the wall, preparing to stab Deagmund. Deagmund ducked down and fired a powerful grenade at him. Blasting Aiko across the arena.

Everyone screamed in excitement, but only Quentin, Suki, and Akarui could discern Aiko's being.

Aiko's breathing became heavier. His sound echoed his breathing, and his suit grew hotter. His steam exhausted out, and his visor stopped glitching out and became sharper, like the visor was attached to his eyes. Aiko charged at Deagmund, who reloaded and fired another grenade. Aiko's eyes focused on the shot approaching him, prompting him to dodge sideways. Again, another grenade shot was fired at Aiko, who, this time, used his blade to deflect the shot, which hit the window above where people were watching. Akarui's heart became more fearful of what was to happen next.

Deagmund, remaining grounded, continued to fire multiple grenades at Aiko. Aiko continued to speed up before Deagmund's predicted shots managed to hit Aiko hips. Deagmund backed off and continued to send grenade shots toward Aiko, with precise timing, managed to cut directly in half. Stunning everyone above, Acheron continued to monitor while walking behind the battle. Aiko throws his blade at his gun, causing his gun to break; Deagmund grabs a shotgun-like weapon out from his backpack, preparing to fight Aiko up close. Aiko jumped him as he released continuous punches that were too hard to see. Deagmund couldn't match Aiko's speed, relying on its predicting where Aiko is going to strike. Aiko began to stab violently at Deagmund's torso, giving Deagmund time to land a shot to Aiko's belly, damaging his suit. Some blood spilled out from Aiko's, but Aiko, using his strength and anger with his blade, cut through Deagmund's chest, disabling the core and shutting Deagmund down. Already broken and tired, Aiko walked off, distancing himself from Acheron, who stared down at each other. Aiko, with his arm, reaches back for the blade to return.

Everyone above remained silent, waiting for whoever was going to draw first. Akarui glanced at Aiko's sync levels, seeing his level already surpassing the limit. She worried about Aiko's condition, seeing his fighting style as violent. She took note of how he cut like a savage animal hunting its prey.

"We need to stop this, Kenryoku."

Kenryoku nodded with agreement and went towards the comms, reaching to Acheron.

"Acheron, stop this. You already proved your point to him; is he not worth it to you, sir?"

"He's not worthy."

"YOU'RE GOING TO DIE, PREMIER; I'M SHUTTING HIS SUIT OFF!"

"YOU WILL NOT DO SUCH A THING! Aiko wants me. If he is worthy of being a Knight, he must strike me down."

"WHY DO YOU WANT DEATH SIR! YOU'RE NOT FEELING RIGHT!"

Akarui screamed through the comms, interrupting Acheron.

"I AM WRONG IN THE BEGINNING. This boy entered my life, reminding me of my failures as a human. I watch this boy struggle with my own actions and arrogance. He is not worthy; he is not ready for what the future will bring him!"

Acheron grabs a wire inside his helmet, cutting off communication from Akarui and Kenryoku. They both worry about Acheron, seeing Aiko's steam grow worse to the point that it clouds the area.

"Aiko."

Acheron said to Aiko directly.

"You want to know where I've been and where I was in your life when you needed me?"

Aiko didn't say a word.

"You're going to have to get that answer from my cold body."

Immediately, Aiko and Acheron charged at each other, both being hit by each other. Both share similar speed and strength with each other.

"Why is Acheron fighting his son? Why is he doing this!"

Akarui pleaded at Kenryoku, who shook his head and stood resolutely.

"It is his orders, and I am to listen to what he commands me, Akarui. Even though my feelings on this are mixed, I can't interfere with this affair. "We" can't interfere. I fear it is more than challenging Aiko's worthiness as The Melancholic Knight. Acheron has always been stern against Aiko becoming the Knight since the beginning. They're not on great terms, you know that Akarui."

"They kill each other!"

"I can't do anything against Acheron's wishes."

271

Akarui gripped her hand on the module, feeling a surge of will to do something, but she felt powerless.

"He has been through enough already."

She said to herself.

Quentin and Suki couldn't do anything but watch, everyone shouting as if they were watching a gladiator ring. Watching them try to kill each other, madness shrouds around them.

Acheron's speed and power had the same impact on Aiko; Aiko blocked and blocked. It was like a tug of war, whoever was more vital in this fight. Aiko released the fury of punches that Acheron blocked and tried perfectly to catch his arm, then elbowing Aiko in the face. Staggering Aiko, Acheron took the offense and beat Aiko on his damaged chest. Aiko's inner body felt the pain, his suit was already damaged by Jax, Ernaline, Deagmund, and now by his father; he wondered why life was against him. Aiko could feel his body giving up on him, his bones with his muscle fibers tearing apart, his body cooking like a stove. He can't focus. More steam exhaled out, and around his jawline, more steam released like a train exhaling out air. With his blades, Aiko tries to slice down Acheron, who merely dodges and has both arms behind his back.

"Are you really worthy of the title of the Melancholic Knight? Are you ready to bear the responsibility of what the world expects from you? Are you ready to die for the greater good!"

Acheron headbutted Aiko and, with his hands, gripped Aiko's armpit hard. Gripping so hard on Aiko that it tears through the suit and stabs Aiko's skin with his fingers. Aiko yelps a bit from the pain.

"How can Acheron fight if he isn't in good condition? He is killing himself more! That's why he had to wear that chest plate to stabilize his body!"

"I assumed Acheron still has synara energy left. Time heals old wounds, but Acheron wounds are permanent. He's hurting himself…"

Akarui and Kenryoku exchanging words.

Aiko throws a blade at Acheron, who dodges perfectly. With his arm extended, Acheron pulls out Ernaline chain rope and uses it to restrain Aiko's movement for his blades, the two having a staring contest while holding their attacks off.

"This is what you wanted, Aiko. You have wanted me since the day we met. You thought about hurting me by telling me the truth. The truth is, Aiko… I thought you were dead!"

This statement only triggered Aiko more, retaliating by headbutting Acheron. Both take back a leap distance from each other.

272

"That suit is capable of many things that you're not ready to handle. Are you truly ready to risk your life in that suit, AIKO?"

They charge at each other, Acheron dodging Aiko's blade attack and kicking his leg, which damages Aiko's leg a bit. Acheron, with the chain ropes locked behind Aiko, begins to choke Aiko. The Acheron suit starts steaming from behind on the back, whether from the shoulders or out from its helmet as well.

"This suit carries the Armageddon genes, the powerful beings that killed your race, Aiko. Are you ready to have the genes consume you? Are you letting that power you feel right now control you? Do you want to be the Melancholic Knight so badly?"

Aiko said nothing, breathing heavily as Acheron kept choking Aiko's throat so tightly.

"You're not ready to die, Aiko; give up the suit! Gave up the life you're setting up."

Aiko choked and started reflecting. He remembers Inoue, the woman who looked over him and took care of him; Albie, a person he feels responsible for and watches over; and Anbu, someone who was like a brother to him.

"*Hold on to Hope...*"

Anbu's voice echoed to him.

"*Promise me! To never look back.*"

A voice he remembered, Inoue's voice piercing him.

"We're not brothers. I guaranteed you that."

Aiko said to Quentin when saying Albie is not his brother.

"I'm sorry..."

Aiko said to himself softly.

"I am worthless..."

Aiko's heart softens down. Everyone from above watches as Aiko continues to struggle to fight. Akarui, who had her eyes closed, refused to watch. Kenryoku, who remained still, only watched the events unfold. Quentin and Suki watch Aiko, who grows tired and weak, giving up slowly. Aiko breathes more softly, thinking about the words he remembers. Hearing Anbu, Albie, and Inoue scream, attacking Aiko with his thoughts. The suit around him growled with his breathing, and he could feel the suit heat up. Aiko's head started to feel like it was melting, and his synara energy started to drip down more. With his mouth already releasing steam from his mask, Aiko's eyes widened intensely.

"I CAN'T LOSE THEM!"

Aiko screamed and headbutted Acheron, catching Acheron off guard. Aiko quickly leaps to Acheron, grabbing both his arms, holding them tightly, and then releasing a powerful kick that sent him flying at the wall. Everyone above was shocked. Quentin and Suki couldn't say anything about what they were looking at. Kenryoku's face became fearful of what he saw. Akarui's face was also overloaded with fear, making her look over Aiko's sync level. Seeing his level exceed the system maximums. Aiko's suit began melting, with steam releasing out from Aiko's exposed areas. His cape was catching on fire from suit heat, and some of the metal pieces from his suit dripped from the heat.

"He is overextending his synara energy."

"The suit is one of its only kind to carry the Armageddon genes; Aiko is touching the power a bit!"

Akarui and Kenryoku were surprised and shocked by the revelation.

Dizzy from the hit, Acheron looked up, seeing Aiko leap and charge at him, forcing him to dodge Aiko's charge. Aiko's eyes were directed at him, and his mind ran from rage to hearing the words.

*"Where were you when I needed you!"*

All Aiko could think of was ending him. Acheron, realizing that Aiko had overextended his suit, still got up and readied himself to fight. Both Akarui and Kenryoku scream to end this but do not reach Acheron. Acheron used the chain ropes to parry Aiko's blade, but even the blade matched the heat from Aiko and melted through the chain, Acheron realizing that Aiko was too dangerous up close. He dashed towards Deagmund, who still had the gun attached. Reaching there on time before Aiko could tackle him, getting the gun and firing upon Aiko. Smoke appeared, and everyone watched to see what happened, waiting for the smoke to clear. Aiko's suit, already taking damage, released more smoke, red hot from the explosion. Aiko's helmet jawline crack released even more steam. Understanding what he has done, Acheron drops the gun and embraces Aiko's punishment. Aiko grabbed Acheron and threw him against the wall, pinning him down with his blade. Now accepting that he can't fight Aiko in this state, Acheron could only watch his son take his anger out on him.

Aiko, with his heated hands, releases a series of punches against Acheron, breaking Acheron's suit all around. Arm, legs, and tear open the suit. More memories appeared, the same memories as those from earlier. A flying fist slams on the person, and screams are echoed. The same pain from that memory affects him here. Aiko breaks through Acheron's helmet and sees his mask with synara energy tearing down from his eyelids. Aiko, grabbing back one of his blades for his right arm, prepares to strike Acheron's helmet.

"AIKO NO!"

Quentin and Suki both screamed at Aiko.

274

"MOVE IT! STOP THE KNIGHT FROM KILLING THE LEADER!"

Cade Valente and the other captain ordered their troops to march down to apprehend Aiko.

"AIKO!"

Akarui yelled out.

Kenryoku readies himself to push the button to shut down Aiko's suit.

Aiko was prepared to stab Acheron in the helmet; his yell to strike came near to Acheron's face.

"Aiko."

The memory voice reaches him, seeing Albie holding Aiko left arm. Looking at him tearfully, Albie looked at Aiko, making him stop, looking at what he was hitting. Realizing who he is hitting at. Anbu, who is covered by blood and bruises. For a split second, Aiko stops his strike on Acheron. His mind slows down, and his steam slows down. Acheron slowly falls to the side of the wall. Acheron's breathing was heavy from the damage. He looked up at Aiko.

"GO AHEAD! KILL ME! MY LIFE ISN'T WORTH IT TO YOU, AIKO!"

Acheron's words strike Aiko, and Aiko breathes slowly. Understanding what he is doing, he drops both his blades. Turning around, he reveals a dozen troops surrounding Aiko.

"HANDS UP, KNIGHT!"

"NO."

Acheron yelled back at Cade.

"Sir BUT-"

"LET HIM GO; he proved himself."

Acheron orders Cade and everyone else to stand down. Aiko looked around, seeing the shock and people's fear from only looking at him. He looks at his hand, seeing blood and his exposed hand bleeding out. Remembering his own hands being damaged from the train and the hands that were about to kill Anbu. Aiko breathes in panic. The door where Aiko entered slid open, revealing that Akarui opened the door for him; she reached for the communication.

"GO, AIKO, LEAVE!"

"WHAT ARE YOU DOING? HE NEEDS TO BE PUNISHED!"

Kenryoku yelling at Akarui, which was heard from the communication but cut off—

Aiko looked around and saw the people who acknowledged him: Quentin, Suki, Odie, Jerome, Joule, and Maverick; Akarui and Kenryoku, who all stood in shock. Aiko felt guilty in his heat, making himself retreat out from the situation. He ran away, running in the dark corridor to get away. Aiko found himself in the darkness, with the light reflecting his silhouette. He looked at his hands again.

"I'm sorry..."

Aiko's broken heart and eyes swell, slowly turning into anger. He immediately punches the hallway walls. Screaming so loud that he contained it inside of him. Each punch unleashed his scream from pain and anger. After one final punch against the wall, he falls. Tearing up and covering himself with the burned cape. Letting his emotions take over him and darkness cover him.

Quentin and Suki look at each other, concerned over Aiko. Akarui, reached through her ARC, messages Saskia, texting her that they need to meet.

"He needs our help."

# ACT 3: Without Anguish

# Chapter Twenty-One: Reunion

Aiko's breathing grows heavier; the suit temperature slows down. His body feels like he is trapped due to the amount of heat. Aiko could barely feel his heartbeat, and his mind, being the only thing he could do, was think. Reflecting on the battles he fought, the pain he can see and feel around his body, and the words returning to him.

*"You're going to have to get that answer from my cold body."*

*"Promise me! To never look back."*

*"Hold on to Hope..."*

Quotes from Acheron, Inoue, and Anbu haunt him. He feels his body drawing colder the more he thinks about it. He remembers Quentin and Suki watching him fight and seeing what he has become. Rethinking his time with them was a nice, new change in his life.

"Just come back here. You may not think he doesn't care about you, but he does. You may think, don't push yourself away from him or others."

Yume's voice calls back at him, bringing up images of Albie's face and the hateful manner Aiko gave him. Aiko feels his body colder, and his synara energy drips down from his mask. Aiko remains hanging back in the same room, in his mind a prison, letting the ambiance and void consume him.

"Aiko!"

Saskia ran out from the sliding door, stopping when she saw Aiko's condition. Her face was in disbelief.

"They—he—put you through hell, didn't they…"

Aiko didn't say a word; his arms and legs were left hanging, exposing damaged pieces and part of his wounds. Aiko sniffs but hides it from her.

"Akarui told me what happened... I'm very sorry, Aiko... I had another assignment to do around the area."

Saskia stepped forward, checking everything around him. Aiko could feel her presence, the tender inspection he felt.

"This suit is strong, durable, and relentless but costly to the person wearing it. I hope this burden isn't heavy on you."

Saskia grabbed a ladder near her to reach Aiko's height. She put her hands around the helmet, inspecting it as she did so. She gently pressed two buttons on both sides of the helmet, almost activating his helmet to come off until Aiko shook his helmet away, preventing her. Saskia, taking notice, paused.

"Please, I need to see you fully."

Aiko let her remove his helmet. Pressing the helmet opened up the top, separating it from the jawline attachment. Seeing Aiko's mask that has black smudges from the fighting and damage. His synara energy dripped down from the eye lens of his mask, and she could see how much despair Aiko was in. Grabbing something from her suit pocket, she pulls out a wipe. Cleaning Aiko's mask, he felt the sense to move away from her hand but couldn't force himself. Looking at her, he saw someone who cared. Aiko didn't know how to feel, but he accepted it. Looking at her made him recall more memories, seeing Anbu's face as he looked up at them. Sending Aiko a little grin from thinking about it but forcing him to look from the realization he isn't here. Saskia took notice of Aiko's feelings.

"Aiko. You want to leave?"

Aiko's head looks up from the question.

"Akarui and I planned to take you out of here for a break. We want to do something special for you. We can understand how hard it is to be like this. And don't worry, you're already healed from the Jax first encounter. It's just the suit putting a strain on you."

Aiko pauses slowly, opening his mouth for a response.

"I want to see them."

"Who?"

Saskia asked.

"See a boy I'm responsible for. He was part of why I became a knight; I failed to keep a promise to someone to take care of him during my service. It has been a long while; I don't know if I can show my face or-"

"Say less; we can visit them."

With her response giving Aiko closure, she prepares to take Aiko out of his suit. With her tools, she unscrews bits from each of his body parts. Aiko's being disconnected from his suit caused him to yelp from the pain. She sees his skin all red from the heat and burned skin that peels off in bits. He screams as he is taken out of the suit, which causes her to pause and removing him from the suit. Aiko began to shiver; Saskia got up and realized that Aiko was cold. Understanding how hot and steamy the suit was to him, she went over to her hanger to grab a coat, wrapping it around Aiko. Then she took her scarf from around her neck and wrapped it around Aiko, soothing his neck and body from the immediate coldness. Aiko struggled to walk; holding onto Aiko's shoulder, Saskia led him out of the room, out from the area he was imprisoned in.

Outside the main area where vehicles and troopers leave URDT, Akarui waits as she leans on the back of the car. With her sunglasses on, she surveys her surroundings, seeing many troopers patrolling and aerial vehicles above her taking off. Wearing a long coat, she fixes herself and waits for Saskia and Akarui. She grabs a phone case from her jacket. She starts putting in the names of everyone Aiko knows. From a distance, she sees Saskia carrying Aiko on her shoulders. Once they got close, she approached them, helping Aiko in the back of the car. She sees that Aiko is wearing a black bodysuit, which is a normally protective layer for his suit. Noticing his exposed hands and skin were red, she helps Saskia set him resting at the back of the car.

"I got his clothes."

I brought out the bag with Aiko's green jacket and the clothing he wore before joining the URDT.

"Let's move out."

Saskia acknowledged Akarui; she sat beside Aiko, ensuring his well-being. Akarui got into her driver's seat and made her way out from the giant escalator from URDT. From above, seeing everything, the window curtains opened slightly, revealing Acheron, wearing bandages around his arms and legs but a suit with noticeable welding to repair, watching above.

"Premier. Aiko, Akarui, and Saskia are leaving the URDT."

"I know Kenryoku."

"But sir, Aiko's service for the URDT required his presence to remain here."

"I know... not directly here at the base but in the nation. He can leave."

"You're just going to let him off the hook easily; he's why you're like this!"

"No, I am. I am responsible for what has happened to me. Let the boy be. Akarui is with him, and she knows she can't break any of the rules against the URDT. That's an order, Kenryoku."

Acheron turned around, looking at him from his office door.

"Yes."

Kenryoku is making his way out the door. Acheron, left alone in his office in darkness, looks at his dog Yasuka, who gives him a curious nod.

"Come, Yasuka, let's rest."

Acheron heeled Yasuka and asked her to follow him out the door.

Akarui continued to drive on the busy street, looking forward to doing so. Saskia looked at the side of the window in a disgusted way. Aiko glimpsed out the window, seeing a protest of people holding signs: "NO TO MELANCHOLIC KNIGHT PROGRAM." A sign that has the Melancholic Knight helmet with an X mark on it. Another sign that said: "No waste of funds for something that was lost." A picture of Earth is shown on the sign, showing how hated the program is to the people. Saskia took notice of Aiko's shakiness and put her hand on his lap. Taking notice of Saskia's presence, Aiko made himself lean back and close his eyes. Feeling the air around him relaxes him and stabilizes his body temperature. They continued out from the Republic of Melancholia, entering to the south near the outskirts.

***

Driving on a familiar route, Aiko recounts when he was walking behind Quentin and Suki, who were all ahead of him. He remembers sharing moments that were good enough for him before transitioning into the Melancholic Knight. Akarui looks at the house, trying to see carefully.

"Is this the house?"

Aiko looked at the house.

"Yes."

He said softly. Aiko got out of the car, slowly walking as his stiffness eased. Upon seeing the familiar house, his heart froze. He felt a surge of shock, feeling that his words were twisted. He walked back slowly, bumping into Saskia by accident.

"Hey, what's wrong?"

Saskia asked. Akarui leaned back on her car while waiting.

"Like I said, I haven't seen them for a while."

"It's fine that you're nervous. I still haven't seen my dad's face and am nervous about ever seeing him. Just walk up and embrace whatever happens."

Saskia pats Aiko on the back, gently getting Aiko to walk up to the door. He knocked until his mind spoke to him.

"Just come back here."

Aiko felt guilt coming through his throat, making him retreat to the car.

"It was a mistake coming here! I failed to return to her, and it didn't last long!"

"Aiko. Look."

Saskia reassured Aiko to remain calm, pointing at something that made Aiko turn around. Aiko saw someone at the door, a woman he recognized. Yume walks out the door, looking at Aiko, who is far away. Immediately realizing it was Aiko; Yume ran up to him and hugged him. Aiko, caught off guard by her hug, didn't know how to react.

"You finally came back…"

Yume said, Aiko, taking her words for granted, couldn't help but put his face on her shoulder. Thinking about Inoue, the feelings and love he remembered felt like they passed over here. Aiko let his feelings out through silence, acknowledging her words. Saskia grins a little after seeing Aiko and how free he is without his suit.

"I'm sorry, I knew that I couldn't come back. Knowing that I don't keep promises is true, and that feeling of that promise floating away just brought me guilt."

"It's ok."

Yume ushered Aiko inside.

"I'm glad you came back. I know I'm not your guardian or your caretaker; I just know how having a son or daughter disappear is stressful enough. I considered you a part of the family regardless, Aiko."

Aiko's head remained still, but she listened to her words in acknowledgment.

"Is Albie here?"

"Oh yes! He has been playing with the boys! I can bring him out for you."

Walking back to her house, Yume turned around and saw Akarui and Saskia, who waved to Yume and nodded to them in pleas. Aiko's heart pounded; he didn't know how to respond to seeing Albie. Part of him thinks he doesn't care about him or how he treats Albie. The ruthless journey Aiko set upon himself to take care of someone he despised. Aiko couldn't help but see himself as Acheron, seeing someone in their life that shouldn't exist. Aiko realized how much of Acheron he felt in him. Aiko took notice of footsteps and sounds. He glances up to see Albie. Albie walks up slowly; he only approaches him cautiously. Aiko remained still, not sure if he should hug him. Albie continued to stroll to him, both exchanging looks. Aiko steps forward slowly.

"Hi Albie…"

Albie nodded to Aiko's response, and their silence continued with the wind blowing around them.

"Albie… I don't know what to say."

Aiko pauses for a moment, Albie only listening to him.

"It's nice to see you. And I'm sorry for… everything. It's the only thing I can say, Albie."

284

Aiko extends his hand out to Albie, both shaking hands. Aiko didn't feel the surge in his body to hug Albie from the guilt he had.

"My friends and I are planning to go out somewhere. I was wondering if you wanted to spend time together. That is something I want to try to do. I want to try my best to take you to places together."

Albie nodded, agreeing with Aiko's statement. He reached into his pocket, pulling out a folded paper. Aiko reached for it, and he was about to open it when a familiar voice pierced him.

"Aiko?"

Aiko turned around and saw Quentin and Suki walking together. Both of their faces were fazed, seeing Aiko after a long while. They both ran up, Quentin being the one charged to hug Aiko, who again was caught off guard. Suki followed suit and only patted Aiko on the shoulders. They both notice Aiko's hands that have surgical lines traveling through his arms, seeing his skin slowly turning red.

"Ah."

"Oh, sorry, I might have squeezed too much."

"It's fine. I haven't been able to walk this freely for a while..."

"Oh... yeah..."

Quentin and Aiko both share the silence, knowing what they experienced.

"I still knew we would meet again."

"It's great to see you again."

Quentin said softly, Aiko again understanding by his silence. Quentin noticed Albie and waved at him, which he did back. Quentin then turned his attention towards Akarui, who surprised him.

"It's you."

Quentin walks to Akarui, who is slightly surprised but grins a little.

"I see that you passed."

"So, he's the person you mentioned back then? I can understand why now."

Quentin glanced back to Aiko, seeing his skin and his hands having surgical marks.

"We came to visit; we're just going to places in the city for him. He needs a break. You all are welcome to come with us. There is still room, but someone is going to have to carry Aiko's little friend on their lap."

285

Quentin looks back at Suki from Akarui's reply. Suki nodded yes to Quentin.

"Um, yeah, we can tag along. If it's possible, we can go to the mall later. Is that fine with you?"

"Sure, it's no problem. We can plan that later, too, anyway."

"Yeah, much thanks."

"I assume it's for the graduation party that has been delayed over and over?"

"Yes, actually, just looking for clothes or suits we need for that occasion."

"Great, let's head out."

Akarui smiled a bit while getting in the car. Saskia sat on the passenger side; Suki got in the back while Quentin got in the middle, and Albie followed Quentin to his lap. Aiko was about to get in when he turned around, looking at Yume, who nodded at him. Both see each other back; Aiko keeps his promise, and Yume is pleased to see Aiko again. With that in mind, he went in the car. They went off from the road, Yume only grinning at the fact that Aiko was back together with them.

Driving by tall skyscrapers to local vendors on the busy street of Republic Melancholia. The roads carried a lot of activities, and she continued to drive to her destination while they all looked out the window. Driving by the west-north of the city reveals a large building that has many square meters. The name of the building is: "Republic of Melancholia Natural History Museum."

They all walked out, with Albie between Aiko and Quentin, Suki following suit, and Akarui and Saskia walking up the stairs, meeting the museum workers.

"URDT employees? There is a discount for each ticket."

"Yes, we are."

Akarui, with her ARC, slips out a card. Using her PCS to pay with credits.

"Don't worry, I'll cover everyone."

She said, with everyone nodding with gratitude.

"Ok, enjoy your time here!"

The workers bow while they all head inside. They walk around, seeing various signs indicating what was in each of the exhibit rooms. Two signs read: "Gaea Native Species." To "Earth Native Creature." Albie, leaning on Aiko, pointed to Earth Native Creature, and Aiko nodded to his point.

"Albie wants to visit that area if that's fine with you."

"No problem. Suki and I are just going to stroll around here."

286

Aiko nods his agreement; Aiko, Albie, Akarui, and Saskia walk towards Earth Native Creature. Quentin and Suki both walk through the Gaea section. Many kinds of creatures exist on display, such as illustrations and models of different creature works that inhabit the planet. Seeing a creature called: "Red Muzzler." A rodent-like species that can fit on your hand, with large circular eyes and eye spots. The description notes that their red spot defies any predators or humans to try near, using it as a defense system to strike fear in anything found anywhere.

More creatures like the "Thicket Colt." Sharing resemblance to the horses back on Earth but with sharp horns on their heads and a long tail used to stabilize the temperature and direction of the wind. From the description, domesticated species used by humans and even from the URDT for survey and patrolling are found anywhere but in open plains.

Another creature called "Talon Starwhisk." which is a tiger-like creature but with longer nails and horns stretching back to ram anything in its way, with a sharp, long knife horn on its tail that can act like a defense system or communication to its own kind, is being found in the inhabitant's zones.

A creature like the "Stubborn Mule hound" that is as big as a horse but with a mix of a hybrid of a dog and a mule, hence the name.

Giant creatures like the Ice Claw Placental Mammal that humans can ride to travel around plains, mainly around tundra areas to forests when temperature changes in Gaea.

Quentin and Suki continued to inspect each creature. Suki's mind dazed off. Memories of her father reappear and hit her instantly, making her fall and collapse.

"Suki! You're alright?"

"Yes, just memories."

"I knew that the powder effect was hurting you."

"It's not Quentin..."

She sighs.

"Quentin, can you make me a promise?"

Quentin turns to her.

"Never leave me."

"I did promise you that, Suki..."

"I know. As time passes, we may grow out of who we are but not our memories. As I experienced more thoughts of my father. The more I want to kill him..."

"Suki..."

"I'm sorry, Quentin. You know how much it hurts to have someone in your life leave."

"I do..."

"I just want you to promise me not to give in to your hate. It's something we can't return or stop. I can't help."

Quentin put his hand on her shoulder.

"I promise…"

Both Quentin and Suki locked eyes, acknowledging each other.

Aiko and Albie, both walking together, look at Earth's animals. They see animals in frozen ice. Aiko reads a description of the frozen elephant.

"Due to the animals having different body functions for this planet, planning to introduce this animal to Gaea is canceled until further development to enhance the animal's ability to be introduced."

Albie points around for Aiko to see bears, buffaloes, pandas, birds, fish, and whales all in cryo-freeze, showing their bodies still preserved. Albie continues to point around while Aiko follows him everywhere. Akarui and Saskia both walk around behind them.

"It's good that he is out of his suit. I don't know how much he can take from wearing it. You were the one that added magnetic for his Valor blades to his gauntlet?"

"Yup, I realized he wasn't protected well against long-range enemies. I hope that gives him an edge in combat."

"I appreciate your help. Following his orders is just getting out of hand. I can't do much against their orders; the more results they want, the more they abuse Aiko."

"Why?"

"I don't know, but Aiko's presence with Acheron changed him. I have never seen him this fanatic or strict. Seeing his son, whom he thought never existed, sparked in him or tried to erase him in his mind. The war back on Earth affected him dearly. Even when Aiko was barely done with his training wearing the prototype suit, they sent him to attack Jax. I believe they intentionally did it to get Aiko in the Melancholic Knight suit. Seeing if his synara energy as Aiko is Harmonian would work on the suit; if not, Acheron would have terminated him; such, they were pouring resources without any of the nation knowing. We were working in secrecy, and I'm sorry if you were involved in all this."

"It's fine, Akarui; I always lived like this. Especially when I lied to my mother about my father doing work without her blessing. I still live like this, so I relate to where Aiko comes from."

**288**

Akarui and Saskia continued to follow behind Albie and Aiko, who were walking around and seeing animals that once existed on Earth.

***

Afterward, they all went to the Republic of Melancholia Mall, located in the downtown city. Walking in reveals large offices as well as stores where people are shopping. Akarui lent her hand to Albie, who was hesitant until he turned around to see Aiko nodding. It was fine. Albie reached for her hand and walked forward, taking the escalator. Saskia follows them, while Aiko, Quentin, and Suki follow suit but must catch up. The escalator was long and high due to the many stores and areas in this tall building. Quentin mumbled his words to Aiko until he regained his thoughts.

"Is Premier Acheron your father Aiko?"

Aiko remained looking forward. He didn't say a word until he realized that he was talking to Quentin, someone he hadn't seen for a while.

"Yes. But I don't want to believe so."

"How come you don't mention him?"

"I had never seen him, nor had he ever thought about me. I don't remember him or even think he remembered me. Even when I asked him questions about where he was when I was little, he dismissed them. All I wanted was my parents, who I thought didn't exist, but I wanted the parents who left me or lost me. I regret that thought now."

Quentin and Suki both look at each other, nodding to Aiko's statement.

"Aiko, don't abandon him."

"What?"

"Listen, he may not see you fully, but later in life, it will change. Believe me, believe us. Don't ever leave him. Even if he dismisses you, some people we care about always push us away. These are just thoughts you can think about. I wish I could see my dad again, Aiko…"

Aiko was about to speak but silenced himself, realizing Quentin's dad was gone. Aiko only looks back and down, letting those words sit with him: "Some people we care about always push us away." Letting the quote rest on him, traveling up the escalator to the clothing store.

Upon entering the store, Quentin and Suki start looking for clothes. Quentin finds a suit while Suki looks for a dress. Saskia takes care of Albie as they sit on the bench. Aiko only looks around, seeing clothes ranging from biohazards to casual clothing, ranging from slip-on shoes to automatic coats to zip-ups. Aiko continues to walk around.

"Psst."

**289**

Aiko turned around and saw that the door to the dressing room was open. Seeing Akarui's face pop out.

"Can you do me a favor, Aiko?"

Aiko walked forward a bit.

"Can you help zip up my back for my dress? I can't reach it. Come in."

Aiko walked in a bit hesitantly. The dressing room was big enough for both of them. He looked around until he noticed something on Akarui's back. He examined her back closely. A large scar stretched from low to top, with other little scars near it. Aiko was stunned and wasn't able to produce words.

"Yeah… I forgot I had that."

Akarui looks at the mirror and her reflection.

"During my time back on Earth, I was a little girl in my hometown on the continent known as Europe. The Nekrothian's spread across the hemisphere and reached the nation I am from. All I remember were screaming, explosions, and Nekrothians shooting. They hunted the people down. I was there when they attacked us."

She sighs, knowing how hard it is to tell him.

"I lost close relatives, people I knew in my life. It is crazy how much time can change in a snap; the people we know just vanish. Without the URDT creation, our race wouldn't thrive like we are now. Your father, Acheron, saved me. I saw him charging at the Nekrothians, a creature that can stab and penetrate anyone. I survived because of URDT when people close to me ran. I survived because of your father, Aiko. He is not what you think he is; just understand that time can heal old wounds."

Aiko didn't say anything, but he was learning about his father. This shows him a different perspective from his father's. He can imagine his father in the suit now. Breaking his daydream, he zips up Akarui's dress.

"I forgot to give you this."

Akarui grabbed something from her coat.

"It is a phone that you can use. It has everyone's name that you know. I let Saskia and the others know so that you can contact each other."

"Oh, thank you."

Aiko put it in his jacket.

***

Leaving the mall, they travel to a playground as the sun is setting down. Aiko, Saskia, and Albie got off.

"Albie wanted to go to the park; sorry if it was a drive to get here."

"Don't say sorry, Aiko; you deserve this time for yourself."

Akarui, responding to Aiko, turned around to see Quentin and Suki holding their clothes.

"I assume we're going to head back to the URDT?"

"Yes, we're going to get ready and change."

Quentin and Suki look at each other in acknowledgment.

"We're heading back to the URDT It's not far from here, so if you're done, just let me know. I'll return you, Aiko."

Aiko nods in response, and Akarui drives off.

"Wonder if Odie and Jerome even know that there is a graduation party tonight?"

Suki whispered to Quentin, who just laughed and nodded sideways, knowing they didn't remember the date.

Aiko and Saskia walked while Albie ran up to the playground. The sun was shining at them, its light orange reflecting on them. They both sat down on the bench, watching Albie play.

"How long have you and Albie known each other?"

Saskia asked.

"Since he entered my life. He was brought in by a man we didn't know who claimed he couldn't take care of him."

"If you don't mind, how was your life back then?"

Aiko paused, reflecting on her words. He leans his head back.

"Peaceful..."

Saskia looked down at the ground.

"Was it nice back then? Akarui told me how much power you used for your suit. I want to know what caused you to feel like that."

"Acheron. Mainly myself. The suit reaches my thoughts, memories I try to bury. This mask keeps reflecting on me. When I said my life was peaceful, it was. When I looked back on it, I regretted how much better it was."

291

"I'm here for you. I'm not your mechanic here. Just someone who cares. If you're blocking what got you here, don't. Let it all out; I'm all ears."

Saskia looked at Aiko, who looked towards the sun. He breathed slowly as he told his echoes from his past.

# Chapter Twenty-Two: Dust and Echoes
## Part 3

"I used to stay at a foster care; all I know is that I was raised by a caretaker named Inoue. I didn't know who my parents were or why I was left with her, so I questioned who my parents were. Where were they at? Who am I? I only knew that I had had this mask since I was born. All I wanted to do was to find my parents and be in a family that might've forgotten me. Inoue kept insisting on letting it go, and they never came home. Years passed, and a new kid was in her care; he didn't have a name, so she named him Anbu. He was older than me; he was someone Albie, and even looked up to as sort of like an older brother. He was happy with his life, and he never questioned who he came from. He never cared about who his parents were; he was just a young boy who wanted to help others for his own goodwill. I waited time and time again, looking at the sky from away the place I called a temporary home. I didn't want a life like this. I wasn't happy and didn't even consider the people I grew up with as a family. All I did was run out, wait, and wait until the family or parents who might have lost me returned. That day came for someone else."

*** 

*May 13, 2125*

It was the same forest that Aiko was familiar with, with the wind and critters scattering around him. Aiko looked up at the sky once more, and slowly, he felt that he was moving down.

"AIKO."

Anbu was holding Aiko in place. Aiko regained his thoughts. Looking around him, he saw that he was on the Olive, the Thicket Colt.

"Weren't you listening to me? Have your stirrups fixed and balance yourself."

"I know."

"You sure? You almost fell out."

"I just gaze off in the distance."

"You always gaze off in the distance."

Anbu groans, walking while leading Olive on the route home.

"That's all you do. Do you even daydream every time?"

"Always."

"About what?"

"Where they're at? My people. Do they even care about me?"

Anbu looked down while listening to his response.

"Aiko, we sometimes need to accept the fact that our expectations may not be what we get."

Aiko turned his head towards Anbu.

"What are you saying? That I shouldn't care about being found by my people! Isn't that the point of a lost child trying to find his way out?"

"That's not what I'm saying. You need to accept that maybe they are there, but..."

"But what? Inoue has sent out many posters of you and me for lost children. Shouldn't they come for us?"

"I don't know Aiko. This planet has barely been settled; it's new to all of us. Slowly, people are trying to recover their lives, or what is left for them."

"And leaving us behind. Like echoes."

"We're not echoes to anyone, Aiko; you and I are here. Right now, that's all that matters. It also matters that we have each other and are responsible for each other, you and me, Albie and Inoue."

Aiko looks away from Anbu, and Anbu understands Aiko's anger.

"I'm sorry, Aiko. I wish I could give you the life you want, but I can't. We need each other, helping Inoue while paying those pirates for their scam service. It is terrible. I need you, Aiko; she needs you, even Albie; don't carry your hate to him. He was born into the world like that; the last thing he needs is the feeling of hate rather than compassion."

Anbu continued leading Aiko and Olive on the route.

"You still holding the letters there?"

"Yeah…"

"Just hang on; we're almost there."

They continued to walk out from the forest, making their way near their home. The sun was setting slowly, creating an orange shade on everything. Albie, who was playing with the plume chickens, ran around while Inoue carried a sack of vegetation. Her face struggled as she left and dragged the bag out to the front porch. The sack ripped, dropping all the vegetation, causing her to fall and cough as she did so.

294

"INOUE!"

Anbu ran off to the front of her porch. Aiko, seeing her collapse, immediately got off and led Olive to them. Albie, who was surprised, ran up to Anbu to see what had happened.

"Are you ok?"

"Yes, dears."

The boys surround her, looking at her in distress.

"I must get these orders read—"

Inoue's cough was so heavy that it caused her to spit out blood, and her cough grew more uncontrollable.

"No, you don't need to do this; take a break."

"We can't take a break. This is barely a fraction of what they demanded!"

"We shouldn't be doing this for pirates that weren't even offering us protection. Have you called URDT for support against this matter?"

"Anbu, the URDT doesn't recognize anyone outside their walls as citizens. The price of becoming a citizen grows higher and higher as there is more demand; people are buying more while prices increase. It is going to get harder for us to survive and earn any credits. Anbu, I can't rest knowing what can happen to us in the future."

"Don't worry about it, Inoue; please rest!"

Anbu set Inoue down on the stairs of the porch, and she shed tears. Her response overwhelmed her, and the boys just stood still, recalling her quote and understanding how tight their situation was.

"I'm worried too; we all are."

Anbu, speaking on behalf of the foster brothers.

"Whatever happens, we shouldn't give up. We push through and keep moving forward. You taught me that, Inoue."

Inoue looked up to Anbu, seeing the rest of the boys. She opens her arms, and Anbu and Albie embrace her hug. Aiko remained still; he hesitated until he moved slowly but stopped. Recalling his words:

"Where they're at? My people. Do they even care about me?"

Aiko couldn't help but stop, feeling too cold and worthless to even hug her.

"I love every one of you; you are my children no matter what."

**295**

Her words pierced Aiko's heart; he looked away. Anbu and Albie looked at Inoue in happiness.

"Ok. Oh, did you all bring in the letters?"

"Yes, we did, Aiko."

Aiko, hearing Anbu and Inoue, walked up to give her the letters and retreated due to her words affecting him. She looked over the letter, reading each name until she saw a letter that stood out. Reading:

"Inoue Caretaker, Anbu Ashin Guardians found."

Putting her hands on her mouth, Inoue looked over to Anbu, who was confused.

"Anbu…. Your parents found you."

Everyone's heart froze; Anbu was too stunned to say anything. Albie was watching in confusion while Aiko, from a distance, heard what she said, creating a mix of emotions in him. Inoue handed over the letter to Anbu, who started reading. His heart dropped, and his eyes couldn't produce a tear from this revelation. Inoue only walked up and hugged him; Anbu didn't know what to say. Aiko's heart started to race, hearing Anbu finding out his parents had discovered him. Aiko felt sad, and his breathing slowed down until it became heavier. Hearing Anbu's parents exist made him angry. Thinking that can't be true. Aiko immediately lunged out, took the letter away, and ran off back to the forest.

"AIKO!"

Inoue yelled out; Anbu was caught off guard and chased after him.

"WAIT, COME BAC-"

Inoue got up and tried to chase after them but collapsed due to her coughing.

Albie didn't know what to do. He walked up to Inoue but looked back at where they had run off to. His feelings grew mixed, and he worried about what he should do next.

Aiko continued running far away from Anbu, trying to reach a distance where he could inspect the letter, not believing the letter's words to be true.

"AIKO, COME BACK!"

Anbu yelled while trying to reach him. Anbu's breathing continued as he caught up to Aiko, but Aiko's speed exceeded him. Upon reaching a safe area, he hid near a tall tree.

"AIKO! AIKO!"

Anbu yelled his name out. Aiko, hiding behind the tree, leans out carefully until the coast is clear. Aiko rushes to read the letter, examining the words to see if they are true.

Aiko's heart grows heavy, realizing that the letter is true. The letter shows Anbu's parents' names, signatures, and pictures. Aiko's heart drops slowly, causing him to fall. Anbu, finding Aiko, could see his position still, noticing the letter Aiko had slipped away.

"Aiko… I don't know what to say."

Aiko's hands slowly shake, and Aiko's mind devolves with him having sentences tossing back at him:

*"Where they're at? My people. Do they even care about me?"*

*"What are you saying? That I shouldn't care about being found by my people! Isn't that the point of a lost child trying to find his way out?"*

Aiko, looking only from the corner of his eye, saw Anbu, who, on his face, looked worried. Aiko's mind slowly pieced together thoughts about the Anbu parents finding him.

"You knew they were coming for you?"

"Aiko, it's not like that—"

"DID YOU?!"

Anbu pauses, restructuring his sentence; Aiko fully stares at Anbu for the truth.

"Yes, she and I knew. These letters we've been receiving were from my parents; they discovered my poster and immediately contacted Inoue. After Albie was adopted by her, we reviewed the letter. Confirming it was them, a picture of my parents that was them. Given how much you want to leave us, she and I thought about how this news would affect you. I knew how devastating it would be for you to hear it; I'm sorry. I'm sorry I had to lie to you all this time; keeping it away from you was-"

"Only beneficial that I didn't know. I now know."

Aiko breathes heavily.

"Aiko, I am sorry. But I realize that—"

"Realize what? I'm not important to you anymore. The hope you gave me disappears like that?"

Aiko's breathing was slow, and he was slowly gripping his fist. Aiko immediately charged at Anbu, pushing themselves down a hill. Aiko started slamming his fist on Anbu's body, directing his attention to his face. Aiko felt a heavy rush of adrenaline rushing through him, flowing through his arm. Anbu's arms were still and moved when Aiko's strike penetrated him. Aiko starts to recall Anbu's words:

"Just remember to hold onto hope."

297

Aiko's anger grew, and he believed those words didn't mean anything to him. They kept him calm, and he believed that he could hope to find his people, his parents.

"LAIR!"

Aiko's mind raced; each slam he threw at Anbu grew worse. Aiko's hands were now covered in blood, using both of his hands, throwing them at Anbu's throat as he proceeded to choke him down. Aiko's breathing grew heavier as he continued to be squeezed more tightly. Aiko's attention was on Anbu's face, and he saw his eyes only looking back at him. Aiko could feel his adrenaline flowing down his arms, feeling the urge to hold him down. His thoughts justified his action; doing it so, he could feel something after doing it.

Out of nowhere, Albie ran up and tried his best to grab Aiko's left arm off to stop him from choking Anbu throat, who was gasping for air. Albie's persistent effort only annoyed Aiko. Prompting him to do a heavy backhand slap on Albie's face and sending him to stumble back on the ground. Albie, motionless, caught Aiko's attention, easing him to lower his guard. His heart started to be colder, realizing that he hit Albie. His breathing slowed, his muscles lowered, and he looked at Anbu, who was turning red. Aiko sniffed and gasped at what he was doing but left his hand against Anbu's throat. Anbu noticed Aiko's tearful impression behind his mask, opened his arm, and touched Aiko with a stroke of his hand on his mask. Feeling the affection, Aiko was stunned; it was not a punch or retaliation but a gentle touch from him. The touch was so affectionate that his body lowered, his adrenaline gently removing his hand from Anbu's throat.

"I'm sorry."

Anbu's raspy voice strikes Aiko, noticing how much damage he has done to him. Aiko stepped back and looked around, seeing Albie looking at him. His eyes glare, and his face is covered by the slap print, becoming red. His breathing was like Aiko's when angry, Anbu slowly breathing in and out as he rested on the floor. Aiko continued to step back, letting the realization set in. Albie got up and ran away into the forest; Anbu, taking notice of Albie's fear, only got up and glanced at Aiko and turned his attention to finding Albie.

Anbu wandered around, screaming for Albie, who didn't attend to him. Aiko followed suit but slowly. Anbu's voice was weakened so that he could yell or yelp. Anbu started to think, figuring out how to get Albie out from hiding.

"Albieeeeeee."

Anbu's raspy voice turned into a cheerful tone, echoing around the trees. Aiko's mind was lost as to what Anbu was doing, but he didn't want to talk to get near him. Anbu continued to joyfully call out Albie's name, clapping and singing. Slowly peeking from the tree, Albie noticed Anbu's joyfulness, encouraging him to get close to Anbu. Anbu continued until Albie appeared to him, and he opened his arms to Albie. Smiling a bit,

Albie ran forward to Anbu, embracing each other. Aiko only watches. Aiko's mouth hesitated but fully opened.

"Anbu. I'm."

"Don't be; you were just angry. I know how much it means to you to find your family and your people; I understand that pain very well."

Both only stared at each other, Aiko and Anbu sharing the silence.

"Let's head back, we're worrying Inoue too much."

Anbu, holding Albie's hand, walks back. Albie only stared at Aiko, who understood his anger. Letting the thought rest with him. Aiko, let them walk ahead. Aiko began to reflect on what got him like that: jealousy. Anbu has a family, but he doesn't. Aiko's heart twisted all around, feeling guilty for his action. Walking through the quiet trees, no wind blew, and the silence remained in the air. Aiko looked at his hands. Seeing Anbu's blood around his fingers and skin torn off from his knuckles, he covers his hands with his shirt, soiling it.

As Anbu and Albie walk, Albie keeps looking at Anbu's throat. Which catches Anbu's attention, he rubs his hands on Albie, who grins a little. Aiko and Anbu didn't want to make eye contact. The sound of distant destruction was heard, like something was collapsing slowly. Anbu, walking up, reveals a shocking event taking place.

Seeing smoke rising, traveling down to their home. Many colts were parked outside the house, and many pirates were raiding from the outside. The same pirates that offered had service returned. One of the pirates drags something that is fighting back, revealing it to be Inoue, whose hair is pulled by the pirates. Anbu felt a sense of shock but immediately felt pure anger. Anbu, without thinking, rushed towards them; Albie and Aiko, both shocked by the event, immediately followed suit. Anbu, hopping over a fence, charges at one of the pirates. Tackling down the figure and pushing in everywhere and on the face, one of the pirates kicked off Anbu and, with the butt of their rifle, smashed Anbu's head. Aiko and Albie are immediately halted by the pirates pointing their rifles at them.

Aiko promptly holds back Albie from instinct, and they both back around near the porch, having a standoff. The pirates' appearance was identical, with their masks showing their eyes. The pirate Anbu tackled got back up, revealing his face. The same man who offered their service got up and looked down at Anbu. His appearance was more transparent, with an angular face with high cheekbones, his eyes tan like before, thick dark eyebrows, and a proportional nose that complements his facial structure. His lips are medium, carrying contemplative authority. His hair is naturally dark, which reflects his dark horse appearance. One of the pirates dragging out Inoue throws her down, coughing erupting from her. The man walks up to her, noticing his tan eyes as he stares straight at her.

"Why… are you doing this?"

The figure remained silent from her question.

"As I said before, we need supplies immediately. Not later, not in a month, I got my people to feed."

Anbu fighting against one of the pirates who had his restraints.

"WE NEEDED MORE TIME!"

Anbu shouted at the figure, and the figure turned to the boy.

"You did have enough time. There is increased pressure from the URDT activities around, and our organization decreased with recent firefights. I am losing the manpower to hold up against the URDT; I was forced to do anything necessary to keep my men alive."

The figure focuses his attention on Inoue.

"You, whatever sacrifices we must make, protecting the people we know and hold dear to us. Whatever you have, I must take it."

The pirates behind him start taking the bags of supplies Inoue had, and everything in the home is taken out while it burns up.

"WHY ARE YOU BURNING OUR HOME!"

The figure looks towards the home.

"Because if the URDT questions you or searches around your property, clues of our affair will be compromised, and even the slightest detail of our involvement will trouble our work. At the end of the day, consider this a punishment for not meeting our needs and URDT from reaching your home."

"BASTARD!"

Anbu yelled while kicking out and back, the pirate trying his best to restrain him.

"Your service isn't done yet."

"WHAT ELSE DO YOU NEED! WE GAVE YOU EVERYTHING!"

Inoue cried out, but her coughing continued to grow worse.

The figure draws his attention towards her.

"Not everything."

The figure marks his eye towards Aiko.

"The boy."

Everyone looked at Aiko; Aiko didn't know how to respond. He didn't move or flinch, as the pirates had their rifles drawn at him.

"That boy with the mask is nothing, but he may be important to our other agendas."

"LEAVE HIM OUT. I CAN'T LET YOU TAKE HIM!"

Inoue yelled out, but the pirate pointing his rifle at him smacked her head.

"Trades are happening in The Imperium of the Choleric; they are looking for children ages 5 through 18. They offer a handsome reward for it. I can make this worthwhile."

The figure now looking at Inoue.

"We're taking the boy, completing our service, and leaving your family alone. I can guarantee you that no harm will be done."

"NO, YOU CAN'T!"

Inoue got up, but being restrained, Albie looked up at Aiko, to whom Aiko didn't know how to respond. He reflected on his actions and recounted how worthless he felt here, never helping himself clean, helping, or showing love to any of them. Aiko closed his thoughts and opened his mouth.

"I'll GO!"

Anbu screamed out, catching everyone's attention, including the figure. The figure stared at Anbu.

"Why would I take you? Look at yourself. Your throat is badly hurt, you're all beat up, and your own appearance alone wouldn't meet my end deal."

"You're wrong... That boy alone can't even lift up a log, run as fast, or properly care for himself."

"How am I supposed to believe you if that is true?"

"Like you said, I am all beat up."

Anbu coughing out blood.

"He wanted to fight me, so I agreed. I let him take many swings and hooks at me to test his strength; he couldn't even take me down."

"I know you're bluffing."

The figure strolls to Anbu.

"But I can understand what you're trying to do. Are you willing to take that boy's spot? He carries a mask that can fetch a higher price to the Choleric. You would have to work your hardest to meet my deal."

"NO, ANBU, DON'T DO IT!"

Inoue yelled out more but yelped from his pain. Aiko and Albie slowly realized that Anbu was trying to protect them by volunteering himself. Anbu paused for a moment from the figure statement. He glanced towards Aiko, who nodded no to him. Anbu grinned at him a little and turned his attention towards the figure.

"Yes..."

The figure stepping back looked around and looked towards Aiko. Breathing heavily, he turned back to Anbu.

"Fine then."

"NOOOO, ANBU, NOOOOO!"

Inoue cried out. Albie, sensing what had happened, was about to charge towards Anbu, but Aiko, wrapping his hands around his stomach, prevented him from getting near him. The pirates holding Anbu took him with them out near the fence.

"Wait, I need to give him something."

The figure paused before exiting the fence.

"Fine. Watch him."

The pirate was closely monitoring Anbu as Anbu approached them. The pirates continued to aim their rifles at Inoue and even at the boys if they tried to fight back. Anbu and Aiko both stared at each other.

"Anbu... I'll go."

"No. They need you! I can't let them waste your future. There is still someone, your parents, out there looking for you. They need you more than I need them. I am already grateful that people are looking for me; I am satisfied."

"Anbu, NO."

Aiko grabbed both sides of Anbu's green jacket, tightly squeezing him toward him, but Anbu resisted.

"I'm sorry, Aiko. I value you and them the most. You are my family."

Anbu took off his green jacket and wrapped it around Aiko.

"You are my brother. Take care of them; don't leave them. Hold on to Hope..."

Anbu was then dragged out by the pirates. He looked at them with small tears coming out of his eyes. Aiko was stunned but shaken. He put his hand around the shoulder of the jacket Anbu wrapped around him. Albie punched the ground, not being able to scream. He charged at the pirates, but Inoue grabbed Albie and hugged him tightly. The figure and Aiko both exchanged looks, leaving Aiko alone as he let the event settle in him.

\*\*\*

Aiko's tears slowly drip from his face; his mask hid his face but showed the tears trickling down his throat.

"Aiko…"

Saskia puts her hand on Aiko's chest. Aiko gasped but regained his thoughts. Aiko slowly breathing, noticeable from his mask echoing his sniff. Aiko only looked at the sun, didn't move, but let the retelling of his story shatter him. Saskia noticed Aiko's refusal to look at her and respect his space.

"What happened afterward?"

Aiko pauses from her response, regaining his memory.

"We stayed at the rancher we trade with, moving on from the event. Inoue would cry each night. Albie would leave dirt drawings, drawing on paper, of us… Anbu with us. We still couldn't move on; year after year, I helped out here and there but couldn't find myself looking at Inoue and Albie. Albie despised me no matter what. I still had that grudge when Albie came into our lives, and I can't blame Albie for all this. I tried here and there to cheer him up, offer meals, and keep my promise to Anbu. It pains me to look at Albie when I know I am not his brother. Eventually, the rancher offered enough money for us to move into the Republic of Melancholia. Upon reaching the nation's walls, we were met with security at the tunnel entrance."

\*\*\*

*December 22, 2133*

Flashback. Aiko, Albie, and Inoue all look up at the wall. Inoue in her hands carrying passports. They approach the entrance gate, with FIREBIRDS guarding every corner and on top of the walls. One of the guards holding out their hands. Aiko and Albie with their bags on Olive the Colt while Inoue leads them to the entrance.

"Passports?"

Inoue walks forward, with Aiko and Albie holding their bags and watching intently. After giving the guard the passport, checking with their ARC monitor. Inoue turns around to Aiko and Albie, helping them get off the colt, her face lower and fearful.

"Whatever happens, run and never look back."

Aiko and Albie were confused. The guard, after checking the card, turned around.

"Check out, enter."

Inoue was pushing Aiko and Albie out from the wall entrance. Aiko's confusion rose as he turned around, the gate closing behind them. Inoue stood behind the gate.

"Inoue?! WHAT ARE YOU DOING?!"

"There weren't enough funds for me, only for you and Albie. Run. RUN!"

"These cards are fake! Arrest them!"

Inoue is being grabbed by the guards while Aiko and Albie freak out about what is happening.

"I SAID RUN! Promise me! To never look back. DON'T LOOK BACK!"

Aiko grabbed her hand through the gate while she was dragged out. Aiko panics but looks around, realizing they will get captured if they stay longer. The troops hold down the colt while Inoue is getting grabbed. Olive the colt fought back and fled to the inhabitant zone, leaving them alone. Albie tried to open the gate, but Aiko, grabbing him by the stomach, carried him out while he ran out from the forest. Albie pounds his fist on Aiko's back, wanting to get out and return, but Aiko continues running. Upon hitting Aiko's back, Aiko threw Albie on the ground.

"ALBIE, SHE'S GONE! SHE'S GONE..."

Aiko kneeled on the ground; his hands covered in his mask. Albie heard his sorrow, stunned but understanding Aiko's emotion.

Aiko looks at Albie, then glances back.

*"Promise me! To never look back."*

*"Hold on to Hope."*

The words keep attaching to Aiko like a broken record. He breathes and looks down. Letting the silence while Albie could watch, with his tears flowing down as well.

✳✳✳

Back to reality, Aiko breathed softly. He turned his attention to Albie, who was joyfully playing around the playground.

"It's my fault."

"What?"

Saskia was caught off guard by Aiko's statement.

"It was my fault Anbu was taken away, and for Inoue giving herself up for Albie and me. I am not what Anbu expected me to be. I am not a brother to Albie; I don't deserve this life."

304

"Aiko…"

Saskia's tears slowly drop down.

"Giving their lives for me. I've been selfish for myself, yet they still cared."

"AIKO!"

Saskia wrapped her arms around Aiko. Aiko breathed softly, letting his tears and pain slow down.

"I chose to become a knight for myself then because I can't forgive myself."

"They loved you; Albie loves you. Please, don't blame yourself. Anbu and Inoue saw something you, even if you don't know it. They let you be free to take care of Albie. He needs you, and they need you to be strong. Even if they're gone. Please, Aiko. Forgive yourself; I am here for you."

Saskia tightly hugged him, and Aiko's breathing slowed down. He was thinking of the hug of Anbu, Inoue, Yum, and Quentin. Aiko closed his eyes, letting their feelings flow in him.

Aiko, Saskia, and Albie walked together on the sidewalk.

"I'm going to head back. Sorry to ask you, but can you take Albie back home?"

"It is not a problem! Don't mention it. I want to explore more around here, so I'll watch him. Don't worry about it."

Aiko looked down for a bit.

"I know how much is going on, but don't let it get to you. I'm just happy you shared yourself with me. You're a good person, Aiko. Forgive yourself; you've been given a chance to change."

Aiko looked at Albie, who was looking around. Aiko walked up to Albie.

"I'll see ya later."

Aiko offered a fist bump to Albie, who fist bumped back. They shared a moment together, and Albie smiled at Aiko. Aiko went to the stairs.

"I'll see you later, Saskia. Thank you."

Saskia smiles in response to Aiko. She grabs Albie's hand as they walk away from him, taking Albie back to Yume while Aiko watches them fade in the distance. Aiko turns his attention up the stairs until he sees a figure waiting for him at the top.

"Aiko."

Acheron's voice pierced Aiko's heart.

**305**

# Chapter Twenty-Three: I know you till then

Aiko didn't believe what he saw. Acheron waiting for him, catching him off guard.

His heart was mixed with cold and heated after seeing Acheron, and Aiko still felt the pain from fighting him. Both sharing the silence and only looking at each other's masks. Locking in their relationship, acknowledging what happened earlier. Aiko didn't even move an inch, only observing and waiting for anything Acheron would say.

"Didn't expect to see me? Don't be alarmed by my presence. You're out on break, so there's nothing to worry about."

Acheron's words lowered Aiko's guard; he walked up slowly and around Acheron, who maintained eye contact.

"Akarui contacted me about where you were at. I assumed we would cross paths; I was on my way to pick up an order for Yasuka."

Acheron whistles over Yasuka, who is sniffing around building corners. Yasuka, alerted by Acheron's whistle, turned her attention to him. Acheron grabs something from his bag, a tennis ball, throwing the ball at Yasuka, who catches it and returns it to Acheron. Acheron turned his attention to Aiko. Offering Aiko the tennis ball, who hesitated but slowly grabbed it. Upon holding the tennis ball, he felt Yasuka's saliva, which disgusted him and prompted him to throw it far, and Yasuka started to chase it. Acheron, realizing what caused Aiko to panic, only laughed, which caught Aiko off guard. Aiko looked at his hands and saw Yasuka's saliva dripping off from his hand.

"Here."

Acheron offered his coat to Aiko, whom he didn't want to, but with a wave, Acheron wiped off the saliva on his coat.

"It is strange to you why I am like this to you. You're not wrong to be guarded by my presence. Are you heading back?"

"Yes."

"Well, I was heading to the cemetery. Paying a visit to the people I knew..."

Acheron walks off from Aiko while Yasuka gives back Acheron the tennis ball.

"You're welcome to come with me."

Acheron said while walking forward, with the sun starting to settle down. Aiko didn't know what he should do. Follow him or go back to URDT.

*"Listen, he may not see you fully, but later in life, it will change. Believe me, believe us. Don't ever leave him. Even if he dismisses you, some people we care about always push us away. These are just thoughts you can think about. I wish I could see my dad again, Aiko…"*

*"I survived because of your father, Aiko. He is not what you think he is; just understand that time can heal old wounds."*

Quentin, Suki by his back, and Akarui's voice reaching to Aiko. Aiko didn't know what to do: trust their words or follow his instincts. Reflecting on their words, Aiko followed suit to Acheron.

***

Following Acheron led them to a large area with structured pillars that stood tall. Each has a series of names of people who died from any circumstances. Acheron walked by each grave, Aiko following as he looked at different names of people, feeling nothing but sorrow. Acheron continued marching forward, reaching the sign: "Memorial of the Earth Lost Souls." Aiko, reading the sign, was shocked; he didn't expect there to be a memorial for the people who once existed on Earth. As Aiko looked away from the sign, he saw millions of pillars, each with rows of names. Aiko understood that these people had lost their lives on Earth. Acheron moved forward while Aiko looked around, seeing more series of names as he continued to look, still growing more sorrowful as he traveled. Aiko bumps into Acheron's back and sees Acheron frozen. Aiko looked to the side and saw a name Acheron was staring at.

"Yasuka Tachinbana."

Aiko was confused, looking at Acheron's dog and at the grave name. He looked back and forth until Acheron grabbed something from his coat, a photo, and firmly placed it near the ground. Aiko looked closely at the photo, seeing a woman wearing the same mask as Aiko and seeing Acheron's real face. He looked younger and cleaner, with gentle cheekbones and deep brown hair around his eyebrows and brown eyes. He smiled at the camera.

"She was your mother, Aiko. I named my dog after your mother. As a remembrance and so I can say her name every day."

Aiko, hearing his words, spooked him. Causing him to collapse while kneeling.

"I met your mother when we were back on Earth. When the URDT was formed, I was a FIREBIRDS walking up to another scheduled meeting I had. That is when I bump into a lady, causing her mask to drop off from her face. I went to retrieve her mask, and she grabbed it upon making eye contact with her as she was going to grab her mask. I was taken away; her beauty and eyes were stunning. I didn't move; I just stared at her soul, which I had stumbled upon. We both stared for a moment, just the two of us. She quickly hid her face from me and grabbed her mask back. I didn't know how to respond but immediately followed her up the stairs."

Acheron paused for a moment and stepped back for a bit.

"I apologized to her, and she nodded to me. I wanted to say words I couldn't, but my heart and mind raced across each other. Then I said this: "You look beautiful." I remember hearing her gasp; I felt stupid based on what I said. I was going back down from my embarrassment until she tapped my shoulders. Saying to me, "Thank you..." I looked back at her, and we both stared for a moment. I said my name is Jabez Acheron. She said, "Yasuka Tachibana.""

Acheron looks up at the sky.

"During the Nekrothian wars, your mother and I connected more to where we were fully together. The problem was that your mother was from a Harmonian nation, people that converted to what Harmonian left behind to mankind. Practicing peace, serenity, and pacifism. They were against violence, and URDT's involvement with the Harmonian sparked national attention. Making our alliance with them, their nation would split due to whether to aid the URDT, going against their teaching, or remain neutral. They had no choice; the Nekrothians were approaching people's doorsteps. We had our relationship a secret, knowing that her people would despise me and my secret from URDT, wanting more from the Harmonians. That was when you came along."

Aiko looked up to Acheron.

"Your mother was pregnant with you; we didn't know what to do when you were about to be born. The war continued to worsen, and nations and countries lost their ground. I spearheaded the Melancholic Knight Project, hoping the Harmonians would pledge their allegiance to fighting against the invaders. URDT and Harmonains' relationship grew worse as the day continued. The suit I wore that you now wear was created before you were born. It was the first experimental suit with Harmonains and URDT engineers putting their minds together. It was the only experiment where we imprinted the Armageddon genes, amplifying the wearer. Her people accepted me, gifting me their mask, but we had to keep our relationship a secret. I had hoped the suit would be enough to fight the Nekrothians and their Armageddons."

Acheron pauses from his words and stutters a bit while speaking.

"I wished I did enough. The suit wasn't enough to save everyone I knew. Resulting in the Nekrothians continuing their advance. She lost her life and many of her people, the Melancholic Knights, as well. Everything I was fighting for was lost; I only survived because the suit wanted me to survive; the Armageddon genes left in me pushed me to continue. I thought I lost everything until you came."

Aiko looked up to Acheron.

"She gave me that exact stare with her mask, nothing but innocence and warmth. I wish—"

Aiko felt much sorrow flowing in him, so Acheron kneeled. Staring at her name and photo, Aiko's mind was open. Listening to his story made him think more about her, wondering what she was like and why he couldn't remember her.

"She gave her life to you; you were still young, and your mind was fresh. I thought I lost you both; she was strong even if her condition was weakening. I'm sorry, Aiko, I didn't know you were here. If I had known sooner, I would've taken care of you. I wish I was a father as she wanted me to be."

Acheron continued to look at the grave. Aiko, quoting back to his voice, said, "Where were you when I needed you?!"

Thinking back on their fight, he realizes they are two broken people fighting for answers and for themselves. Aiko walks up near him, kneeling with him.

"I wish I knew her more."

Acheron and Aiko looking at each other. Aiko slowly put his hand on Acheron's shoulders. Aiko opened his mouth.

"Father."

Acheron, who was shocked but nodding to his response, remained still. Sharing the moment of peace and serenity as the sun slowly sets and the wind calmly blows.

***

The evening settled in, almost closing the day. Acheron, with Yasuka walking alongside as Aiko watches the dog follow. Thinking of the dog named after his mother, wondering if that is how Acheron remembers her. Walking out of the memorial, Acheron checks his ARC. Seeing the time, he turns around.

"Going to head back?"

Aiko noticed his question but focused on Yasuka.

"Yeah."

"Not just yet. There is someone you need to meet."

Aiko was confused by his response. Acheron got closer, showing Aiko his ARC screen. Acheron displayed an address and clearance code: "Republic of Melancholia Detention Center."

Acheron pressed a button to swipe the location to Aiko's phone.

"Head over there and let them know that Premier Acheron sent you. They should check the log and allow you in. They will guide you to the person you're going to meet."

Aiko's hands lower, wondering who he is meeting.

"Who am I meeting?"

Acheron walks away from Aiko, with Yasuka following suit.

"You'll see... when you're done. Report back to base. There is a party tonight."

Acheron walked down the empty sidewalks, and Aiko thought about their shared moment. Slightly opening his mouth.

"Ach, Dad."

Acheron stopped and turned his head around.

"Thank you for sharing."

Acheron didn't respond, only nodding to his response. He continued walking toward the URDT. Aiko, noticing he didn't respond, acknowledged how painful the experience he shared was. He traveled off to the destination Acheron sent him to, the dark area of the city.

***

Reaching the destination, only walking and taking shortcuts, revealed a medium-sized building with few guards patrolling. The sign above him read: "Republic of Melancholia Detention Center."

Walking into the building shows metal detectors from both sides, and guards check Aiko's body scans.

"What is your business here?"

The guard asked Aiko.

"Premier Acheron sent me."

The guard signaled the other guard, who was checking on their computer check and saw his message to allow the boy in. The guard gave him a thumbs-up.

"Follow me."

The guard walked away, and Aiko followed. The area was tight with corridors, and the white-gray light dimmed it slightly. Doors with offices and even cages were visible. Aiko began to wonder who he might be meeting but couldn't be sure. The guard continued and opened the door to Aiko, seeing the sign: "The Parlor."

Walking in shows glass that divides the room; each space has a spot for people to sit and talk to someone behind the glass. Aiko, the guard waiting near the door, walked cautiously as he wondered who he was meeting. Aiko continued past each space until he saw half a face, revealing someone; his heart dropped. Inoue's face was shocked at first, but they slowly smiled. Aiko dropped nearly missing his seat but managed to get himself fixed. With both locked eyes, Aiko couldn't help but sniff and shake. Inoue, who remained still, grabbed the phone.

"Aiko…"

Aiko didn't speak. His heart combusted from his reaction to seeing her. Everything he shared about his past, from his feelings and guilt to Saskia, shattered in pieces. Seeing Inoue being dragged away, he thought he wasn't going to see her again.

"It's okay…"

Inoue reassured Aiko. Aiko, who refused to look at Inoue, continued sniffing more.

"Look at me. Look at me, Aiko."

Aiko slowly refused to look at her until hearing his name. He thoroughly looked at her. Noticing some bruises and cuts on some of her face.

"Inoue. Are you ok?"

"Don't worry about me. Just minor injuries. How are you and Albie doing?"

"We're doing… fine."

"I was worried about you and him. How would you both survive or find a place to live? I didn't know what I was doing, but I knew that I wanted you both to be free from out there. I believe in you, Aiko, and that you can care for him and yourself."

Aiko looked down from her response.

"How did you and he get to do or live here?"

"We've met new friends; one of them offered their place for Albie to stay."

"And you?"

Aiko remained silent but spoke his mouth slowly out.

"I met my father, Inoue…"

Inoue's mouth opened wide, but her eyes lowered.

"Acheron, isn't it?"

Aiko was caught off guard by her response.

"How did you know?"

"Everyone knows who he is. I didn't expect or think he would be your father, Aiko. Just because he has a Harmonian mask like yours."

"I didn't want him to be, but he is. He didn't want to believe I existed. He told me about my mother."

Inoue continued to listen in, but her eyes lowered as she talked.

"Told me what she was like, even if everything he said was surface level. He fought hard to protect me and me but lost us. The people, the Harmonians, are all gone."

"They're not all gone; there just aren't many around much anymore."

Inoue sniffed a bit.

"So, you find your family, your guardians, a family you wanted?"

Guilt started flowing in Aiko, and he nodded no to her.

"No, Inoue, God. NO."

Aiko put his hand on his mask as he felt pain from her response and the memories he had.

"That is the reason why I became the Melancholic Knight Inoue."

Inoue's face became more shocked.

"WHY AIKO?"

"BECAUSE I WANTED TO SEE YOU. I WANTED TO FIND YOU AND RETURN US ALL BACK THE WAY IT WAS!"

"AIKO... Aiko... my dear..."

Inoue, shedding a tear from his response.

"I told you to never look back…"

"Why. WHY CAN'T I LOOK BACK?!"

"Because I don't want you to guilt yourself over what happened. I know you didn't like that life, and I get it. I tried my best to give you the life you wanted, but in this world, it is hard, Aiko. I know it is hard for you. It was worse when Anbu—"

Inoue broke down from mentioning his name. Aiko's heart broke off. He slowly got close to the glass, putting his forehead on it.

"I miss him too, Inoue."

Inoue slowly looked up at Aiko, both locking eyes.

"I don't want you to look back; you can't change the past. You will hurt yourself more when dwelling on what preceded it. And you became a Knight, Aiko, which is even worse."

"It's temporary! I agreed to offer my service in exchange for them to find you."

"Aiko, after being transported back and forth for months. Even dealing with this abuse, I didn't care about myself; I was happy that you and Albie were free to make your choices. I don't want you to waste your freedom."

"I'm not using it for yours..."

Inoue smiled a bit and put her hand on the glass. Looking at her hand, Aiko couldn't help but think how much he rejected Inoue's love, Aiko's love, and Albie's innocence. He slowly pressed his hand against the glass as well. Breathing softly, he thought to himself that Inoue had forgiven him in a way for how he was.

"I don't blame you for anything that happened, Aiko. You were just a kid, and life isn't fair anymore."

Inoue erupted, coughing, catching Aiko off guard.

"Inoue, my god. I forgot."

"Don't worry. I'm already used to it."

"I can-"

Aiko's frustration kicks in, but sorrow is mixed inside of him.

"I'll get you out of here!"

Inoue smiled.

"Take care of Albie for me; just remember what Anbu was like to you. You'll be fine."

"Inoue. I'll get you out. I'll get you OUT! I'LL GET YOU OUT!"

A hand pressing on Aiko's shoulder.

"Time's up..."

Aiko turned slowly to the guard who was waiting for him by the door.

"I'm sorry."

Aiko wanted to speak more, but looking at Inoue's face, seeing her pure smile, he couldn't help but listen to the guard. Aiko turned and followed the guard out. Inoue watched as he left her sight. Her mouth hesitated at first but opened.

"AIKO!"

314

Aiko turned around to her.

"I do—"

Aiko wanted to know what she was going to say, but the guard ushered him to go. Leaving the void of her condition to worry him more. He turned to the guard.

"Is it possible for one of my significant others to visit her, if that's fine?"

The guard looked away but then looked at Aiko.

"I'll allow it; ensure they get here before we close. They still have time."

"I appreciate it!"

Stepping out of the building, Aiko looked up at the night skies. He has his phone like the case, and he texts Saskia.

"Are you close to the place he is staying at?"

"No, we're just done exploring. Geez, he liked to travel a lot. Why?"

"I found our caretaker. I was wondering if he could go see her. If not, I understand."

"He can! Where is she?"

"Republic of Melancholia Detention Center."

"Ok, on our way. Maybe for a while. Hey Aiko, is she ok?... Are you ok? Since you haven't seen her."

"I'm fine. I will head back to URDT. Take him home when you're done."

Aiko saw Inoue, and his heart was repaired but also broken. Tears dripped down his throat. His mask hid his face, and he looked at the sky for any hope or serenity he needed.

# Chapter Twenty-Four: Blowout Fun

The URDT opened the area, and aerial vehicles docked. Troops are installing more straps around the aerial vehicles while other troops are changing the spotlight lights to red, green, or blue. Many volunteers set up booths, tables, and the deck where Maverick gave his orientation. Troops grabbed the disco ball and hung it near the docked aerial vehicles.

***

Back at the "Bunker" Quarters, many cadets that now are official FIREBIRDS are wearing nice suits, and some wearing the finest dresses. In his room, Quentin starts putting his suit on, tying his shoes, and buckling his pants. He has his ARC monitor a video of a man explaining how to make a tie knot, which Aiko struggled with at first but got right the second time. He put his poncho on his bed and combed his hair back, ensuring it was nice and neat. Quentin fixed his smile, trying to figure out how he should smile. Grabbing his shopping bag, he revealed a cologne. He sprays it on himself but doesn't like how intense it is, only spraying a few bits on himself. Once ready, he walks out from his door. Looking at Suki's dorm next to him.

"Suki, I was wondering if you want to dance? Hmm, it's too generic. Suki, care for a dance? This is stupid. How would Dad ask Mom out for a dance? How did you do it, Dad?"

Suki's door slid open, revealing her in a purple dress that reached down near her ankle. Her long hair was down. She looked towards Quentin's attire, a nice black suit with a vibrant brownish-tan tie and a white shirt. She got closer to him and stopped.

"Argh, what is that smell?"

Quentin's face lifted.

"What you're- got to be kidding me. I thought this cologne would change my vibe."

"It's getting to me, dude."

"Gosh..."

Suki noticed Quentin's tie sticking out from his collar. She walked over to him, put her hands around his neck, and tried to fix his tie.

"I notice this is your first time making a tie knot."

Quentin was caught off guard by her approach but regained his thought of speaking.

"How did you know?"

316

"You did a four-in-hand knot. That is the most beginner knot; also, your tie's tail is sticking out."

"Oh…"

"My mom would teach my dad how to make a knot tie. Even my own mother knows how to make a knot better than my dad when they used to…"

Suki shook her head and coughed a little to skip over his sentence. Quentin, taking notice of Suki's erupting, paused.

"I tried my best. My dad never taught me how to make a tie knot, which is the same thing you do. My mom taught me when we go to these types of occasions."

"I guess we both aren't so different."

"I guess so."

After fixing his collar, Suki pauses to look at Quentin's eyes. They both look into each other's eyes before backing off a bit.

"Yeah, this cologne isn't working."

The door to the whole room opens, revealing Odie and Jerome, who are wearing casual clothes. Quentin, noticing their clothing, puts his hand on his face.

"Guys… Seriously."

"What do you mean seriously? The party never emphasizes the clothing dress code."

"Yeah, but Odie, it's just dressing up nicely and properly around people. Common courtesy."

"We're not going to dance or do much there; we're going to head out to the weapon range since I want to test my rifle. Noticing it has a bolt malfunction. Jerome is going for the food like always."

"Don't call me out like that, Odie."

Responding to Quentin while calling out Jerome, Odie is leaning on the slide door's side.

"I'm not into dancing anyway."

Odie grabbed his bag containing his rifle and ARC and headed to the door.

"We're down there and head out for a bit."

Odie waves bye to Quentin and Suki while Jerome nods his head down and follows Odie. Quentin is still looking at the door.

"What the heck were they doing all day then?"

"Beat me; I should take my ARC too."

"Why?"

"Just for emergencies, and I find it very useful wherever I go."

"It's a party, Suki."

"I'll put it on the side. You don't have to take yours if you don't like it."

"Yeah, I don't. Not carrying a weapon around my waist for this occasion."

Suki is walking to her room while he looks away. Odie and Jerome are already walking from the bunker area and making their way to the elevator. They see people wearing coveralls, with one of them pushing a cart with wires and boxes. Odie and Jerome make room for them. Odie can't help but look at their waists; they are wearing ARC, which is unusual. But Odie doesn't care that much. Both reach the elevator and venture off to the party.

The giant escalator continues down, the sound of metal creaking as the gears slowly lower vehicles and people. Aiko, resting by the railings, only looked down, thinking about Inoue's words:

*"I told you to never look back..."*

Aiko looked at his hand, seeing the surgical remains of his bond with the suit. He couldn't help but remember each time he looked at his hands. Looking at his burnt hands, Anbu's blood on his hands. Aiko started feeling fear from rethinking about it.

Reaching down, he is met with changing lights, music blasting softly, and people in dresses and suits walking around. Most people going down the escalator are here for the FIREBIRDS graduation party, while some are personnel who bring in their vehicles. Aiko, getting off, looked around; he couldn't help but notice a bit of déjà vu that reached him. Seeing this open area overshadowed at first but now a sparking light show with people's smiles on. Walking forward with people walking around and having fun, his mind zones away from the voice of Saskia, Acheron, and Inoue; the secrets he kept in himself, now being expressed to them, opening himself fully after months and years.

"Hey."

Aiko turned to his side, seeing people he didn't know confronting him: a slim, short boy with glasses and a big guy with uncombed hair.

"Aren't the Melancholic Knight?"

The glasses guy asked, and Aiko was caught off guard and didn't know how to respond. He feared that they would taunt him or say anything to scare him.

"If you are..., can you tell me what wearing the suit feels like!?"

Aiko, amazed by his response, was baffled.

"Uuhh…"

"Don't let his question get to you, man. I know he is jealous of you wearing the suit."

Jerome intercepted the conversation. Odie's eyes widen.

"I'm not. Only people like him can maintain the suit calibration and power. I am curious about how your body functions and reacts to the suit energy. Does your mind shift into the suit function when you're in combat? Do you feel a surge from the suit that can change you?"

Aiko, overwhelmed by his question, could only shake his head no.

"I guess...?"

The guy with glasses scoffs.

"Don't mind him. He got distracted from seeing you and wanted to ask you these questions. Since seeing a Melancholic Knight reappear in public was new, I couldn't care less. I'm Jerome Aguilar, Odie Ulysses."

Odie walked away but waved his hand back to say hi to Aiko. Aiko waved until he took a closer look at both of them. Aiko remembered seeing their faces, Odie with Quentin while fighting with Nerdhard troops and Jerome's face in pain from the restraints and stupor lotus.

"What, aren't you both with Quentin?"

Both of them look at each other and at Aiko.

"Yeah, we are. Why? Do you know him?"

Odie asked.

"Yeah, we met when I got here to this nation."

"Wow, what are the odds? Your friend is our team leader, which puts you in charge of us, too!"

"Really? I guess. I didn't expect Quentin to get that role. Last time when he took the lead, it didn't go well."

"Oh wow, really."

Odie laughed.

"But no, he is good. He took accountability for us all and understood our peaks and weaknesses. I love the guy. He doesn't quit easily nor give up on us."

Odie turned around and saw Quentin and Suki walking over to them.

"Speaking of which."

Aiko and Jerome look over to see them as well.

"Aiko?"

Quentin noticed him. Running up to him, Aiko remained still but smiled a bit from his presence.

"Where are Albie and the girl you were with?"

"I asked her to take Albie to visit someone we knew; she'll drop him off back at Yume's place."

Suki and Aiko making contact.

"Aiko."

"Suki."

Both nodding in seeing each other.

"How are you doing?"

"Good, it was good during the day. I haven't felt that happy like that for a while."

"It's nice to see you."

Aiko chuckles for a bit.

"Thanks. My energy is tired, so I'm sorry if I can't talk that much."

"Don't worry."

Quentin joined in the conversation.

"We understand what you're going into. It's just like what she said: nice to see you."

Aiko and Quentin look at each other in acknowledgment.

A mic sound screeched, spooking everyone.

"Oof, sorry about that, everyone. Mic checks 1, 2, 3."

One of the URDT volunteers checked the mic quality. Quentin and Suki noticed Maverick still wearing his uniform, waiting at the bottom with Captain Curtis and Dahlia. Wearing nice suits and dresses. Cade, with his helmet and military attire on.

"We're going to head out already."

Odie signals over to Jerome, who is holding a big bag of all the food from the tables. Quentin nods no to himself.

"Go already."

Quentin waved at them.

"You got it!"

Odie and Jerome turn around to Aiko.

"Hey, it was nice meeting ya, Aiko."

Odie offered his handshake to Aiko, who shook firmly. Jerome saluted Aiko while holding the bag on his back. They walked over to the entrance of the main office, leaving the party behind their backs.

"Finally. I mean—"

Quentin fake coughs himself. Redirecting his attention to Aiko.

"You're going to stay here? They're going to be a dance; it is a blast."

Aiko was about to reject his offer but remembered the joy he felt when being with people close to him: Inoue, Anbu, and Albie. Today was fantastic and peaceful as I was surrounded by the people who cared for him. I did not want that joy to end.

"Sure, I'll just watch from the side."

"That's fine; your presence here is enough. Alright, enjoy your time, Aiko."

Both Quentin and Suki waved goodbye to Aiko. Aiko nodded at them. Aiko rested by the side of the table, watching and admiring the view of the party and taking in the peace he found himself in.

"Hello and welcome FIREBIRDS. What a great afternoon to finally welcome you to the brotherhood of being a FIREBIRDS and pledge to the URDT. I would like to give the attention to Captain Maverick for your achievements."

The URDT personnel gave the microphone to Maverick, slowly fixing himself.

"Finally, we can have a party to celebrate everyone's success in becoming a FIREBIRDS Give yourself a clap.

Everyone around the room clapping, Quentin and Suki clapping with everyone else.

"I am proud to say that you have shown unwavering dedication, courage, and commitment to excellence. From the first day I saw you, you overcame challenges and obstacles and broke your limits. Be proud that your strength and responsibilities took you here in the first place."

Being a FIREBIRDS is a privilege. You are carrying the legacy of your fallen comrades and those who have served before you. You defend and uphold honor, duty, and respect in everything you do. You are URDT soldiers.

As years pass, you will continue to face challenges that test your caliber in many circumstances. Remember that we move as a unit, cry as a unit, and stay together as a unit. You are part of a brotherhood and sisterhood, sharing a common goal and trust. You have each other; remember that.

"As I close off, you still have a long way to go. So, continue to strive in your field and service with pride. Everyone looks to you with great hope and confidence."

Aiko, Suki, and Quentin, along with everyone who looked at Maverick in amazement,

"Valor Unto the Skies."

Maverick said.

"Valor Unto the Skies."

Everyone repeated. Aiko didn't say anything but watched on.

"Grounded in Courage."

"Ground in Courage."

"Till our last breath!"

"Till our last breath!"

Everyone yells after Maverick finishes the URDT motto. Maverick stepped back. With Cade Valentine walking up with the FIREBIRDS walking up. Aiming their ARC at the sky. Shooting three per shot in salute and honor, showing the FIREBIRDS commitment to their cause.

Music breaks out, and everyone heads to the center of the dance floor. Many people dance to the gentle state of the music, making everyone go in the same motion of speed. Some went to the bar to drink or play beer pong. Some make out near corners, trying to find a spot to do their own thing. Suki remained still, only watching people dance, and Quentin saw an opportunity to display his dance moves. Suki took notice of Quentin's moves, making many dance moves that were quicker than the blink of an eye.

"What are you doing, Quentin?"

"I'm *panting* trying to *pant* show off."

"That was actually quick, impressive dance moves."

"Yeah, my dad would have dance competitions with other guys at parties. *Pant He wasn't into drinking or in a strength battle. He settles it on the dance floor."

Maverick, from a distance, took notice of Quentin, seeing Suki's embarrassed face as he danced. He chuckles to himself.

"Look, Cade."

Cade is looking at where Maverick is pointing. Making him chuckle as well.

"Those dance moves, only one person could've taught him that."

"Indeed. Surprise, he can move exactly how his dad moved. I remember I tried to challenge him in a dance; he was of a different caliber."

Cade agreed that Quentin's dad was impressive.

"Here, I try to teach you."

Quentin grabs Suki's hand, moving her frantically in response to his body language. Suki wants to restrain his movement until she finds the right time to call it off.

"Whoa, Quentin, with the moves I see."

Joule was dancing to the same beat as Quentin. Quentin noticed both of them dancing to disco-like music. They both tried to dance off, performing kicks that showed off their signature moves. Suki backed up from the embarrassment.

"I can't move like you, Quentin. Joule, don't encourage him."

"C'mon, this guy is by far the most impressive dancer I have ever seen. I must challenge him for fun."

Quentin put his hand out but a few seconds later lowered it down from her response. Suki chuckled but kept her seriousness. Quentin regained his voice.

"You just need to *pant stretch."

"I don't dance like that; I prefer dancing..."

The music suddenly shifts from hip-hop funk to slow jazz. Quentin, caught off guard, notices the music shift. He looks around, seeing people dancing with each other slowly. He slowly turns to Suki, who has her hands out already.

"This is my style."

"Well, you two enjoy yourselves. I got a date with my fiancé."

Joule leaves both Quentin and Suki. Suki extends her hand out to Quentin, who has a slow smile but is uncertain about taking her hand. Suki grabs his right hand and places it on her left hip while Quentin's left hand and hers are up. They do a slow dance in sync motion.

"Hmm, I didn't know you liked this."

Quentin said softly.

"That's because my mother liked to dance like this when my dad… was around."

"Well, I'm not great at dancing like this. See, I'm already stepping over you."

"It's fine; you're doing better than I expected."

Aiko watches them as they dance, feeling a bit of joy inside of him. He looked up at Acheron's window, staring at Acheron's closed curtains. Inside, Acheron, with his head on his arms, looks at the photo, and Yasuka, near her dog bed, looks at him. The music echoing from outside his room is the only sound source he listens to as he stares at the void of the picture. The same picture with Aiko as a baby and his mother wearing his mask.

"Aiko?"

Aiko turns to his right. Seeing Akarui in the dress she got earlier.

"I didn't expect you to be here."

"I just came to be with them. Accompanying them."

Akarui leaning with Aiko.

"Where are Saskia and your little brother?"

"I asked her to visit my… caretaker."

Akarui's eyes widen.

"She is at the Detention Center. I wanted Albie to see her; it's what I can at least make up for him since my absence."

"Don't blame yourself. We're here at this moment. Enjoy it and be happy with what is around you."

Aiko breathes in and out as he looks up. Staring but embracing what she said around him.

"Seems we're the only ones who aren't dancing."

Akarui extended her hand to Aiko. Aiko, looking down now, notices her hand. Feeling shocked.

"Me? I can't dance Akarui."

"It doesn't matter; I'll teach you. I tried asking Curtis, but he was already dancing with Dahlia, and Kenryoku is antisocial."

Putting her hand closer to Aiko.

"Care to dance with me?"

Aiko, hesitant at first, didn't want to but didn't want to leave her alone. He slowly put his hand on hers, and she dragged him out onto the dance floor. Upon reaching the dance floor, she moved in a rhythmic motion, moving her feet back and forth while their hands moved side by side. Aiko, not in sync, was panicking a bit. He kept looking at her feet while looking at their hands, trying to keep up with her pace.

"Don't worry, you're doing great."

"I don't even have a suit."

"Doesn't matter; you dancing with me is all I care about."

"You're older than me."

"Who said age doesn't matter?"

Aiko is trying to come up with a way to get out of the dance, but she just wants to embrace her kind of dance. Aiko is slowly regaining his focus on how to move with her.

"See, 1, 2, 3. 1, 2, 3. And 1, 2, 3. Now look down."

Aiko looked down, seeing how she moved her feet, sliding and moving her legs to get the footing correctly. Aiko focused and followed closely to her motion. He could hear her metallic leg clanking while her right heel clipped the floor. Aiko watched intently and did what she said.

"Nice. Just like how I help you in your mission, I'm helping you dance."

Aiko couldn't help but smile a bit. Quentin and Suki notice that Aiko is dancing with Akarui.

Quentin laughed.

"I never thought Aiko could dance."

Suki remarked.

"I guess he's learning like me."

"Well, let's not stop then."

Suki said towards Quentin.

325

Quentin, Suki, Aiko, and Akarui continued to step up with the music beat, reaching faster and faster movements. Suki and Akarui taught Aiko and Quentin how to lower them to spice their dance. The music reached its climax, and everyone danced in sync, treating the dance like a ballroom. Once the music reached its end, Akarui and Suki both neared their ears.

"Now."

Quentin and Aiko both dipped down to Akarui and Suki. Aiko struggled, but due to the exposure to the suit, the strength from the suit passed through him. Quentin managed to pull it off while Suki smiled and gasped at how excellently Quentin executed it. The music ended with everyone clapping and bowing to each other. Aiko, noticing that everyone was bowing to their dance partner, did the same. Akarui did the same, with a little chuckle coming from her.

"I was quite worried that I was too heavy for you. I guess the suit made you strong enough to do anything. The training must pay off."

Aiko couldn't help but chuckle a bit. He looked at Quentin and Suki, who smiled and nodded to him. They were happy to see Aiko dancing out on the dance floor. Roars of clapping and cheering filled the air.

***

Back inside the building, multiple people wearing attire from various companies equipped with ARC communication devices. A group is in the communication breaker room, wearing a uniform from URDT. Another group is above the party near the aerial vehicles, placing a sticky substance with a box attached near the vehicles. The last group, the cabling company, is in the power source room, which provides electricity for the building.

"Set charges in 3."

After placing their charges, the groups relocate far away. Each group has a member with a detonator.

"2."

The groups keep their distance while the announcer says, 1.

"1."

Each member pressed their detonator, and an explosion erupted in multiple areas.

***

Aiko, looking up, notices fiery debris coming down. He immediately grabbed Akarui's hands and pulled her to safety with all his force. Raining aerial vehicle parts. Came down towards the people, many took notice of and, with their ARC, grappled out to safety.

326

Quentin was caught off guard by the explosion and knocked over; Suki pushed him off to safety. The debris trapped Suki, with flames engulfing the area.

"SUKI!"

Quentin ran to Suki, but the flames forced him to retreat. Multiple explosions were heard from each of the rooms where the groups were. The light went out, pitch black; the flames served as the only light source. The emergency lights kicked in, and everyone around was panicking until a voice rang out.

"WE'RE UNDER ATTACK! EVERYONE GET TO THEIR BATTLE STATION. I NEED SECURITY SQUADS TO HEAD INSIDE AND INVESTIGATE. GO, GO, EVERYONE!"

Maverick, in charge, ordered everyone to get ready and find the attackers. Everyone listened and obeyed without question. Squads assembled and ran inside with their ARCs to investigate the unknown danger.

"The communication isn't WORKING! KEEP IN MIND EVERYONE!"

Maverick yelled out.

"Joule! Join with Cade; he's going to need the forces there."

"Understood, sir!"

Joule followed Cade and the other troops. Maverick grappled up to where the aerial vehicles were, following the attackers.

"SUKI!"

Quentin tries to get the debris but burns his hands. Akarui took notice of Quentin's yell.

"Aiko. Suit now!"

Both Aiko and Akarui ran to the entrance to the buildings but stopped to see the Melancholic Knight suit on a stand, with Acheron and a few mechanics leading the suit to Aiko.

"The Excesses must have infiltrated inside here, but how did they bypass the clearance!"

Akarui yells while the fire and smoke surround them.

"Because someone let them in here. Our security wouldn't let just anyone in. Only by personnel's entrée."

Acheron said as he walked up to him. Acheron looked at Aiko, both nodding to each other. Aiko ran up to the suit, letting it stick to him and around his body. The wires and connection reached the eyelids of his mask, letting the suit calibrate with him.

"SUKI, I'M NOT LEAVING YOU!"

"You're *cough* getting yourself burned!"

"I DON'T CARE!"

Quentin tries to pull with all his might while his hands are firmly on the heated metal, melting his skin away. A footstep is heard behind him, grabbing Quentin and moving him to the side. Aiko, in the suit, pulls the debris out and goes inside, grabs Suki, holding her, and uses an extinguisher to take out the smoke and fire. Placing Suki on the table, Quentin reaches for Suki, checking on her raspy breathing. Akarui comes in and checks her neck.

"She is fine; it's just the heavy heat and the smoke. You two need to get to safety."

"No… I can fight."

Suki gets up from the table. But Quentin was holding her off.

"You can't, Suki; I don't want you."

"Well, too bad! I NEED TO HELP!"

Aiko, watching them argue, felt a vibration from his jacket. His phone began to relay messages on his HUD, a message from Saskia.

"AIKO, PLEASE HEAD OVER TO THE ABANDONED RADIO TOWER IN THE CITY'S SOUTHEAST. I NEED YOUR HELP!"

Aiko's heart raced. He immediately rushed out of the building entrance. He ran up the escalator and out from the building to the city outside, sprinting and grappling with the city skyline as he desperately tried to get to Saskia.

"AIKO, WHERE ARE YOU GOING?"

Acheron shouted.

"Sir, I'm heading to the tactical operation room to track him."

Akarui called to him.

"You're not going without protection."

Curtis, with his shirt sleeves ripped, revealing his muscular biceps, showing his battle readiness. They all ran inside the building, heading to the tactical operation room.

"Quentin, let me go!"

Quentin was holding Suki off, but she put her hands on his. Quentin lowered his hands and let her get down.

"I'm fine *cough. Plus, you didn't even bring your ARC."

Suki runs inside the building. Quentin is hesitant but follows suit.

Excesses members, still dressed as cabling company employees, armed as they barricade themselves at the communication circuit room; the man with the mask code-named Romeo was there, waiting for anything that comes at them.

# Chapter Twenty-Five: Fortuitous Clash

Aiko continued to rush through the busy city, wall-running, grappling, and hooking onto buildings. Managing to cause property damage from his weight and speed, rushing so fast that people could only see the blue light from his suit dazzle from his speed. Aiko's mind ran through many thoughts, thinking of Saskia and Albie. Then, remembering Inoue and Anbu's faces, his face grew lower and tighter as he rushed to the Republic of Melancholia radio tower.

"REPORT!"

Acheron leads the way, with two FIREBIRDS soldiers guarding him. Akarui follows suit, while Curtis is behind them to protect them.

"It indeed is The Excesses; they access infiltrate inside our building using the outside access."

"Who allowed them in!?"

"We weren't able to determine that maybe one of the people working here might have let them in by using pirate sources to hide their tracks."

"Where are The Excesses at right now?"

"We detected them to be in three main areas in the building. One is at the power station on floor 20. The second is the communication circuit on floor 33. We suspect the third group that caused most of the aerial vehicles to be destroyed are going to target the vehicles next. Maverick and the other captain are going to stop them, sir."

"Very well. Has the tactical operation room been compromised?"

"No, few members tried to get in but were repulsed."

"Strengthen the security!"

"Yes, Sir!"

Kenryoku is following alongside Acheron as they march to the tactical communication room. Two guards stand by the door to the area with their ARC pointing sideways, with three members down from the stun shot. Opening the door, the workers are hiding underneath their desks, some in their dresses and suits, hiding from the unexpected attack.

"Get to your station; I need a location on Aiko NOW!"

The worker, feeling confident from Kenryoku presence immediately listened. The emergency power kicking in as each of the workers started navigating on the modules, the city camera systems and activities from Aiko that were about.

"Curtis, your assistance isn't needed. We are good here. I require your help with the other captains."

"Understood."

Curtis, with his ARC, presses a different type of ammo on the screen, selecting the slug type set to stun. He runs off, navigating and regrouping with Maverick.

"Use the power sparingly and be exactly where Aiko could be."

"Sir, we found him."

"Put his visor on the screen."

"We can't; we don't have enough power to do it."

"Track his location. Can we at least reach his communication?"

"Yes."

"Put me on."

Aiko continued to wall run and managed to grapple onto a building roof, running across while jumping onto different rooftops. He felt the suit as it was but remembered the pain it brought him. He was still feeling the pain continue to swell him, but he pushed onward.

"Aiko, your presence is needed back at URDT. WHAT ARE YOU DOING?"

Acheron barked through his helmet.

"Forgive me. Saskia needs my help?"

"What about her?"

"She is in trouble, Dad. She is at the abandoned radio tower. She has my brother."

Acheron wants to say something back, but realizing that Aiko's little brother Albie is in trouble, he only listens in.

"I don't know what happened, nor if they are—I'm sorry. They need me."

As Aiko closed off communication, he continued to rush. Seeing the radio tower in the distance.

✳✳✳

"Come quickly; stay by me."

Quentin checks his corners as he peeks.

"Don't try Quentin; you don't even have your ARC."

"Yeah, but I'm trying to protect you."

They both run up the stairs, navigating the emergency lights as they reach up.

"Maverick should be up there; let's continue!"

Quentin yelled while checking his corners. Upon reaching floor 27, FIREBIRDS charged from the hallways; Suki followed suit with Quentin while covering his back.

"Have you seen Maverick?"

Quentin asked one of the FIREBIRDS troopers.

"Yes, he is—"

An explosion nearby sent the trooper flying away and caused Quentin to stumble down. The other two FIREBIRDS getting shot at immediately but only at their leg and chest, leaving them down and breathing.

"Take cover by the walls."

Suki peeks by her right side while Quentin is on the other side of the wall. The Excesses members with rifles continue blind fire due to the heavy smoke. Suki returns fire, shooting in the direction of The Excesses location.

"I can't get a shot!"

Suddenly, someone fired from behind Suki, shooting straight at the two Excesses members. Stunning them down and leaving them immobilized. Quentin and Suki turned around, seeing Odie with his casual clothes on but with his FIREBIRDS helmet with the goggle attachment on.

"These are the party poopers. We heard screams and explosions, so I and-"

Odie turned around to see more Excesses members running, but they were immediately stunned by Jerome Gatling's gun, who was behind Odie.

"Jerome and I came out to find this."

"Have you seen Maverick?"

"Yeah, he was speeding past us. Seemed to be heading upstairs."

Odie points Quentin in the direction that Maverick went.

"Let's go."

Quentin ordered everyone, and they stormed off to the stairs. Reaching Maverick while watching their corners and navigating through the dense darkness of smoke.

Upon checking multiple floors, they saw Maverick and the other FIREBIRDS, who were wearing their dresses and suits, having a firefight across the hall. Walking up, they saw some of the troops wounded and being pulled back.

"Maverick!"

Maverick turned around to see Quentin and the others.

"Where's your ARC boy?!"

"I left it behind by mistake.

"Why would you do that?!"

"That's what I told him, too, sir."

Suki jumped to embarrass Quentin. Maverick palmed himself and made his attention forward.

"Here, use mine."

"Are you sure, Captain?"

"I'm very sure I have other utility at my disposal. They have this hallway closed off tight in their favor. They have a minigun stationed on both sides of the entrance, preventing us from entering the communication room. They have their hands on ARC, so that's why they're still shooting with reloading. We hope they can overheat their weapon, but we need that communication back online!"

Quentin looked around, seeing how dark it was and how the smoke from the bombs had cleared the area. He looked at Odie and Jerome, who were standing by him.

"I got a plan."

***

Breaking into the radio tower, Aiko observes the tower. Seeing an escalator and poster of a URDT radio. Looking up, he noticed how open the interior is; he started to climb up by grappling. He could feel his pumping adrenaline as he grappled. Upon reaching the final floor below the rooftop, he ran straight at the door. Breaking the door open revealed a prominent figure covered by a cloak on the stage. He couldn't see Albie nor Saskia; he prepared himself for anything.

A door opened, prompting Aiko to turn around. His eyes widened from what he saw: a man with a Harmonian mask like his but altered a bit, wearing a large trench coat and suit with a tan tie.

The figure walked towards the stage, staring at Aiko.

"Aiko Ashin."

Aiko is caught off guard by the fact that the figure knows his name, or his voice sounds slightly altered.

"Yes, I know you. And I pity you for what you are doing."

And gripping his hands tightly from his response.

"Who are you?"

The figure sees Aiko's relentless action and the need for an answer.

"Homura Kuragari or Mr. Mortis by The Excesses. Their leader."

Aiko's heart spooked, seeing the leader standing before him.

"Ever since we left Earth due to humanity's failure to sustain its survival, I lost faith in what we did. I had trusted the URDT with all my heart until the people WE LOST Aiko from their failure! Aiko, I am like you."

"You're not like me!"

"Yes, we are. We are from the same race as the Harmonians. And we served the same master, the URDT."

"That makes you a..."

Aiko said softly.

"A Melancholic Knight as well."

Homura said to Aiko.

"Yes, I have served as humanity's last hope, but only to our race; I feared we would lose. That promise left us when Harmonian's alliance with URDT was tightening. Forcing our men to take on the role of Melancholic Knights. We lost everything on that day; you don't need to remember anything to know what I mean."

Aiko was hesitant and wanted to fight against his hate towards the URDT.

"WHERE ARE THEY!"

"I'M NOT DONE YET! That is why I created The Excesses in the first place; many people who joined had been neglected by the URDT. During the colonization of Gaea, many people were forced to live outside of this nation, the poor and the weak. Only the wealthy could afford to live in URDT protection, only select people who could benefit them. They stopped being humanity's source of protection, forming a government nation that needs to be the strongest to exist. Lasting longer than anyone. They only see you as useful. That's how Acheron sees you, Aiko; yes, I know him; a fool he was."

"Was this all about telling how bad URDT is?"

"So, it seemed. Depends on the outcome of this meeting. I know you very well, Aiko, and I can help you. Arranging this meeting wasn't easy; having one of our spies working at URDT wasn't easy. Giving us intel on your suit and planning an attack like at the meat factory. Jax was too arrogant to listen, and Nerdhard escaped to continue our plans."

"What are the plans?"

"You'll learn soon enough. You're distracted with me while they are fighting off what remains of The Excesses; I forgot to mention that Nerdhard is there. But communication here is off, so you can't do anything. He will continue our plan of bringing URDT down, no matter what."

"What's stopping me from ending you?"

"Because you can't, you can't lose what you have, can you, Aiko? You can't lose Albie, you can't lose Inoue; losing Anbu wasn't easy for you, was it!"

"WHO THE HELL ARE YOU?!"

Aiko charged at the figure to tackle him until someone ran up before him. He stopped to look down, seeing Saskia blocking him from attacking the figure. He gasped, his heart and words shaking from her appearance, but part of him was happy to see her.

"Aiko, wait!"

"Move, Saskia!"

Saskia protesting Aiko down.

"Saskia? Is that the name you chose? Unbelievable."

With the figure disapproving of what she said, Aiko's mind went slow. Saskia? Her name being dumb? Aiko backed off a bit.

"You two know each other?"

"Yes."

"Of course, that's why you provided that information to me. Right? Aria?"

Aiko's mind froze. Aria? Who is Aria?

"You think Saskia is her real name? Go ahead, say your real name."

Homura put his hand on Saskia's right shoulder. Saskia was nervous and scared, but she moved her mouth.

"Aria Kuragari..."

Aiko's heart dropped. Aria Kuragari is his daughter, and the spy in the URDT Homura takes off his mask and reveals the pirate, who took Anbu away and left them all alone. Aiko backed off, and his body felt a surge of cold. His heart was broken; he looked at her and him simultaneously, not wanting to believe she was his daughter.

"Don't be surprised, Aiko; how else did I know you? Besides telling me stories about what had happened long ago, I had Aria operate under URDT's nose, giving The Excesses an edge to strike URDT when the time was right. I didn't expect her to make friends."

Homura walked away, uncloaking the prominent figure. Revealing a suit. Segmented angular look and overlapping plates that carry out a heavy build and medium mobility. There are layers of segmented armor that mirror both the chest piece and lower and upper arm guards. The armor shared similarities to Aiko's suit, but its waist guard had overlapping plates that hung down to cover the upper thighs and ensure that the hips and torso were guarded. More layers of plates are overlapped around the legs. The armor was molded and heavier than Aiko's, similar in stature to Jax's armor but shorter. He got inside the suit, wearing a helmet that had a transparent visor to show his face. The helmet was like Aiko's but sharper around the jawline, with a sharp Hachi helmet structure covering his head.

"Aiko... I can expl—"

"Saskia..."

Homura looking at Aiko intently now.

"HER NAME IS NOT SASKIA!"

A whip from his arm launches towards Aiko, wrapping around his neck. The spike on it restrains his throat a bit.

"Without her help, I couldn't upgrade this suit."

Saskia looks back and forth between her father and Aiko, her thoughts racing.

"Aiko, it is not what it seemed!"

"WHY SASKIAA! WHERE ALBIEEE!"

"Aiko, I—"

336

"I know I keep interrupting you, but you served your purpose; that's all he needs to know. If you want to know where Albie is at, like you said, take him to see Inoue. There has been a complication with that request. You have two choices, what you choose determines their outcome. Join me, Aiko. I heard stories about how wearing a suit can be a burden to you. You don't have to die like the rest of our race. You are your own master; that is what I want. I don't want to have a quarrel with you; fighting each other would be pointless. Unless you stay with the URDT, that's when I will give the word to my man to transport your close one away from here."

Aiko shakes violently, trying to break the restraints from the whip but can't from how much he struggles.

"CHOOSE AIKO! YOU DON'T HAVE TIME TO THINK; DO IT!"

For a moment, Aiko wanted to side with him, knowing how much pain the suit, the URDT, is and the burden he carries. Even Inoue urged him to never look back and face the future. But simultaneously, he remembered why he was fighting for it. Trying to save the people close to him, Quentin, Suki, Akarui, Albie, and Inoue, even if it hurts him; he can't lose them. Can't experience the trauma.

"I DON'T WANT TO KILL YOU, AIKO, BUT I GOT TO DO WHATEVER IS NECESSARY TO FIGHT FOR OUR RACE!"

Worrying about Aiko, Saskia began to feel hesitant. Part of her wants to stay by her father's side, but, at the same time, she feels Aiko's pain. Their experience and his trust in her loyalty to Aiko. Grabbing something from her bodysuit pocket, she pulls out a screwdriver and stabs Homura's hips. Homura yelped, causing him to loosen his grip on Aiko. Saskia makes a run to the other door that takes her downstairs.

"AIKO, THEY'RE TAKING THEM TO EVERGREEN HUB STATION! EVERGREEN HUB STATION!"

"GET BACK HERE!"

Saskia, ignoring her father, dashed out the door, headed downstairs, and disappeared from them.

"I guess it has to end like his. I'm sorry, Aiko, but I can't have you in my way. I need vengeance for our people."

Aiko and Homura look at each other, ready in a stance, awaiting who will strike first.

\*\*\*

"OK, WE'RE GOOD."

"YES."

337

Maverick Odie and Suki are behind Jerome. The other troopers are behind cover elsewhere, providing cover fire for Quentin's plan.

"GO!"

Jerome, with his table they used as cover, pushed and continued to push it.

"We need to reach the other hallway. This table isn't going to hold off the firepower! Odie, get them."

Odie is listening to Quentin's request. With his sniper rifle, he aims at the gunners, but because of their endless shooting, it is hard for him to get clear shots. He manages to get a few Excesses members down, but the constant fire forces him to take cover. Suki and Maverick are blind firing while Jerome is struggling to push the table, and he notices that the table is heating up.

"It's heating up!"

Quentin notice.

"Everyone pushes till we reach the next hallway!"

They all pushed and managed to reach the next hallway, Suki, Jerome, and Odie taking a position on the right side while Quentin and Maverick were on the other side.

"What now?!"

Suki yelled over to Quentin. Quentin tried to think and look around but was hesitant and struggled to come up with a plan.

***

"ARRAGH!"

With multiple blades from underneath his arms, Homura strikes Aiko while Aiko blocks off his attacks. Aiko notices his fighting style is like his but with Ernaline's movement. Homura performs a kick that sends him launching back. Homura throws multiple blades at Aiko, who, with his Valor edge quick draw, blocks each of them. Homura's blade returns while he charges straight at Aiko. They both clash their blades, showing how equal their strikes and clashes are. Aiko takes advantage of Homura's speed. Noticing how he jumped, Aiko timed a well-hit on Homura's hip where Saskia struck. Causing Homura to stumble back, angering Homura even more. Homura flips a switch on his arms. Electricity sparks from the blades and his whip. Immediately, Homura, using both of his whips from his arms, launched at Aiko with the whip, tangling Aiko and forcing Aiko to his knees. The electricity shocked his body and his head, and he couldn't think anymore, paralyzing his body more and more.

***

"Quentin."

**338**

Quentin looks to Maverick.

"I have enough armor and an EMP grenade. I'll use my back, and the bullet will bounce off my armor, but we have to make it quick."

"All due respect, sir, I can't let you take the hits."

"I don't care what you think. You go behind me with the grenade. AND YOU ALL COVER FIRE FOR US!"

"YES, SIR!"

Suki, Odie, and Jerome yelled in agreement. Quentin was hesitant but nodded. Maverick rushed out, putting his body down; Quentin followed his back closely, but a bullet sliced his arms.

"Throw it and duck down!"

Maverick ducks down, and Quentin throws the charge grenade, getting it near his hips from the ammo. He ducks down while the charged grenade releases an EMP burst that turns off the ARC system and Gatling gun.

"CHARGE FIREBIRDS, CHARGE!"

Maverick ordered everyone who wasn't affected by the EMP to charge. They began stunning down the hall and took cover by the door entrance.

"They're more in the room, sir!"

"Get them!"

Maverick rests by the side wall. He looks at Quentin, who is bleeding.

"You're good?"

"Yeah, just scratches."

"Okay, everyone, charge in!"

Everyone, including Odie and Jerome, followed suit. Suki stayed behind Quentin, checking on his wound. Both of them smiled at each other.

"One of them is escaping!"

A trooper echoed from the entrance, and one of the Excess members ran outside. Quentin and Suki saw it was one of the members, code-named Romeo, from the last encounter. The figure dashes out to his left, forward and away. Suki tries to shoot but realizes the EMP radius reached her ARC, so she pursues him. Quentin, taking notice, stands up.

"WAIT, SUKI!"

Quentin follows Suki as she chases Romeo. Her face is red, and his eyes are lowered. They pursue the figure through the emergency light flickering and smoke-filled hallways.

***

Aiko, trying to break from his restraints, used all his force and escaped the whip. Aiko, realizing Homura has electricity, must keep his distance from him. Homura performs a flip as he throws his electrified blades. Aiko manages to dodge the multiple blades. Homura catches Aiko with his whip, wrapping it around Aiko's chest and neck. Restraining Aiko, Homura throws another batch of blades. Aiko manages to dodge slightly but gets stabbed three times, hitting his armor chest. Feeling the electricity charge him, fueling Aiko's anger even more.

Aiko, releasing steam from his suit, overheated the whip, grabbed it and tore it off. Homura, shocked by his strength, threw his other whip at Aiko, which Aiko grabbed and used against Homura, throwing Homura out of the building. Aiko ran and looked out. Suddenly, a whip lashed out and grappled onto Aiko, dragging him out as well. Both began wall running on the skyscraper, clashing and throwing their blades.

The wall ran up to the roof. It was a standoff; which one of them could hold their strength? Homura felt Aiko's energy and suit overheating; Homura could feel his old body giving up; his energy and body didn't match Aiko's. Aiko's mind ran angrily, thinking about Albie, Inoue, and Anbu, especially Anbu. Aiko's mindset moved forward, and he headbutted Homura so hard that he staggered him back. Aiko quickly, with his valor edge, disarms Homura's whip and blades; Aiko even kicked so hard at Homura's leg that Homura felt his bones crack. Aiko stabs directly at Homura's armored chest, pressing him down and putting both his blades against Homura's throat.

"DO IT! AIKO. YOU VERY MUCH EARN TO KILL ME!"

Aiko could feel his tears dripping from his eyes and going down his face.

"WHAT ARE YOU WAITING FOR? I DESERVE TO DIE!"

Aiko thought about it; killing him would remove the anger he had but at the same time. He saw himself in the position he was in. Having his hand against someone's throat, Acheron, Anbu, remembered the anger he felt towards them. With his fist, Aiko smashes Homura's helmet, tearing off his mask to truly see his face. Seeing a man with his face all bloody and tears showing from his eyes. Sees himself about to end someone's life, the same life he did to Acheron and Anbu.

"You very much deserve to die. But. I can't do it. Human life is too precious to give up."

Aiko got up and walked away. Leaving Homura pinned down, broken.

"AIKO, WHAT ARE YOU WAITING FOR! KILL ME! I CAN'T BE A PRISONER TO THIS LIFE ANYMORE! NOT TO URDT"

Aiko ignores his words and stands near the edge of the skyscraper. Aiko reaching from his side of his helmet, records a message to Akarui.

"Mr. Mortis is defeated; he's all yours."

"YOU'RE NOT GOING TO MAKE IT TO THEM, AIKO! YOU'RE TOO LATE! COME BACK AND END ME!"

Ignoring Homura's screams, Aiko's anger grew but didn't let it get to him. He leapt off the skyscraper, grappled onto other buildings, and headed towards Harmony Station. His mind ran with many thoughts: Are Quentin and the others are okay? Is he too late for Albie and Inoue? Why did Saskia betray them? He swings to different sides of the buildings while people below him watch him running on rooftops. Hoping the outcome doesn't end the same for his past again.

# Chapter Twenty-Six: Don't leave me

Kenryoku asked Acheron.

"Why is she at the tower?"

"I don't know, Akarui; she was with you, right?"

Acheron turning his head toward Akarui who is sitting on a chair with only the emergency light displayed. The darkness makes everyone's vision hard to see, even with some light modules on.

"She was. She stayed with Aiko and his brother. He came back alone, so I can assume she went to take his brother back home since that is where I went first during the day."

"She and his brother must have been taken hostage by The Excesses. Distracting him there. It's a trap, sir."

Acheron looked at the blank, the power not turning on.

"I know."

Acheron looked at his card, which was the access to the LYN underground.

"Can you both look at your LYN access cards?"

Kenryoku took his out of his coat. Akarui, with her dress still on but still carrying her valuables, checked. Her face dropped.

"It's not there."

Kenryoku and Acheron looking at Akarui.

"Did you carry it with you? You are supposed to have it all the time!"

Kenryoku yelled at her.

"I did. When I got the dress, I placed it in my dress when I was about to drop off Aiko and—"

Akarui turned to them, and Kenryoku's eyes widened. Acheron still looks at the blank monitor screen.

"She's the spy we've been looking for. GET THAT COMMUNICATION BACK ONLINE! GET ME CADE!"

The workers check on their modules and connect wires while doing so.

"It is good that not many people know about LYN; everyone is occupied with The Excesses. We continue with our plan."

A stern voice, Nerdhard walking the same hallway that Acheron and the others walk. Looking at the insertion, he swipes the card. Opening the door reveals the three monitors, Lycoris, Yvette, and Nicodemus. Nerdhard makes his way to a nearby terminal, inserting a chip and turning off the AI's monitors. He accesses the system using the Akarui card. Seeing the Humanity history log and many projects, he continued to look through the terminal. Finding a specific project that widens his eyes: "Project Revival." His face lowers, and his teeth grind.

"So, this is your plan, Acheron. Humanity makes me sick! Screw this race then!"

Nerdhard looked up Gaea's coordinates, then logged into Harmonian history. He found many technologies belonging to the Harmonians, including one technology he was looking for: space travel. He got what he came for; he made his retreat away from LYN. Upon leaving, he was met with a sharp cannon ARC pointing at him.

"Cade."

Nerdhard said, looking at Cade with his modified ARC.

"I was alerted that The Excesses may have invaded here. You don't belong here."

Nerdhard chuckles from his response.

"Cade, Cade, Cade, why are you still working with them?"

"Always been loyal to URDT since it began. URDT cause is important for humanity's survival."

"You don't understand what URDT's intent is. They are only protecting us since we are essential to their survival. We're only useful till they can dispose of us."

"I'm not. Direct orders from him are to."

"Arrest me, that soft law they installed. To farm us more and more for their benefit."

"No. Acheron personally asked me to kill you."

Nerdhard's face widens.

"I was their top scientist. I believed what was right back then before they started meddling with the Harmonian, and that was when I lost faith in humanity. What we became after the Nekrothian wars. What URDT has in plan isn't going to work."

"You weren't supposed to know about that. Humanity will survive, no matter what. We will do what is necessary."

"Like I said..."

Nerdhard grabs a grenade from his back.

"We're only useful till they can dispose of us."

Nerdhard throws a grenade at Cade, who jumps out of the way and fires a projectile, electric and sharp, hitting Nerdhard's jaw. Cade is caught by the explosion and knocked unconscious. The explosion triggers the fire alarm. Nerdhard puts his hand on his bleeding jaw and runs to the elevator. Nerdhard, going up the elevator, made his way to another port where aerial vehicles are docked. Piloting the aerial vehicle out from the port, leaving URDT behind.

*** 

"We got an unauthorized vehicle leaving URDT without permission!"

Acheron taking notice.

"SHOOT IT DOWN!"

Guns from the base open, firing upon the aerial vehicle. Damaging the right engine but escaping the shots.

"It's heading up north!"

"TRACK IT!"

Acheron order.

"Can't we have our troops take another aerial vehicle to chase it down?"

"We can't; we aren't sure if there are still active bombs lying around. They know it, and we don't. We're waiting for the bomb squad to check around corners. We can't risk our supplies being damaged more than they are."

Kenryoku looked away from Acheron's response. Akarui looked at her monitor and saw that Aiko's vitals were not high. She remained still, with workers chatting through the microphones. Communication was back online, but not the power.

*** 

"SUKI, WAIT UP!"

Quentin continued to chase Suki and Romeo. Romeo grabbed a pistol from his pocket and proceeded to fire at Suki, but he missed.

They travel up the stairs while Romeo continues to fire. Suki dodges but grows angrier. At the end of the stairs, take them out to the roof of the URDT. Romeo runs towards the front, where the building faces the city, seeing the lights and skyline of the Republic of Melancholia. He walks over to a square pillar structure, hanging over the entrance below. Ambling away from Suki, who is approaching him. Reaching the edge of the rooftop, he pointed his pistol at Suki, who stopped.

The pistol ammo is finished. Romeo throws the pistol, looking at Suki. Quentin caught up to them but stopped a distance from them. Romeo looked at his ARC, which caught Suki's attention. Immediately, Romeo tried to pull his ARC, but Suki was quick enough to disarm him. Romeo stumbled back near the edge. Suki walked up slowly, pointing and standing over Romeo. Quentin follows slowly behind her, getting her back. Once she aimed her ARC at Romeo, he spoke.

"SUKI!"

Suki stopped. The voice coming from Romeo sounded familiar since—

"SUKI, SUKI, wait."

Romeo pulled off his mask, revealing a face Suki tried to erase from her mind. The same face she saw from her hallucination when prepping for the raid on the meat factory and getting sprayed with stupor lotus.

"Suki…"

Suki's dad has bruises and cuts around his face. Suki didn't want to believe it, causing her to step back. Quentin took notice until he saw Romeo stand up.

"Dear, it's been a long time. I can see you fully without that mask."

Her father got closer to her, but Suki immediately pointed his ARC at him.

"What… are… you… doing here?"

Suki's voice hesitated. Her arm shakes as she tries to process with her mind.

"When I left you all, I felt nothing but shame. I knew I couldn't come back to your life. Your mother didn't want me anymore. I had nowhere to go; this was the only thing I had in life."

"JOINING THE TERRORIST GROUP!"

Suki points her ARC at her father's face.

"YOU LEFT US BECAUSE OF WHAT YOU DID TO US."

Suki's tears dripped slowly down from her eyes.

"The hits you gave to Mom left marks on her. Did you know that? She couldn't find any job, and we starved for weeks until she healed and was able to provide for us."

Suki walked closer to her father while pointing at him, forcing him to step back slowly.

"Boe and Kaito don't even know who their father was!"

345

Pushing him far to the edge of the rooftop.

"You remember this!?"

Suki showed a bit of her skin from the side of her arm, revealing a heavy scar.

"You gave me this when you cared about drinking."

"I DON'T. I couldn't live with the fact that I couldn't provide for my family. We lived here before there were opportunities when only the powerful could live while the rest tried to mangle at each other. I loved your mother, your brothers, and you."

"NO, YOU DIDN'T!"

Suki shoots his left leg, causing him to yelp and fall to his knee. His heart pounds, and his face grows apprehensive.

"If you did, you should have stayed with us! You don't understand how difficult our life was after you left. You made it worse when you left. I ran away trying to find you; I ran away from home, thinking you were lost. I didn't care what Mom, and her parents said. I hated my life when you left. I felt alone. I didn't know how I could help my family when you were gone. I hated my life because of YOU!"

Suki proceeded to shoot at his right leg and his chest. Causing him to stumble back on the edge of the cliff and cling to the edge. Suki looks down at him while he is holding on for dear life. She slowly points at his face, pressing her ARC to reveal that she had changed her ammo type to lethal. Quentin, taking notice, rushed and grabbed Suki by the stomach before she fired her shot that nearly missed him.

Suki tried to fight back, but Quentin dragged her back. Quentin managed to disable her ARC screen before she kicked him out of her way. She sprinted back to her father, who was struggling to hold on. When she positioned her hand to open fire at her father, nothing happened. Her ARC barrel and screen malfunctioned, causing her ARC to smoke a bit.

"QUENTIN!"

"SUKI, STOP!"

Both locked eyes with each other.

"Do you realize you are going to kill a man?"

"HE DESERVED IT! FOR ALL THAT HAPPENED IN MY LIFE, QUENTIN. You... don't UNDERSTAND!"

"No, I don't. But when my dad left, I tried to find him, too, until I got lost, and my mom called his friends to find me. When I was lost, I felt alone and scared, but I wanted to see my father because I knew he wouldn't leave us when he came back."

"This doesn't help me, Quentin. I don't care; his affection was false. My life is still a mess if he is still alive."

Suki didn't look back but at her father. She pressed against her father's foot, causing him to let go with that hand. Quentin, realizing what she had done, ran over to the edge, grabbing her father's hand while grappling to the edge. Their combined weight was heavy; the cable struggled to hold them. Suki only looked at them and turned away, leaving him and her father. Quentin struggled to hold on, too; his heart broke when he saw Suki leave.

"Why... why save me?"

"You deserve to be punished... but not like this..."

Quentin continued to look up while his cable slowly brought him up.

"HEY DOWN THERE, YOU NEED HELP!"

Two FIREBIRDS reaching the rooftop notice Quentin.

"HELP, I got one of The Excesses members!"

The two troopers grabbed the cable and pulled them up. Upon reaching up, they immediately restrained Suki's father. Both Quentin and Suki glanced at each other, closing their eyes with tears. Quentin thought that he held dear to his life and was about to lose it from Suki. Suki. He looked around to see her, but she wasn't there.

"Where is the girl that was here?!"

"She rushed downstairs; we didn't know what upset her."

Without asking many questions, Quentin rushed to the door, heading back downstairs.

Asking each person he ran across, each said that Suki had run downstairs to the open area. Upon reaching there, he looked up at the escalator, which he grappled out from the building entrance. Still trying to figure out where she would be, he looked around to only find firetrucks outside. He kneeled, thinking where she could be, trying to think where she would go when her emotions became too much for her.

*"I always visit this bridge when I feel like this. Staring at the currents moving through the stream, away to somewhere else. Far away from where I am, forgetting where it came from because of constant movement. Doesn't need to remember where it came from."*

The quote hit him. He didn't think she would be over there, but she is relentless without thinking. With that place in mind, he grappled on the building's swing across the cityscape, trying to reach her before she could do anything for herself.

Reaching the same route to her home, he walked on the dusty road as his mind began to ponder. Wondering if Suki is ok? The most obvious question, but he asked why she left him hanging. Because he saved her father, but she didn't want that? This caused her to go, and she was unsure what to do. With that in mind, he ran straight to the bridge, turning to the right where she would be. Quentin could hear the water rushing heavier, waves crashing upon each other from the current. Upon reaching the bridge, he saw her there at the same spot. Looking down at the rapidly moving waves.

"I always visit this bridge, right here, when I feel like this."

"I get it..."

Quentin finished her words.

"Do you always repeat that to yourself?"

"At times."

She moves closer off the edge.

"Suki! Don't"

"Why did you save him!? Don't you understand what I got from him when he left my life? This feeling of being left alone hurts when someone leaves me. That hope he left me shattered when I grew up."

"I know Suki! He deserves every right to be punished, but this isn't right. This isn't justice; this isn't going to help you."

"Quentin, I can't live with the fact that he was alive all this time. My mother, my brothers, and my grandparents all suffered because of him. Quentin, you got out of my way. I can't live like this."

Quentin notices her hands lifting, and he runs straight at her. She jumped off the bridge and into the running water. Quentin, without thinking, jumped into the water as well. He swims towards her, but the current keeps striking his face and mouth, flipping him over as the waves push him. He notices her floating but not fighting; he knows she is doing it on purpose. He looks at the side of the river, seeing cement walls towering over them as they are guided down the river. He swims toward her, grabbing onto her while she drowns. He aimed at the wall with his ARC, grappling a hook attached. The force from the water and the cable tightens his arms. He wants to let go of the pain but can't let go of Suki. The cable slowly pulls them back up, and the water continues to fight them. Once reaching the wall, they lay down uphill near the river. Quentin spit out water, making him lay back. Suki immediately reaches him and tackles him. Both slide down near the water. Suki put both her hands against Quentin's throat.

Suki's tears were dripping down on Quentin's suit; his arms were down. He didn't try to fight but saw her face lowered with her eyes watering up. Quentin couldn't breathe or talk, so he did one thing he could have. He places his right hand on her left face cheek. She continued to choke him but slowly let down her force on him. She cried down on his chest, slowly letting her hands off Quentin's throat. Quentin slowly wraps his arms around Suki. Securing her and letting her cry as she presses her face onto his chest. Both Quentin and Suki share the moment while the wave near them roars.

"Quentin..."

Suki whispered.

"Don't ever leave me, even if our past hurts me..."

"I know. I promise not to give in to my hate; we can't return from it."

She rests on Quentin while Quentin continues to breathe and gasp, letting the wind blow on the side and the sound of the wave's echo.

# Chapter Twenty-Seven: Familiar home

Aiko continued to swing across the skyline, running on the rooftops while grappling and swinging around different locations. As he could see Evergreen Hub Station with his visor enhancing the image, his mind raced back to when he and Albie were at Harmony Fall Station, meeting Quentin for the first time. He remembers how much they traveled before losing Inoue and Anbu; their path to get here was troublesome.

Now they're heading back to the Inhabitant zone, to The Imperium of the Choleric. He continued to wall run until he noticed the train's steam blowing out, departing from the station. Aiko needed to think fast. He decided to increase his energy, knowing that he would deplete and must recharge, but he didn't care. He walls run while using the grapple to propel him faster with the momentum. With enough force, he launched across the remaining distance and crash-landed near the station. With the last railcar leaving him and his energy depleted, he grapples at it and has it drag him.

Aiko gasped for air, the energy draining from his body, but he knew he couldn't give up. He slowly grapples up to the railcar and rests there for a bit. Steam emits from his shoulders and jawline; his body grows hotter, but he ignores the heat. Redirecting his attention, he notices that this train is carrying many supplies. Noticing the label on the cargo: "Property of URDT"

Homura's men are stealing supplies from the URDT and transporting them to The Imperium of the Choleric. Using the surprise attack at the base was a distraction for him to leave and this transport, with Inoue and Albie on it. A door slides open, catching Aiko off guard.

Revealing an armored individual with a pauldron around its shoulders and a knee guard with lines. The figure is wearing a mask, covering its mouth but not its eyes, and wearing a cloth hoodie attached, with wiring connecting around the armor.

The color scheme is tan, with a few reds from tiny pieces of armor, like the cuneate around the leg, and the armor is black. The figure panicked until Aiko immediately sucker punched them so hard that he sent the figure flying. Upon sending the figure out, Aiko detected more than one of them. Many figures share similar armor, with some having different attachments surrounding their body but carrying the same overall theme. One of them yelled, but the language was unrecognizable to Aiko. He felt like he had heard the language, but he couldn't remember. Immediately, the figures all start firing rifles that have wrapping around, holding their rifles in place. Shooting at Aiko only made Aiko charge at each of them, performing powerful swings that sent each

353

figure down. Punching each in the face so hard that each of them is knocked out from the blow.

"This must be the choleric mercenaries. Not The Excesses."

Noticing their armor was different and a bit more advanced but put together piecemeal. Aiko turned around, seeing three axes swinging down at him. Aiko, with quick reflexes, grapples one attacker and brings him so close to him that he punches his face, knocking him out. Activating his gauntlet, Aiko unleashed his Valor blades to block off the other attack.

Aiko has both his blades locked with their axes, and Aiko's strength proves to be enough to overpower them. Aiko notices them pressing a button around their wrist, and then an orange energy is emitted from the line around their suit. Aiko realized their strength was now equal to his. Aiko overcame their duo strength by kicking one Choleric mercenary's leg and deflecting the other's axe. Aiko proceeds to elbow him, then performs a powerful kick strike that sends the choleric warrior against the wall.

"They have the same energy as me?"

Aiko pondered on what energy they had flowing in their suits. Aiko redirects his attention to incoming rockets flying towards him. He immediately dodged to his left but saw another one coming, forcing him to jump off the train and grapple with the wall of the next railcar. He notices a bike-like machine floating in the air with two of the Choleric members. One is piloting the bike, and the other is holding a rocket launcher while aiming at Aiko.

The bike had two plates underneath its machinery, showing the ability to hover and move. Seeing an incoming rocket, Aiko dodged off the railcar and grappled back onto the railcar. Aiko noticed the bike, and he grappled onto it, which prompted the members to try to knock him off.

Aiko noticed another bike, and one of the members shot a missile at Aiko, who dodged it by dropping and grappling again. Aiko retaliates by throwing his Valor edge at them, which destroys part of their bike and sends them flying. Aiko cable zips him up, and he manages to get on top and kick out the Choleric members.

While he tried to figure out how to use the bike, he noticed a red dot pointing at the bike once his eye met with what was aiming at him. His visor enhances the image of a woman in Choleric armor with a substantial mechanical scope sniper.

Without a thought, Aiko jumped out and landed on the rooftop of the railcar; the Choleric woman fired upon the bike, which destroyed it instantly. Aiko realized how powerful the rifle was and saw how she needed both arms to reload another chamber. Aiko was about to his blade at her but was met with more choleric mercenaries jumping out, some carrying rifles on them while some carrying blades and heavy armor to fight against Aiko. Aiko blocks and parries hits with bladed warriors; he dodges hits while getting shot at. He knows that bullets don't affect him but make his suit weaker with more hits applied to him and overheat his suit more, which he starts feeling. He disarms one of them and headbutts him off the train. Another, managing to get on top of his back, has his blade against his throat, and the other choleric warrior starts attacking Aiko, exposing the area of his suit, which Aiko, with his left arm, blocks off the attacks.

Aiko pushes the first attacker, swinging himself so hard that it sends them plunging. Plunging down off the train. The second attacker came running towards Aiko, but Aiko managed to strike the second attacker's hand with the Valor Edge so hard that he cut off its hand, leaving the second attacker screaming from the disarm. Still getting shot at, he rushes at the warriors until he sees the sniper woman aiming at him. Which forces him to dodge and wall-run on the far side of the rail car.

Upon reaching where the warriors were, he disarmed them with a precise strike. Using his armored knee to do deadly blows on their chest or heavy hammer arm swings to bring them down. Aiko, noticing his suit was overheating, had to retreat until meeting two more homing missiles. He dodged one, but the other hit Aiko around the chest.

He started to breathe heavier until he looked up when he stood, seeing the red dot aimed at his right knee. He partially dodged, but the shot broke his knee wings on his right, sending Aiko to hang off the railcar. He notices the wind blowing against him, and looking down, he reveals they're on a high mountain hill. Looking to his right, he noticed the exact nature he was looking at before getting to Harmony Station. He sees more homing missiles coming and throws one of his blades to cut the rocket. He grapples onto the next railcar rooftop.

This time, his sync level increased as his body grew hotter. He strikes and cuts down each member to disarm them while dodging more homing rockets, throwing more of his blades at the bikes, and stabbing the member with the missiles. He traded blows with the warriors until grabbing one by the side and throwing him against the other bikers. More warriors with rifles and rockets meet at the end in front of the rail car.

He charges straight at them; all firing upon Aiko, increasing his energy with his suit. He used his blades to block the bullets, then leaped forward to dodge the homing missile that caused the railcar to shake a little. Aiko threw his blade at one of the members, causing them to shoot at their comrades; the other kept focusing his fire at Aiko, and one of them managed to hit Aiko, damaging an already crippled knee.

 Causing him to stumble a bit. He looked up to see the red dot aiming at his chest. He moved down, but he was too slow. The sniper hit and compromised his right chest.

Aiko's steam grew worse, appearing from his chest now. He charges at one of the homing rockets aiming at him. He grapples the rocket and performs a swing to aim down at the Choleric members, and the explosion radius sends them flying. The woman with the rifle reloads fast. Aiko charges at her, and he throws his Valor blade at her but misses. Aiko leaps to her railcar and throws his blade. Damaging the backside of the rifle, he ran to her while calling back his blade. She managed to reload her rifle and to aim at Aiko close up but was too slow for him. Aiko, grabbing the gun, aimed it at the roof, shooting and causing a huge hole. The railcar began to shake due to the car being damaged by the rifle. He kicked the gun out and tackled her and elbowed her face. Aiko continued to run up the train, remembering that he ran on the train with Quentin and Albie; he couldn't help thinking about that. He noticed that he was close to the front, and he grappled and leaped by momentum forward against the wind.

Upon landing in the open space between the two front cars, he approached the front, the final railcar, until he noticed more Choleric members with rifles and rockets, all pointing at Aiko. His steam grew, and he burst his blades out to attack.

"WAIT, AIKO!"

Inoue's voice breaks his focus.

The railcar door slid open, revealing to be one of the Choleric members, but he had a red pauldron, indicating that he was in charge. He had his rifle against two people, causing Aiko's heart to drop. Albie and Inoue were forced out, with the Leader's rifle pointed at them.

"Put your blades down, Knight."

Aiko wanted to charge at him, but he knew he couldn't move. Aiko, dropping his blade, made himself unarmed. He could only stare at the Leader; he felt his body growing hotter from looking at them.

"These clients are given to us by order of our recent Kaiser. They must be delivered to our nation!"

Aiko poses himself ready to fight, which heightens the members to aim at him intently.

"Aiko..."

Inoue pleaded.

"Please... go back."

Aiko grips his hands tighter.

"Please, let the boy go. You can take me instead!"

Her cough grew way worse, and she pleaded with the Leader.

"Homura assured us that you two were identified; our Kaiser wants the both of you in their presence at once! There is not, but. Knight, surrender. None of us wish for bloodshed or a war between the two of our nations.

***

"Is the communication back online?"

Kenryoku asked the workers.

"Yes sir, broadcasting Aiko visor."

Once the big monitor is turned on, it reveals Aiko having a stand against the Choleric Warriors.

"Are those Choleric?"

"Yes. GET ME TO HIS COMMUNICATION."

Acheron yelled. Akarui looked at the monitor more intently, seeing Albie and Inoue being held. She gasped at seeing them and was shocked.

"Aiko, I know you are listening. You are traveling to The Imperium of the Choleric. If you enter their territory, you will be compromised and will draw us into a war. You will head back to base; that is an order."

Aiko remained silent, not caring what he heard. He focused on the Leader and Albie with Inoue. Akarui looked back and forth, worrying about Acheron's orders and the Aiko family.

"Stand down, Knight. You have 5 seconds to comply. 5"

Aiko tightened his fist more.

"4"

"He's not listening, Acheron."

Kenryoku pointed out.

"3"

"YOU NEED TO RETREAT BACK TO BASE NOW! THAT AN ORDER, AIKO!"

Acheron pierced Aiko's ears.

"2"

Inoue looked up, seeing the rocket aiming at Aiko above her, then focusing on Aiko.

"Aiko... I'm sorry again."

"1"

Inoue, kicking the leader's foot, manages to grab his rifle, and she starts shooting the person holding the rocket launcher above her, causing the explosion to erupt around them, sending them to fly out to different spots. Albie, who is crying and pinned down, is grabbed by Inoue, who is hurt, dragging him to Aiko. Aiko stumbles back to the other railcar wall and regains his thoughts. Seeing Albie thrown against Aiko.

"Aiko... I told you to not look back..."

Inoue's voice hit Aiko; Aiko wanted to talk back, but suddenly, the Leader grabbed her.

"FIRE!"

The Choleric warriors fire at Aiko, and Aiko calls his blades back to block off the bullets for Albie. Aiko notices they're on the bridge so high up that the water is below them. Aiko wants to fight them all, but he can't due to his protection of Albie.

"TAKE CARE OF ALBIE! BOTH OF YOU! TAKE CARE!"

"FIRE!"

Inoue's voice breaks through while the Leader drags her away. Aiko, overheating, realizes he can't protect Albie for too long. He ran straight out the train side and rolled down to the water. Holding Albie close to the chest, he grappled with the nearby cliff, taking in the impact to protect Albie. Albie tried to scream and weep for Inoue but couldn't, the fear he felt right now. Albie's screams reach Aiko, causing him to shed a tear. His heart froze, breaking slowly from realizing that Inoue was now gone. First Anbu, now Inoue. Aiko slowly grappled up the cliff top, reaching up and dropping Albie down. Aiko collapses, and Albie goes to a nearby tree and cries away. Aiko lies down, now turning himself around. Looking at the stars, hearing a voice in his head.

"*Hold on to Hope...*"

Aiko didn't know how to respond, just letting Albie's cries match Aiko's feelings while the ambiance of nature surrounded them, and Aiko's suit released the steam.

"Aiko... you are reported back at base now..."

Acheron's voice reached out to Aiko, who, in return, grabbed a wire from his helmet and opened it. He grabbed it out, disrupting the communication connection and removing the image from the screen. But the sound was only heard still, Acheron making a fist.

"Send a patrol to track Aiko."

"Our troops aren't ready yet."

"Send them when they are..."

Acheron left Kenryoku and Akarui behind. Akarui looked down at her module. Saying to herself

"Was he ready? For the life challenges he must face."

Aiko slowly got up, which caused Albie to panic. Aiko, noticing Albie's panic, opened his helmet to Albie. Albie, seeing Aiko's mask, was surprised.

He started running where the train direction wanted him to. Aiko grabbed Aiko's arm, which he started hitting.

"Albie... she—"

Albie wept, and tears were so tearful that Aiko couldn't finish his sentence.

"She—"

Albie punched fully at Aiko's arm, which prompted him to grab Albie by the side of his body.

"She's gone!"

Aiko's voice breaking Albie.

"She's gone..."

Aiko was whimpering to himself, his voice showing his emotion. Aiko lets go of Albie, and they both drop to cry. Slowly regaining his thought, Aiko got up and dragged Albie's arms while he walked back to the nation. The travel was far, with Aiko's suit still having energy and helping him and Albie to travel greater lengths. Managing to find a dusty road, he runs back to the nation. Albie sniffed while the trees blew at them, reminding Aiko how he and Albie were alone again when Inoue gave herself for them. He couldn't deal with this trauma again, but it returned; it hurt.

He continued walking, holding Albie by the arms, letting the silence reach both. Aiko continued to look down until he looked up and saw someone on a colt. Closer, the figure was revealed to be Saskia with her bag, cloak, hoodie, and scarf on. She got off, sauntering to Aiko, who remained still. Both looked at each other, and Albie noticed Saskia was surprised. Aiko felt a surge of adrenaline reaching him; he let go of Albie's arms and speed walked to her. She remained still until she realized what Aiko was going to do. Aiko, grabbing Saskia by the throat, lifted her up and pinned her against a tree, causing the colt to roar and Albie to freak out.

"Aiko..."

Aiko continued to grip hard against Saskia's throat; she began to breathe heavier and her voice raspier.

"Aiko..."

"Shut up..."

Aiko's anger slowly turns worse with a mix of sadness.

"How could you... why.... WHY!"

Saskia's breathing slowly dies. Then Albie, out of nowhere, tries to pull Aiko's arms down, but his strength isn't enough. Aiko looked at Albie and then realized something:

memories flow in. In his exact position of power, he choked Anbu. Seeing Albie's fearful face. Aiko was shocked by what he was doing until he felt a hand touching the side of the helmet. Saskia put her hand near his helmet.

"Aiko... please... Let me explain..."

Feeling her affection, Aiko dropped her down, and she slowly gasped for air.

"Aiko... I didn't know he was going to take them away. I did what you asked, Aiko; I took him to Inoue. They both were able to see each other and embrace each other. I swear, Aiko..."

Saskia began to cry out and bowed to Aiko.

"I wouldn't put Albie in harm's way. My father broke through the building out of nowhere, taking me, Albie, and Inoue away! I only aided him because I can't escape from him."

"Were those stories of your past true?..."

"Yes! They are true. My mother discouraged my father from committing robbery and actions he had done in the past. My father forced me to be silent, and I was unaware he did all that. I didn't know what he had done until you told me about your past. That was when I wanted to make it up to you, but I can't escape from him. My mother died when I was a teenager; it was me and him. I can't escape Aiko; he forces me to spy on URDT, everyone, and you. But our relationship, Aiko, was real. I didn't want our relationship to get in his way, so I tried to hide it, but he saw me everywhere. I'm sorry, Aiko, I'm sorry."

Saskia is crying down, and Aiko is slowly stepping back from hearing her plead. Albie slowly walking up to her, only to hug her, which shocked her. She embraces her hug, acknowledging that Albie forgives her.

"I understand. You don't have to forgive me. You have every right to hate me, Aiko. I just want you to know that I still care about you."

Hearing her words, Aiko felt some sorrow for her. He didn't want to believe her, but her voice and plea were sincere, leaving him silent. He held his hand out to her, and she noticed it and slowly put her hand on his, helping her get up.

"Albie, go over there, please."

Aiko said softly to him; Albie was confused but listened. Aiko gets closer to Saska.

"I can't do this... I don't like myself..."

"Aiko. What are you saying?"

"I failed. I failed everyone I know. This life... I hate it. I hated my foster family; I hated my father. I hated...Albie... I tried to fight against life, to only have people taken because of me. I don't deserve this suit; he doesn't deserve me; I don't deserve this life they gave to me. Everything is my fault; they don't need me, he doesn't need me, and I'm not needed!"

"AIKO... Aiko..."

Saskia slowly puts her hands on Aiko's helmet, which moves but slowly accepts her affection. She opens his visor to reveal his mask.

"You are needed. She wanted to protect you so you could rebuild and start over. Giving you a chance to be someone, he needs you."

She slowly moved his mask up, revealing his mouth, but Aiko put his hand on her until she stopped.

"They need you. I can't stay here, and you can't go with me. I'm sorry, Aiko. You don't deserve my affection after what I've done. I'm sorry."

She slowly put his mask down. Aiko's heart dropped, pressing his helmet back together.

"They are going to need someone like you, Aiko. I know you are capable of many things."

She slowly takes off her scarf.

"Please, don't look back, Aiko."

Wrapping around Aiko's neck.

"Don't give up on hope."

Grabbing her music box with wire headphones, placing it in his hand.

"They need you, and I want you to heal."

Saskia whistles over her colt. She slowly steps back, both locking eyes. She gets back on, rides a bit away from him, and looks back.

"Take care, Aiko Ashin..."

She shed a few tears but hid by riding away from him, leaving Aiko alone with her scarf and her music box. He only stared, letting the wind blow around him.

"Aria..."

He said to himself. He slowly turned around to see Albie. Walking over to him, he extended his hand to Albie, which he accepted. Both holding hands, they walked back home.

Traveling back, Aiko carried Albie while sprinting. Hopping over the tall wall, traveling the same path they had gone since the beginning. Aiko looked down and saw the same drawing Albie had left, muddy and printed on the ground. He continued to run, hooking onto a train from Harmony Station while holding Albie close to him. Reaching Evergreen Hub Station, he travels the path Suki introduced to him. Heading back to their home, Yume embraced them. Upon reaching there, Aiko dropped Albie, looking at each other and Suki's home.

"I'm sorry, Albie, for everything. You don't deserve me..."

Aiko kneels to Albie. Hearing Aiko sniffing, Albie slowly gets close to him and hugs him. Aiko, feeling his unexpected hug, slowly wraps his arm around Albie.

"Aiko?"

Quentin's voice comes from the door. Both Suki and Quentin are covered by towels. Aiko and Albie are staring at them in a confused manner.

"It's a long story..."

Suki remarked. Yume burst out, seeing both Aiko and Albie in surprise. All sharing the silence of relief of being together.

Quentin checking his ARC screen:

"WANTED: AIKO ASHIN. LOCATION:"

Showing the location where Aiko is at.

"Aiko... They're coming..."

Aiko's heart dropped, but he understood why. He slowly got up, taking off his chest piece and pulling out his jacket—the jacket that Anbu gave him—and wrapping it around Albie, which surprised him.

"He would've wanted you to wear this."

Aiko put back his chest piece, kneeling once more. Hugging Albie, the hug lasted until aerial choppers were heard hovering above them. Quentin and Suki didn't move, knowing they couldn't do anything. Aiko grabbed Albie, taking him back to Yume. Aiko slowly walked back, and vehicles rushing in their direction were heard. FIREBIRDS is dropped down by cable and surrounding Aiko. All pointing at Aiko, Aiko, knowing the action he had done, put his hands up. They attached Aiko with wires, dragging Aiko up the aerial chopper, which dropped from his weight but hovered up. Albie tried to fight and reach Aiko, but Yume restrained him. Yume is in tears at seeing Aiko go again but is calm when he promises to return to their home.

Taking Aiko back to the base, he could see the city skyline. He thought about everything, his past and now. Accepting what had happened, the people who affected him lowered his head. His arms are restrained by shackles, preventing him from moving. He accepts what will happen to him but is grateful to the people caring about him. He looked up at the sky, seeing the sun slowly rise. Leaving the sun rising, they approach the URDT building awaiting. Aiko doesn't know that whatever happens.

# Chapter Twenty-Eight: The Harbingers of The End Part 1

Kenryoku yelled out to the personnel.

"What is the status of our headquarters?"

"The majority of our aerial fleets are destroyed by The Excesses attack. Our other docks are secured and being watched on high patrol! Some active fires are still being removed while engineers and workers do their best to restore the building's integrity. And the number of troops who were hit in the firefight and many fatalities from this attack..."

Kenryoku slammed his fist on the modules. Akarui noticed his anger but didn't watch on. She was focused on Aiko's sync levels, which dropped as his heartbeat slowed. She began to reminisce.

*"Please, don't look back, Aiko."*

When he took away the camera feed but not the audio, what was left of Aiko's audio? She wondered about Aiko's condition and how he felt. She didn't believe that Saskia could betray them or that Aiko let her go, but she understood why he did. She thought to herself that she would have done the same if she were in Aiko's place.

"Sir, The Melancholic Knight is back to base; security is watching over him."

"Alert Acheron and take Aiko back to his repair room."

Kenryoku responds to the personnel who are monitoring Aiko.

***

The aerial chopper approached a side of the URDT building that The Excesses didn't destroy. Upon docking, a crane hooking on top of the aerial chopper brings them to the docking bay where land vehicles are. Aiko got off, waiting for the FIREBIRDS to get off and having their ARC pointing at him. Hearing orders to take Aiko back to his repair bay. Aiko thought he could easily beat them down and make an escape out of URDT, but it was pointless to him. They continued to the hallways, making their way.

Aiko looks at the floor while being unhooked from his body parts. He could move his arms because the suit gave him so much strength, but again, he thought it was pointless. This suit was cold; his body grew colder, and he let the void consume him. Inoue's voice echoed to him. He didn't care what would happen to him; everything he had done was to repay his guilt for years; this undeserving chance, he didn't feel grateful for; this suit alone was enough to be his prison. He imagines seeing Saskia's hands touching his suit and then putting her hand on his helmet. Aiko leaned his head against her head but realized she wasn't there, making himself feel colder when she left him.

The sliding door opened, revealing Acheron, who walked down slowly and approached Aiko. Aiko noticed his presence but didn't say a word. Acheron looked to Saskia's desk, saw the desk cabinets open, and rushed, acknowledging her betrayal.

"Why did you let her go?"

Hearing his words, Aiko wanted to say something but didn't, his feelings conflicting with his mind.

"Not only did you disobey my orders, but you also let a person who was a spy leave. Damaging our headquarters and leaving us vulnerable."

Acheron walks back and forth while maintaining eye contact with Aiko.

"I talked to other nations about our circumstances. While our headquarters are damaged, we had already established other prominent bases of URDT in Phlegmatic and Sanguine's territory. Our vehicles and headquarters are in high demand for maintenance. But you went off, to the point of almost crossing into The Imperium of the Choleric boundaries. If you had, we wouldn't have been ready to go head-on to retrieve you."

"I thought she was with us! I left to save her because I thought she needed my help; she had my Albie. And The Excesses took my caretaker; those warriors took her away. I lost her... I LOST HER AGAIN!"

Aiko began to shake and move from his anger and sorrow; Acheron walked back a bit, seeing how much strength he had to shake the restraint from him.

"I'm sorry, Aiko. While you're in the suit, you're still doing URDT service. But that can end already for you."

Aiko looked up to him.

"You managed to bring down The Excesses' leader, destroying the organization plaguing us since the colonization. Thus, you have completed our contract, Aiko, though the deal isn't what we expected."

Acheron turned around, making his way to the exit.

"Maverick and the other squadron are taking the leader in; we will need an answer about where Nerdhard is, but his presence shouldn't be much of a threat. Once they're done, you will be removed from the suit. You can be with your brother again... And don't have to be The Melancholic Knight anymore."

Acheron leaves Aiko alone, and Aiko lets his words rest in him. He has wanted to be removed from the suit since the start, but now, he wants to stay in it. Letting the suit feel inside of him, letting his thoughts plague him, comforted him and allowed him to forget what had happened to him.

***

Maverick and Cade rode the elevator to reach the prison area. Walking the hallways, we hear screams from The Excesses, and even some of the troopers who are holding and restraining them, trying to put them in their cells. Cade shakes his head violently, and Maverick notices his action.

"You're good?"

"Yes. Nerdhard throwing me a grenade was unexpected, but his aim was terrible. Just shaken up."

"Did he mention where he was going?"

"No, just saying he has plans to finish something. He was vague about what he was saying. Your troops already brought Mr. Mortis?"

"Yes, they've already got him in the holding cells. Next to Jax."

"That traitor..."

They continued to walk until they saw a figure looking down. Revealing him to be Suki's father, he put his hand on his face, and both Cade and Maverick redirected their focus to getting to the leader's cell. When they both approached Jax and Homura's cells, they saw Homura sitting while Jax was leaning to the cell side.

"Mr. Mortis, are you req—"

"Just call me Homura... that name has no meaning now."

"We need an answer from Nerd—"

"Maverick? Is that you?"

Maverick paused. Cade and Jax take notice.

"You're still in service with the URDT, obviously. Your loyalty has always been a trait I admire."

"Care to elaborate?"

Maverick is at odds with Homura's thoughts.

"When Earth was still standing, even when our forces were losing and our lands were captured by the Nekrothians. You remained while others left. Did you ever think how pointless it was fighting a war that was already lost?"

Maverick paused, his helmet hiding his face. He grabbed something behind his pouches: Homura's mask hanging from strings. Maverick examined the mask, noticing its blue color scheme.

"You used to be part of the Melancholic Knights…"

Maverick looks, then looks at Homura, who hides in the shadows.

"What happened to your loyalty? Homura?"

"When the URDT thought the Harmonian alliance was beneficial? You don't know much about the alliance, but our people agreed to serve the URDT to fight off the invaders. That was when I realized we were too loyal that each Knight's death contributed nothing besides URDT contingency to abandon us."

"They didn't abandon the Harmon—"

Homura grabbed both cell bars while looking at Maverick from his beat-up face.

"They did. They saw us only as a resource, like that boy is to them—only a resource. Harmonian energy and technology are scarce, and they will do anything to keep them."

Maverick got closer, both staring at each other intently.

"If that is what is necessary to keep humanity alive from threats like you, so be it. We won't die that easily and will do anything to survive."

"Are you willing to do that, Maverick?"

"I have something to lose other than you."

Homura was about to speak but silenced himself; Jax and Cade glanced at each other.

"To answer your question, no. I don't know where Nerdhard is. He has a project that he kept a secret, and I never took his act seriously. Or taken him as a reliable person, now that he lied about you, Jax."

Jax looking at Homura.

"He abandoned me. He really wanted justice for what had happened all those years; now I realize I am part of his scheme."

Cade looked at Jax.

"What scheme?"

"No one knows. Why else was he here? His project was something only he knew; he never shared it with us. He only served to deliver other work in The Excesses. He did mention somewhere he was going before you raided our operation."

Maverick's attention was now focused on Jax.

"He was heading to New Arcadia after The Excesses succeeded in overthrowing the URDT?"

"What's his business over there?"

"Beats me..."

"Why are you telling us this?"

Jax looked up at the ceiling.

"I don't know. It's pointless to keep it a secret when you're behind bars for life."

Cade looked at Maverick.

"I'll report it to Acheron."

Cade walked away. Maverick wondered why Nerdhard was there at New Arcadia. He looked at Homura's mask, looked at Homura, and tossed the mask down on the cell floor. He left them behind while he left. Homura looked at his mask on the floor, staring back like it was a reflection of his shame.

***

Joule walks over with his ARC; the cleared dock area shows reconstruction was completed and that it is ready for engineers to start repairing the aerial vehicles. He looks down on the dock, where people below are cleaning, and more vehicles are coming with supplies or walking in. He looks up to see Quentin there, looking over the docking bay. Joule holds a cup of green coffee-like material.

"Quentin?"

Quentin turned around to see Joule.

"Hey..."

"Where were you? I didn't see you after we were clearing up the headquarters."

"We chased an escaping Excesses member, chased up all the way to the rooftop until the member revealed it to be. Suki's father..."

Joule's face was surprised, but he fixed his position to look where Quentin was.

"So where is she at?"

"She's somewhere in base, probably in her quarters from the night. She and I had a scuffle; seeing her dad really made her depressed."

"Is she alright?"

"She is. Joule, I'm trying to calm her down. She was grabbing my throat but with no intention of killing me. I look at her face, only to see her eyes fill with water. The only thing I could do was let her hit me, releasing her anger to me."

"You didn't fight back against her?"

"No, I knew she was in pain and needed to be listened to. You can only reassure someone that everything is alright. It was something my dad told me. When I had fits, I would attack my mother since she would fight me the most until my dad came. He lowered himself to my position, and I would punch his chest. Punching did relieve my anger; all he did was to be still like a rock. Absorbing my anger until I stopped, he hugged me and reassured me of what action I'd taken. Looking back to those times, I understand why he did that."

Quentin put his hands on his face, breathing heavily when thinking more about it. Joule put his hand on Quentin's back, rubbing it around.

"My parents and a few of my brothers fight each other a lot; the only thing I could do was wait and let their anger go away. Even if they all have grudges, they will eventually reflect on it. What you're doing, Quentin, is great, letting Suki rest. You should too; I guess this night was… a blowout fun."

Joule fixed his back and was about to walk away until.

"What was Dad like?"

Joule paused and turned around. He walked towards him.

"I guess like you. You have his personality; he was taller than me, but he was great. Our missions were preparing areas for settlement, clearing native life, and fighting evil. We even counted how much we found in our mission and kept the points of how many bottles we shot. Unfortunately, he isn't here, but if you asked me. He would've been happy to see you here; I like to remember that the people who are gone are with us in different forms; we can't see them but feel them, maybe."

Joule gives Quentin the coffee.

"I don't drink espresso."

Quentin called him. But Joule turned his head around while walking away.

"You'll like it!"

Leaving Quentin's sight, he examined the drink. He was hesitant but sipped it. He felt a mix of herbs but with a high sense of vanilla from this planet. He breathed in and out, feeling sincere about the drink.

***

*June 4, 2134*

The street was filled with vehicles designed to resemble the vehicles back on Earth. Many people with bags or cattle travel from one spot to another, getting to their destination. A person is tapping on the metro map screen near the busy street on the sidewalk and street. After they press the desired destination, it displays a message: "Thank you for visiting New Arcadia!" The person walks away towards the unknown, in the large, developing city of New Arcadia.

In the center of the developing city, a building has barricades around the area with a warning sign: "DO NOT ENTER. Chemical hazard spills." Inside the building are a series of stairs and undeveloped regions. Machinery is heard cracking and welding, filling the void area. A radio is heard: "A military helicopter from URDT crashed near the urban areas. It is unknown if anyone survived the crash, but the search is still going on."

A person is turning off the radio as the figure twists gears and presses many of the modules based on the schematics. The figure gets up from fixing the gears but stumbles and falls. The figure gets up and coughs a lot. He walks over to the ledge of the building. The ceiling hides the figure's appearance until it reaches the open outside.

Nerdhard sighs as he watches the people walking and driving below, some on their cattle. He notices a few FIREBIRDS walking by, patrolling the area nearby.

"Useless..."

Nerdhard continues to cough, and he gasps heavily. His right jaw was covered by a bandage from his ripped shirt; his leg showed a wound from the crash. He struggled to pronounce words, walking back to reveal a big machine with wiring attached to different compartments. The specific compartment he set his eye on had an open slot for a disk; he reached into his jacket pocket. Revealing a disk he got from the URDT headquarters, he placed the disk in the open slot. The module screen displayed loading a sequence. An image displays Harmonian fuel. He grabbed a metallic case containing tubes; only three survived, and one broke. He touched it and examined the spilled liquid; he caught the other three tubes and placed them in three compartments. Near the modules was a blueprint of what he built, but not exactly.

"The E-xcess wer-e helpfu-l."

Nerdhard struggles to speak as he inserts the tubes.

"For a whi-lle. We ca-n-t fi-x our nature, we be going- t-o su-ffer! Th-ere no- m-eaning- to our ex-sitence- if ou-r fu-ture-wh-at it-becomes."

Nerdhard began coughing hard and collapsing. He crawled over to the module with the disk, seeing the screen displaying: "Loading Fuel…" The compartments all start smoking intently. The screen then shows the text: "Portal Extend?" Nerdhard pressing yes. The text: "Open portal to Earth?" Nerdhard, pressing yes, crawled back to where he looked down at the people. He leaned on the pillar by the side, saying to himself.

370

"And ye sh-all he-ar of w-ars...s-ee t-ha-t ye be n-ot tro-ubl-ed...f-or a-ll t-hes-s t-hings m-ust c-ome-to-pass..."

He turned around, seeing energy forming in the center of the compartment.

"B-ut t-he e-nd -is n-ot y-et."

The energy formed a portal, but suddenly, it opened abruptly, causing a large whiteout to burst that blinded Nerdhard and then filled the building. Many people down below, families and workers, took notice of the blinding lights, sonic booming with the light as if it was an explosion.

*** 

Quentin is on his bed in his quarters, with his eyes closed. Opening them up, he stares at the ceiling, breathing, then looks at pictures of Aiko, him, and Suki together. He rests on his side while letting the silence surround him; his eyes were tired and closed instantly...

Quentin opened his eyes immediately, grabbing his ARC, which was buzzing off. He opened it to announce to everyone: "National Threat Alert: An attack has occurred in New Arcadia! Report to the hangar bay of the building." Quentin immediately put his gear on and ARC on, and he walked out the doors. Seeing Odie and Jerome both looking at each other, Suki walked out. Both looked at each other, revealing the troubling news.

*** 

"What are the reports?"

Acheron and Kenryoku walk together.

"From what was gathered, a large whiteout blinded the city. It was reported that the sign of a man with a large coat and blood injuries was sighted in the area."

"Nerdhard. Whiteout effect..."

Acheron paused.

"What was stolen from the LYN?"

"From what Cade checked, blood samples from Harmonians, coordinates of Gaea and Earth, and then blueprints of the portals that were used to get here to Gaea..."

Both Kenryoku and Acheron looked at each other; Acheron looked forward and ran forward, with Kenryoku running with him.

"Get Cade and the other captains ready for New Arcadia NOW!"

Kenryoku reaching over his ARC.

371

"Your and Akarui's presence is required at the Tactical operation room. We need vehicles, supplies, and troopers in the station. I'm going to get Aiko."

Kenryoku's face was concerned.

"Wasn't the boy released from his service?"

Acheron going to the elevator.

"Not yet..."

Closing the elevator while Kenryoku goes to Tactical Operation, Acheron reaches the floor and walks through the hallways, opening the sliding door to reveal Aiko still in his suit.

"Sorry, Aiko, your service isn't done."

Acheron reached over the module and disconnected the hooks.

"The threat... that nearly ended the human race ended your mother, Aiko."

Aiko got up; his suit is still damaged from his fight with Homura. He looked down at Acheron, and his heart dropped.

"They have returned."

"They have returned. Who has returned?"

***

At the hangar bay, the large inclined cargo lift is halted, not letting anyone in. Cade is above the platform as he looks over thousands of FIREBIRDS who are in rows, together in their squad; they all look up to Cade.

"As if we couldn't get a break, another threat has struck us once more. But not just us URDT, humanity. As I am saying, we are still getting reports that humanoid-like creatures are appearing in New Arcadia. That city is falling more quickly than we are mobilizing. The Nekrothians have returned."

Everyone below him gasped, looking at each other, murmuring about the Nekrothians. Quentin's mind froze, and he looked down. Suki looked at him with concern. Quentin took notice and looked at her.

"I thought those were stories that my father told me. They were real, obviously, but I thought we were safe to tell them..."

Odie breathes slowly while Jerome, near him, starts gasping. He immediately vomited, which spilled down the floor; Odie patted his back and made him step back. Not many people took notice of Jerome's vomit.

372

"Maverick has already proceeded with his force to New Arcadia, where he meets with the enemy. Curtis and Dahlia are at the URDT bases in Sanguine, getting vehicles and supplies for this unexpected attack."

"Isn't Joule with Maverick squad?"

Suki whispered to Quentin; his heart sank.

"Yes…"

Quentin said it while shaking. Suki holds Quentin's hand to reassure him.

"We will meet with the Maverick battalion, hoping that Dahlia and Curtis battalions are ready to send in their forces. Each of the five squads will be in their designated Osprey Eagles. We will head towards New Arcadia, stopping the Nekrothians from finishing us off."

Everyone below looks at each other in worry, some even vomiting like Jerome. Cade looks below.

"It has been a while since we've seen the Nekrothians. There has already been a bombing run in the city to make our approach and meet Maverick's force there. Remember your training; you are not only fighting for the URDT; you are fighting for the survival of humanity. This will not be the end of our story, for we are to tell the stories to our grandchildren. We will win the battles to tell our families of our bravery; we will kill every Nekrothian we see. You are all brothers and sisters in this fight; you have each other; never fight alone! REPEAT AFTER ME! "Valor Unto the Skies, Grounded in Courage, till our last breath!"

"Valor Unto the Skies, Grounded in Courage, till our last breath!"

"Valor Unto the Skies, Grounded in Courage, till our last breath!"

Everyone yelled in unity, filling the hangar bay with various voices, a call of spirit.

Quentin and his squad walk to their designated Osprey Eagle, joining other squads there anxiously waiting. A heavy footstep was heard, prompting them to turn and see a large metallic figure walking in. The cape flapped, and the lights from its suit showed a bright glow. Aiko looks to see everyone; Quentin, Suki, Odie, and Jerome grin at seeing Aiko.

The Osprey Eagles took off after loading. The launch decks near the far back of the URDT headquarters catapulted them out like a slingshot up to the skies. Everyone inside is shaken by the momentum. The pilots controlling the Osprey Eagles communicate with each other as they all travel towards the north of the Republic of Melancholia. The sound of the wind is heard from the outside, and everyone inside is calmed for now. Many Osprey Eagles flew behind and formed as they traveled, heading to New Arcadia.

Quentin checked his time as they traveled, noticing how much time they had traveled from the base. He looked at Odie.

"Odie?"

Odie glances at him.

"What do you know about New Arcadia?"

Odie hesitated to speak but managed to make some words.

"Not much; I heard it was a fast-developing city from various trading and funds URDT was receiving. Even heard that it could replace the Republic of Melancholia due to its massive size and building, which opened many opportunities. Well, now... it's all gone, I suppose."

Odie proceeds to fake cough as he realizes New Arcadia is probably gone. Quentin glances away from his response, noting the danger they're approaching.

Aiko looks outside the window, noticing how much they travel, looking down at the ground, and seeing clouds.

"The weather and turbulence are continuing, so hold on tight! Heavy fog is covering our destination, and we are drawing near. We will drop you all off at the outskirts of New Arcadia."

The pilot made an announcement. Aiko continued to look out. His mind showed various images, including seeing himself give Albie his jacket and hugging him. Voices from Saskia and Inoue matched each other.

*"Don't look back!"*

*"Hold on to hope."*

Aiko's heart sinks as he dwells on and looks at other Osprey Eagles. Suddenly, Aiko noticed something emerging from the fog and clouds, a large spear flying up, and saw smoke coming out. It shot out scattered spikes and sharp debris at the other Osprey Eagles, causing them to explode. Everyone inside is alerted by the explosion.

"WE'RE UNDER ATTACK! EVERYONE, HOLD ON; WE'RE GOING TO TRY TO CONTINUE OFF TO REACH A SAFE DISTANCE!"

The pilot said while swerving to avoid more flying spears that appeared before them.

The large spears were black and covered with heavy smoke upon launching spikes that exploded at the Osprey Eagles. Aiko is still holding near the wall while Quentin, Suki, Odie, and Jerome hold on to the straps. The other squads hold on as they are pushed around from the vehicle swerving. More explosions are heard as more Osprey Eagles get caught by the bombardment. One of the spikes exploded and damaged their chopper's engine, compromising it.

"WE'RE GOING DOWN! BRACE FOR IMPACT!"

The vehicle began to swing and turn violently!

"EVERYONE, HAVE YOUR PARACHUTE ON!"

Everyone reaches under their seat, retrieving parachutes, which some struggle to put on. One of the squad members trying to put his parachute on was suddenly sucked out from the door opening near up, a heavy amount of air sucking the FIREBIRDS, and some got sucked out. Quentin panics while he, Suki, Odie, and Jerome hold on. Aiko, remaining still from the chaos, just holds on.

"THIS BIRD IS DAMAGED ENOUGH, ABANDON SHIP! ABANDO-"

The pilot's words get cut off as the explosion from the dock gets destroyed due to the damage. Quentin, holding on, looks at everyone.

"GET OUT! JUMP OUT NOW!"

Everyone, without question, listened, jumping out from the door and flying towards a different area, going through deep fog and clouds. Quentin and Aiko look at each other for a few seconds; Quentin jumps out while Aiko is the last one. Quentin breathed heavily; he couldn't see what was happening until he fixed his skydive. He looks around to see other Osprey Eagles, some still flying, some falling and crashing even into FIREBIRDS members. Quentin dodges through the chaos, down through the clouds. Reaching out from the cloud are New Arcadia's many high skyscraper buildings and skylines filled with fire while smoke erupts from the ground below or in buildings.

It was hard to see due to the heavy wind blow, seeing the clouds covering the soot and smoke, making it difficult to see any sunlight. He looked down, trying to find a spot to land. He pulled the ripcord to open his parachute, but nothing happened. He panics and tries again, but nothing happens. Without thinking, he flies down to the past skyscrapers, with some already collapsing from the chaos. With his ARC, he grapples and swings to slow his momentum but hurts his arms in the process. He continues to do so until he gets close to land, where he falls, rolling over while Osprey Eagles debris falls. He regains himself and runs towards a building to take cover from the chaos. He looks around, seeing an empty city with nothing but chaos and explosions heard from distances. He reached his ARC, trying to communicate with Suki, but nothing was heard. He tried Odie and Jerome, but nothing was heard.

"There must be a jammer..."

Quentin looked around, seeing how empty the city was. He walked while looking around, trying to reach his friends in this city that was once thriving but is now a warzone.

# Chapter Twenty-Nine: The Harbingers of The End Part 2

Quentin continues to walk while hearing explosions; he keeps close to the buildings, out of sight, while looking at both sides of the street as he cautiously moves to different spots of New Arcadia. He sees burning cars and destroyed areas that once housed people. He made his way forward, thinking it wasn't a great idea, but still pushed on regardless. As he strolls to each building's side, he waits. He examines himself, seeing that he is bleeding from his side. Thinking to himself that he probably got it from a rough landing. He looks nearby, seeing a clothes store. He runs and checks around, grabbing shirts, ripping them into bandages, and binding his wound. He walks outside, looking around until.

"AAAH!"

He heard screaming, and he looked up while holding his ARC on. He changed the settings to lethal rounds. He continues to hear more voices around and above the building tops. The sound of explosions continued, and his mind began to panic as the screams of human voices echoed around him. Prompting him to run straight to a nearby building and cover himself near a desk. He breathes heavily over and over to let out his anxiety, looking around himself. He felt nothing, only imagining Suki, Odie, and Jerome around him. With that in mind, he walked timidly until hearing what he thought were moaning.

"OOOOOAAAAH!"

A cow ran from the heavy fog, and its hooves made heavy steps that echoed on the quiet streets. He observes as the frightened cow runs down the road.

A shot comes out of nowhere, hitting the cow's throat. Then, multiple shots followed suit, which scared Quentin and made him look up while he continued forward.

"What was that? It can't be from an ARC; the bullets sound different. A sniper round? But it sounds like a very aggressive screech that cut through the air."

He didn't want to think much about it, hoping whoever shot that cow didn't know he was there. His mind began to wander, and voices from the past reached him.

*"I knew you would be like this. Yes, I know what I'm getting into and what I'll face."*

*"I've become a FIREBIRDS... Mhm... I did it, Mom... I did it for him."*

*"It's fine... you were worried about my safety... No... I won't end up like him. Just don't think about that, Mom... Talk to you soon then."*

His conversation with his mother begins to haunt him, and he starts to breathe more aggressively, which makes him tighten his shirt to secure his wound. He walks past a broken window. A sound of whimpering was heard; he was hesitant to check but walked in regardless. Pointing his ARC at whatever was making the sound, he breathes slowly as he approaches the counter. Leaping forward to catch the figure behind off guard only widened his eyes. He discovered a mother holding her daughter; both were covered with dust and debris. Quentin lowered his ARC and offered his hand to her. She was hesitant but slowly put her hand on his, and he got her up slowly.

"Are you okay, ma'am?"

"ye-ssss."

She shakes as she stands. Looking around her surroundings, she sheds tears and immediately hugs Quentin, which catches him off guard.

"Oohhhakyy.."

"It was terrible! It was- oh, oh!"

"Shhh…please stay quiet. Whatever is attacking is still lurking around."

"They came out of nowhere! Attacking anything they see on sight. Savages!"

"Please… calm down..."

Quentin puts his hand on both sides of the woman.

"What's your name?"

"Liliana..."

Quentin noticed her hair was covered by the gray debris color from the damage.

"And she is Chaya..."

Quentin put his hand on Chaya's hair, rubbing it to comfort her while removing the dust from her hair. He looked out to the side, thinking about Suki and his squad. Reuniting with his squad was his first goal, but finding this woman with her child made him reconsider his goal. He did not know what to do, so he thought about what Suki and his father would do. He looks at the lady.

"I'll get you out of here."

"Thank you… thank you..."

"I just need to know where exactly..."

"The town map is a few blocks away; it will tell you everything about the city. It just makes it, while being stalked—"

She couldn't finish her words.

"We're going to walk quickly but stick to the side of the buildings. We shouldn't be detected if we don't make noise. Just follow behind me."

They both nod; Quentin's heart drops, and feeling the burden he is carrying, he pushes through. Walking out of the building, they speedwalk by the side, looking around them to see anything unusual. Seeing burning vehicles and one exploding caused them to run even faster. He continues to look above him, looking at the skyscraper. He noticed a window with a hand-like presence lurking but hiding it immediately, giving Quentin chills but making him even more prepared for what was to happen.

Quentin, making his way, noticed the map terminal, but it was out in the open. He looked around and made his way there, where he signaled them to wait. He examined the terminal, noticing the screen was broken and not displaying images. His visible frustration was seen from his kicks around the terminal until his kick revealed an outlet. Quentin looks at his ARC, with his quick-thinking, Quentin grabs the needed wire from his ARC and connects it to the outlet, receiving information while clicking through what he is looking for. Getting a blueprint of the city landscape and navigating the system to reveal that all the routes are just open streets that can lead them to any attack.

"Ouuuu."

Chaya looked above, hearing voices. She leaves her mother's sight while Lilana looks at Quentin. Quentin continues to look around the archive until finding a map of the sewer system, showing that the route leads out to the buildings but to nearby lakes. One stretches far south of New Arcadia, while the other route up north has two large lakes held by a levee system to ensure the lakes don't overflow into the city. Quentin took note of the sewer path to get down to, hoping that this would provide them with enough safety to get out of the city. He looked at Lilana but realized that Chaya was gone; he looked around until he saw Chaya standing in the middle of the street while looking up. Without question, Quentin sprinted and dashed towards her; Lilana, who was so blinded by Quentin's action, realized her daughter had escaped her sight. Quentin managed to grab her by the sides and make it to the side across from Liliana.

Hitting the ground where Chaya was standing. Quentin puts his hand on her mouth to shush her. He looked to his left and right. In the distance, a figure that was hard to make out leaps a great distance to another building. But Quentin didn't see that. He looked up and glanced at Liliana.

"I'm going to grapple you…"

Quentin whispered but loudly to make sure she could hear him.

He grappled Lilana by her waist and pulled her over to him, where they rested by the side. They remained quiet. Quentin looked behind him to see another abandoned shop, which they hid there for now. Quentin examined the map more. Liliana grabbed her daughter by the side, her face fearful.

378

"WHY DID YOU LEAVE MY SIGHT!?"

"I thought I heard dad; he made-"

"YOUR FATHER IS GONE!"

Chaya began to shed tears slowly, and Lilana couldn't contain her face, breaking down in tears.

"I don't know if he survived or not, sweetie. I don't know..."

Quentin noticed Liliana weeping; he couldn't help but feel her sadness. He walked over and just patted her back. Her words about the father being dead or missing, he couldn't help but think about his father being dead or missing. He understood how she felt.

Quentin immediately pointed his ARC around, hearing footsteps above them.

"Ouuu..."

"Ouuuuuoou"

The voices sounded human. Quentin looked to his side, seeing an exit that took them out of the alley. The silence crept in, waiting for anything to happen or strike.

"OOAAAAAAAUU!"

Quentin grabbed Chaya while telling Lilana to follow him. They ran out the exit to the alleyway of the buildings. Quentin didn't look back; he could hear footsteps creeping up on them. He pushed through and made his way out of the alley, running by the sidewalk. He looked at his ARC, seeing they were close, but he just had to cross the street. He turned to them.

"I'm going to run across the street, and I'll grapple you both to me, okay!?"

He looked both ways and sprinted, making sure nothing was above them. He got his ARC ready. Chaya was first up. Quentin grappled her to him so fast that a blink couldn't miss her speed, zipping her fast. He put her to the side and signaled Liliana to get ready. Quentin grappled with her and zipped her to him.

A shot hit her thigh; she yelped. Quentin took notice and held her by her shoulders.

"Hurry, I will get you out of here! We're close!"

Quentin and the girls all follow him to the right. They continue to run while their pursuers chase them. Quentin notices the manhole for the sewer route, but looking around, he notices how open the area is. Quentin looks around, seeing a building on its last footing still holding up, giving Quentin an idea.

"Wait here; I'm going to give us cover."

Liliana and Chaya wait by while Quentin rains bullets on the broken building; he aims at the final pillar holding the building. He shoots to make the pillar thinner, and with his grapple hook, he wraps around it. He steps far back but at a reasonable distance where he can pull the pillar off, causing the building to collapse. Heavy wind and debris flew out, hitting Quentin and the family. Quentin comes towards them with him, now covered by debris and gray particles.

"Come now! This is the only cover we have left."

They run through the smoke while Quentin looks at his ARC to follow straight to the manhole. More unusual yells came out, which prompted them to run faster. Liliana struggled to run but pushed through the pain from her wound. Once reaching the manhole, with his grapple, he opened up the manhole with all his might. He opens it and rushes the girls to get down while he follows suit, closing the manhole cap in the process. Reaching down from the ladders, it was pitch black, and the smell of decomposing matter reeked; Quentin grabbed something from his pouch, revealing a flare that could be extended, and he turned it on. Revealing the tunnel, he looks at Liliana, kneeling in pain.

"Are you okay?"

Quentin reaches down to her level.

"Yes... *sigh*, it hurts."

Quentin grabs more clothes from her shirt, rips it, and ties it around her wound.

"There, you will be fine. I can't go further with you. My job is here; I need to find my squad. Just continue down south. You should be safe, and we can meet by the lakes over there."

Liliana hugged Quentin tightly.

"Thank you. Thank you for saving us!"

"It's just my service, ma'am. I know the people I'm looking for would've wanted me to help others."

"Well, they are proud of you already."

She grinned at Quentin; he gave her his flare and turned her attention to her daughter.

"Let's get out of here, sweetie."

Quentin couldn't help but tear up seeing them together, remembering holding Albie's hands and holding his father's hand. He watches them as they disappear, the lightning leaving his sight. He climbed up the ladder, where he peeked out carefully.

Noticing nothing nearby, he got out and closed the manhole immediately. Sounds pierced his ears, a sound getting louder. He focused on hiding in another building on the forward left, taking cover behind a desk. Quentin hid while hearing heavy footsteps; these footsteps are so heavy that they vibrate around him. He peeks from the desk, looking to see a big figure walking in slow motion, carrying supplies and two large swords. The gray and shadow made it hard for Quentin to see clearly, but it was accompanied by another slim, tall, humanoid creature walking alongside.

Quentin got up slowly and leaned against the wall on his back. Not paying attention, he noticed a humanoid creature walking past, which prompted him to hide under the desk again, catching the humanoid creature's attention. The creature walked slowly in, looking around, which Quentin couldn't see. The creature got closer, and Quentin got ready for its presence. The creature walked past Quentin, but this is where Quentin could fully see the Nekrothians up close.

The Nekrothians had slim, tall bodies, with long legs and arms that reached their knees. Adorned with gray and dark metal-like armor, covered with sharp, jagged edges. The helmet had a pointed visor that extended forward, spikes, and ridges around. The shoulder plates were large and curved outward, with jagged edges and a layered design. Its torso armor has three segmented scales covering its chest and back. Segmented design, with the arms being robust, with overlapping plates and spikes showing at different angles, with the legs following the same theme and with sharp edges. The jaw appeared extended with a pointed end, matching its visor. Upon noticing Quentin, he looks intently at him. Opened its jaw to reveal human-like teeth and a sharp and black mouth. The Nekrothians had a rifle-like gun with a bayonet blade extended out and a barrel showing on top. It has a revolver-like mechanism but shows a sharp aesthetic, with weathered clothes wrapped around it. The Nekrothians' throat was noticeable, sharing similarities to the human throat, which would explain its roars. It pointed at Quentin, Quentin thinking if he didn't move, it would leave, but the Nekrothian with its finger on its trigger had Quentin frozen; he couldn't move. Forcing Quentin to close his eyes.

Quentin, hearing the shot from his left, noticed the Nekrothian was shot from its chest, where it was exposed. Forcing the being to collapse, Quentin gets up and shoots the Nekrothian down immediately.

"QUENTIN, CALM DOWN!"

Quentin paused; that voice was familiar. He turned to his left, seeing Joule stuck underneath the rubble near the stairs; he walked over. Looking up, he saw a crashed Osprey Eagle dangling above him.

"JOULE!"

Quentin gets near Joule, seeing him gravely wounded and cut around his eyes and face. But Joule still smiles.

"You came here for the fun, too?"

Joule's raspy voice was noticed; his breathing was heavy. Quentin examined his condition, seeing that he was pinned down and the debris crushing his chest armor, showing how damaged he was.

"What happened?!"

Joule trying to get his words together, managing to speak.

"We were sent to be the first wave of defense. We head to the city, not knowing what to expect, and walk into a trap."

"Until giant-like spears launch to the skies, taking the Maverick battalion down to the city. Our communications weren't working, and the majority of us are still out there or have died. We tried to warn the URDT it is useless unless there is a way to transmit a message."

He continues to cough and looks at Quentin.

"It's good to see you here. It's crazy how we met the first time; you were new, and now... You're just like your father. He has that same look as you do, and I've never forgotten about him."

He coughs more aggressively.

"I was passed out until I saw you..."

Quentin observed Joule's neck wound and could see he was covered with blood, Joule's voice becoming difficult to hear as he talked.

"I'm getting you out of here, Joule. Let's get this debris off of!"

Quentin tries to pull the debris off of him, but it is so heavy that one of the concrete slabs falls and makes a loud sound.

"Don't worry about me, Quentin; I knew what I was signing up for…"

"Don't say that! I swear I'll get you out of here, CMON!"

Quentin sheds tears while pulling the debris out, but his frustration causes him to slam into the concrete. Joule, taking notice of Quentin's frustration, extends his left arm, with his right arm being pinned or crushed. He puts his hand on Quentin's cheeks, calming him down.

"Listen to me, Quentin, I can't get out. But you can."

Joule and Quentin, hearing sounds of crawling and roaring, approach him.

"You will."

Joule reaches around his neck, getting out a dog tag that Quentin noticed when they first met.

382

"Find your comrades, your friends. Find Suki and protect her; protect everyone. That's what a leader does."

Joule extended his hand to Quentin, giving him his dog tag. Quentin was hesitant, but he grabbed his dog tag from him.

"Win this battle for us; protect humanity! Find Maverick; he has an important package that can end this fight!"

The sounds of the Nekrothians continue to draw closer. Joule goes back in his pouch, trying to grab something out.

"URDT did a lot for me, and it's time to repay them in my favor."

Joule grabbed out a grenade with his finger holding the hatch.

"NO, JOULE, DON'T, PLEASE."

"Listen, Quentin! Go! If my younger brother joins the URDT, promise me you'll take care of him."

Joule's coughing is growing worse.

Quentin stepped away as the sound of the Nekrothians drew near. Walking towards the rear exit, he looked back.

"Joule, I PROMISE!"

"GET OUT OF HERE, FOOL. TAKE CARE OF EVERYONE!"

Three Nekrothians appeared at the front door and started firing at Quentin, who ran out the back door. Joule breathes softly as more comes in surrounding Joule, but they do not notice his arm. Joule's heart froze as he looked at the Nekrothians.

"Valor Unto the Skies, Grounded in Courage, till our last breath."

He said softly until unleashing the hatch pin. This caused an explosion that destroyed the building's foundation, caused the broken Osprey Eagle to fall, and caused more of a blast. Hearing the sound, Quentin continued to run until finding a safe spot where he could hide. By the walls, near buildings around northeast of him. He looked at Joule's dog tag, his tears touching the tag, and began to weep. The ambiance of explosions and roars continued to echo around New Arcadia.

The never-ending explosions and roars continued to plague Quentin as he walked on the sidewalk, not caring what was around him. He walks as he continues north, thinking about Joule's words. He thinks about how they met, even though they had only seen each other occasionally. He couldn't help but think of him as his older brother, someone who knew his father. He continued to walk until noticing a laser pointing at his chest; he looked at where the laser was coming from. Seeing a figure waving at him. Quentin, without thinking, runs towards their direction, to the tall building. Reaching the spot where the figure was at. Revealing three figures, upon closer inspection, Quentin's heart dropped. Seeing Odie with his rifle, Jerome with his minigun ARC, and Suki waiting by the wall. All covered with dust and cuts. Quentin and Suki locked eyes, both running at each other. Quentin immediately breaks down. He tells them about what has happened to him since their arrival. Suki wraps her arms

around him as he collapses. Odie and Jerome look at each other, saddened by what Quentin said. It was hard to hear him from the explosion and roars. He continued to weep while the sound covered his cries from the ongoing battle, what remained of New Arcadia.

# Chapter Thirty: The Harbingers of The End
# Part 3

The calm wind blows the tall trees, whistling to Aiko's ears. Staring upon the night sky, seeing stars together and forming shapes to call out.

"That looks like a colt."

"How?!"

Aiko looked over to Anbu, who stared up. Both lay back while the trees opened the skylight to them.

"You can see the head from those four stars; you just have to line them up…"

Anbu looked at Aiko, who, still wearing his mask, looked at him, but Anbu understood from his blank expression.

"You'll see later when you piece things together; it makes sense to you."

Anbu looks to his right side and sees an empty spot of dirt.

"Why didn't you want to take Albie with us here? He would've loved seeing the stars; it's perfect right now."

"I don't want him here; he'll just get us in trouble."

Anbu just nods, not to Aiko's answer.

"He can't talk, just wave and move us to what he wants. You must understand that he needs help, and this world is unforgiving."

Anbu got close to Aiko, putting his arm underneath Aiko's head and offering his arm as a pillow.

"Aiko, you're my brother. Even if we're not genetically close or aren't the same, I still consider you special to me."

Aiko continued looking at the sky, seeing the colt that Anbu was saying. The piece lined up as he said, and he chuckled to himself.

"You're my brother Anb—"

Anbu's body disappeared; the night sky vanished once Aiko blinked. Seeing debris around him, he turned his head to the sky. Only gray and black smoke filled the air, and his visor picked up the quality of his eye vision.

***

The wind blows heavily from the myriad explosions, and Aiko hears the whistle of the cries of war. His eyes open, seeing the dark gray clouds hovering in the sky. Echoes of explosions and roars are heard. Aiko stares, slowly regaining himself in his suit. Checking all around him and his functions. His visor flashing red to show part of his suit is critical, but he ignores it. He slowly got up, examining where he was. Realizing that he crash-landed due to the bombardment attacks from the Nekrothians. The Osprey Eagle swing pushed him out and made him crash land due to his suit weight. He looked up, seeing that he had broken through a building layer. He sees his own body from his screen, showing every critical damage he sustained. The suit started automatically cooling off the damage by using Aiko's synara energy.

He recalls what happened before his crash landing, remembering that he and Quentin nodded to each other. Promptly, Aiko reached for his suit communication but realized he had ripped the wiring from the communications. He still had the suit on while being hooked; no armor smith was available to analyze his suit.

Getting up, he leaps out from his crash site and grapples up the buildings to reach the top, revealing a city reduced to rubble. Smoke and explosions set off on the streets. Buildings cover the battlefields while roars continue to haunt everywhere.

From a distance, Aiko saw a flare go out from a distance away. Peaking to the sky and catching his attention. Aiko nods to himself, regretting removing his communication adapter. Aiko, without question, leaps off the building, and he grapples onto rooftops and towers. Looking down at the streets shows him what he is fighting.

Multiple Nekrothians like the ones Quentin encountered, but others had hoods on with a different visor style being round but sharp, carrying out a similar round shape approach but having a sharp edge in its design. It carried a bow on its arms, with arrows that had very sharp edges. Walking alongside them is an exceptionally large Nekrothian that is heavier and bigger. Its armor is like its counterpart but exposes more of its skin. Seeing that its skin is mottled gray but peach spots, with the armor only covering its body part and areas to protect it. It carried many Nekrothian weapons on its back, while big slab blades were on its backpack. Its visor has a sharp edge forward-pointing, and its mouth is covered like other Nekrothians, but its eyes are revealed from its visor. Having open eyelids to see, showing green eyes. Aiko continues to observe, seeing them patrolling the streets. He looks forward in the building, seeing an open area for him to jump, avoiding their detection.

Looking up when he landed on the street revealed where the flares came from. He looked around, seeing a crashed Osprey Eagle against the building. The rubble below shows many dead FIREBIRDS and Nekrothians piled near each other. Aiko approached the corpses, Aiko popped out his blades and prepared himself in case a

Nekrothian was alive or anything else was there. Fully seeing the rubble lowered Aiko's guard.

"Knight? I didn't think you would come soon."

Maverick's voice reached Aiko. Aiko immediately lowered his Valor edge and started removing the debris from Maverick.

"What happened?"

Aiko asked. Maverick breathes softly and unleashes his breath in his helmet.

"My battalion and I were the first responders for this unexpected attack. We knew that we were heading to the unknown. I know full well what these Nekrothians are and what they can do. If we were heading into a battle, we could at least communicate back to headquarters warning about Nekrothians traps. But our communication got jammed, and we got ambushed."

Aiko removed more rubble from Maverick. He grabbed Maverick's arm, but he yelled out of pain.

"I can't move my legs; the rubble got them pretty good."

"Can you walk?"

"I can't..."

Maverick holds on to Aiko's arm, leaning so he can stand a bit.

"But I can still fight. My Osprey Eagle got caught in the bombardment; I can assume that some of us survived... I've been trapped and fighting for my life, laying explosives near me and getting as many Nekrothians as I can."

"I'll get you out of here."

"You're not."

Maverick grabbed something from his back.

"Fortunately, this hasn't exploded. Even when we crash-landed."

Maverick pulls out a cylinder, holding it in both of his hands, but nothing appears on the cylinder's screen.

"I was ordered to deliver it to where the Nekrothians are at. So, we can end their invasion fast."

"What is it?"

"Death itself, end of life. A weapon man created from fear of each other; we used it during the Nekrothian war. Killing Nekrothians but humans who were caught in the crossfire. We don't have any choice but to use it for this city, so it seems humanity can't survive another fight with the Nekrothians."

Maverick looked up, seeing buildings and smoke all around him, then redirected his focus to Aiko.

"What's your name, son?"

Aiko moved his mouth slowly from what he said but regained his focus.

"Aiko... Ashin..."

"You must be Acheron Boy. I heard what he did to you. You can't forgive him easily, right?"

Aiko meditated on what he said but responded to what he felt was natural.

"Somewhat. I'm doing this for someone back at home. It's what I got left."

"Me too…"

Maverick is looking around and at the bomb.

"I just became a father, Aiko..."

Aiko looked at Maverick, surprised by his statement.

"My wife was in the hospital after the baby was born. I was going to see her, but. Here we are… I just wished I had time to see my wife's face."

Aiko didn't let go of his focus on Maverick. He saw Albie's face, and their hug may be their last.

"Then it's enough reason for me to get you out of here, Captain."

"No. It is our duty as human protectors to fight the wars, even if we can't win. We still fight for humanity. I know my wife would've wanted me to save the world first because otherwise there wouldn't be a world for my daughter."

Maverick puts his hand on Aiko's arm.

"People in our lives are counting on us; they want us to continue forward. If they really matter to you, end this battle. Then we can all go home."

Aiko hesitated. He wanted to run back home, but people in his mind appeared. Quentin, Suki, Odie, Jerome, Akarui, Acheron, Kenryoku, Yume, Saskia, Anbu, Inoue, and Albie. Aiko breathed in slowly, then out, with his mindset in motion.

"Where are we going?"

Aiko looks at Maverick. Maverick looks up and sees the skyscraper from the distance that reaches peak height.

"When I was falling to my near death, up high, my helmet picked up snatches of communication chatter. If we are up higher, we can reach any nearby forces. Who did you come with?"

"Cade Valente Battalion. With Quentin and his squad."

"That boy, he should be alright."

Sounds of roars and footsteps were heard coming in their direction.

"I can't walk; I propose that."

Maverick pulls cables from his ARC and ties himself to Aiko's back. Aiko feels his weight and steadies his footing.

"You scratch my back."

With his ARC pumps up, Maverick puts the barrel attachment on and changes the ammo to "shells and slugs."

"I'll scratch yours."

The roars and footsteps continue to approach them closer.

"Can you carry me like this, Aiko?"

Aiko is adjusting himself and has his position straightened out.

"Yes, you are not that heavy, sir, with all due respect."

"That's fine. We need to reach that tower, and I'll cover for you. Do whatever you can to get there!"

Aiko pops out his Valor Edge, looking forward while Maverick, wrapped around his back, buckles himself.

The sound of the Nekrothians was near; Aiko dashed forward, which Maverick felt. Aiko runs towards the sound, waiting to see their presence. Once making eye contact with the Nekrothians, Aiko grappled to a nearby building and zipped them across up high. Nekrothian roared at seeing Aiko, which prompted each of them to fire. Dodging inside the building, he runs straight while still hearing more Nekrothians.

"Seem there more of them; let not disappoint them."

Aiko runs out of the building, breaking out the windows where, on the street level, there are more Nekrothians, with heavy Nekrothians pointing at them while the others grab the heavy weapon on their back. All shooting at Aiko while he leaped across to the next building. He runs straight to the destination, neatly dodging their bullets and making it.

The Nekrothians, looking at each other, run up the building and crawl, scaling the building to chase them. Maverick looks as they approach them and chase them down.

"Here they come!"

Maverick loaded his cartridge in his ARC and started to fire upon them. Aiko makes sure to turn so Maverick can protect him while Aiko uses his Valor Edge to block the bullets. Aiko continues to do so while making his way out of the buildings. More Nekrothian approached him while getting the jump on him. Using their rifle bayonet blades, they attack Aiko while Aiko, using his blades, trades blows with both the Nekrothians. He started to pinpoint their opening and disabling their rifle. He sliced one of their rifles and slashed its arms and stabbed its throat. Aiko felt a surge of energy filling him again. He redirected his attention to the other Nekrothians, where he kicked its leg. Aiko grabbed its throat and choked and slammed him while running out the window. With his ARCs, Maverick blasts off Nekrothians that try to reach them while using arms as cover from their bullets.

Leaping out of the building, Aiko threw the Nekrothians down. It crashed onto a car roof, which the Nekrothians nearby noticed. Seeing Aiko, they roar out. Calling more of their kind. Aiko grappled to the building, cracking the windows but getting his footing. Maverick's perspective as he looks down, seeing dozens of Nekrothians starting to crawl up.

"GO UP! GO UP!"

Maverick yelled out to Aiko. With his energy converted to his foot, Aiko leaps while grappling up. Running up to the rooftop while Nekrothians inside the building jump out to get an edge on Aiko, he backhands them. Maverick continues to shoot any Nekrothians that get nearby, switching ammo type to slugs or shells depending on the distance. Gunning them down while reloading different cartridges and overheating his ARC, Aiko noticed that the Nekrothians above him were shooting out the windows at him, which prompted Aiko to block and then throw his valor edge at one of them. Knocking them down to make his way above.

Upon reaching the rooftop, Aiko and Maverick both sigh while looking around. Aiko looked to his side, seeing more rooftops around him, then he saw hooded Nekrothians with their bows pointing at them, prompting Aiko to move. One fired its arrow, which broke through a rooftop.

"What do we call them, sir?"

"Archers…"

Maverick responded to Aiko's question. Maverick took notice of them and started firing at them, hitting their skins through gaps in their exposed armor, while Aiko performed a flip to dodge the other arrow. Throwing his other Valor Edge at them, which stabbed through its torso and returned, moving his blade down to remove its waste. Maverick took more notice of the Nekrothians crawling up on top of them. Firing their rifles for a while, forcing Aiko to run forward off the building.

Aiko began grappling and swinging the building sides. He swings forward to the skyscraper, where they are drawing near. Maverick continues to shoot off any attacker getting near them. He looks forward, seeing Nekrothians, too, swinging towards them, carrying cables and modifying them to swing or get across buildings.

"So, they learned to grapple, eh..."

Maverick fires slugs at the Nekrothians while they fire back. Forcing Aiko to roll down and grapple back, perform a wall run, and grapple to a building near the skyscraper. Once near the building, he runs again and continues to expend his energy, making his suit steam. Aiko notices that the heavy Nekrothian is carrying a chain with a heavy spike ball on the end, which it throws at Aiko. This made Aiko leap prematurely out of the way, dodging the attack.

"What those big dudes!"

"Brawlers!"

Maverick yelled out. Aiko noticed another heavy Nekrothian throwing another spiked ball at Aiko. It strikes Aiko, sending him flying to the skyscraper floors above. Rolling over on the floor of the skyscraper, Aiko coughs while steam continues to come out of his suit. Maverick looked around and saw pillars and support that were holding the skyscraper.

"I got an idea. Draw their attention here; I'll leave them with a surprise."

Maverick is holding out grenades and showing them to Aiko.

"Leave an opening around the supports so I can heave them in. Once we detonate, it will break the support at the top, which will break the top down and cause a domino effect."

Nekrothian started appearing where they were, looking at them freely.

"LET'S DO IT!"

Maverick yells out while Aiko focuses his attention on making an opening and running up. Aiko continues blocking Nekrothian firing and attack, slicing and dashing past them while punching the support. Aiko leans Maverick close to the holes, and he starts putting each grenade inside. They continued to do so while Aiko climbed up and grappled around the building, trying to make it quick for him to move. Archers fire at them, and he performs a slide to dodge the arrow. Aiko blocks off more clashes with Nekrothians, and in the process, he gets shot by an arrow around his chest. Feeling it, Aiko felt a surge of anger, and he cut both the Nekrothian's arms off and kicked the body down. He used his arms to swing at the incoming Nekrothians and even choke a Nekrothian neck. Using his blade, Aiko throws it at the Archers, cutting its top body off. Aiko felt his suit overheating, and he tried to calm himself down by breathing in and out. Knowing that he is carrying Maverick on his back and not wanting him to get burnt.

Aiko climbs up higher and higher, grappling inside while Maverick puts more grenades inside the opening where Aiko punches.

"We're good; get higher! FASTER!"

Aiko acknowledges his words and leaps out the window, feeling the wind around them due to the altitude. Aiko grapples the side of the skyscraper's top side, wall-running around while some Nekrothians continue to pursue them. Maverick continues to fire until his ARC stops firing. Maverick reaches for his pouch, realizing that there is nothing in it.

"I'M ALL OUT, AIKO; GET CREATIVE!"

Aiko noticed the harsh wind, so he let go of his grapple and flew back to the Nekrothians. Using his weight, he grappled the two Nekrothians down. One he stabs in the back, and the other he makes a turn to him, cutting its throat, punching it multiple times, and throwing it away. The other Nekrothians, noticing Aiko, swung down with its rifle, firing at him. Hitting Aiko's chest and hurting the exposed damaged part of his chest from his fight with Homura. Angering Aiko even more, they both darted at each other. Aiko, with both his blades, launches up at the Nekrothians, stabbing its chest and, with his strength, tearing its body off.

Aiko grapples up to the top, where they're at the tip of the skyscraper. Aiko, hanging on by the pole of the skyscraper, looks around to see if there is any danger while Maverick, with his ARC, tries to get communication. Seeing the bar signal move once, Maverick speaks to his ARC.

"THIS IS CAPTAIN MAVERICK! I REPEAT, THIS IS CAPTAIN MAVERICK. IF ANYONE CAN HEAR ME, WE NEED HELP! MY BATTALION IS MISSING, AND I AM PROTECTED BY THE MELANCHOLIC KNIGHT, BUT WE ARE BEING OVERRUN BY THE NEKROTHIANS! WE NEED REINFORCEMENT IN THE NORTHERN DISTRICT OF NEW ARCADIA. WE NEED REINFORCEMENT. I REPEAT, WE NEED REINFORCEMENT!"

Maverick looks down, seeing more Nekrothians crawling up and surrounding them. Shooting at him, Aiko turns and uses his energy with his blade to cut and block the bullets from hitting them.

"LET'S HOPE THE MESSAGE REACHES ANYONE. I GOT IT OPEN TO ANY COMMUNICATION CHANNEL, SO THE HEADQUARTERS SHOULD HEAR IT AS WELL. I HOPE."

Maverick looks down, seeing how high up they are.

"AIKO, JUMP DOWN AND BREAK THE TOP OF THIS AREA SUPPORT!"

Aiko listened without hesitation, jumping out behind him and diving down. Aiko grappled to the side below and swung through the window, where he ran so fast with his arms out to prepare a strike! He smashed one of the building's supports and dashed out the window while dodging the Nekrothians' attack.

"BREAK MORE!"

Aiko continues to do so, swinging all around and slicing any Nekrothian that tries to challenge him, falling to each floor and breaking the supports. The top of the skyscraper starts to shake the more support Aiko breaks, going down to each level. Maverick looks to see the top foundation shake; he checks his hand to see the final grenade on his hand. He hands it over to Aiko.

"HEAD DOWN, THROW IT!"

Aiko follows through, leaping out of the building and diving down, then doing a quick grapple, which strains his arm and makes him yelp. Ignoring the pain, he pushes through and throws the grenade down to the floor.

"DIVE OUT!"

Maverick yelled out. Aiko ran out of the building while the Nekrothians chased him, and all crawling up pursued them.

The grenade explodes, which causes the other grenades to explode, causing other grenades nearby to go off and detonate others. The top of the skyscraper collapsed, causing the whole skyscraper to fall forward from the explosion. Aiko dives forward to the rest of the buildings north of him while the Nekrothians all get caught by the debris and collapse from the skyscraper. Destroying dozens of Nekrothians in the process, Aiko grappled to the nearby building rooftop, where he slid and rolled over, causing Maverick to break out from the cable and roll out. Aiko focuses his attention on the collapsing skyscraper and then on Maverick, noticing the debris and smoke from the destruction coming toward them. Aiko quickly made his way onto Maverick, covering him from the damage and the debris landing towards them. The destruction of the skyscraper pushes many Nekrothians into other buildings, where some crash into the debris and get buried by fragments from the series of explosions.

Once the air cleared and the debris vanished, Aiko got up slowly to see Maverick, who was getting up on his back and holding onto Aiko.

"We make a good team."

Aiko falls down a bit, releasing all the steam from his suit and pressing his hand on the damaged part of his chest. Breathing in and out to get his suit to cool off his wound. Aiko then looked forward, seeing two tall figures of similar stature to Aiko. Both figures are Nekrothians but have taller legs and torso structures different than other Nekrothians. Nekrothians have two arms on their left side while holding a large spear-like blade taller than them, while their right arm has just one. With sharp pauldron edges on their shoulders and their armor covering their bodies. The one on the left has those features and has a gray color scheme all around, while the one on the right is all black and has white clothes wrapping around its arms and legs, sporting around its body. The pauldron on its right arm was sharp on both its tips and had more white cloth around it. Their visors are similar to the Nekrothians' jaw armor, which is sharpened, and their top point is out, exposing their mouth. Showing it a like mouth confuses Aiko.

"Those are the Lancers. Best of the Nekrothian Empire."

Aiko looked at the Lancer's mouth, seeing the same skin color scheme of the Nekrothians, but its mouth was closed. Both looked at Aiko and charged straight at Aiko. He immediately grabbed Maverick and slid him out of the conflict.

Aiko blocked the Lancer's attacks, pinning his blade down. The second Lancer's right arm grabs a rifle from their back and prepares to fire at Aiko. Without thinking, Aiko ducks down and rolls over between them. Both the Lancers took turns trading blows with Aiko. One attacks him up close while the other shoots with its rifle. Aiko began to see a similarity between Gunner and Runner. The Lancer with the gun turned his attention to Maverick, who was crawling from its line of fire. Aiko took notice and threw his blade at the Lancer, which reacted early to its throw, deflecting it with its spear blade. Now, getting both the Lancer's attention, he blocks while making strikes. Aiko could feel his suit overheat more as they continued to strike at him; he knew that he had to take down one of them to even out the playing field. Aiko focused on the gray Lancer's two arms on its left side, noting how strong they were but could be easily exposed.

Aiko's shoulder bashed the gray Lancer with a precise shot; Aiko plunged his Valor edge between both its arms, cutting them off. Aiko jumped on it and started stabbing it to make it collapse. And then stabbing its neck, killing it. Aiko turned his attention to the Black Lancer, who stood still, looking at Aiko. Suddenly, its mouth spews out blue liquid. It charges straight at Aiko, who stabbed part of his left arm. The Lancer, with its right arm grabbing its rifle from his back, tries to stab Aiko's chest, but Aiko continues to block its hits. He looks at the liquid dripping out from his mouth, thinking it has the same energy as his.

Maverick crawls towards the black Lancer, staying out of its detection while Aiko blocks. Aiko began to question. "What are you?" "Synara energy?" "Harmonian?"

His mind wandered as he fought to kill the Lancer, conflicting his emotions. The Lancer pulled its rifle out to prepare a blow. A laser, out of nowhere, pointed at the arm of the Lancer.

A shot out of nowhere disarmed the Lancer, which prompted the Lancer to look back and get shot in the face, releasing Aiko in the process. Aiko stabs the Lancer around the torso, and Maverick holds the Lancer down as Aiko gets his grip on it. More shots disarm the two arms holding the spear blade. Aiko held the lancer tight, keeping it from its blade; he lifted it up and ran forward and launched the lancer out to fall to the street below.

Aiko collapses and is wasted by the edge wall while Maverick crawls near him. Both looked over to see where the shot came from, seeing a laser point on top of the wall. Aiko's visor zoomed to where the laser was coming from. Seeing Odie waving from the distance.

"Who is it?"

Aiko pauses for a moment.

"Friends..."

# Chapter Thirty-One: Turbulent Ride Part 3

Kenryoku called out to one of the personnel on their modules.

"Is there any chatter in comms?"

"Only in bases at Phlegmatic and Sanguine, but nothing over at New Arcadia..."

He turned to Acheron, who was overlooking the large monitor that showed the New Arcadia map, which had different districts of its size, and pinpointed the Nekrothians' area that had been seen. Then, pinpointing the area where the URDT Battalions are engaging.

"Our satellite has every FIREBIRDS location, but the communication is being disrupted. We're trying our best to reach New Arcadia, sir."

The worker looks back at Kenryoku and then at his module; Kenryoku looks to Acheron.

"The only problem is that Nekrothians may have advanced, probably grew smarter than us. What if those trackers are just stolen and baiting any soldiers to come to them?"

"We don't know that we're not there right now. They should be the same as the last time we saw them back on Earth. They destroyed everything in their path, only learning from us and killing us off."

Acheron looked to the northern far district where most of Nekrothian's activities were appearing.

"Nerdhard has opened the portal to Earth."

Kenryoku looked at Acheron.

"The LYN report stated that the only things that were stolen were coordinates with Earth and Gaea, Harmonian energy, and the files were viewed."

"Nerdhard. That genocidal maniac deserves what he gets; he shouldn't get humane treatment if he lives. Wherever he is, pulled out from his own existence or in hell for all I care about..."

Acheron sat down on his chair; he looks at a glimpse of Akarui, who is monitoring Aiko's sync level and condition, which displays his injuries and his level that are moderate. Acheron couldn't help but remember him focusing on Aiko levels. His laser attention on Aiko's performance was crucial to him, seeing him as a hand of the URDT sword, obeying and striking when needed. He leaned forward while he continued to ponder.

*"Sorry, Aiko, your service isn't done."*

*"The threat... that nearly ended the human race ended your mother, Aiko."*

*"You barely escaped with your life, surviving close combat with Jax and taking a direct shot rocket. Armor-piercing caliber to revise that. I was given a choice to either cancel the program and let you die out or try to piece together whatever remained of you. You should be grateful that you are still breathing!"*

*"She gave her life to you; you were still young, and your mind was fresh. I thought I lost you both; she was strong even if her condition was weakening. I'm sorry, Aiko, I'm sorry I didn't know you were here. If I knew sooner, I would've taken care of you."*

*"Where were you when I needed YOU!"*

Acheron's voice and, finally, Aiko's voice start to haunt him around, and his mind begins to reflect heavily on his actions. He looked up, seeing Yasuka. Aiko's mother looked at him with her mask while blinking to see Aiko when they met. He blinked again to see it was just an illusion. He felt a liquid drop on his pants, putting his hands on his mask. He felt liquid dripping from his eyelids, and he continued to understand how he was getting liquid from his eyelids.

"THIS IS CAPTAIN MAVERICK! I REPEAT, THIS IS CAPTA-"

Acheron looked up, hearing sounds from the monitor.

"INCREASE THE FREQUENCY!"

Kenryoku yelled out to the workers; all the workers scrambled around trying to get the message to pass through. Kenryoku and Akarui look on as they fix the message while Acheron sits and covers the liquid from his mask with his trench coat.

"THIS IS CAPTAIN MAVERICK! I REPEAT, THIS IS CAPTAIN MAVERICK. IF ANYONE CAN HEAR ME—"

"THERE, THE MESSAGE WAS TRANSFERRED NOW!"

"Put it on!"

Kenryoku yelled out.

"THIS IS CAPTAIN MAVERICK! I REPEAT, THIS IS CAPTAIN MAVERICK. IF ANYONE CAN HEAR ME, WE NEED HELP! MY BATTALION IS MISSING, AND I AM PROTECTED BY THE MELANCHOLIC KNIGHT."

"Aiko?"

Acheron looked up to hear the Knight.

"BUT WE ARE BEING OVERRUN BY THE NEKROTHIANS! WE NEED REINFORCEMENT IN THE NORTHERN DISTRICT OF NEW ARCADIA. WE NEED REINFORCEMENT. I REPEAT, WE NEED REINFORCEMENT!"

"That was sent by Captain Maverick 20 minutes ago, sir!"

The worker said getting back to his module. Kenryoku looks to Acheron while Akarui turns to look at him as well.

"What is our plan, sir?"

She said to him. Acheron gazes at the monitor, the voices of Aiko striking him back and forth. He began to remember times he spent with Aiko, only working and scolding him down. Then the one last time he felt happy.

*"I wish I knew her more."*

*"Father."*

Aiko's words touched him. He got up immediately and walked over to the modules while looking at everyone.

"We're going to send everything we have to the Nekrothians! Kenryoku, are the captains ready?"

"Captain Curtis and Captain Dahlia are on standby with their battalions. Many Humvees, Osprey Eagles, Bombers, Armored Reconnaissance Vehicles and Armored Fighting Vehicles, more all ready to be deployed."

"Give them a green light to go in. SEND EVERYONE TO THE NORTHERN DISTRICT OF NEW ARCADIA NOW!"

"Wait, didn't we say that our troops are falling into their traps?"

"You didn't hear from the message; they were all chasing Aiko and Captain Maverick. Maverick is carrying a nuke towards that area."

Acheron is pointing north up to New Arcadia.

"Nekrothians are more active around the northern district. This is where Nerdhard must have opened the portal. Maverick's battalion was a strike force that should have eliminated the threats in swift action, but it seemed we underestimated the Nekrothians. Maverick's job is to deliver the Nuke to the portal, destroying most of that district but reassuring the Nekrothian invasion doesn't spread. He is still alive, and so is Aiko. We need to protect them, getting them to the objective."

"Understood. YOU HEARD HIM, EVERYONE IN THE BATTLE STATION. SEND EVERYONE TO NEW ARCADIA DISTRICT! CONTACT CAPTAIN CURTIS AND DAHLIA TO HEAD OVER!"

398

Kenryoku yells out to the workers, who immediately start sending messages to every FIREBIRDS that is available.

"Akarui."

Akarui looked back at him.

"Yes?"

"Continue to monitor Aiko. We don't have communication with him, but we watch over him."

"I will, Acheron."

She continues to look at Aiko's levels and condition while looking at the ongoing situation. Acheron looks at everyone's work while he watches the monitor. He sees Yasuka and Aiko standing together. He tightens his fist while his illusion fuels his mind.

The URDT Headquarters hangar starts opening, releasing every Osprey Eagle with many FIREBIRDS on board. Departing to their battles of humanity's fate.

***

The building stood still while the city continued to be destroyed, windows reflecting the horror that had happened a while ago. Suki looks upon everything, and her eyes reflect from the window, displaying her unease about the nature of things. She looks over to see Odie lying down while having his sniper out, looking over any activities. Jerome is holding Maverick and taking him to sit down near the wall side where Odie is. Aiko, near the middle, looks around and sees everyone busted, dusty, and tired. He looked over to Quentin and then to Suki, where he made his way. He leaned against the wall, shaking a bit around him from his presence, sitting down next to her.

"Aiko…"

"Suki…"

Both exchanged their names with each other. Sharing the moment of silence together.

"How's Quentin?"

"Terrible like all of us. We all got separated by the crash; I managed to find Odie in the building nearby. We managed to catch up to Jerome, who was fighting hordes of those… things. We barely escaped them until they redirected their attention to somewhere else together, like something is controlling them. So, we hid and tried to find Quentin; when we got to higher ground, which is when Odie spotted Quentin getting attacked."

Suki looks over to Quentin, who is looking out his side of the window.

"He just came up and cried on me; I could only comfort him."

Suki looked at Aiko.

"Quentin's friend that we knew died, sacrificing himself to help Quentin escape the hordes. After the news, we have just been depressed until Odie scouted ahead and found y'all."

Suki leaned close and rested the side of her head on Aiko's shoulder. Aiko took notice but didn't mind.

"Can you check on him for us?"

Aiko paused for a moment and looked over to her.

"OK."

"Wait."

Aiko stopped, and Suki noticed wire tangling out from his helmet.

"What are those wires popping out for?"

Aiko touched the wires in his helmet. Realizing it, he removed the wires.

"It was part of my communication; I ripped it out by accident."

Suki got close to his helmet, examining it while having her ARC out to point at the two separated wires.

"Simple fix."

She spoke. She changes her ARC to welding. She twists the wires together and seals them up with protectors, then slightly solders them to make sure they seal.

"There. Even though communication is out, it should be helpful if it is restored."

"Thanks, Suki."

Aiko got up and walked over to Quentin and sat beside him. Quentin felt his presence but didn't seem to care. Aiko just sat near him, letting the silence and the sound of battles take place outside.

"Quentin..."

Aiko said softly...

"I wanted to say that... If I didn't say it a long time ago, then I'm sorry."

Quentin looks sideways at Aiko.

"I wanted to thank you for staying by me when we first met."

Quentin has his attention on Aiko.

400

"I would have never met you, Suki, or everyone else. I am happy you took care of Albie even when I despised him. More importantly, I'm happy to see you alive. He would've wanted us to continue to finish this fight so we can go home and be with the people we protect."

Quentin's mouth began to form a smile. Aiko got up and offered his hand out to Quentin, who took it. Helping him get up, they nodded in gratitude.

Jerome walked over to Odie.

"What?"

"Do you have…a bandage?"

Odie takes his eye off his scope and looks over to Jerome.

"What kind?"

Jerome reveals his neck, showing a tiny cut. Odie just nods and chuckles.

"I'm not playing! What if I continued to move my neck aggressively, and it opened? I don't want to bleed out."

"Fine here then."

Odie, sitting right up, takes out a large blade from his pocket and cuts a large strip from his scout kerchief, offering it to Jerome.

"Here, just wrap it around your neck. Choke yourself. Oh, here, big boy."

Odie grabs a small bandage from his pocket, which Jerome looks at in a confusing manner.

"I don't want to die like this."

"We're not going to die!"

Maverick yelled up.

"We're going to win this battle no matter what."

Maverick tried to get up but collapsed. Aiko took notice and ran over to help him, but Maverick declined.

"I formed a plan while we're waiting for reinforcement."

Everyone got up and walked over to Maverick.

"So how are we supposed to make it north without getting our bodies torn to pieces?"

Maverick took Aiko's arm, and Aiko helped him get to the middle, where everyone was around him. He held out his ARC, but his screen glitched.

"I guess my ARC is acting out. I was going to show the map, but I guess not."

"Wait, I have the map, sir."

Quentin walks in the middle, where everyone huddles together, looking at the map on his screen.

"Nice work, Quentin. My objective is to take the Nuke to where the Nekrothians have been coming from."

He pointed to the very northern district but in the middle.

"That's the district they are coming out of, but that district south of it has two lakes; if the Nekrothians destroyed the dams holding the lakes, most of the area below the north might've been flooded."

Maverick pressed buttons to expand the map.

"We're on our own unless we find more squads out there, but the communication is jammed in this city. We're going to have to push forward and go in hard."

"Strike force."

Jerome stated.

"Yes."

Maverick said while looking away.

"I can't guarantee you that we are going to survive. That's why we're going in fast and swift."

He points and drags their path to reach the flooded area.

"We are going to be grappling across the sideline of the buildings; we are each going to help each other if one of us gets attacked. We will stop to help, none of that lone wolf crap. We have each other. Upon reaching the flooded district, we will either have to wait for reinforcement or even swim across unless there is some god's miracle we can pray for."

"Why don't we wait for reinforcement, sir?"

Odie questioned Maverick.

"The Nekrothians are approaching the city. If we wait too long, this planet will be compromised by them. Even if one survives, it can assure doom to humanity. We must do everything in our power to stop them."

Everyone's faces were lowered, looking down.

"I'm scared, too, even as a captain. It's normal to feel like this. We are taught to restrain it, but sometimes, we need to have it with us. But are we going to give up that easily, the lives we all work for? Everyone is counting on us; they wouldn't want us to see ourselves like this. We have the Knight with us; Aiko will protect us. You're the anchor of this operation; you're needed."

He looked to Aiko, who looked back. Acknowledging his words.

"We are humanity's soldiers; we have each other's back. You all train not for yourself but for each other. We strike and move swiftly. Aim around the Nekrothians exposed chest and drop them. All of us will kill as a unit, assuring we can all move swiftly. Aiko will lead us to the destination. He will kill anything that gets in our way, assuring our safety while he leads us. We got this."

Everyone looked at Maverick with determination set.

"Valor Unto the Skies."

"Valor Unto the Skies."

They repeated after Maverick.

"Grounded in Courage."

"Grounded in Courage."

This time, it gets louder, and Maverick gets on Aiko's back. Maverick grapples with the cable around Aiko to hang onto. They all walk outside the window, forming together as they prepare to drop down. Their eyes open wide, facing the travel they must overcome.

"TILL OUR LAST BREATH!"

"TILL OUR LAST BREATH!"

Aiko jumped out first while everyone followed behind him. Diving down, they reached the other building, where Aiko grappled and swung up high and continued to do so. Suki and Quentin followed suit while Odie grappled, slid, and repelled on the rooftop while having his sniper stored on his back. Jerome landed on the ground, grappled to the side, but leaped a distance to make up for his lack of speed.

They moved in unison, moving and swinging through windows, sprinting inside the buildings, and grappling with each other. Odie, with his rifle, looked ahead in his scope, seeing multiple Nekrothians from Troops, Heavy, and Archers all together in a block.

"LOT OF NEKROTHIANS AHEAD OF US, MAVERICK!"

"OK, AIKO! LEAD US THE WAY!"

Aiko grapples to the top of the building; he sprints fast, popping out his Valor Edge. The Nekrothians took notice, shooting their rifles, bows, and spike balls at Aiko. Below Quentin and Suki, covering Jerome as he fired his minigun ARC and got multiple Nekrothians. The Nekrothians fired back at Jerome. He feels their bullets when he uses his back as a shield. He grappled up while Suki and Quentin together tag-teamed, swinging and shooting their ARC at the Nekrothians's necks and torso. One of the Nekrothians tackles Suki above by crawling up, but Quentin's quick reaction is that he grapples at it and changes his ammo type to shells. Shooting its torso and disposing of it, they were about to get fired upon until Jerome swung very high from his grapple, zipping himself. Jerome mows down each Nekrothian.

Aiko fights off any Nekrothians who try to slice him and throws his blades at any Archers who try to fire. While Maverick is on his back, firing at any Nekrothians while changing his ARC to shells and slugs. Maverick provides covering fire for Odie, who sprints while aiming his scope at each Nekrothian near his line of fire. He fires, missing some of his shots but getting clean kills when having precise timing, aiming for their necks.

They all continued to press their charge, taking sharp turns at each corner of the city blocks. Aiko continued to swing across and even sliced the Nekrothians in half. Jerome continued to mow down Nekrothians while grappling and leaping to catch up, while Suki and Quentin continued to cover Jerome. Odie challenged any Archers who tried to shoot him, getting a headshot with his visor detecting any head popping out.

"HOW CLOSE ARE WE QUENTIN!?"

Quentin, hearing Maverick, grappled near Aiko, who was swinging and wall running.

"WE'RE GETTING NEAR!"

"WE ARE!"

Suki pointed at water flowing down the streets. Quentin was about to turn to Maverick until he got tackled by a Nekrothian. More Nekrothians on the ground follow to shoot and charge at Quentin while Jerome provides covering fire. Suki joins in with the firing while getting hit by Nekrothian bullets. Odie fires at them while Aiko goes down and charges at the Nekrothians. Cutting and clashing with the Nekrothians while Maverick provides covering fire for Aiko. Getting the Nekrothians out of their way, they charge on foot.

"GRAPPLE!"

Maverick yelled out. Everyone grappled behind Aiko and zipped across buildings. They saw the water level increase as they drew near to their destination.

Upon landing down, they all catch their breath. Their eyes widen as they see what they see before them: the lakes have flooded the district; only the tops of buildings show while the water covers their remaining structures.

"They got to the dams..."

Suki said. They all looked around, seeing how the lake's waves had demolished this district like nothing. With his scope, Odie looked forward, seeing the light from a distance.

"Is that what you're talking about, Maverick?"

Aiko turned to Maverick to look where Odie was pointing.

"That is the destination. Nekrothians are coming out from the portal over there."

"What now then!? Are we going to swim over there then?"

"COOL IT, ODIE."

Quentin is getting after Odie. Jerome looks away but notices an Osprey Eagle tilting by the side of a building on his left.

"There is an Osprey Eagle!"

Everyone turned to see the vehicle. They all ran towards the Osprey Eagle, getting inside. Everything is uninjured for the most part; just the door and back are opened.

"Take me to the cockpit."

Maverick told Aiko, walking up to the cockpit. Two dead pilots were at the controls. Aiko moved the body to the left and settled Maverick on the seat. Then Aiko carried both bodies out. A moment of silence filled everyone as Aiko carried their pilot's bodies and gently placed them down on the floor. They all looked down and nodded, Aiko, noticing their dog tag, having a name but life before it ended.

"It's operational!"

They went inside to Maverick.

"I assumed the pilot managed to land perfectly on its side besides getting damage on the wings and repelling. I can pilot this, but we can't fly her high. It would damage the foundation of this vehicle. I'm going to have to drive her like a boat. Aiko, gently push this bird down onto the water; we'll go drifting."

Aiko acknowledged Maverick, grappled out the door, and moved the bird down on its belly. Everyone inside could feel Aiko's strength as he pushed the Osprey Eagle onto the water. Maverick started up the engine, which shook violently but managed to start. The Eagle began to move while floating on the water, coasting forward slowly.

"WE'RE OFF! EVERYONE HANG ON!"

Everyone in the cargo bay grapples on the top and bottom, securing themselves and hanging on. Maverick accelerates the Eagle, cruising toward The Nekrothian's portal.

405

Odie, looking out the window, noticed something flying at them. It has a slim, long body with its head and tail pointing like a spear. Having wings that are the same length as their body. It has a greenish-gray color scheme with armor pieces attached to it, part around the body. Its head has no eyes but has horns on its side top and two prominent horns sticking out like hooks. On top of it was a Nekrothian, riding it while shooting at them. Odie takes cover.

"FLYING NEKROTHIANS! SIR, WE GOT INCOMING... I DON'T KNOW WHAT THEY ARE. FLYING NEKROTHIANS..."

Odie calls while trying to shoot.

"WE CALL THEM VULTURES! DON'T LET THEM GET ON THE SHIP OR ATTACK US! WE NEED TO REACH THE OTHER SIDE! AIKO, GET ON TOP OF THE SHIP; MAKE SURE THEY DON'T LAND ON US!"

Maverick yells at everyone to get to their battle station. Aiko runs up and climbs on top while having his grapple on the top of the ship while his blades are out.

One of the Vulture charges at Aiko who threw his blade, which missed. Dodging before the Vulture could tackle him down. Aiko continues to grapple onto the ship, his visor showing clearly where the Vulture will try to attack. He looks at the distance and predicts where it will come from. Sending it down and retrieving back his blades. Aiko continues to get shot from behind, prompting him to switch his position back and forth on the top of the ship. Anticipating how it will turn, he throws his blade in that direction, and when it turns, it gets stabbed in the stomach.

Maverick continued to navigate the bird while using the water to steady it. He struggled with the Osprey Eagle's steering, as the water's forceful nature and the Eagle's already damaged condition made it difficult for him to pilot. He looked at the Eagle's fuel, seeing it depleting fast.

"I'M GOING TO GO FAST; HANG ON!"

He yelled out; he pushed the gears forward. Increasing the engine speed. Sending the Eagle to bounce up and down and getting water in the vehicle. Everyone bounces in motion to the bumpy ride. Having their cables held inside, they peek back and forth while shooting at the Vultures. Odie manages to get clean hits while Jerome shoots his bullets in a widespread, hitting many targets. Suki begins to get them at a distance once she aims ahead of their direction, getting damage on each Vulture. Quentin focuses his fire on the Vulture's wings, seeing that it has a large area of exposed flesh, getting three down while making sure he doesn't slip out.

Aiko continues to get shot, feeling his body growing warmer and getting annoyed. Getting familiar with how they fly, he gets clean kills with his blades. Two Nekrothian jumped from their Vulture, in a team-up clash against Aiko. He struggled to hold his position due to the ride, only using one arm to attack and defend himself. He put heavy force on his right arm, slashing one of the Nekrothians and kicking it overboard. The last Nekrothians managed to stab Aiko, damaging part of his chest. This only angered Aiko more; he released his grapple and threw the Nekrothian out against the wind. He quickly grappled back on the plane's tail, making him fly with the wind. Aiko's system began to cool his wound but ruined his focus. He grapples back into the cargo compartment, where everyone is struggling. Jerome continues to fire until getting slashes from the bullet on his face, nearly hitting his head. Quentin's armor protects him, but he knows how dangerous it is if he continues to peek.

More Vultures are coming to where they're heading, shooting at the Osprey Eagle, damaging the engine more and penetrating its armor.

"TAKE COVER! USE YOUR BACK AS A SHIELD!"

Aiko immediately dashes over to Suki and Quentin, where his armor protects them. Jerome protects Odie while the bullet releases hell on them. Maverick knew that he would lose control of the Osprey Eagles if he let go of the controls. The bullet traveled to him, shooting the cockpit. Once shooting ends momentarily, Aiko redirects his focus to Maverick.

"AAAARH!"

Maverick, yelp. Aiko steadily walked over to him, and he could see his blood pouring out. His right arm was down while he was operating the Osprey Eagle.

"MAVERICK! ARE YOU OKAY!"

"I survived worse back then. There are too many of them..."

Maverick looked up and noticed that they were near the Nekrothian base.

"I'M GOING TO DISTRACT THEM FOR Y'ALL TO GET DOWN THERE. I'M TAKING THIS BIRD UP HIGH WHILE YOU ALL GRAPPLE ONTO AIKO. HE WILL GET YOU DOWN SAFELY; GRAPPLE ONTO THE BUILDINGS WHEN YOU GET NEAR."

"WHAT!"

Quentin ran up to Maverick, seeing him able to pilot the Osprey Eagle. Maverick tilted the Eagle up, getting it off the water and taking it to higher levels but not too far from the ground.

"SIR, I'M NOT LEAVING YOU AGAIN!"

"YES, YOU ARE; THE OBJECTIVE IS TO STOP THE NEKROTHIANS FROM ESCAPING FROM THE CITY. YOU ARE NEEDED FOR THE OPERATION; YOU BETTER OBEY!"

Quentin backs off from his statement and nods to him.

"UNDERSTOOD, SIR!"

"VERY WELL."

Maverick coughs heavily.

"AIKO, YOU MUST COMPLETE MY MISSION!"

Maverick, using his weak right arm, hands Aiko the Nuke.

"IT IS HEAVILY PROTECTED, BUT DON'T GET IT DAMAGED!"

Aiko's heart pounds, realizing he is holding a bomb that can wipe out a cityscape. He hesitated and almost dropped it.

"LISTEN TO ME! ONCE YOU'RE NEAR THE PORTAL, PRESS THE BUTTON, AND IT WILL START A COUNTDOWN. YOU HAVE 2 MINUTES TO GET OUT UNTIL IT EXPLODES! YOU WILL BE FINE IF YOU ARE FAR AWAY!"

Aiko looks back and forth at the Nuke and at Maverick. Suddenly, Maverick put his weak arm on Aiko's chest.

"WE DO WHATEVER WE TAKE TO PROTECT THE PEOPLE WE'RE FIGHTING FOR! WE CANNOT LOSE THEM! PROTECT WHAT YOU HAVE LEFT, AIKO!"

Maverick's words reached Aiko's mind, remembering Albie back at home.

"VALOR TO THE SKIES!"

"Valor to the skies!"

Aiko repeated Maverick's speech. Aiko walks back, where everyone is waiting for Aiko. Aiko is holding on in the middle, and everyone grapples around Aiko.

"ON GO, DROP WITH AIKO. I'LL SWING YOU OUT NEAR THE BUILDING HEIGHT; YOU NEED TO GRAPPLE AND NOT HURT YOURSELF TOO MUCH."

"3!"

Everyone tightens themselves, holding on to Aiko.

"2!"

Jerome and Odie look at each other in concern, and Suki and Quentin both show fear but are still willing to act.

"1!"

Aiko looked forward, holding the bomb near his chest. Breathing in...

"GO!"

Maverick turned the Eagle so sharply that it sent them flying, diving down near the ruined buildings. They all hold on to Aiko and take each side to where they can grapple and land safely. Jerome holds Odie while both grapple near the rooftop, but their landing is rough. Odie's landing with his foot causes his leg to be damaged from impact, but Jerome's heavy suit protects him from the effects. Quentin and Suki dart at the right side of the building; using the momentum of the dive, they swing fast so they can't damage their arms. They manage to slow down, but Quentin's missing grapple causes him to fall on his side, damaging his arm. While Suki manages to land on the side of the building, she falls on the rubble nearby. Aiko grapples near the buildings and manages to wall run but slips, falling down but managing to protect the Nuke from further damage. Aiko immediately looks up, seeing Maverick in the Osprey Eagle continue getting shot at but drawing their attention away.

Maverick coughs as he brings the Eagle higher into the sky. Noticing the engines were smoking, he knew he had to jump out or else he would get caught in the explosion. Maverick went to the cockpit compartment to find the emergency kits and parachute. He grabs the parachute and immediately grabs the emergency kit while he crawls out while grappling with safety. He holds the morphine injector and applies it to his damaged right arm. Once the Eagle cockpit started smoking, he let off the grapple cables and zipped out. The Eagle flew up and exploded, Maverick barely escaping the explosion.

"Maverick…"

Quentin looked up as well, seeing the Eagle explode. Everyone turned their attention, with the explosion shattering their hearts.

"We can't weep! We're exposed out here if we don't continue the mission!"

Jerome yelled out. He turned around, widening his eyes more.

"It's even bigger up close…"

Everyone turned to where Jerome was looking. Seeing a large fortress with a series of open gaps all around, like a dome but exposed to light. The fortress was red due to the material it was made from; the fortress stretched taller than the buildings.

"It's almost as big as the URDT Headquarters."

Suki said. The fortress's height looms over them, creating a feeling of doom in them.

"We're supposed to fight them all!"

Jerome yelled out.

"Calm down, Jerome!"

Quentin put his hand on his shoulder, but Jerome moved away.

"You do you mean calm down! This is suicide!"

"We're already here; we can't go back!"

"Yes, we CAN!"

"ALRIGHT, FINE, GO BACK. SWIM ACROSS THE GODDAMN LAKE WHERE YOU GET RIPPED TO PIECES BY THAT VULTURE!"

Odie and Suki looked at each other, noting how truly hopeless they felt. Odie turned around to look back up until his eyes widened. He put on his visor and looked at the sky with his scope.

"Y'ALL STOP FIGHTING! LOOK!"

Quentin and Jerome look at it, and Suki and Aiko look at it well.

While parachuting down, Maverick reloads his cartridge and aims at the flying Vulture. Managing to get a clean headshot when it draws near. More firing came around him, narrowly missing him. He breathes in and out, thinking he'll die out here. He took his aim as the Vulture came charging at him. Then his ARC starts statically buzzing, a voice trying to connect to him.

"Maverick? - Captain Maverick?"

"Is that you, Curtis?"

"YOU KNOW IT, BABY! WHOOOO!"

A series of shots coming out of nowhere knocks the Vulture out of the sky, saving Maverick. He looked to his right, his eyes widening, which prompted him to switch cartridges and shoot out a flare, going to his ARC.

A fleet of Osprey Eagles is seen. Some carry troops, while others are carrying AFV vehicles that are like tanks but with wheels, ARVs with turrets, and tank-like Humvees. They are making their way to the Nekrothian fortress.

"It's good to see you in one piece, Captain Maverick."

"Is that you, Cade? Where were you at?"

"I got trapped underneath rubble until Dahlia's force was performing a sweeping operation. They found five Nekrothian-built communication jammers, and eventually, we got the communication back online. I'm with Curtis and Dahlia now! With some of yours and mine, the battalion is still ready to fight."

"Pick me up; I'm sitting bait!"

Curtis Osprey Eagle is swooping in, and FIREBIRDS is grappling with Maverick. Bring him inside.

"Rest easy, Captain. You've done enough. LET'S GET DOWN THERE! VALOR TO THE SKIES!"

"VALOR TO THE SKIES!"

Many FIREBIRDS skydive down to the ground, with many Osprey vehicles deploying their ground vehicles.

Quentin, Suki, Jerome, Odie, and Aiko all look at many FIREBIRDS drop down. Parachuting or gliding down to buildings on the ground, the URDT army is here.

"The cavalry is here then..."

Jerome smiles, along with Odie, who bump into each other in excitement. Quentin and Suki sigh in relief, look each other in the eye, and grin. Aiko hears static coming from his helmet.

"Ai-ko, AIKO! Can you hear me?"

"Akarui?"

Aiko responded.

"How are you? WHY DID YOU BREAK YOUR COMMUNICATION WIRE? I WAS WORRIED SICK FOR YOU!"

"It was an honest mistake..."

"That doesn't matter right now."

Acheron intercepts their conversation.

In the Tactical Headquarters, Acheron is looking at Akarui.

"Acheron, can you hear me?"

"Yes, Maverick, seeing you alive is very good."

"Me too, sir. Aiko is carrying the Nuke, sir. I sent the mission to him because of my condition."

Acheron paused, looking at the monitor, which showed Aiko's visor holding the Nuke. Both Akarui's and Kenryoku's eyes widened, looking at Acheron.

"Very well."

Acheron said. He looked at Akarui.

"Put me on all frequencies, everyone."

"Yes, sir."

Akarui listening to Acheron.

"Proud soldiers of the URDT This may be humanity's final stand against a threat that nearly wiped us out. But this will be a victory for us all. We must hold our ground and get The Melancholic Knight safely across to the portal in that Nekrothian fortress."

Dahlia, Curtis, Cade, Maverick, Akarui, Kenryoku, Jerome, Odie, Suki, and Quentin, along with soldiers that drop down, all look at Aiko. Aiko feels his heart getting heavy as his attention is gained.

"Carry a nuke to eliminate the Nekrothian advance and secure our protection from the invaders. We must do our part to make sure he gets there safely. You all have each other, and you help each other out. Humanity is counting on us; our fallen comrades are counting on us. Our loved ones are waiting for us all at home, wanting to see us victorious in this fight for humanity's fate. FIGHT TO WIN, FIGHT TO LIVE, FIGHT FOR THE KNIGHT!"

Aiko looked forward to the looming fortress. Images of Anbu, Inoue, Saskia, and Albie, who were smiling at him, appeared to him, and his heart pounded more and more. His eye lowered as he held the Nuke with his right arm, with his left arm unleashing his Valor Edge. Quentin, Suki, Odie, and Jerome were behind Aiko's back, preparing to charge.

"FIGHT FOR VICTORY!"

All the FIREBIRDS grapple or charge on the ground. With Humvee, AFV, ARV, and Osprey Eagle charging in. Many of the FIREBIRDS surround Aiko, offering their protection. They all charge into a fight for humanity, willing to lose themselves so as not to lose their new home planet.

# Chapter Thirty-Two: Holding on to hope

The fate of humanity is pulled between the Nekrothians and Humanity's last hope. Aiko is protected by two squads of FIREBIRDS as Aiko charges towards the fortress.

"WATCH OUT FOR INCOMING DEBRIS FLYING!"

Quentin looked behind, seeing the AFV cannon taking aim at the fortress's dome-like wall.

Many AFV fire upon the dome, breaking its walls. Aiko and everyone else notice the debris. Aiko immediately took the lead, grappling with each piece of debris falling off. Everyone else follows suit with him as they grapple with each piece of debris, reaching where the cannons break through the Nekrothian's defense. Upon reaching there, Aiko's and everyone else's eyes widened from what they had seen. A series of bridge-like constructs span around the large dome areas, connecting each other from top to bottom. Aiko's visor zoomed in on the ample light shining in the middle, with bridges breaking through destroyed buildings and the ruins of New Arcadia scorching the battlefield. The light shone and was large enough to allow Aiko to see more Nekrothians being thrown out from it; Aiko took a survey around the dome and the distance he had to travel.

"It's so far away..."

Odie noticed the portal in his scope.

"We'll give you enough cover to get across to the portal; that bomb needs to be delivered no matter what!"

One of the squad members speaks out, Aiko, and the others acknowledge the other squads.

"I can't travel or run that much."

Odie kneeled, pressing against the foot that he damaged upon landing. Quentin and the others look down at him.

"I can survey from here, give you a heads up, and take some baddies down. I'm a bird watcher anyways."

Jerome put his hand on Odie's shoulder, with Odie grinning a little.

"If you don't mind, Quentin, I want to stay with my friend. We'll watch each other's backs, and he would be defenseless up here."

"That's fine. Be safe, you two!"

Quentin pointed them out, reassuring them to watch each other's backs. Quentin and Suki look at each other.

"You got mine?"

"I got yours."

Both offer a slight grin, then tighten themselves. Quentin felt pain around his arm from the landing but still pushed it. They all looked down, seeing URDT forces breaking through and started firing. They look forward, seeing a horde of Nekrothians Soldiers, Archers taking a position from the top or bottom and Heavies charging in with their spike ball and large blades. The URDT charge with war cries while Nekrothian roars mimic humans but are distorted, giving an unsettling sound they make.

"Rematch at last; I'VE BEEN WAITING FOR THIS A LONG TIME! YOU SON OF"

Aiko and Others' communication shattered and cut off before Curtis could finish the line.

"With my FIREBIRDS!"

Curtis and the other squad of FIREBIRDS grappling up and clashing against Nekrothians. Aiko and the others see the battle taking place.

"When you are ready, sir!"

One of the squad members is waiting for Aiko to take charge. Aiko, looking down, knew that the fighting was taking place elsewhere thanks to the URDT drawing the Nekrothian's attention. Aiko took a step forward, and everyone else got ready themselves. Once enough Nekrothian forces made their way over to the fighting.

"NOW!"

Aiko jumped out, and Quentin and Suki, along with the other two squads, followed suit, jumping down with him. They grappled to a nearby bridge, going underneath and on top. Aiko, not wanting to draw too much attention, continued to grapple and ran on the extended bridges, matching the same level height as where the portal was.

"VULTURE INCOMING TO Y'ALL!"

Odie yelled through the communication. Aiko and everyone else noticed six vultures with two Nekrothians in each, while two of the vultures carried Archers. They all took aim at them and fired upon them, prompting them to dodge out of the way, but Aiko continued to run while using his armor as shielding.

Quentin and everyone else grapple back up but clash with each Nekrothian, jumping off and fighting against each other. Quentin, getting air tackled by the Nekrothians, opens his jaw, but Quentin's eyes widen. He notices that their armor is dark gray and chrome but still dirty. A shot through its neck sends the Nekrothian off the ground.

"They're like ashes, their armor."

"I think they were using the dust and debris as cover. Camouflages in the destruction they made."

Quentin and Suki continue to run with Aiko and the other two squads on the bridge.

"Unless their armor can camouflage, like those chameleons back on Earth, they could do that to hide from predators. But only this time, the role is reversed; we're their prey."

Odie mentions to them that he continues to shoot down Vultures and Nekrothians that come across his scope. Jerome watches him back, guns down, crawling Nekrothians while some grapples are near them. Jerome sweats himself off as he looks around to secure their protection.

"How many kills have you gotten, Odie?"

"Sir?"

Cade speaks through his communication line.

"I said, how many kills have you gotten?"

"9 so far..."

"DO MORE!"

Cade exclaimed. He grappled past them, landing on the construct with his modified revolver scope, gunning down three Vultures and two Nekrothians who came to charge at him.

"Can you beat us all?"

Cade remarked. Odie and Jerome looked to their right side, seeing more snipers taking position on top or on the bridge, shooting down vultures and Nekrothians from top to bottom.

"You're on!"

Odie grinned as his motivation pumped up his eyesight, shooting more Nekrothians within seconds. Jerome continued to offer protection to Odie as more crawled up.

At the bottom of the floor, FIREBIRDS clash with each Nekrothian, but two FIREBIRDS, or four each, take down Nekrothians one after another. Doing precise teamwork but getting stabbed or hit by the spike ball out of nowhere by Brawler. A brawler prepared to throw its spike ball forward to another squad until getting shot in the chest by the ARV vehicles. Another Heavy Nekrothian slash and dash at each team.

"Get some of this!"

Curtis swung and landed on Brawler, placing a grenade around its neck and jumping out.

Exploding it to bits, Curtis and other squads follow his example. One of the squad members gets shot in the chest by the Archer, with more jumping down and firing at them.

"AAAARRH!"

Curtis and the other FIREBIRDS charged at them while firing from their ARC, clashing with them and switching their ammo type to shells. Shooting in their chest, getting each side to die. Curtis, bursting out with his knife from his chest, stabs relentlessly at the Nekrothian's neck.

"AAARRRH!"

Yelling out in a war cry, he notices another Archer taking down another of his men. He reaches for his ARC.

"SOMEONE TAKE THAT FOOL DOWN FROM UP THERE!"

ARV, with its cannon, takes aim  where the Archers were at.

"Thanks."

"WE'RE GETTING OVERRUN BY MORE NEKROTHIANS!"

Curtis looked up, where one of the squad members had spoken with Aiko and Saw Hordes, shooting at them and grappling with them.

"DAHLIA! CAN YOU ASSIST ON THEM!"

"ON MY WAY!"

With her ARC, Dahlia runs while the other two squads follow. They were so fast they dodged every fight. They grappled up more to each bridge constrict, three of the members getting shot at in the process but still pushing to where Aiko and the others were.

"AIKO, WATCH OUT!"

Akarui yelled through Aiko's communication. Aiko saw a Nekrothian getting a jump on him, but he kicked it off the way. The squad members started getting pulled away. The second got stabbed and thrown off. Quentin and Suki, shooting with their ARC, both worked together, tackling and getting each Nekrothian that was thrown at them.

"THERE ARE TOO MANY!"

The last member that followed Aiko got shot at and pushed off the ledge of the bridge. Suki blocked but got shoved off to the ledge, and Quentin's heart pounded. He immediately dashed and grappled to the spot and grappled to her.

"I won't lose you too!"

Quentin struggles to hold due to his right arm feeling pain. Suki holds on to the cable until she notices more movement below her. Dahlia and the other two squad members follow up near her, getting on top of the bridge and forcing off the Nekrothians. Aiko grabs a Nekrothian jaw and head, opening it to break it in half. He grabs another Nekrothian, but it has arms; he repeatedly kicks it so hard that its arms break and send it falling down.

"AIKO! HELP YOUR FRIENDS! WE'RE COVER!"

Aiko, redirecting his attention, ran over to Quentin, grabbing him and Suki up. Quentin kneeled as his arm felt more pain.

"Quentin, we need to get you out of here. Your arm isn't well!"

"I'M FINE!"

Quentin yelled from the pain.

"NO, YOU'RE NOT; SHE'S RIGHT!"

Dahlia ran to them while shooting.

"You are not fit to fight now; you must retreat and be at the backline. You got Aiko far, but more Nekrothians and the Nuke will kill you. Suki help Quentin out of here."

Dahlia looked over to the final squad that was with Aiko,

"GET THEM OUT OF HERE. YOU DID YOUR JOB. LET US FINISH IT FOR YOU!"

"YES, MA'AM."

The squad retreated back to Suki and Quentin. Aiko follows them, both looking at Aiko.

"You be safe, Aiko. Return!"

Suki patting Aiko on the arm. Aiko and Quentin look at each other.

"Take care, Blue Face!"

Quentin and Aiko embraced in a hug. It was fast since the battle was still going on. Suki supported Quentin while they retreated with the squad. Aiko looked at them while they ran back.

"They're fine, Aiko. You're nearing the portal, but there are a lot more Nekrothians coming in."

"GET THAT BOMB DELIVERED AIKO, FIGHT FOR YOUR LIFE!"

Aiko heard Acheron's voice, making Aiko ready himself. He sprints with full force off the bridge and continues to grapple up. Dahlia and the two squads block and wrestle with the Nekrothians that try to get near Aiko. They reach the big construct that connects the bridge to the portal. Many more Nekrothians are there on Vultures, more on the bridge, and Archers are covering the top bridge on other sides. Many heavy Nekrothians, all varieties, meet at the top, looking at Aiko.

"PROTECT THE KNIGHT! EVERYONE!"

Acheron message reaches everyone at ARC. Kenryoku is at the bottom of the room and goes to each personnel. Everyone is working to get communication for the soldiers and assure the signal is operational.

Dahlia and the two squads run in front of Aiko, shooting but grappling back and forth to get every Nekrothian that charges at them. Aiko sprinted, noticing how long he had to run. One Archer aims at Aiko but gets shot in the head by other snipers. Each exchanging hit and killing the other. Finally, one of the Archers aims at Aiko's armored knee guard, damaging the broken piece Aiko had when he fought Homura. The snipers continue to get the Archer off Aiko's back.

"WE GOT THE HIGH GROUND COVER!"

One of the snipers communicated with Dahlia. Aiko was on his knee, feeling pain around it. Feeling the bones snap in, he breathed in a while, his energy trying to cool his damage.

"AIKO! YOU NEED TO CONTINUE, FIGHT AGAINST IT!"

Aiko looked up, seeing Saskia's face, but regained his thoughts that it was Dahlia. Who is covered by cuts and bleeding across her face.

"CMON!"

Aiko got up but limped. He continued to sprint while using his Valor Blade to slash and dodge. Brawler's heavy chain spike ball demolished the whole squad that protected Aiko.

"WE NEED REINFORCEMENT!"

Dahlia communicates in her ARC.

418

"ON MY WAY."

Curtis responds; he is grappled by the Osprey Eagle that got into the fortress. FIREBIRDS members in the vehicle begin to rain fire with heavy machine guns, gunning down Nekrothians near Dahlia area and some on the side of the other bridges. Curtis and the other squad jump down to assist Dahlia.

"GO KNIGHT! WE'RE HOLDING THEM OFF!"

Curtis yelled while wrestling with a Brawler and stabbing it. The Osprey Eagle that was shooting was swarmed by many Vultures that slammed against it. More Osprey Eagles joined in and assisted with covering fire. One of the Osprey Eagles had Maverick, who was controlling the machine turret. He reached for his ARC.

"DON'T LOOK BACK, GO AIKO! GO!"

Maverick yelled while he shot more Vultures and Nekrothians around. Cade, with more snipers following his lead, shooting multiple Nekrothian necks and chests.

"WE GOT YOUR BACK. GO!"

Cade joins in; he and other snipers continue to shoot and run on the other side of the bridge. Aiko looks behind, seeing Odie, Jerome, Suki, and Quentin's faces as an illusion in his head. With that in mind, he charged forward. Jumping over Nekrothians and stabbing each that got in his way. Aiko continues to make great distance forward as more URDT forces and the captains support Aiko. They continued to fight, but each of the URDT forces and captains got pushed back by the overwhelming Nekrothians. Aiko was getting overwhelmed, and he is pinned down. Aiko's suit grows hotter as he can feel his right shoulder piece fall off, and his big armor breaks off. He used his energy to stab each Nekrothian, breaking free and charging forward. His suit releases steam from his shoulders and jawline.

"His levels are the same as when he fought you, sir… but they're increasing. He is going to hurt his body MORE!"

"WE CAN'T DO ANYTHING ABOUT IT. KENRYOKU! ARE THEY THERE YET?

Acheron looks away from Akarui to Kenryoku, who is monitoring two names.

"Gunner and Runner."

Aiko continues to slash and cut, feeling his body giving him the power but setting his mind to the objective. Two heavy Nekrothians, one with a heavy slab blade and spike ball, hit Aiko. Causing Aiko to breathe heavily, he feels blood coming out from his suit. The two heavies approach him until a whip chain strangles one of the heavies' necks and follows up with a slam.

Ernaline pushed back the heavy look to Aiko.

419

"GO!"

Her voice has a cybernetic sync. The other heavy gets shot away by Deagmund, who is dropped down behind Aiko and helps Aiko up.

"GO!"

He gives the same response, his voice being cybernetic as well. They provide Aiko with cover, prompting Aiko to run across the bridge.

"START THE COUNTDOWN!"

Akarui yelled to Aiko; Aiko looked at the nuke button and pressed it. Starting the countdown.

"2:00"

"AIKO HAS STARTED THE COUNTDOWN; BEGIN TO RETREAT TROOPERS!"

Cade got words from his ARC, and everyone started retreating. Aiko continued to run while slashing and breaking through the Nekrothians' forces. His mind ran through many images; he couldn't think of many, but he focused his eye on the portal. Aiko continued to examine the portal but noticed that it was shrinking, closing.

"IT IS CLOSING!"

Akarui yelled out, Acheron and everyone else looking at Aiko's visor.

"What, sir, was that why this fortress was about to be made? These portals were used for space travel but created a dangerous, huge shockwave. That's how they were able to launch their attack."

Kenryoku paused, but his eyes widened, looking at Acheron. Acheron looks around.

"TELL EVERYONE TO RETREAT FAR AWAY; GET OUT OF THE FORTRESS AREA!"

Acheron yells out to the personnel on their module and gets his message out.

"IT'S GOING TO WHAT!?"

Quentin yelled at Odie.

"THE PORTAL IS CLOSING, AND IT GOING TO SEND OUT A POWERFUL SHOCKWAVE THAT WILL SEND THAT FORTRESS DOWN; IT IS NOT FROM THE NUKE!"

"WHAT ABOUT AIKO? HE NEEDS TO GET OUT!"

Suki grabs Quentin. Looking at each other in concern.

"THERE IS NOTHING WE CAN DO; WE NEED TO GET OUT OF HERE!"

"NO, I'M NOT GOING TO LOSE AIKO AGAIN!"

Quentin was about to grapple until Jerome grabbed him by the waist. An Osprey Eagle approached them, revealing it to be Maverick!

"GET IN!"

Each got in while Jerome held Quentin, trying to break free.

"MAVERICK! AIKO, HE GOING TO GET-!"

Maverick put his hand on his shoulders, not offering any words but reassuring them. They escape out of the fortress while other FIREBIRDS grapple out on the vehicles or Osprey Eagle while some get shot down by Nekrothians. All the Nekrothians turned their attention back to the portal, returning to stop Aiko.

"AIKO, YOU ARE TO RETREAT BACK. IT A LOST CAUSE, GET OUT NOW!"

Acheron yelled through his helmet, but Aiko continued to move. Ignoring his response, he presses on.

"1:15."

Aiko slashed and stabbed every Nekrothian; upon reaching the portal, it started to shrink down more and more.

"AIKO, GET OUT! WHAT ARE YOU DOING! AIKO!"

Akarui yelled out to him, but Aiko continued to ignore them. The steam and overheating made his suit red. He ran and ran, ignoring the damage he was getting from the Nekrothian.

"I'm sorry. They will come back, but with more numbers, I can't lose more people. I just can't... I'm sorry, Dad. I'm sorry, Inoue. I'm sorry…. Albie."

"AIKO!"

Akarui yelled while Acheron sat back down, his body too stunned to move as he watched Aiko's visor. He saw Aiko run up to the portal and seeing it shrink down. Aiko grappled, slid, and dived forward, nearly making it into the portal. His visor disrupted and cut his connection, along with the condition that Akarui was monitoring; she began to tear up while Kenryoku looked down. Acheron got up and walked away, leaving them. Akarui looked down, continuing to weep.

"Was he ready to give himself up for us?"

She said to herself.

Every trooper was on an Osprey Eagle as they flew away from the shockwave that demolished the fortress. Bringing the whole area down creates a powerful disturbance that spins high from the shockwave. Many Osprey eagles felt powerful waves hitting them. Maverick, Cade, Dahlia, Curtis, Ernaline, Deagmund, Odie, Jerome, Suki, and Quentin look at the destruction, noting that Aiko is there somewhere. Quentin's eyes are sorrowful while Suki comforts him and hugs him. The brightness of the blast blinds everyone, escaping to their near end.

***

Aiko opens his eyes and sees white light surrounding him like a tunnel. Pushing him through it while slowly turning red. Aiko began to feel coldness from his suit. The light vanishes, turning into darkness. Aiko looked up, and his eyes widened. A series of Vultures of Nekrothian flying towards his direction and many big ships near a planet. They share the same aesthetic sharp edge but are so large that many cruisers come out and start to approach Aiko. Aiko notices the Earth and sees the continents around it, which are brown and less green.

"Earth..."

Aiko examined Earth but redirected his focus to a series of ships that were far away. Aiko understood that the series of vessels would continue coming, but he could damage their fleet for a long time. With his strength, Aiko held the energy he left, holding the Nuke.

"10 seconds."

Aiko, twisting his arm around, prepares to throw the Nuke. His steam grows more on his arm due to his energy being redirected to his arm, making his arm hotter. Aiko throws the Nuke towards the Nekrothians cruisers. Traveling a great distance towards the Nekrothians cruisers, which the Nuke detonates. Creating a large whiteout explosion that spread around and reached the ships, causing each to explode from the radius. Aiko was getting close to the Nuke radius; he tried to grapple back but understood that the portal was gone. He looked forward, seeing the Nuke radius reaching him, expanding it. Aiko remembered that the Nuke was powerful enough to destroy a full-scale city, understanding how devastating it truly is, being called death itself.

Many images come out of Aiko's head. Quentin, Suki, Odie, Jerome, Maverick, Dahlia, Cade, Curtis, Kenryoku, Akarui, Acheron, Yume, Saskia, Inoue, Anbu, and Albie. Thinking about the time he spent with them, remembering their words.

"*Hold on to hope.*"

"*Never look back.*"

"*Where were you when I needed you!*"

"*You are needed here.*"

*"You, my brother, Aiko."*

*"Take care of each other!"*

*"Please come back!"*

Hearing various voices sends Aiko screaming as he moves with space, being spun around as the Nuke shockwave reaches towards him. He continues to cry and breathe heavily as the radius reaches towards him. Growing whiter and whiter, Aiko's suit starts cooling, and he immediately shuts off his visor. His eyes black out, and his mind slowly brings back memories. He slowly embraces the nuke explosion, engulfing him and whiting out around him.

# Epilogue: The Metallic Crusader: The Melancholic Knight

Whiteness remained, no sound, only the void of white. Aiko opened his eyes, only seeing whiteness. He began to wonder where he was; had he died? He looked at both his sides, and nothing but voidness. He continues to look ever more around until he sees a figure blackened, obscuring his vision. It floated near him, but he couldn't tell what the figure looked like. Examining around him, it put its arm above Aiko. Pressing around Aiko's damaged chest piece, feeling it around until reaching Aiko's flesh, it was caught from the burning.

"No, you're not dead."

The figure's voice was metallic and heavy, as if struggling to speak. Aiko's heart pounded, but slowly. He couldn't feel his body; it wasn't responding. He didn't feel his blood pump around him; he breathed more slowly than ever. The figure is placed firmly around Aiko's damaged piece, releasing some liquid. Liquid that looked similar to Aiko's synara energy, but this was dark red; it dribbled down into Aiko's flesh. Aiko could feel it surround it and enter its body.

"But your time is not over..."

The figure's hand had sharp ridges and was as wide as Aiko's chest. He left his hand out of Aiko's sight.

"We're meeting again when you don't expect it. Aiko Ashin..."

Its voice left Aiko. He breathed more but struggled. He couldn't panic due to his low energy and his body's inability to respond. The light got brighter, blinding Aiko and making him pass out once more. The sound disappeared from him, and the void filled the air around him.

***

"WE FOUND HIM! THE MELANCHOLIC KNIGHT!"

Echoes and voices peered out, but Aiko could only slightly hear them. A glimpse of the light from the sky appeared. He could feel himself getting carried but then knocked out.

"Aiko?"

He opens his eyes, seeing familiar faces. He couldn't see fully, only glimpses of faces.

Quentin, Suki, Odie, and Jerome. Standing by some entrance and leaving him. More faces appeared. Maverick, Dahlia, Curtis, and Cade then leave out the door. Two more faces appeared, Akarui and Kenryoku, leaving out the door as well. Albie, along with Yume, appeared with her boys behind her. Albie walked up and hugged his armored chest. Then leaving out the door. Aiko's eyes flicker repeatedly, seeing Saskia putting her hand on her cheek but blinking at another person. Inoue smiles at Aiko but disappears when he closes his eyes. Aiko looked down, seeing Anbu. His younger self, smiling. Aiko blinked, and he disappeared as well. His eyes close, pausing his mind and body. His suit began to growl, like how he felt when he first got into a suit.

"AAAAARRRRRH!"

Aiko screamed out.

***

*June 8, 2134*

"AIKO! AIKO! ARE YOU ALRIGHT!?"

Acheron is in front of him, putting his hands on his chest. Aiko gasps as he breathes in, now feeling his body but feeling off. Aiko tries to move his arms, but they are restrained. He looks around, seeing that he is in the same room where he is always hooked up.

"Dad…"

"I'm here, son. I'm here…"

Aiko looked down at his chest and armor, seeing that it was also repaired.

"We got an armor smith to repair the suit."

"I feel off…"

Acheron acknowledged his word, walked forward, and opened his chest piece, revealing Aiko's body chest. He looked down; his heart dropped, along with his eyes. A cylinder-like object in the center of his chest appeared in front of him.

"AAAARRH!"

Aiko screamed.

"AIKO, CALM DOWN, CALM DOWN!"

"WHAT DID YOU DO TO ME!"

Acheron pauses, slowly walking forward. Putting his hand around the cylindrical object.

"It was the only way I could save you."

**425**

Aiko wondered what he said.

"This is the synara core. Only one of three left by the Harmonians. The Imperium of the Choleric and The Nekrothians possess them. It carries out heavy Harmonian energy, allowing life to continue through energy flow. It is the only reason why you are still alive, but barely. I made the choice to have the surgery around your chest, implanting the core in you. Now, that is keeping you alive. You can finally move, talk, and think, but… you're stuck with it…"

Aiko's heart dropped, breathing more heavily.

"Your brother and everyone else came to visit you. They're waiting to hear if you're alive. I'll tell them that you're fine."

Acheron walks out until stopping.

"Your service is fully complete. We are safe for now. URDT is expanding its enlistment more than ever. Each nation has responded to the Nekrothians' return. We, as humanity, are more concerned than ever."

***

Suki stands by the URDT escalator with Odie, who has a cast on his leg, and Jerome, who is supporting Odie. Quentin walks slowly to the URDT escalator as a woman in her 30s or 40s with long hair approaches Quentin. She shares the same hair color as Quentin and is as tall as him; their eyes are the same color. They embrace in a tight hug. Quentin begins to shed tears repeatedly, and so does his mother.

Albie is back at Yume's home, playing with Yume's son around the front yard while Yume and Suki's grandparents watch, smiling at the boys' joy.

Homura and Jax look outside from their cell, feeling vibrations and sounds coming from above.

Back at the entrance of the URDT, Maverick is on the platform, talking to many new recruits.

A dozen recruits look up at Maverick's speech. Alongside him are Cade, Curtis, and Dahlia. Jerome, Odie, and Quentin's mom, behind Quentin and Suki, watch as Maverick continues to speak. Both Quentin and Suki look at each other, grinning in a hopeful manner with a soft smile.

Acheron's continued voiceover to Aiko.

The chant of the recruiter's lips spelled out the URDT motto.

"Valor Unto the Skies, Grounded in Courage, till our last breath."

"Valor Unto the Skies, Grounded in Courage, till our last breath."

"Valor Unto the Skies, Grounded in Courage, till our last breath."

The next area is LYN headquarters, where Kenryoku examines Ernaline and Deagmund's condition and reports them as charging. Kenryoku watches on as he goes to the module and enters a password, revealing a project that scared Nerdhard.

Akarui was at the Tactical operation area, watching the big monitor of many news reports showcasing reports of "Nekrothians returning!" "URDT recruitment has increased!" She closed her eyes, breathing slowly in and out, then opened them and embraced what was to come.

***

"With the Nekrothians advancement being stalled over time, our reaction was slow... They now know where we're at."

Acheron continues to speak voiceover while Aiko listens.

"I thought I destroyed them; a fleet of ships held Nekrothians."

Aiko said.

"That's only a fraction of their race; there are more of them back on Earth by now. On that planet's surface, already preparing for their invasion of Gaea. It's only a matter of time..."

Acheron looking down with doubt.

"We're preparing if they return; we need more help than ever if humanity is to survive once more. Aiko..."

Acheron coming back to Aiko.

"You can leave this suit, this life I put you in. You can be with your brother; forget about me. I don't want to see you hurt like this anymore."

Acheron looked forward at the door entrance.

"I won't..."

Acheron turned around to Aiko's response.

"If I'm stuck in this suit, so be it. I can't lose anyone... I won't lose everyone I know... I can't go through it again."

Acheron walks up to Aiko.

"If that is your choice, I'll do everything possible to make you happy. Just know that whatever happens in the future, we can't change it. I'm sorry for what will happen later because of my actions. I promise to help you no matter what."

**427**

"It is my choice."

Aiko looks straight at Acheron, his helmet showing Acheron's mask reflection, getting closer to show his determination.

"This is what I mean. Being The Melancholic Knight..."

# THE MELANCHOLIC KNIGHT

www.ingramcontent.com/pod-product-compliance
Lightning Source LLC
Chambersburg PA
CBHW030540260626
47157CB00006B/2125